WHERE ALL PATHS MEET

THE ADVENTURES OF HOLLOWAY HOLMES

BOOK 3

GREGORY ASHE

H&B

Where All Paths Meet
Copyright © 2023 Gregory Ashe

Published by Hodgkin & Blount
https://www.hodgkinandblount.com/
contact@hodgkinandblount.com

Published 2023
Printed in the United States of America

Version 1.03

Trade Paperback ISBN: 978-1-63621-061-2
eBook ISBN: 978-1-63621-060-5

I found myself regarding him as an isolated phenomenon, a brain without a heart, as deficient in human sympathy as he was pre-eminent in intelligence. His aversion to women and his disinclination to form new friendships were both typical of his unemotional character, but not more so than his complete suppression of every reference to his own people.
    — "The Adventure of the Greek Interpreter," Sir Arthur Conan Doyle

Work is the best antidote to sorrow.
    — "The Adventure of the Empty House, Sir Arthur Conan Doyle

My hand had drawn him back from that dark valley in which all paths meet.
    — "The Adventure of the Greek Interpreter, Sir Arthur Conan Doyle

Chapter 1

The Incredible Growing Boy

I stared at myself in the mirror. "I'm going to do the mature thing."

Dad didn't exactly sigh, but he did rub his forehead.

"I'm going to do the only sensible thing," I said.

"They don't give out enough good parenting awards, you know that? And they never give them out for moments like this."

"I'm going to skip prom, spend the rest of my life single, and die alone, at home, a virgin."

"A little late for that," Dad muttered.

I broke away from the mirror and rounded on him. "Excuse me?"

"It's not that bad," Dad said in a soothing voice. "You look very handsome."

"That's what parents say. Because they're legally obligated." I held out my arm, so he could see the tux's sleeve sliding up past my wrist. I showed him the trousers hitting me above the ankle. I crossed my arms for emphasis, and in the silence, you could hear the seams in the shoulders straining. When I'd asked about renting a tux, he'd produced this abomination from under his bed. He probably thought I didn't know what else he kept down there. The gun safe, for one. That was new.

"Ok," Dad said. "You're a little bigger than I was when Mom and I got married. God knows you've been working out enough."

"I look like Frankenstein."

"I thought Frankenstein had cut-offs."

"Dad!"

"We'll figure it out, buddy. We'll get it tailored."

"Tailored? No. This thing needs to be burned. And then somebody needs to perform an exorcism on the ashes. And then I can die at home, alone—"

"A 'virgin.' Yeah, I heard you."

Proof of bad fathering: he even drew the air quotes with his fingers.

"I'm glad this is funny. I'm never going on a date again. I'm never going to fall in love. I'm never going to move out. I'm going to die alone, in your basement—"

"We don't have a basement."

I drew myself up—which, ok, was kind of hard because the jacket was so snug—and glared at him.

Dad was rubbing his chin suspiciously and refusing to look at me. "What about Glo? You two are cute together. Oh, wait—what about Rowe?"

"Don't do that."

"He's a nice-looking guy."

"You are not going to weasel out of this by pretending to be supportive of my bisexuality."

"Hey, hold on, I am supportive—"

"Glo is dating Rowe!"

"Oh." Dad rubbed his chin. Vigorously. "Well, how was I supposed to know that?"

"They sit on your couch and suck each other's faces off!"

"What about Emma? You're always hanging out with Emma."

"Emma is going with Rowe and Glo. They're together."

"Why—

"If you ask me why I don't go with them, I'm going to Hulk out!"

"You're halfway out of the tux already."

I was still trying to Hulk my way out of the tux when the knock came at the door.

"It's not that I'm mad," Dad said as he headed down the hall. "I'm just disappointed."

"That's not how you're supposed to use that!" I shouted after him.

"Perfect timing," Dad said at the other end of the cottage. "Will you please be a gentleman and ask my son to prom?"

I couldn't stop my squawk of "Dad!"

"Sorry, Mr. Moreno," Rowe said, his voice moving toward me. "I'm going with Glo and Emma."

"Can he go with you?"

"Stop embarrassing me!"

Rowe appeared in my doorway. He was one of those obnoxiously masculine guys: he had a few inches on me, as well as probably fifty pounds of muscle, and he had that Minnesota-Scandinavian look of perpetually ruddy cheeks. Combined with puppy-dog brown eyes, an annoyingly full beard, and disheveled blond bangs, he was pretty much the whole package.

So, if he'd asked, I probably would have said yes. To prom, I mean. Not that he was bi. And not that he would have asked me if he was. Not that I even thought about him like that.

He took one look at me and burst out laughing. "Holy cow, man. That's hilarious!"

"It's not a joke," I snapped. I tried to squirm out of the jacket, but I couldn't. "For fuck's sake, help me!"

"Jack," Dad bellowed from the front of the house.

Rowe was still laughing as he tugged off the jacket. When it came loose, I said, "Knock it off. It's my dad's fault."

"Rowe, please tell him to be polite to his elderly father."

"Stay out of this," I shouted back. "You're the whole reason I'm in this mess."

"Dude," Rowe said with a smile.

I glowered at him too because Rowe was like a teddy bear, and he could take pretty much any amount of glowering. It didn't have any effect on him. I shucked the tuxedo pants, found a pair of shorts and one of Dad's old Nirvana tees, and pulled them on. It might have been my imagination, but the shorts seemed to hit me higher on the thigh than I remembered, and the shirt might—might—have been a tiny bit too small. I considered changing again. But what if it wasn't my imagination? And by then, Rowe was straddling my chair backward, waiting. He was already geared up: running shoes, mesh shorts, a *Sin City* t-shirt in a bro cut.

"Ready?" Rowe asked.

"Yeah, almost, hold on. Let me finish dying from parental neglect and internalized humiliation."

Rowe worked a finger in his ear.

"Rowe's not going to want to date you if you treat your father like that," Dad called back.

"Everybody's a comedian," I said.

I flipped off the lights, and Rowe trailed after me. "So," he said, "I was thinking we'd change things up. We'll finish with sprints this time."

I groaned. "No. I changed my mind. I'm not going."

He bumped me, and I stumbled into a half-jog and caught myself on the counter. I stopped when I saw the envelope there—the kind of reinforced cardboard mailer that official documents might come in. Lord knows I'd seen enough of those in the year after the accident. Only instead of Dad's name, it had mine, and there was no return address.

"What's this?" I asked.

"Rowe brought it in," Dad said from his recliner, where he was flipping channels.

"I found it on the porch."

"What is it?" I asked.

"Well, son, there's this thing called an envelope—"

"I'm going to run away," I said as I grabbed the mailer. "I'm going to join the circus."

"The incredible growing boy," Rowe said. "No clothes in the world will fit him."

Dad sounded like he was choking, but he managed to say, "It's probably a college packet."

"Yeah," I said as I opened the envelope. "With my grades."

Two pieces of paper lay inside. The first looked like a greeting card, but when I touched it, it was different—heavier, with a feel and texture that said it was seriously expensive. I pulled it out and gave it a closer look. It wasn't a greeting card; it was an invitation.

You are invited to the Zodiac "Fabulous Five" Anniversary Party. Below that, it gave details—the party was Saturday, tomorrow, and I was allowed to bring a guest. The only people I knew at Zodiac, the tech conglomerate located at the north end of Utah Valley, were Maggie Moriarty and Blackfriar Holmes. Both of them, I was pretty sure, had tried to kill me. So, all things considered, that was a pass.

I shoved the invitation back into the mailer and took out the smaller piece of paper. It felt different from the invitation—cheap, like copy paper. On it was printed a single sentence: *Come if you want to know the truth about your mother.*

"Well?" Dad asked. "What is it?"

Giving Rowe a warning look—because, nosy, he'd seen the invitation—I dropped the paper back into the mailer. "Like you said. College stuff."

"What college?"

"BYU."

Dad snorted a laugh.

I took the mailer to my room and shoved it under the mattress. When I rejoined Rowe, he was giving me a look, which I chose to ignore.

"All right," I said. "We're leaving."

"Go easy on the sprints," Dad said. "If you puke on my porch, you're cleaning it up."

"See?" I asked Rowe as I ushered him out of the house. "See what kind of love I get?"

The May evening was soft in the twilight, the air sweet with the smell of the water from the sprinklers, the new growth of grass. Rowe was giving me that look again.

"We're not going to talk about it," I said. "And you'd better not say anything to my dad."

"If you need to—"

"I don't," I said. And then, because I couldn't help myself, "I'm not getting caught up in that mess again."

Rowe made a face. Then he said, "Race you to the athletic center?"

"Are you stupid? We're doing sprints—God damn it, Rowe!"

I tore off after him.

But as I ran, words thundered in time with my steps.

Come if you want to know the truth about your mother.

Come. Come. Come.

And the answer rose inside me: You'd better believe I fucking will.

Chapter 2

It Was Wonderful Meeting You

I was the proud owner of a 2000 Dodge Dakota (ok, it was still Dad's, but I got to drive it), and I had my driver's license, and I even asked permission to go to a party. So, I wasn't breaking any laws or parental commandments as I drove north on I-15 Saturday night. I was lying by omission, that's all. And running into whatever trap the Holmeses or the Moriartys had laid for me. And, if anything happened to me, it would kill my dad. I tried to balance the gut-clenching guilt of that against the hope, however small, that whoever had sent that invitation was telling the truth.

Almost two years ago, my mom had died in the same car accident that had left my dad coping with the long-term effects of a traumatic brain injury. Until a few months before, I had believed it was an accident. Now, I wasn't sure. Now, I knew my mom was a Watson. And I was a Watson. And someone had tried to kill me in a car accident in December. And that made a guy wonder.

In May, Utah was at its most beautiful—the days were warm, the evenings cool, the cottonwoods and plane trees in the valley were coming back to life, and mountainsides were green with scrub oak and pine. Granted, I-15 was never beautiful. It was a hellscape morass of endless construction and bumper-to-bumper traffic, bracketed by the strange mixture of strip malls and fast-food restaurants and holdout agricultural and industrial buildings that told the story of a different time in Utah's history—one that actually wasn't all that long ago.

Lehi, a city at the north end of the valley, was one of the places that had changed the most. A number of big tech companies had come to Utah, taking advantage of the business-friendly state government and the natural beauty, and created what some particularly annoying people had taken to calling Silicon Slopes. Among those businesses was the multinational tech conglomerate Zodiac. It did something with social media and AI. And that was about the extent of what I knew, unless you counted the fact that Blackfriar Holmes was the majority shareholder and the CEO, and Maggie Moriarty was his chief of AI. A Holmes and a Moriarty working together. What could go wrong?

With the sun settling behind the mountains to the west, great raven wings of shadow closed over the valley, and I-15 became a pinball machine of lights and cars. It was hard not to think about the past. In September, I'd driven to Zodiac to confront Maggie, part of my investigation into the death of Sarah Watson—my distant cousin, it turned out. Or maybe my aunt eighteen times removed. Or something. I wasn't sure how it worked. In the process, I'd become entangled with a boy named Holloway Holmes. He'd stowed away in the back of the Dodge, hiding under a tarp. And then he'd popped up like my own personal nightmare jack-in-the-box, and from that moment, we'd been tied together. Inseparable. The quantum reality, I guess, of a Holmes and a Watson finding each other. I'd been stupid enough to think it had been more than that.

When I reached the Zodiac campus, I followed the signs toward the Scorpio building, and that sense of déjà vu swept over me again. Scorpio was where Maggie Moriarty had her lab and office. Scorpio was where Holmes and I had gone all those months before. And tonight, Zodiac's party would be celebrated in Scorpio. Of course it would be. Why not?

I parked and joined the people trickling toward the building. Cars and trucks and SUVs filled the lot, each one costing somewhere between five and ten times what the Dodge was worth. Ok, maybe even more than that. I mean, it was an old truck. The people heading inside the building looked fancy: an Indian woman in a pale linen dress, her neck strung with gold; a Latino guy in a tailored suit and shoes that had obviously been handmade; a pink-cheeked lady in a Chanel belt and Louboutin heels (I only knew what they were because Ariana had shown me a million pairs she wanted). I was wearing my only pair of black jeans, a white button-up that was (please, God, let it be my imagination) a little too tight across the shoulders, and one of Rowe's blazers: a wine-colored velvet that he had pronounced fire and that, more importantly, Glo and Emma had signed off on. The Stan Smiths finished everything off. I'd even cleaned them up; I was classy like that.

The Scorpio building, like the rest of the Zodiac campus, was a future-tech hybrid of glass and concrete. At night, it glittered coldly, trapping the valley's smaller lights in its reflection. Security at the main entrance required everyone to show their invitation, have their bags inspected, and then pass through a metal detector. My phone and keys and wallet went in a little basket, and I held my breath as a dour-faced woman scanned my invitation.

Then she waved me through. The metal detector didn't even beep, which was kind of amazing considering I felt like I had a steel plate in my head.

After stuffing keys and wallet and phone back into their respective pockets, I headed into the lobby. It was a vast space, and the concrete redoubled the echoes as people milled and chatted and congregated in the little pods of seating done in expensive, neutral-colored leathers. I kept my head down as I crossed the lobby, following the crowd down a hall. I hadn't been this way on my last visit. That visit had been all about sneaking and snooping and getting to Moriarty's offices without being stopped by security. This visit—well, I wasn't sure what this visit was going to be like. I could go up to Maggie or Blackfriar and demand the truth about my mom, but I figured that probably wasn't my best idea. One thing you could trust about the Moriartys and the Holmeses, though, was that they loved drama. I figured someone had brought me here for a reason, and at some point, there'd be a nice, big spectacle that would, doubtless, involve me somehow.

I watched the crowd in sidelong glances and quick, stolen looks, and after a couple of minutes, the knots in my shoulders began to loosen, and I brought my head up. I'd been worried I was going to stand out, but the more I looked around, the more I realized that I'd struck the jackpot. I knew I looked young, but then, a lot of these geeks looked young—they had that pale, slightly translucent look of people who got zero natural sunlight. Like Dad said, I'd been working out a lot this year. Ok, what he said was that I worked out like a psycho. And so, I'd added inches to my chest and arms that made me look, in some ways, at least, older than some of the pencil-necked tech bros in their quarter-zips and their dark-wash jeans. A lot of them looked visibly as uncomfortable as I felt, and they clumped together in little bands, talking with their backs to the crowd. Others stared at their phones or—in one case—tablet. Drag everybody out from behind their computer screens and force them to socialize. Overall, it was going about as well as you'd expect.

The hall ended in an enormous multipurpose room: forty-foot ceilings; exposed ductwork and rigging where colored lights offered enough illumination to temper the darkness; high-def displays mounted high around the room displayed a montage of the Zodiac campus, their logo, and Blackfriar Holmes's smiling face.

Tables broke up the space, gleaming with white linen and floral centerpieces, and twelve ice sculptures stood at intervals. It took me a moment to make sense of the gleaming, dripping blocks—the Zodiac signs. Jesus, I thought, on the nose much? Caterers mixed with the partygoers, offering canapes and crab rolls, melon wrapped in ham, mini Yorkshire puddings, even edible flowers. I know because I tried them. All of them. The edible flowers were a big pass, but I hit the crab roll guy so many times he started trying to dodge me, which only meant I had to work a little harder. I'd gotten carded at two of the four bars spaced around the room, and I was really regretting my lack of fake ID, when someone spoke behind me.

"Excuse me, sir." He was about my height, probably twenty years older, and dressed in the kind of suit that said security instead of executive. "Will you come with me, please?"

"I've got an invite," I said.

"This way, sir."

He didn't grab my arm. He didn't have a cattle prod. He'd even said please. But something in his body language made me tense. Other people must have gotten the vibe too because he cut through the crowd like a hot knife. I'd seen movies like this. They usually ended badly for the guy who wasn't supposed to be at the party. Like, strapped-to-a-chair-with-a-car-battery-hooked-to-your-'nads bad. That kind of bad.

The transition happened so quickly that it felt like popping a bubble: one moment, I was following the security guy through the crowd, and the next, I was in a clearing. It was disorienting, like floating in outer space. Then I saw the cluster of people ahead of me, and I started to understand.

Blackfriar Holmes stood at the center, his dark hair combed back, his eyes like chips of tarnished tin. The woman next to him was tall—almost as tall as I was—and slender, her blond hair threaded with silver, the off-the shoulder dress revealing clean, elegant lines that were disturbingly familiar. She had to be Holmes's mother, and even in that moment of terror, I was surprised to realize that I'd never thought about him having a mother. I'd assumed she'd died. Or been a mad scientist. Probably both. She met my eyes for a moment, and her gaze was cold and hard and knowing. She recognized me; that was the first message she wanted me to get. And she didn't like me.

"Jack," Blackfriar said. "What a surprise."

He looked like he was about to say more, but a shrill voice interrupted him: "What's he doing here?"

The words came from a guy who might have been a few years older than me. He had sun-streaked brown hair, blue eyes, and thin, stooped shoulders. His suit and skinny tie were hipster chic and obviously—annoyingly—expensive, although the suit didn't seem to fit him quite right. In the dim lighting, it was hard to make out what he held low against his leg, but it looked like a black leather doctor's bag.

Blackfriar threw the guy an annoyed look and then glanced across the small group. I hadn't spotted Paxton Adler until then, which was saying something—Paxton was the kind of guy genetically engineered to draw every eye. He had dark hair in a faux hawk, thick eyebrows, almond skin. The last time I'd seen him had been at a bus station, where Holmes and I had caught him trying to collect a payoff. He'd looked worn out that day; tonight, in navy trousers and a silk shirt with a plunging neckline that left nothing to the imagination, it was obvious he'd bounced back.

At Blackfriar's look, Paxton burst out laughing. He sounded genuinely amused, and the longer he laughed, the more annoyed the guy with the doctor's bag looked.

Blackfriar's expression revealed nothing, and after a moment of watching Paxton laugh, he turned back to me. "This is Tom Watson, Jack. Say hello. Tom, meet Jack Moreno. One of the…branches of the Watson tree."

In the past few months, since learning the truth about my family, I'd spent a lot of time learning about the Watsons and, of course, the Holmeses. I'd never seen the name Tom Watson anywhere. I stared at him, and he stared back. His jaw was set, and a flush speckled his neck. After a moment, I stuck out my hand, and he switched the bag to his other hand and shook.

"My wife Cecilia," Blackfriar said, indicating the woman I'd recognized as Holmes's mom. "And my daughter Noneley."

The final member of the group had her father's dark hair, her mother's hazel eyes and build, and when she moved, she looked like Holmes. My Holmes. Not the same cold-chiseled perfection, but the mannerisms. She was his older sister, I had learned from my research—because Holmes, of course, had never told me anything about his family. But watching her move, I knew in that moment that, at some point in his life, for what must have been a long stretch, Holmes had idolized her, studied her, copied her. The way younger kids do with older siblings. Where have you been, I wanted to ask her. Why haven't you been helping him?

Noneley was grinning at me, and it took me a moment to process what I was seeing. Instead of something suited to the semi-formal dress code, she wore a cheerleader's uniform: a blue and silver top that left her arms and midriff bare; a pleated blue skirt that revealed long, toned legs. On the front of her top was printed the name of my old high school, along with the bulldog mascot.

"Don't you love it?" she said, laughing. "I couldn't wait to see your face." And then, as though her father hadn't introduced her, she said, "I'm Noneley," and kissed my cheek.

The last few minutes had been a lot, and most of my processing power was being taken up by serial realizations: the presence of someone calling himself a Watson, the uncanny similarities between Noneley and Holmes, the fact that somehow she'd known I was coming and managed to get a cheerleader uniform in time, and her sudden intrusion into my space, followed by that kiss.

All of which is to explain why I said the smartest thing possible: "You're supposed to be dead."

That cracked them up. Paxton and Noneley laughed, and even Blackfriar allowed himself a twitch of his lips. Tom didn't laugh, though; he stared at me, color still mottling his face, holding the doctor's bag in front of him with both hands now. Cecilia didn't laugh either. She studied me. Her fingers were white around the glass she was holding.

"I made a miraculous recovery," Noneley said with a huge smile. "We Holmeses are notorious for it."

Apparently, my brain couldn't leave well enough alone: "But I read the articles—" I managed to drag myself to a halt there. I fished for something better and came up with nothing.

"A misdirection." Noneley paused to hit her vape, and I got a whiff of cannabis. "Government work is so boring, shuttling back and forth between D.C. and London, but every once in a while, I get to do something fun."

Blackfriar shot her a dirty look—whether because of the vape or the statement, it wasn't clear—but his focus settled on me again. "Tom asked the pertinent question, I believe. What are you doing here, Jack?" He threw another look at his daughter, who struck a cheer pose and did jazz hands. "Or are you simply another of my daughter's misdirections?"

The silence seemed to demand an answer, so I said, "I was invited."

I showed him the invitation itself. He studied it for a moment. Then he looked up at me and bared his teeth, a mockery of a smile. "Well, here we are. The Holmeses, the Watsons, and the Adlers. This promises to be an interesting evening."

As though that had been some sort of cue, Cecilia passed her glass of wine to Noneley and produced a small enameled box from her clutch. She withdrew a pill, placed it on her tongue, and accepted the wine from her daughter. We all watched as she sipped at the wine and swallowed the pill. It had the feeling of a ritual.

I pulled my gaze away and, by accident, caught a glimpse of Blackfriar's face. What I saw there startled me—some intense emotion that I couldn't parse, breaking through the wall of reserve he normally hid behind.

Something buzzed, and Blackfriar's face emptied itself again as he took out his phone.

"Daughter," he said after a moment, "why is my head of cybersecurity asking me about a backdoor in the company firewall?"

Noneley's face was cartoonishly innocent. She even spread her hands.

"From my personal device, Noneley. Really?"

"I don't know what you're talking about, Father."

Blackfriar scowled, pocketed his phone, and stalked away from us. Tom lingered for an extra heartbeat, giving me a double whammy of his glare, and then hurried after Blackfriar.

"His little Boswell," Cecilia said drily, her voice tinctured with an English accent. Her face looked different now, the tiniest bit slack. Her movements seemed slower, her attention fogged. Whatever she'd swallowed, she probably shouldn't have taken it with wine. "It's grotesque; I don't know why he permits it."

"Next, Tom will be following him into the bathroom," Noneley said. She turned to Paxton. "Tell the truth: did you invite Jack?"

"I fink I'm a little smarter than that, luv," Paxton said with a smirk. Like Cecilia, he had an accent that Noneley, probably for the same reason as Holmes, did not. The problem with Paxton, though, was you never knew how much he was faking. "Kind of thing you'd do, innit?"

"Don't be silly; I didn't invite him."

"Spoze you had the uniform lying around."

Noneley grinned. "I did, actually. As soon as Holloway started up with Jack, I thought of it. Holloway will go insane when he finds out."

"Don't antagonize your brother," Cecilia said in that same affectless voice.

"Come off it," Paxton said to Noneley. "You had that lying around, and you just happened to put it on tonight."

"Of course not. As soon as I knew Jack was in the building, I got it out of my car and changed." Her grin widened. "It made Father furious, didn't it?"

Paxton shook his head and took a drink. He caught the eye of someone across the room, passed me his empty glass, and straightened his shirt. The dark wedges of his nipples pressed through the linen. "How do I look, bruv?"

I chose not to answer that.

He smirked at me anyway, but his attention roved back to the other side of the room, where a young blond guy in catering digs was leaning against the door. "Right, then. 'Bout to make this lovely boy see God in the bog. Evening, evening." Some of the swagger dropped from his voice when he said, "Evening, Mrs. Holmes."

"Be careful," was all she said to him.

He nodded—no comeback, no cocky bullshit. And then he was gone, sliding through the crowd, and I was alone with Noneley and Cecilia Holmes.

"I'd love to stay," Noneley said. "I want to ask you all sorts of embarrassing questions about my brother—and I will, I promise. But right now is the perfect opportunity to set Father's desk on fire, and I'll kick myself if I don't take it."

"Uh—"

"Bye, Jack. It was wonderful meeting you."

She darted in for another quick kiss on the cheek, and then she was gone.

And then there was one. Cecilia stared at me. Even swaddled in medication, that gaze was intense. I tried to think of what people said at parties. Hello, maybe. But I'd already said that. Or had I? Hello, how are you? How are you doing? How are you doing tonight? How are you doing tonight, Mrs. Holmes? And then something short-circuited, and all I could do was stare, hearing my own breathing inside my head, wondering if my jaw had dropped and I was currently mouth-breathing in Cecilia Holmes's face.

I was still staring when she handed me her glass and walked away.

For a moment, I stood there, a glass in each hand. Then I retreated, trying to get away from—it wasn't exactly the scene of a crime, but maybe the scene of death from sheer humiliation? I found one of the staff collecting empty glasses and got rid of the ones I'd been carrying. I wriggled through the crowd until I had my back to a wall. And then I tried to regroup.

That had not gone well, I informed myself. That had not gone well at all.

I suppressed, for a moment, the thousand different ways that little debacle had gone wrong. I made myself focus. The whole point of the night was to get information about my mother. But had I gotten information? Maybe a little. By accident. I'd learned that Cecilia Holmes might be even more frightening than Blackfriar, who at least pretended to be human. I'd learned that Noneley was legit psycho. Oh, and that apparently she'd been carrying around a cheerleader uniform from my old school on the off chance that she bumped into me. Or had that been a lie? Maybe she'd sent the invitation. From the way Blackfriar had responded to my presence, I didn't think he had—but then, I didn't think Blackfriar would send me anything in the mail except possibly anthrax. Except he could have been lying too, and maybe he'd invited me here to lure me into a trap—

And if you wanted to impress them, a part of my brain spoke over the rest of my thoughts, if you wanted them to think you were smart and sophisticated and, at least potentially, an acceptable match for their son, no matter how much better he is than you, well, you really did a wonder-fuck on that one.

"You look like you're having fun." The voice was cool and cultured, with a kind of dollhouse, Oxbridge coquettishness. I knew it, and a frisson ran up my spine.

Maggie Moriarty stood to my side. She wore her usual getup: a fashionably ripped red shirt under a leather jacket, leather pants, knee-high leather boots, every piece of gear bristling with studs. "Hello, Jack."

I did a quick scan. There were probably two hundred people in the room, and not one of them was paying attention to us. When my gaze came back to Maggie, she was smiling, the expression predatory.

"Hold on," I said. "Let me get my Taser."

She laughed. "I understand you're a Watson now. Remarkable how things change, isn't it? How do you feel?"

"I had to send a lot more Christmas cards than usual."

She didn't laugh at that, but her smile grew.

The babble of the party, the heat of too many bodies, the smell of alcohol and microwaved pastries and sweat—it all pressed in on me.

"Well," I said. "Did you want something?"

"I always want something; that's the nature of being a Moriarty. What about you, Jack? Do you want something?"

"Do you have those little pretzel dogs?"

Her smile tightened. "We should talk, Jack."

"Uh, sounds great. Tell you what: you get a head start, and I'll catch up."

"There's a great deal I could tell you. Information that helped Sarah. You and I could be friends, Jack, and although you may not realize it, you need friends right now. You're in very real danger."

"Trust me, I know."

"Not from me, you imbecile." Then she paused, and her mouth slanted with amusement. "Not exclusively from me."

A list of names ran through my head. I hadn't only been doing research on the Holmeses over the last five months; I'd done some family history as well. Brian Roe, June Watson, Florrie Sheahan, James Watson. On and on. They were a drumbeat at the back of my head.

This time I met her eyes, and I said it just loud enough for her to hear me over the hub of the party. "I said I know."

For a moment, her face revealed nothing, but those dark eyes had an intensity to them that hooked me, held me. In a low voice, as though speaking to herself, she murmured, "Who brought you out to play?"

"Yeah, yeah, I'm his toy. I get it. You used that one before."

Her voice was stronger as she shook her head and said, "No, Jack. Not a toy, not anymore. A piece on the board. And don't you wonder whose hand is moving you?"

My phone buzzed before I could follow that particular strand of madness; I reached for it, and when I looked up, Maggie was gone.

The message was from a number I didn't recognize: *Moriarty's office. Now.*

For a moment, I considered ignoring it. Two facts weighed pretty heavily in favor of that: one, out of all the people who might lure me into a trap by inviting me to a Zodiac party, Maggie Moriarty was near the top of the list; and two, I'd just seen Maggie, and I didn't like the idea of having a follow-up, private chat with her. The last time I'd done that, she'd let her goons try to separate my shoulder.

But I was kidding myself. I was going to go. On the off chance that this was legit, on the off chance that I could learn something about my mom, I had to go.

I left the party, and the corridor was cool and quiet in comparison. My steps rang out on the expensive concrete. When I got to the elevators, I remembered they all operated on keycards; I'd have to jimmy the lock on the fire stairs, the way Holmes and I had our first time. But one of the elevators dinged, and the doors slid open.

Jesus Christ, I thought as I stepped into the car. That wasn't creepy at all.

The door glided shut, and the elevator took off without me pressing any buttons. My ears popped as we raced up the building. The digital display changed as we hurtled past each floor. I thought of the Wonkavator, or whatever it was called, bursting out of the top of the building.

But this wasn't a Wonkavator, and it slowed as we approached the final floor. The doors slid open, and I stepped out into the hall.

And all the power went out.

Chapter 3

The Thief

The darkness dropped over me, and I froze. It wasn't total darkness — emergency lights still gave a weak glow, but they were spaced out along the hall, and they didn't do much more than offer an impression of the space: the long, empty hallway, a sketch of doors.

I listened, but I couldn't hear anything. No footsteps. No voices. No shouts of alarm. My pulse beat in my throat, and my face felt hot. The darkness seemed to magnify that silence. I was surprised I couldn't hear anything echoing up the stairwell, but maybe the power outage was limited to this floor. Gee, wouldn't that be a coincidence?

I fumbled around until I found the wall, and then I felt the elevator doors, which still stood open. I wasn't sure if that was supposed to happen — were they supposed to seal automatically if the power went out? Shouldn't there be some sort of backup generator? A business like Zodiac, which had plenty of money, should have had state-of-the-art stuff. So, I told myself, the generators would come on in a minute.

Sure.

The smart thing to do would be to stay in the doorway, right by the elevator. Or, even smarter, find the fire stairs and get the hell out of here. I'd seen plenty of movies. I'd even read a few books. And when you got mysteriously summoned to a meeting in a supervillain's secret lair and the power went out, good things didn't happen. Not that Moriarty's office was technically a secret lair. But I thought I was still making some valid points.

On the other hand, I was an idiot. So, I kept one hand on the wall and started walking toward her office.

I remembered the way, not that there was much to remember — this floor, unlike the others in the building, had only a handful of doors, and Moriarty's office was located at the end of the hallway. So, there was no way to get turned around or to open the wrong door by mistake.

Running footsteps broke the silence. The noise startled me—one moment, there was nothing, and the next, the sound of steps was only a few feet away. A shadow loomed, metal jangled, and I drew back instinctively, trying to get out of their path. The figure sprinted toward me, and I got a glimpse of a woman's face when she passed under the emergency light. She was short, dressed in dark colors, and had dark hair. She threw glances over her shoulder as she ran, and her ID badge flapped and fluttered on its lanyard. In her other hand, she carried something small. Her jewelry rattled and clanked, almost as loud as her panicked breathing. If she saw me, she gave no sign of it. One moment, she was hurtling toward me, and the next, she was past.

"Hey, hold on!" I called.

She kept running, and a moment later, the fire door at the other end of the hall crashed against the wall.

Ok, I thought. Up goes the creep factor. Not that it could get much creepier.

A groan came from the end of the hallway.

Ok, I thought again. I was wrong.

I moved toward the noise. I didn't have a gun or a knife, so I settled for slotting my keys between my fingers and making a fist. It was an ugly weapon, but it was better than nothing. Then I remembered how smart I am—Jack Moreno, boy genius—and got out my phone and turned on the flashlight. It seemed a lot weaker than I remembered, but it carved a cone out of the darkness.

Muffled noises from ahead suggested movement. They grew louder as I got closer. The doorway to Moriarty's office took shape, the door standing open. The darkness on the other side broke up as I came closer with the light. The chair that was more like a throne. The coffee table with a trayful of acid and shrooms. The skull. All Maggie Moriarty's lovely little accent pieces— what makes a house a home.

A figure stood at Maggie's desk, steadying themself on it. Behind them, the digital frame—the one that was supposed to show Maggie's face age-progressed through the processes of decomposition and skeletonization— had been removed from the wall. The heavy metal door of a safe was open, and the interior of the safe was a black socket.

When the light brushed the figure, they moved. I had a blurred impression of overalls, a hat pulled low, and then the figure was vaulting the desk. They came straight across the room toward me, charging me.

Because I'm a Boy Genius, I shouted, "Hey!"

The thief—or whoever they were—crashed into me. It was a solid tackle: shoulder set to strike me in the chest, the move designed to knock me on my ass while they kept going. But I'd played football (ok, a little), and I knew how to take the fall. I also knew to grab on to their jersey. Or, in this case, overalls.

We both went down, and the force of the impact sent me skidding along the carpet tiles. I rolled onto my side, trying to get to my feet. The thief was trying to slither out from under me, but I still had my grip on the overalls, and I hauled them back toward me. They grunted, a sound that my brain decoded as a guy's noise. The thief twisted, and his knee came up and caught me under the ribs. The breath whooshed out of me, and I lost my grip.

The next moment, the thief was on his feet, sprinting down the hall. I got myself upright and lumbered after him. He hadn't gotten me in the solar plexus, thank God, and after a couple of deep breaths, I put on the gas.

For the last five months, I had fueled every workout with my rage at Holloway Holmes. And, if I were being honest, with my hurt. Working out with Rowe. Working out by myself. Training in the silence of the athletic center and practicing the moves Holmes had taught me. Lifting weights to add strength and mass. But mostly what I'd done was try to run and swim myself into unconsciousness. And apparently the old saying was true, because it hadn't killed me, and I flew down the hall after the thief.

He hit the fire door at full speed. It crashed open, and the metallic bang of it hitting the wall sounded like thunder inside the stairwell. It was almost closed again by the time I reached it, but I put my shoulder into it and kept going, and the sound boomed through the stairwell again. My feet hammered the steps as I went down. The thief was half a flight ahead of me. I was fast. Maybe even faster, if we were running flat out on open ground. But the stairs changed that; every time I put on some speed, I had to brake, turn, slow down again.

Fuck that, I thought, and threw myself over the railing.

It was one of those things that wasn't as dramatic as it sounded and, at the same time, was an absolutely terrible idea that seemed pretty ok at the time. I swung myself over the railing, lowered myself toward the flight of steps immediately below, and dropped. I didn't swing out over the void at the center of the stairwell. I didn't do any dramatic jumps over that vast, yawning emptiness. There were zero Jason Bourne moves, which would have disappointed Dad, since we'd watched those movies approximately a hundred times.

Still, I did have a prickling sense at the back of my skull that I'd done something stupid, and when my heels jarred against the concrete, the rush of relief caught up with me.

I didn't have much time to think about it, though, because the thief was barreling down toward me now. With his hat pulled low, I couldn't see his face, but I still caught his surprise when he realized what I'd done. He probably looked even more surprised when I tripped him.

He went flying down the stairs, and I threw myself after him. I landed on top of him at the next landing, and for a moment, I thought I had him: I twisted one of his arms behind his back, locking it into place. But the next moment, he was twisting and thrashing again. He was boneless. He was a human gummy worm. He grabbed my ear and twisted until I screamed, and when I released him, he did something where he flipped both of us, and then he was on top of me, straddling my back. He released my ear and caught my arm, trapping me in a wrist lock, and pain lanced to the front of my brain. I bellowed and tried to move, but he had me pinned.

And then he eased up, and the pain died down to embers.

It wasn't possible.

But it was, of course.

It should have been obvious, actually.

He tensed, readying himself to run again.

And I said, "H?"

Chapter 4

What the Hell Are You Doing Here?

At the sound of his name, his body tightened even more. I knew what he felt like against me. It had been five months, but I knew. I knew how he moved. I knew his eyes. I knew what his breathing sounded like, for heaven's sake. I should have figured it out as soon as I saw him in Moriarty's office, but now, in hindsight, I realized he'd been holding himself funny, as though he'd been hurt, and then there'd been the hat, and the darkness—

"What are you doing here?" His voice, normally so controlled, was knotted with frustration.

"What am I doing here?" I reached back and slapped his leg, and he eased off me. I flopped onto my back, got myself into a sitting position and stared at him. His blond hair was mussed and staticky from the hat, which was gone now. Eyes the color of moon dust. Cheekbones and nose and jaw that would have given sculptors wet dreams. The corner of his mouth was raw where he'd been chewing on it. "I'm whipping your ass, that's what I'm doing. What the hell are you doing here?"

"You shouldn't be here. Why—"

A door boomed above us, and heavy, coordinated steps thundered down the stairs. Flashlights swept cones of light over the concrete.

Holmes was on his feet in a heartbeat, dragging me up by the blazer with apparently zero effort. Hauling me with him, he started down the next flight of stairs.

I tried to shake him off. "What—"

"Silence."

It was déjà vu all over again, or however that saying went, and it was surreal—being here again, Holmes bossing me around again, every minute of the last half hour's worth of insanity. I opened my mouth to tell him this when above us, a voice called out, "Stop right there!"

"Run," Holmes said, and he followed his own order, sprinting down the stairs and yanking me after him.

Gunfire erupted. A bullet struck the stairs ahead of us, throwing up chips of concrete and dust. Bullets stitched a line across the next landing. Men shouted above us, and then, in a series of flickers, lights began to come back on. Not all of them. Not all at once. But enough, especially compared to the darkness we'd been operating in. An alarm blared, and a woman's soothing voice encouraged everyone to find the closest exit, but it all sounded distant after the thunder of the shots. Someone had gotten the backup generator online, I figured. Perfect.

A final burst of gunfire tore up the railing above us, and then it stopped. A man shouted an order, the words garbled by the fading echoes, and then a different sound came. This one was strangely familiar, a sound I associated with airsoft and paintball—the kind that used CO_2 canisters. Something clanged, the sound of metal on metal. Holmes grunted. The silence after left my ears ringing. When I risked a look, Holmes's face was grim, etched in strong lines and shadow, tombstone marble. He shook his head at my unasked question and, if anything, he ran faster and pulled me along with him.

When we hit the emergency exit at the bottom of the stairs, a fire alarm blatted, and cool spring air slapped me in the face. The sun had set behind the mountains to the west. The dusk was purple only by gradation, deepening instantly to black, and it smelled like dust and sage—I hadn't realized, until then, that my lungs had been full of the stink of gunpowder. People were streaming out of the Scorpio building, voices high and panicked as they evacuated the Zodiac party, and the building itself was a dark, chitinous shell glimmering with reflected starlight. Even the parking lot had gone dark aside from a few emergency lights.

Holmes juked right, but I caught him and yanked him in my direction.

"My vehicle—"

"No," I said. "We're taking the truck."

"Jack—"

"I'm mad at you, which means I'm in charge." He opened his mouth like he might argue with that—or, more likely since this was Holmes we were talking about, like he wanted further explanation—so I yanked him hard enough to raise his heels from the sidewalk, and he followed me across the lot.

All around us, cars and SUVs were starting up, headlights coming on, taillights flashing. The men in the stairwell—Zodiac security or, perhaps, Moriarty's private contractors—would only be a few seconds behind us, but the chaos in the parking lot would buy us some time. As I watched, a tech bro hit the accelerator too fast, and his Tesla lurched backward and smashed into the Mercedes behind him. A woman shouted. Tesla bro rolled forward, with more crunching of fiberglass and metal, and a wide-eyed boner in a Beamer tried to squeeze through the opening. Everyone in the entire universe, it seemed, was choosing that moment to use their horn.

I checked Holmes; his head swiveled as he scanned the area around us. He looked tired, and he was moving slower than I expected. I was still watching him when he pulled me backward. I opened my mouth to tell him again that I was in charge when a Corvette rocked over the curb where I'd been standing a moment before. The woman behind the steering wheel had a look on her face like she was going to run down anyone who got in her way.

"Jesus Christ," I muttered.

"They're not prepared for emergencies," Holmes said. "And most of them are not suited for them."

"No kidding." It cost me a little to say, "Uh, thanks."

Holmes wavered. His eyes had the same chitinous glitter as the glass husk of Scorpio. "The truck?"

"Yeah. Right. Over here."

I'd gotten one of the stalls at the end of the lot, and at the time, it had seemed like a good spot—the truck didn't exactly blend in, and it would draw less attention there. But as I unlocked the passenger door, I realized we had a new problem. The lot was deadlocked with honking vehicles and furious drivers. As I watched, a guy in one of those micro-penis trucks smashed into a tiny sedan, and more screaming erupted. When the door opened, I pushed Holmes inside.

"Is this necessary?" he asked.

"You tell me."

"You realize that if I chose to leave, I would be perfectly capable of doing so."

I looked at him.

"I have chosen not to leave," Holmes said. He relaxed, for a single instant, against the seat, eyes closing. Then he forced his eyes open, and it looked like it was hard for him. Not sleeping, I guessed, although he'd picked a hell of a time for it to catch up to him. Then he added, "For the time being."

"For fuck's sake," I said and slammed his door.

I got behind the wheel, started the engine, and considered my options. We weren't that far from the main road, but we'd be here hours trying to get through the quagmire of the parking lot. In the rearview mirror, I saw the emergency exit door we'd emerged from swing open, and men in black tactical gear swarmed out into the lot.

"Hold on," I said as I shifted into drive.

"Why aren't you driving the truck I bought you?" Holmes asked.

"Oh, right, the truck you bought me," I said. I gave the Dodge some gas, and we bumped over the curb. "I burned it and drove it off a cliff."

"Why?"

We rocked across the uneven ground as I steered us toward the street. It actually was pretty easy going—say what you will about evil tech conglomerates, they didn't cheap out on the landscaping, and the spring fescue did fine under the Dodge's tires. "Because I hate you."

"Yes, of course, but why would you burn it first and then drive it off a cliff? Why wouldn't you drive it off a cliff and then burn it?"

"Stop talking."

"Or simply do one or the other?"

"I said stop talking."

When we rolled onto the asphalt, I let out a breath. Then I checked the rearview mirror and swore. Headlights bobbed across the grass, coming straight toward us.

"Are they pursuing us?" Holmes asked. His voice was muzzy, and I risked another glance. His pupils were dilated, which wasn't normal for him—if anything, he was usually speed skating on addies, which turned his pupils into tiny dots.

"What are the odds that they know exactly who I am and what kind of truck I'm driving?"

"It's not a possibility; it's a certainty."

"This is—this is fucking ludicrous."

"Would you like me to drive?"

In answer, I hit the gas, and the truck lurched forward. We shot down the street. I blazed through a red light, laying on my horn to warn the cross traffic, and kept my foot all the way to the floorboard. I-15 unspooled ahead of us. The headlights behind us grew brighter.

"This is why we should have taken my car," Holmes said. "Or, conversely, you should have been driving the truck I bought you—"

"If we'd taken your car, you would have ditched me the first opportunity you had. You might have left me at Zodiac. You were probably thinking about hogtying me and leaving me in a trash can where I'd be nice and safe until somebody found me."

Holmes's silence lasted a beat too long.

"Jesus Christ, H!"

"It would have been for your—"

"If you say safety, I'm going to pull over."

He yanked on the overall's straps and looked out the window.

"Do you want to finish that sentence?" I asked.

His voice was brittle with frost. "I do not. And if you're considering the highway, you should be aware that they will pursue us and catch us. This vehicle is not suited for a high-speed escape."

"Yeah, cute butt," I said. "I know."

I repeated my trick with the red lights, flying through the I-15 interchange, hammering on the horn. We almost got T-boned by a semi, but we jinked around it at the last moment, and then it was between us and the guys following us. It didn't buy us much time—when we reached the opposite side of I-15, the headlights were back again, zooming toward us.

But it had been enough. I hoped.

Thanksgiving Point rose to our left, and on the right, another of Utah Valley's never-ending strip malls. I turned left and cut down a street lined with office buildings. The rest of the traffic had dropped away, and for a moment, we were alone. I cut the headlights so we were driving dark. Please, God, let me be right, I thought. Please, this one time, give me something to shove in Holloway Holmes's face. Please, please, please let these dumbass rednecks be lazy one more year.

Ahead of us, the bristle of last year's corn came into view, and I let out a whoop of triumph.

"Yes! Yes! In your fucking face, H!"

"In my face?" he asked.

Behind us, the headlights swerved onto our street, but I took another sharp right. The corn maze spread out to our left, with a service drive for the food trucks and equipment trailers that came and went all fall. I cranked the wheel left. The Dodge rattled as we went over the rutted dirt tracks, and then the corn rose around us, a wall of brittle, drooping yellow that had been bleached by the sun until it was almost white. Husks hissed against the sides of the truck. A few dried-up ears of last year's corn thumped against the hood and rolled to fall off the side. And then I stopped and killed the engine.

In the silence that followed, the only sound was the corn moving—a vast, rushing noise like the ocean—and the tick of the engine cooling.

"They may have seen us turn," Holmes said, his voice strangely soft.

"The lights were off. And there's a million places around here we might have disappeared. And I'm doing the best I can. Do you have a better idea?"

He touched his side, winced, and shook his head.

"Then say thank you."

For a long moment, he was still. Then he turned toward me, and his eyes were the color of morning light on snowmelt. "Thank you, Jack."

I couldn't look at him for too long. Blinking, I shifted in my seat. I grunted. I flipped the visor down and flipped it back up again.

His breathing was quiet and slow. The maze had stilled around us. The weak ambient light made a picket line of the drooping heads of corn.

"Jack—"

I pivoted toward him, and five months' worth of fury erupted, and I heard myself talking before I could stop myself. "Hi, H. Hello. Great to see you again. Nice to know you're not dead—I've spent a lot of time the last five months thinking you might be dead. Nice to know that you were thirty fucking minutes away from me this whole time, and you could have at least told me you were alive."

"Jack—"

"You know what? I don't want you to explain why you couldn't say goodbye in person. And I sure as fuck don't want to hear you tell me that you were doing this for me, that this was your way of keeping me safe. I'm sick to death of hearing that from you. I don't want anything, H, except for you to answer one fucking question. Can you do that? Can you answer one fucking question for me?"

His eyes looked glassy. His breathing was shallow.

"How fucking dare you? That's my question. That's the only one I want you to answer. How fucking dare you, H?"

"Jack," he said, his voice thick, and the next words were slurred. "I think I am about to lose consciousness."

Chapter 5

Every Teenage Rebel Who Had Ever Lived

His eyes drifted shut, and he started to slump. I steadied him and called his name, and then I saw it: the dart syringe lay in the footwell, where Holmes must have discarded it after we got in the truck. After he'd pulled it out of his side. I remembered the sound from the stairwell, the one I'd associated with paintball and airsoft—the sound of an air gun. In this case, a dart gun. Holmes had been shot with, what? A tranquilizer dart? And because he was basically the teenage version of the Terminator, he'd powered through and kept running.

Until now.

All of that rushed through my mind in a matter of heartbeats. Holmes's jaw was slack, his face soft in the absence of his usual ferocious control. He looked younger. And what if it hadn't been a tranquilizer dart? What if it had been some kind of poison? What if he was slipping into a coma, or he was about to have a heart attack, or some sort of irreparable damage was being done to his brain? I dragged out my phone, googled hospitals, and found an emergency medical center less than three minutes away. I slid the key into the ignition—

And I forced myself to take a deep breath. No. No, that didn't make sense. They'd stopped firing their guns. And they'd switched to darts. Because they'd recognized Holmes. Or because their orders had changed. But they wouldn't have switched weapons if they'd wanted to kill us— they'd have kept shooting their guns until we were dead.

I did a quick vitals check. Holmes's breathing was even, although he wasn't taking very deep breaths. His pulse was steady. His color was good. If he could talk, I knew what he'd tell me to do: wait, let him recover on his own. Going to a hospital meant doctors, questions, police.

"As long as you're breathing," I told him, and I caught his overalls and dragged him closer. "As long as I think you're ok. If you scare me again, though, we're going straight to the hospital."

He made a sound deep in his throat and half-fell against me.

It took some maneuvering, but I got him lying in my half-assed version of the recovery position, his head on my lap. His hair was so soft, and it was still sticking up all over the place, so I combed it with my fingers. I tried to be gentle, but as the adrenaline drained out of me, I started to shake. I let my head drop back against the seat. I closed my eyes. I didn't trust my hand anymore, so I settled it on his nape, where the skin was warm and smooth, and the bristles of short blond hair tickled my palm.

He started to snore. Just a little.

When Holmes had left—when he had disappeared from my life, after I had learned that he had lied to me, after I had learned he had known, for months, that my mom was a Watson, and that I was a Watson—he had given me a notebook. It had been his explanation. And although I hadn't been able to bring myself to read it, not at first, eventually, I'd had to know. I'd wanted some reason I could accept. I'd wanted something better than *to keep you safe* or *it's better this way*.

What I had found had sounded like Holmes: the detailed explanations, the anatomization and atomization of his feelings, the reasons and logic and evidence. Hell, he'd even included some diagrams.

But as I'd read, and reread, and reread yet again those pages of dense handwriting, I'd started to see the slippage. The circular reasoning. The leaps of logic. The vague, half-formed reasons that trailed off into unwritten ellipses. And then I'd known why he'd left. Not for any reason I could argue against. Not for any belief or opinion I could debate. He had left because he didn't want to be with me, and because he was, at heart, tremendously kind, he hadn't been able to say it.

And now, here he was again, his head warm in my lap, and the tears came even though I tried to stop them. I mopped my face with one sleeve of that damn velvet blazer.

Holmes's breathing changed, so I gave my face one last wipe and looked down at him. His eyes were open. The word from eighth-grade Language Arts, the word Mr. Scholz made us learn, was lambent. His face still had that unfamiliar vulnerability, the lines of cheek and jaw and chin smoothed out. His mouth worked once, soundlessly, and then, in a cracked whisper, he asked, "Is this a dream?"

I shook my head and carded his hair once.

Some of the armor fell into place, and he struggled to sit up, his breathing becoming labored. I gave a little tug on his hair and said, "Hey, dummy, you don't have to do anything right now. Relax."

For another moment, struggle played itself out in his face. Then he lowered his head again, and his breathing quieted. The wind moved through the corn, and that rushing sound came back, and it was vast. And his breathing rose and fell like the wind. And I felt, again, what it was like to be with him, to touch the edge of something bigger than myself.

After a while, he moved against my hand, like a cat pressing against touch, and I stroked his hair, and his eyes opened slowly. He reassembled his armor piece by piece and sat up. He wiped his mouth. I was a gentleman, so I hadn't planned on mentioning the drooling.

"How long was I out?" he asked, and his voice was flat and detached, and the distance fell into place between us again.

"Fifteen or twenty minutes."

He nodded. "Ketamine." He twisted to look out the back of the cab, and then he did a full scan. "Any sign of our pursuers?"

"Nope."

"I suggest we leave. If you can take me to a TRAX station, I can—"

"Are you fucking kidding me?" I hadn't meant to shout, but he was so stupid sometimes. When he didn't answer, I said—er, shouted—"I asked you a question."

His chin came up.

"I just caught you trying to break into Maggie's safe. And then some lunatics tried to gun us down before they switched to dart guns and tranqed you. And then they chased us through Lehi, and I had to sit here and wonder if you'd been poisoned and were going to die, only I knew you wouldn't want to go to a hospital, so I fucking sat here and waited and hoped your brain wasn't shutting down because for some reason I still care what you think. I got that creepy invitation, and I got that weird text, and I've had a few seriously fucked-up days. I haven't seen you in five months. And instead of explaining any of that, you want me to take you to a fucking TRAX station. What the fuck is wrong with you?"

The corner of his mouth trembled. An unfamiliar tightness marked the corners of his eyes.

"Get out," I said. "You want to do this on your own so bad? Get the fuck out of my truck." He reached for the door handle, and I grabbed him and shouted, "What the hell do you think you're doing?"

"I don't understand what's going on," he said—ok, he was shouting a little too. "You told me to get out!"

"Because I'm mad, you jackass! Not because I want you to go!"

I released him. He stared at me, and then he looked away and straightened the sleeve of his shirt. One hand came up to rub the side of his head.

"Are you ok?" I asked gruffly.

"Fine." He bit the word off. After ten or fifteen seconds, though, he said, "The ketamine is making it difficult to think."

"Maybe you should take an addy," I said. "I guess that makes me a hypocrite, but if you need something to help you, I guess now's the time."

His hand slowed. "I do not...have any."

I snorted.

He shot me a look and then, just as quickly, pulled his gaze away. As he resumed rubbing his head, he said, "I no longer use it." He labored over the silence that came after and then, with a note in his voice that I couldn't make sense of, he said, "You did not approve."

What I wanted to say was, *Since when does it matter what I want?* But what I said out loud, because I'm so smart, was, "Oh."

A flicker of something—amusement, possibly—crossed his mouth.

So, I shoved him. "Don't laugh at me, dumbass. I mean, that's good, right?"

He risked a longer look, amusement mixing with wariness in his face. "I suppose. There was some dependency. It was not pleasant."

"That's good, then. That's good that you're not using it anymore. I mean, that's good."

He didn't do anything. He didn't smirk, and his eyes didn't get big, and he didn't laugh. But I heard myself, and my face got hot.

"Yes," he finally said. "I suppose."

And then there didn't seem to be anything to say, so I said, "Are you sleeping any better?"

"Yes."

"Liar."

He shrugged, but some of the stiffness in his shoulders eased. "Better, Jack. Not well."

Then there wasn't anything to say. *I gave up my chemical dependency for you after I abandoned you* wasn't exactly a prime conversation starter, and I could still hear myself saying, *That's good, that's good, that's really good,* so silence seemed like the safest option.

Holmes, of course, couldn't read any of the fucking social cues that made this so fucking agonizing. He took a longer look at me, and his gaze seemed to touch every part of me: chest, shoulders, arms, lingering on my face. "You look well."

"I'm not."

"I'm sorry to hear that."

"I'm terrible."

He moved the seatbelt away from his throat. He was clutching the polyester strap.

"You abandoned me," I said. "And you lied to me. And you didn't even have the guts to tell me to my face. I hate you. And I will never, ever forgive you."

"Nor should you," he said, a hint of the posh-boy English slipping into his voice.

"No. Don't even try."

His hand slid along the belt, tightening and relaxing, tightening and relaxing. "I am sorry, Jack. I'm so very sorry I hurt you. I know that doesn't mean anything, but if it's any consolation, I will never forgive myself either."

I wanted to look relaxed. I wanted to look casual. Like nothing could touch me. Like zero fucks given. I slouched against the seat, and I wrapped a hand around the steering wheel, and the old, cracked vinyl was sticky against my palm. "Whatever."

Every teenage rebel who had ever lived was staring down at me from heaven and rolling their eyes.

I needed fresh air—I needed to do something with my hands besides hold on to that goddamn steering wheel—so I rolled down the window. Cold air washed in, stinging against my fevered cheeks, weirdly comforting with the mixture of moldering husks and damp earth. The maze looked pretty sad by this point, but it hadn't been harvested, and they hadn't tilled it under yet—they wouldn't do that until July when they put in the silage. A truck rumbled past us on the other side of the corn.

"I don't know what to do right now," Holmes said in a small voice.

"You could apologize a million more times."

"I am sorry—"

"Save it; I don't want to hear it."

"But you said—"

I turned in the seat, and Holmes pulled back a little. "I want to know what's going on. Who sent me that message? Why? What the hell were you doing breaking into Maggie's safe?"

Holmes grimaced. "Jack—"

"Think carefully about how you're going to finish that sentence. If it contains any version of 'it would be safer' or 'I can't tell you' or 'this is for your own good,' then you might want to consider how attached you are to your balls, because I will twist them the fuck right off if you try that shit with me."

He broke down and chewed his lip for a moment. It was hard to watch; Blackfriar had tried to break him of the habit, and even now, when he gave in to it, I could see him struggling with himself, trying to force himself to stop.

"Tell me about the invitation," he said. "And the message."

So, I told him.

"But that doesn't make any sense. Why bring you into it tonight? Why involve you at all?"

"Gee, thanks."

"No, Jack. It's not that you're irrelevant—"

"What every guy wants to hear."

"—but you are a complication."

"The second thing every guy wants to hear." I sat up straighter. "I want answers, H. No more stalling."

He picked at one buckle of the overalls. He had long, slender fingers, and right then, in the moonlight filtering in through the windshield, his skin looked like marble.

"I don't know about the invitation. And I don't know about the message you received tonight. As I said, those actions do not make sense to me, and I can't explain who orchestrated these events. But—" He stopped to draw a breath. "But I will tell you the rest of it. I'm afraid you are going to be angry with me."

"Huh. Really."

He threw me a look that, on anyone else, I would have called nervous. "I...did what you said. I lied to you. By omission. Watson—Sarah—had prepared a contingency. In the event of her death. Last November, I received a package in the mail that included, among other things, the Watson family tree. The one you took from Paxton. It's not clear what she intended or why she sent it to me. It's possible that she had planned, eventually, to send you that package if she had lived longer."

"But she didn't," I said. "Because your dad killed her."

Holmes froze. Color drained from his face until he looked gray, but his expression stayed locked in that unyielding neutrality. Finally, he said, "Explain."

"Your dad arranged for Burrows to kill her. He set the whole thing up." And I told him about that night in September, about returning to the cottage and finding Blackfriar searching my bedroom, about Sarah Watson's laptop, which Blackfriar had found where Holmes had hidden it. "He as much as admitted he killed her."

But Holmes was already shaking his head, and I thought it might have been my imagination, but his color looked better.

"H, I'm telling you—"

"I'm not saying you're lying, Jack. Or even that you're wrong. But what you've described—my father didn't admit to killing Sarah, did he?"

"He didn't have to. It was the way he—" I stopped; there wasn't a way to put into words the aura of menace Blackfriar carried, the half-verbalized threat, the way he had looked at me, and I had known—known—that he had killed Sarah Watson. "H, I was there. I'm telling you. What about her laptop?"

"Yes, that makes sense. The laptop's hard drive had been reformatted using a program that makes it virtually impossible to recover the data. Sarah was dealing information about the Holmes family, and she had information about Zodiac as well. It only makes sense that my father would want that information destroyed."

"He killed her, H. I'm sorry I didn't tell you, but I'm telling you now. I know he did it."

Holmes shrugged. "And I believe you're mistaken. For the moment, it doesn't matter."

"How can it not matter—"

"Sarah sent me more than the Watson family tree. She sent me a portable safe."

"And? What was in it?"

"I don't know. She didn't send the combination to open it. And, because of the possibility of a failsafe device that might damage or destroy the contents, I did not attempt to open it." Holmes stopped. "The instructions in the package were to have you open it."

"And you didn't."

"No."

"For fuck's sake." I rubbed my eyes. "So, you hid that stuff in my room. Again."

"I believed it had been a successful hiding spot before," Holmes said. "If I'd known about my father's visit, I would have altered my plans."

"No, don't try to pin this on me. Ok, you got the package in November. Then you hid the family tree and the letter and the portable safe in my room.

And then—" I stopped. "Maggie was behind all of that stuff in December? Sending Paxton to distract us, having someone to search the cottage—that was her?"

Holmes nodded.

"How?"

"Hm?"

"After—" I almost said, After you left. Instead, I said, "After everything calmed down, I started to wonder: how did anybody even know you had something worth stealing?"

Holmes gave me that look he usually reserved for when we were doing chemistry and I'd flubbed a particularly easy problem set.

Then it hit me. The Walker School was a prison. It was fancy, and it cost a lot of money, and nobody would call it that, not out loud, but that's what it was. That was the whole reason, Holmes had told me when we first met, he'd been sent there. The staff were regularly paid—by Blackfriar and presumably by other people, people like Maggie Moriarty—for information on Holmes and other students. Mr. Taylor, Dad's boss, had even tried to squeeze information about Holmes out of me once.

So, of course, somebody was opening student mail.

"Oh," I said.

"Yes."

"But, like, all your mail?"

"Jack," he said, and it was chemistry all over again.

"Ok, ok." I thought for a moment. "How'd you figure it out?"

"I tracked the operative who tried to meet Paxton at the bus station. The process was…circuitous, but it led me back to Maggie." It was hard to tell in the dark, but I thought he blushed. "Paxton confirmed information I had acquired."

"Jesus. Ok, and then what? You waited for the perfect opportunity for your heist?"

"The anniversary party was ideal. It would be held in Scorpio, so I would have easy access to Maggie's office, and security would be stretched to its limits keeping track of the guests."

I stared at him. "And that was your disguise?"

He touched one of the buckles again. "What?"

"What are you supposed to—oh my God."

"We're getting off track."

"A plumber?"

"The point, Jack—"

"In the first place, you copied my idea."

"That's ridiculous."

"Second, you don't even have a toolbox."

"I did have equipment—"

"I mean, Jesus, H, the obvious disguise for every fancy party ever, in the history of fancy parties, is catering staff."

"Yes, well, I did not have your expert opinion," he said, "so I did my best."

"Ok, well, aside from the dumbest disguise ever—well, except for that Junior FBI one you tried to use last year—what went wrong? Oh damn. Someone beat you to it."

"A third party had already accessed Maggie's office when I arrived. They were in the process of opening the safe when I engaged them."

"And they handed you your ass."

"They tased me," he said, his voice heating, and he touched his side. "Fifty thousand volts renders any question of competence or ability moot."

"They handed you your ass," I repeated. And then I remembered. "Holy shit, H. That's who I ran into in the hall; she went right past me—I thought she was a tech or staff or something, freaking out because of the power outage. Wait, was the power outage you?"

"Of course. What do you mean you saw her?"

"I saw her. She ran right past me." Memory struck, and I added, "She was carrying something."

Holmes shifted in his seat. "Yes, Watson's portable safe. It had been removed from Maggie's vault. Jack, I need you to think very carefully: would you recognize her if you saw her again?"

I made my thinking face. I scratched my noggin. I hemmed.

"Jack!"

"Yes, dumbass. 'Think very carefully.' Jesus Christ, I don't need to recognize her. She was wearing her ID badge. I saw her name."

It was one of the few times I'd left Holmes speechless. I wanted to buff my nails or something.

Instead, I added, "That's why it's going to be so easy for me to track her down."

"What do you mean—Jack, you can't!"

I leveled a look at him.

In the night's ambient light, Holmes's blush was the color of cinders, but he forged ahead. "Please, Jack. You—you mustn't." His words tumbled out, more of the English slipping into them. "I promise you that I will bring you the safe. I promise you I will give you everything. But you must trust me—"

"Oh, yeah, but here's the thing about that: I don't. I hate you, remember?"

He breathed hard for several long moments, and then he bit his lip so savagely that beads of blood rose when he opened his mouth again. They glistened like black mercury. "You do not understand the magnitude—"

"I don't care. Watson—I mean, Sarah—wanted me to have this stuff, right?"

"Yes, but—"

"And it's about my mom, right?"

"We don't know that. We have no idea what Sarah sent in that package. The message about your mother, the invitation to the party tonight, they could have been nothing more than bait to lure you into a trap. Correction: someone is definitely luring you into a trap."

"Then why did the instructions in Watson's package say for me to open the safe?"

"I don't know. Jack, you're not listening—"

"Here's what's going to happen. I'm going to find Sarah's portable safe, or whatever it is. I'm going to open it. And I'm going to do it whether you like it or not. But because I'm such a nice guy, I'm going to let you tag along. How does that sound?"

His hands tightened into fists at his side, opened, tightened again. He chewed the corner of his lip. A part of me wanted to tell him it was going to be ok, wanted to find a way to remind him to breathe, wanted to hold his hands while he struggled with whatever was scaring him so badly. But that part of me had gotten fucked over five months ago, so I watched.

"Please." The word sounded broken. "I know I have no right to ask this of you—"

"No," I said. "You don't."

For a moment, he looked like he was going to start crying. But, as usual, his tremendous control won out. His breathing flattened into an artificial rhythm. His long, pale fingers uncurled. He sat up straighter, wiped blood from the corner of his mouth, and nodded, but he wouldn't meet my eye. "Very well."

"Great," I said as I started the truck. "See how easy that was?"

Chapter 6

Popcorn Sock

Her name—at least, according to the ID badge she'd been stupid enough to wear—was Lynnissa Baca, and Holmes found her address in about thirty seconds.

"Do you have all the Zodiac employee information on your phone or something?" I asked as we drove north on I-15. Traffic had died down—as much as it ever did on this particular highway—and we swam through the night in loose schools of red taillights and the occasional lonely semi.

"Of course not," Holmes said absently, still scrolling on his phone. "My father would never give me that kind of access."

"Would he give it to Noneley?"

Holmes barked a laugh. Then his head came up and something like horror rimmed his eyes.

"Oh yeah, buddy. I met the whole fam."

It took him a long time to say, "I see."

"Your mom particularly seemed to like me."

"Mother is…wary."

I let him dangle.

We made it around Point of the Mountain, and the dark glitter of the Salt Lake Valley was opening up ahead of us when Holmes asked, "Did you…say anything?"

I smirked at him. I even gave him the eyebrows.

It took a moment, and then he huffed one of those little amused sounds. "I suppose I deserve that."

After a laugh, I shook my head. "I stared at them like JoJo the Idiot Circus Boy, H. I didn't know I was going to meet them. I definitely had no idea what to say."

"Noneley likes you," he said as he went back to his phone.

"She told you that? When?"

"She's been spying on you for ages."

"Jesus Christ."

It might have been the light from the dash, but I thought the little shit looked way too pleased with himself.

"To answer your question," Holmes said a few minutes later, "I pay for a subscription to a private investigator database. Well, a collection of databases, actually. It simplifies things."

"Like finding out where someone lives."

"Among other things."

"Such as?"

"Well, Lynnissa Baca has been employed by Zodiac for two years. She's got a PhD in computer science from CALTECH, and her work there involved machine learning."

"So, AI. Like Moriarty."

"Precisely."

"Which is why she'd have access to that floor of the Scorpio building."

"Yes."

"But it doesn't explain why she'd be stupid enough to wear her badge."

"She's not a professional thief, Jack. Besides, she might have thought the ID badge would actually make her less noticeable; remember, on an ordinary day, choosing not to wear the badge would have drawn security's attention, and she likely would have been stopped."

"Ok, well, why is she stealing from Maggie Moriarty? Does she have a death wish?"

Holmes made that little amused noise again. "She is, apparently, tremendously in debt."

"Oh. Shit."

"Yes."

"What else can you turn up on those databases?"

"I don't know. Someone keeps interrupting me."

Grinning in spite of myself, I said, "Hot damn, everybody. He's a live one."

"Stop talking now."

"It's more fun when you say it the other way."

Holmes bent over his phone.

"Like a cartoon villain," I prompted.

Holmes rubbed his head.

"I could sing to you while you work," I offered.

"Silence," Holmes snapped. "Will you please leave me alone?"

I did. After I ruffled his hair once.

Baca lived in a condo building that had been squeezed onto a block of north Salt Lake. It was a mixture of brick and white vinyl siding, and it looked relatively new—ten, fifteen years, tops. Each unit had a covered deck that bristled out over the sidewalk, and many of the units were warm with yellow light. At Holmes's direction, I parked another street over, and we walked back.

The condo building's main entrance was protected by a locked vestibule. Eyeing the intercom panel, I said, "Want to be a plumber again?"

"No," Holmes said as he continued walking down the block. "I want to see if her vehicle is here."

"Oh, maybe you can be a mechanic. Mechanics wear overalls."

"I don't understand why you find this disguise so amusing."

"Where to start—"

"Silence," Holmes said and walked faster.

We accessed the parking garage by following a ramp down from the street. It had one of those barrier arms that go up and down if you have the right fob or remote; we ducked under it. The smell of cold concrete and motor oil and piss rose up to meet us. This was close enough to downtown Salt Lake that they probably still had to deal with some of the city's massive homeless population.

Holmes's database had given him the vehicle information for Baca: a white Subaru, which we found on the garage's lower level in a spot marked 4B. Holmes used the flashlight of his phone to look through the windows. It was pretty clean—a Maverick fountain drink cup in the cup holder, some bonus ketchup packets in the change tray, a few wadded receipts in the passenger footwell. The back seat held plastic shopping bags: Target, Home Goods, Anthropologie. The lady liked to spend.

"I guess she's home," I said.

Holmes made a noncommittal noise.

"Do you want to break into her car?"

"Not without a Tyvek suit," he said.

I couldn't help it; I laughed. "H, it's not that bad."

"Remind me: what is the acceptable number of toaster pastries for a desk drawer."

"Hey, sometimes I get hungry when I'm studying!"

"I found popcorn inside a sock one time, Jack. Inside the sock. How does one even manage that?"

"One is bored and one is playing popcorn sock all by himself and one is really fucking good at popcorn sock." I crossed my arms. "You want to ask me what popcorn sock is, don't you?"

"I cannot," he said to himself, with what might have been panic tinging his voice as he turned toward the door that connected the garage with the condo building proper. "I cannot do this."

He needed a win, so I didn't even say anything about how cute his butt looked when he bent over to inspect the lock.

"Camera." I pointed above us as we waited for the elevator.

Holmes nodded; he didn't even look.

When we got into the elevator, I pointed overhead. "Camera."

"Yes, Jack."

When we got out on the fourth floor, I pointed again.

"We have nothing to worry about," Holmes said. "We've not committed any crimes."

"Yet. Well, technically you did by picking that lock. And maybe me too? I guess this is trespass."

Holmes shrugged, and we made our way to 4B in silence. He knocked.

"Why are we knocking?"

"What is the alternative? Do you want to surprise her in the bath?"

"No, but shouldn't we have a plan?"

"Yes. You'll restrain her while I search her condo."

"Uh."

"She's a thief, Jack. She won't report this to the police."

"That's not the part I'm worried about. Not the only part, I guess."

Holmes hammered on the door.

We waited a minute. Then another. Still nothing.

"Maybe she's asleep."

"That seems unlikely."

The way he said it, what lay behind the words, made my arms break out in goose bumps. "Maybe she took a sleeping pill because she's, you know, amped up from tonight."

He picked this lock too.

I couldn't help myself this time; the words had a nervous edge I couldn't totally smooth out. "You still have a cute butt."

"Jack."

"What? I haven't seen you in five months. It might have gone flat or something."

Holmes let out a few strangled words that were totally indecipherable but sounded like a prayer. The door popped free from the jamb, and Holmes straightened. "Remain in the hallway until I have cleared the condo."

I licked my lips. "Right."

Then I followed him inside.

He turned and gave me a furious look, but I nudged him forward, and then we both stopped.

We were standing in an open space at the front of the condo, a combination of living and dining areas, and the light off the deck, filtering through the vanes of the vertical blinds, left the room black and white, everything surreal and inverted like a photographic negative. Farther back, I was aware of the kitchen, and then a hallway. But most of my attention was on Lynnissa Baca, the woman who had run past me in the hallway. She was slumped in a chair at the table, an empty glass in front of her, and I was pretty sure she wasn't breathing.

Chapter 7

You and Mainframes

Holmes stared at Baca for a moment, his breathing steady and controlled. Then he turned on the light and moved across the room toward her. He produced a pair of disposable gloves from those ridiculous overalls, pulled them on, and took her head in his hands. He checked her pulse. After a moment, he stood and shook his head.

"We should call an ambulance," I said. I swallowed. "We should call the police."

"In a moment. Shut the door, Jack."

"What if she needs help—"

"Shut the door, Jack."

He sounded calm. Even, strangely, kind.

I guess it worked because I shut the door.

"She—" I began.

"She's dead," Holmes said, and he turned to face me. "The body is in primary flaccidity, before rigor ensues. Perhaps an hour. Not yet two. Is this the woman you saw running from Maggie's office?"

I swallowed again. Now, mixed with the faint perfume of an air freshener, I could smell urine again and made out the dark, inverted Y staining the chair between Baca's legs.

"Jack." Again, almost gently.

She had glossy dark hair in a bob, and her skin was brown with reddish undertones. Her eyes were partially open, but I couldn't look at them. She was short, solid trending toward heavy, and she wore silver and turquoise everywhere she could: hanging from her ears, around her neck on a dragonfly pendant, rings on every finger, even the concho chain belt.

I nodded.

"Step out into the hallway and make sure no one surprises us," Holmes said with that same quiet, assured authority.

But I shook my head. It wasn't the first time I'd seen a dead body. It wouldn't be the last. But it was the shock of it, I told myself. After a night of shocks. After finding Holmes again, and the havoc that had done to my well-calibrated system of giving no fucks. After seeing him hurt, worrying he might be—

"Jack—"

"I'm fine."

The words came out rougher than I would have liked, but they must have sounded convincing because Holmes studied me for another moment and nodded. He produced a second set of disposable gloves and said, "Begin in the bedroom."

So, I searched her bedroom. The furniture all looked new. It all looked like it matched. Thanks to too many hours of being forced, along with Rowe, to watch HGTV with Emma and Glo, I recognized the pieces as having a "mid-century modern influence": clean lines, neutral-colored upholstery, dark wood. I didn't find anything interesting in her dresser, or behind her dresser, or under the dresser. Ditto with the nightstands. I did find a box full of sex toys in the closet, including a wicked-looking alien tentacle dildo, but I left those for Holmes to discover. I wanted to see his face.

The guest room-slash-office had a similar design with even less of interest, and while the office had an abundance of paperwork—all of it neatly filed in hanging folders—there wasn't anything that I could make sense of, nothing that seemed to be immediately and obviously significant. Holmes would have to take a look as well.

In the main area at the front of the condo, Holmes had moved into the kitchen. He held out a sandwich baggie that held a powdered white residue. Then he nodded to a wine bottle left on the counter.

"So, what?" I asked. "We're supposed to believe she committed a major theft, broke into Maggie's vault, raced home, and—what? Used a bottle of wine to pulverize her pills, and then drank them down?"

"It's impossible to tell without a toxicology report, but her death appears to be consistent with an overdose. The glass on the table still has the dregs of the wine and a granular residue."

"But that's bullshit."

Holmes cocked one perfect blond eyebrow.

"She didn't steal from Maggie, run home, and kill herself. In the first place, that makes no sense. Why commit the theft at all if you're going to kill yourself? And it's not like she got caught, so she's not trying to avoid prison or—or whatever."

I decided on *whatever* because it was easier than saying, *Or having your dad and his pet Moriarty feed her to sharks with lasers on their heads.*

"Perhaps she did get caught," Holmes said. "Did you find the portable safe?"

I shook my head. "Wait, you think someone beat us here?"

Holmes returned the plastic baggie to the counter. He was silent for several long moments. The stillness in the condo was incredible; blood rushed in my ears like static.

"I believe you are correct that, taken at face value, the pills and the wine and the way she is positioned are meant to suggest suicide. And I believe you are correct that such a conclusion does not seem borne out by the events of the evening, what we know of them. And I believe you are correct that someone wants the police to believe Lynnissa Baca killed herself."

"But?"

"No buts, Jack. I don't know who did this, but I believe I know why. Someone...recruited Baca to steal Watson's safe from the vault. And that same person came here tonight, took possession of the safe, and killed Baca to silence her."

"Jesus."

"There's bruising on her jawline—faint, because the process didn't continue after death. Some broken hairs. It suggests a struggle. Someone held her head, perhaps."

"You think she fought whoever did this?"

"Perhaps. Or—or she was partially drugged, and then, when she was disoriented, she was forced to consume the remainder of the lethal dosage. She may have struggled, but by then, it would have been too late."

"Someone killed her. Someone planned this. Someone knew they were going to kill her." I could hear myself, hear how repetitive I sounded, the way I had earlier. *Good. Good. Good.* I was trying not to say, *Your dad did this.*

"Did you find anything in the bedrooms?"

I shook my head. "There were some papers. In the office."

He nodded. "I'll look at them. Perhaps you'd like to wait in the hall?"

"No, I—did you already search out here?"

"Briefly."

"I'll take a look."

"If you're uncomfortable—"

"What, being alone with a dead body? Go look at those papers so we can get out of here."

Something creased Holmes's mouth, not quite a frown, but he nodded, and after another moment, he hurried down the hall.

I shuffled around the front room. I looked at the art prints hung on the walls. I slid them aside, in case they were hiding anything, and let them fall back into place. I checked the teak-and-wicker accent cabinet near the door and thumbed through the mail she'd tossed there. Her bag was propped against the base of the cabinet, and when I opened it, I saw a laptop, phone, tissues, a tube of lipstick—that kind of stuff.

She was dead, so she wasn't staring at me. You couldn't call it that, anyway. But every time I looked over, her gaze seemed fixed on me: half-lidded, the eyes themselves barely visible, but following me. I stared back for a while. Death looked different at different times. Right then, it left her features drooping, her body limp. Her concho chain belt was twisted, and I thought about going over and fixing it for her. I was supposed to be getting used to it—to her, I mean. I thought I'd stop feeling it. Or it would stop affecting me. Or whatever I was supposed to say, however I was supposed to say it.

I didn't know why finding her, seeing her, hit me so hard. I didn't know her. What I did know—she was a thief, in debt, and had been dumb enough to get herself killed—wasn't good. Finding Watson hadn't affected me like this. Or Mr. Campbell, or Kazen Bates. Not even Dawson, and he'd been something like a friend. I'd been shocked. Frightened. Upset. But not this.

Since December, though, everything had been different. It was hard to pinpoint exactly when. The night I'd been run off the road in the middle of a blizzard, and a man had tried to kill me—with all those eerie echoes of the night my mom had died. Or learning that she had been a Watson, and by extension, I was too. Or losing Holmes. After Mom died, I hadn't thought anything could hurt me again. Not like that. But, once again, I'd been wrong.

I tore my gaze away from Lynnissa Baca. The door mat was askew, which I hadn't noticed. For lack of anything better to do, I bent to straighten it, and when I pulled it into place, I found that it had been covering a dark stain. Crouching next to it, I gave it a longer look. Oily. Black. Still wet, I thought. And definitely shaped like a shoe.

"H," I called.

He appeared next to me like a ghost, his face intent as he studied what I'd found. "Men's size eleven, I believe. Or twelve. Part of the print didn't take—" He gestured to where the print was incomplete and then used his phone to snap a picture. "—so it's difficult to say for certain. Well done, Jack."

"Did you find anything in the office?"

"Nothing obvious. There may be something significant, but it would take more time."

"We've got time."

"I'm not sure we do, and there's something else we need to check while we have the opportunity. Bring her bag; the police will wonder, but I'm not willing to leave it behind."

Holmes set the lock on the latch and pulled the door shut behind us. Then he took my disposable gloves, balled them up, and stored them in a pocket of the overalls. We rode the elevator down, but instead of returning to the parking garage, Holmes stopped on the first floor.

When we got out, it looked like the lobby of your typical apartment building: the locked vestibule that connected to the street, a mail room, a multipurpose room currently filled with children's toys, and then a door with MANAGER on its pebbled glass. Holmes picked this lock too. The door inched open as the elevator dinged, but Holmes moved without any apparent haste as he hip-checked the door and tilted his head for me to go first. I did, and Holmes slipped into the office behind me, and the door began to swing shut.

From the elevator came a man's voice, older, rough: "I'd throw my own son out of a moving car if he talked to me like that; the fuck chance do you think you have?"

A younger, campier voice answered him: "Daddy, I said I'm sorry!"

I caught Holmes's eye by chance, and for some reason, his face lit up with a blush.

The office was small and crowded with too much furniture: hardbacked, stackable chairs that probably got hauled out and set up in the multipurpose room for condo board meetings and book clubs and maybe the occasional light cult worship; an L-shaped desk with a computer; white laminate filing cabinets. Everything was a little battered, a little chipped, but you could tell they'd been going for Crate and Barrel by means of Ikea. Again, too much HGTV with Glo and Emma. Someone had spoiled it by hanging a poster on the wall that showed what was, by my best guess, a guitar-playing rock-and-roll wizard. I got the sense that whoever had designed it had believed fervently in psychedelics. From the trash can next to the desk wafted up the reek of microwaved turkey loaf and brown gravy.

Holmes moved unhesitatingly toward the desk. He donned a fresh pair of gloves, held out a pair for me, and then powered up the computer.

Perched on the edge of the desk, I took my time with the gloves, snapping them against my wrists so that Holmes flicked me a look.

"How are you going to do this?" I asked. "Let me guess. You're going to rear-admiral the cloud-connected synthesized intermodulation. And if that doesn't work, you'll copy the 1080 HTTP feed into the mainframe."

"What is it with you and mainframes?" he muttered in a distinctly un-Holmes-like manner. Then he tapped a few keys and made a satisfied noise.

"Are you kidding me?" I asked.

"Password is still the most common password. Even for admin accounts."

"Good Christ. So, what now? We poke around and hope we find something interesting? Actually that kind of sounds like what we did that night in your bed."

Holmes's shoulders tightened, and he hunched over the screen, but his clicking and typing didn't slow down.

"Are you looking for—"

"The security camera footage," he said. "And I've found it."

"You have got to be kidding me." I slipped off the desk and came around to see if he was lying, but he was Holmes, which meant he never lied about anything—well, apparently only earth-shattering stuff. On the screen, he'd pulled up what looked like a cloud-based dashboard for the building's security system. "Ok, fine, I'll ask. How?"

He pointed to a sticky note at the corner of the monitor, where someone had written in blue ballpoint a web address and, below it, a username and password.

"For the love of cocks," I said.

Holmes shrugged, but his words were clipped. "Most people do not imagine they will themselves be the victim of a crime, so they fall into patterns of what is easy, not what is best."

"Are you mad at me about the poking around comment? Because I had fun poking around. You know. In case you were wondering."

In the glow of the screen, the color in his face deepened, but he sounded more like himself when he said, "I saw some alphabet blocks in the nursery next door. As well as a train. Perhaps you can find a way to keep yourself amused."

"Ok, that was pretty solid."

"Less talking, Jack."

I pitched my voice higher. "Daddy, I said I'm sorry."

"I will remove you from this office if I must."

That was how you knew he ate this stuff up.

Instead of leaving, I watched as he checked the feeds of the security cameras. They showed the outside of the building, as well as the lobby, the second floor, and the third. The feed from the parking garage, however, was only a black screen. As was the camera from the elevator. And the fourth-floor hallway.

Holmes took a moment to delete the footage that showed us emerging into the lobby, and he deactivated that camera. Then he went back to the parking garage feed and scrubbed backward. For a little over an hour, the feed was black. And then it changed to white. The white lasted for several minutes, and then the camera feed looked normal again. Holmes let the video play forward again.

As we watched, a black car came down the ramp into the parking garage. It didn't have any plates, but Holmes made an annoyed noise.

"What?" I got closer, leaning on his shoulder.

Holmes tried to shrink away, but he couldn't do it without both of us ending up on the floor, so finally he said, "Jack."

"Uh huh?"

"It is—could you move your arm, please?"

"What's the deal with that car?" On the video, it was pulling into an accessible parking space. "Do you recognize it?"

Holmes was still grumbling and muttering and trying to shoulder himself free of me.

"H?"

"It is my car. Would you please—"

"Holy shit. Is that a Bentley?"

"Jack, please."

Before I could tell him to cowboy up, or something similarly encouraging, the door to the Bentley opened. I waited for our killer to emerge, but instead, I only had a glimpse of a hand, and then the screen lit up with white. Moments later, it went black.

Holmes swore under his breath.

"What?" I asked.

He played the video again. And again.

"How'd they do that?" I asked. "With the camera, I mean."

"A high-lumen flashlight. Followed by a piece of tape."

"Do you know who it is?"

"No, Jack, I do not know who it is."

He switched the feed to the elevator, but we got more of the same—barely a glimpse of a hand before the flashlight blinded the camera, and then, moments later, the screen went dark.

"I can't even tell if it's a man or a woman," I said. "Light skin, I guess. Relatively light, anyway. That's something, right?"

"Yes, Jack. In the state of Utah, where the population is over ninety percent white."

"Hey, dummy, I'm trying to help."

"If you want to help, get off me."

"Nope. I'm too comfortable, and besides, you were mean to me about the letter blocks."

Holmes did some more grumbling, some more of those plaintive, distressed, totally fake noises. But he didn't break my arm or flip me on my head or use even a single pain compliance hold, so I figured deep down, he was loving this stuff. I figured it was like catnip to him.

The rest of the blacked-out camera feeds tracked the killer's progress through the building. In each one, we'd catch the momentary appearance of a hand, and then a white-out that made it impossible to see anything else. I wanted to say it was a guy because I wanted it to be Blackfriar Holmes. But if I were being honest with myself, I couldn't tell. Man or woman. Young or old. It could have been almost anybody.

Holmes was uploading the footage to what looked like a private cloud server, presumably so he could obsess over them for the foreseeable future. I tried to think about what it meant, that the killer could move so easily through the building, could make sure that the only possibly identifying feature was the car, which looked conveniently like Holmes's own. I tried not to think about what it meant to be this close to Holmes again, my hip bumping his, the familiar architecture of his rib cage, the dense musculature of his shoulder. I tried not to think about having a semi, which was totally inappropriate, but also, I was seventeen, and I wasn't made of stone.

From the hallway came another ding of the elevator, and then a woman's voice. "—because it's simple. Do you know how to read numbers? Do you know numbers one through ten? That's all you have to know. They're on the front of the fucking building." She paused and must have spoken over whoever was on the other end of her call. "I should not have to put up with this to get my fucking Enchirito!" More distantly came the sound of the vestibule's door crashing open, and then I heard her shout, "Excuse me!" Then, mercifully, her voice cut off.

"Let's say it's a he," I said, and I tried not to think Blackfriar's name too loudly. "Whoever he is, he knew the layout of the building, right? He knew where every camera was. He was prepared."

Holmes made a noise of acknowledgment as he uploaded the video files.

"On top of that, he was prepared to kill her. Right? I mean, the way he came into the building, making sure none of the cameras caught sight of him, and then taping them, and then getting into her apartment, and—oh shit. H, did he get here before or after Baca?"

Holmes shot me a sharp look, and then his hands flew over the keyboard. A moment later, he replayed the footage from the parking garage. Baca's parking spot was empty.

"Well done, Jack," he murmured. "Very well done."

Ok, most of the time, I know I'm Jack Moreno, Boy Genius. But it was hard not to let that go to my head. "He gets here before her," I said. "How? Why?"

"For the killer to arrive before Baca, he must have anticipated her behavior."

"Or been working with her. He knew where to go because he was in on it."

Steps squeaked in the lobby, but no talking accompanied them. Hopefully she'd gotten her goddamn Enchirito.

"He arrives early because he intends to kill her," Holmes said. "Probably to drug the wine. He would have offered her a drink — celebratory, congratulatory. She had, after all, successfully stolen something incredibly valuable. They both would have wanted to celebrate."

"Wouldn't she have found it creepy that he was inside her apartment waiting for her? Wouldn't that have set off her internal alarms?"

Holmes was silent. Headlights reached us through the window, tracing a pale arc across the wall, and then the office was dark again.

"I understand that you believe my father was behind this—"

"I didn't say that."

"Jack, please." His voice was flat. Heavy. On someone else, I would have called it defeated.

"Ok," I said. "But I'm open to other possibilities." Not technically true, but hey. "What do you think?"

"We don't know the nature of the relationship Baca had with her killer. He—or she, Jack—"

"Yes, I know, it definitely could have been a woman."

"—might have been a lover, or a friend, or for all we know, they might have arranged for him to be in the apartment, waiting for Baca, so that the transaction could be completed as quickly as possible. We simply don't have enough information, and it is a mistake to theorize without sufficient data."

I recognized the second half of that statement, with its slightly antiquated sound, as one of Sherlock's favorite sayings. I didn't have to guess why Holmes was trotting it out now.

"I'm not saying it was your dad—"

Holmes shoved me hard enough to send me crashing into the filing cabinets. The surprise of it, and the force behind the shove, threw me off balance, and I lost my footing and fell. I had a disorienting moment in which I thought Holmes had been tricking me, that he'd been waiting for this the whole time—a chance to get away from me again. And then glass shattered, and the door crashed open, and the thud of bodies colliding filled the room.

I pushed myself up. And then, for a heartbeat, I stared. Holmes, in his dumbass overalls, was a whirlwind of movement as he fought a figure dressed in black. Someone had broken the pebbled glass in the door, and the door hung halfway open, and the light from the hallway cut across the office in a rhombus. Holmes snapped out a punch that should have put our attacker on his ass, but somehow the man dodged it, and he darted forward. The blade of his knife glittered as he stabbed at Holmes.

But Holmes had already moved out of the path of the blade. He was water and silk. He was a storm of light. Every movement was a grace. His foot caught the side of our attacker's head, and the man grunted and stumbled, but when Holmes followed up with an elbow, the man had already recovered and moved out of reach.

The office seemed too small for them to be fighting like this—too small for the fight to go on for more than a heartbeat. And, I realized, I was just standing there behind the desk. I might as well have been stepping on my own cock.

When the man lunged at Holmes again, I picked up an old, heavy stapler—some millennial's dream of *Mad Men* chic, a part of me registered— and chucked it. It caught the attacker in the chest, and it couldn't have done much damage, but it was enough that he made an annoyed noise and threw a look at me, while Holmes drifted out of reach of the blade again.

Throwing the stapler, I decided instantaneously, had been a mistake.

The man in black hurdled the desk in a single, easy movement, and me, Jack Moreno, ultimate street fighter, I stood there, slack-jawed, and watched the knife come toward me.

Then Holmes was there, sliding between me and the man with the knife. Holmes grunted, twisted, threw a punch that went wide. Our attacker pressed his advantage, slashing viciously at Holmes's face. Holmes slipped past the blade once, then again. But his movements were slower. And the man with the knife seemed as fast as ever.

And I was still standing there like a dumbass, so I picked up the desk phone and slammed it into our attacker's face.

He let out a pained sound of surprise, and Holmes delivered a heel strike that drove the man back a step. Our attacker shifted his weight, angled his body toward the door. Holmes lunged and caught his sleeve, but the man tore free—literally, leaving a scrap of his sleeve in Holmes's hand—

and threw himself across the desk. I glimpsed something on his forearm, dark ink, the suggestion of geometry. Then he sprinted through the open doorway.

Holmes charged after him.

Sirens moved towards us, but Holmes kept running.

"H!"

He pulled to a stop long enough to glance back. "Stay here—"

"Police!"

The sound of sirens grew. For a moment, nothing registered on Holmes's face. His expression was a stranger's: a frozen, murderous intensity. Then, slowly, the bloodlust drained away, and he shook himself and winced, favoring his arm.

"Are you ok?

"Pulled muscle."

"Do we—"

"We must run, Jack. Now."

Chapter 8

Thanks

We flew out of the parking garage, the Dodge going so fast we bounced coming off the slight lip at the top of the ramp. Holmes grunted again, and when I glanced over, his face looked white in the ambient glow from the street. He shook his head before I could ask and curled up against the door.

"H—"

"Drive, Jack. Away." He closed his eyes as though concentrating. "West."

So, I drove west, and we were half a block away before the flashing lights appeared in the rearview mirror. They didn't come after us, though; someone must have called the police, maybe the DoorDash lady. I remembered the way she'd said, *Excuse me,* as she'd left the building. In hindsight, she must have been talking to the man who had attacked us as he passed her on the way in. He wouldn't have been wearing a mask then, but there was no chance we could go back and check the security footage, even if the police hadn't been swarming the condo building. Holmes had disabled the lobby camera.

"He wasn't our killer," Holmes said out of nowhere.

"He might have come back—"

"And used the front door this time? No, Jack. He came for another reason. Like us, I imagine, he was trying to find Lynnissa Baca."

"Someone else wants to find her?"

"Someone else wants to find what she stole."

I thought about that for a while.

I was still thinking when Holmes said, "Turn here."

I turned, and we headed up into the foothills at the north end of Salt Lake. The capitol building glowed south and west of us, the stone luminous under the floodlights. The city itself spread out in a gold-dust glitter. And beyond that, the desert, the stars. But where we had turned, the road was wide, and the hills were dark.

"Haven't they heard of streetlights?" I muttered.

"The residents don't have much need of them," Holmes said drily.

That made me take a closer look. Thick, well-tended grass rolled away from us on either side, and headstones formed serried rows in the gloom. I would have noticed them earlier if I hadn't been worrying about, I don't know, super spies and thieves and a secret about my mom, and all the other shit from the last twenty-four hours. The Salt Lake City cemetery was one of the oldest in the city, where people had been buried—including a lot of the early Mormon leaders—since the pioneers had come into the valley.

"Stop," Holmes said. I stopped, and Holmes opened the door. "Wait here, please."

"H—"

"I need a moment alone."

He slipped out of the truck without another word, and the door clicked shut behind him. He strode off into the dark, his pace even and smooth. He was cradling one arm.

"God damn it," I said to no one in particular.

I got out and poked around under the seat until I found the first aid kit. Then the flashlight. Then I headed after him.

He'd gone behind some trees, and by the time I found him, he'd rolled the overalls down, and they hung off his hips. Starlight made his shirt glow like it was under a black light—everywhere except where it was stained with blood.

"Hey!"

His head snapped up, and even in the faint light, red circles marked his cheeks. "Jack, please wait in the truck—"

"You're hurt?" I told myself, Don't shout, don't shout. My voice rose anyway. "You're bleeding?"

"The injury is superficial—"

"Be quiet."

He opened his mouth to say something.

"Do not fucking test me right now."

Holmes eyed me, but after a moment, he shut his mouth.

By then, I'd reached him. "Let me see."

He hesitated.

"You are determined to piss me off tonight, aren't you?"

A beat passed, and with a note of worry, Holmes asked, "May I answer that?"

"No. I told you to stop talking."

Helplessness flurried across his face. He angled his blood-soaked side toward me. The sleeve of his shirt was rolled up, partially exposing a long, lateral slice across his biceps. It was still bleeding—not pumping blood, but a steady trickle.

"I tried to remove my shirt."

"How is it possible that for someone who is literally a genius, you don't understand what I mean when I tell you to stop talking?"

This time, I got anger from him. That was good. I was pretty fucking angry myself.

I got the scissors out of the first aid kit and dropped the kit on the ground. Holmes shivered when I took his arm. Or maybe it was a flinch. His breathing quickened for a single intake, and then it evened out again. His blood filled the air with the scent of copper, and this close, his breath reminded me of what he had tasted like when we kissed.

After snipping away the sleeve, I cut up along the shoulder seam, then down his side. The shirt opened like a book, and Holmes helped me slip it off his uninjured arm. His chest was even more clearly defined than it had been a few months ago. He'd lost weight, not that he'd had any to lose, and he'd added muscle. The blond fuzz between his pecs was a darker gold, like the hair under his arms. Goose bumps rose on his chest. His skin was ivory hills and smooth swales of shadow.

"This is going to sting," I said as I produced a disinfecting wipe.

Holmes nodded, his expression unreadable again.

I cleaned the wound as best I could, and the edge of the alcohol mixed with his blood and the smell of the freshly watered lawn. When I'd finished, I wrapped a bandage around his arm and taped it in place. "It needs stitches." I crouched to pick up the paper. The grass was still wet, and the cold was pleasant on my hands. I felt like I had a fever. Maybe I needed to yell at him some more. When I looked up, his eyes were silver, and shadows limned his cheekbones. "I'm guessing you're going to say no hospital."

"It would not be safe."

I grunted. "Maybe we can find a vet who will do it."

"That is a workable alternative."

"Jesus Christ, H. That was a joke."

I'd gotten all the trash, so I stood. He was still looking at me.

"Thank you."

I grunted again. But it felt like more was required, so I added, "It's my fault. You got stabbed protecting me."

"It's not your fault."

"It pretty much is. Unless you jumped across that desk for the fun of it."

"This is why I didn't want you to know. I didn't want you to blame yourself. I didn't want you to worry. You should not be inconvenienced or discomfited because of my incompetence."

I tried to wrap my head around that particular brand of *Looney Tunes*, but all I came up with was, "Well, that was a particularly stupid idea, wasn't it? What were you going to do? Tear off a strip of your shirt and tie it with your teeth?"

His silence lasted too long.

"Oh my actual God!"

"I was improvising."

From somewhere nearby came excited voices, and flashlights cut a trail in the distance The group took shape in the gloom. Excited voices. The rustle of paper. Laughter. They had to be young—they might have been our age, although they sounded so much younger.

"President Monson's next," a girl said. "This way."

A boy launched into a song I didn't recognize, some sort of hymn, and another girl began to harmonize with him. Mormon kids, I guessed. A scavenger hunt. A fun romp through the graveyard that felt safe and appropriate because it was church related.

Their voices faded, and then Holmes and I were alone again, alone with the smell of the wet grass, damp soil, the water in a vase where the flowers had started to turn.

"What's next?" I asked.

"I have an alternative to the veterinarian. If you're willing to—to help me. A little longer, anyway."

He said it the way he said most things—his voice untouched and untouchable, everything a statement that had been weighed and considered. The only hint of how much it cost him was that tiny slip in the middle.

I nodded. "Who is it? Some down-on-his-luck doctor who deals with gunshots for the mob? Or are we going another direction—a med student who's got gambling debts, or an undertaker, something wild?"

"My sister."

I managed not to say anything about that. Not out loud, anyway.

"She'll be at Sundance," he said. "She always stays there."

I didn't ask why she didn't stay at the family home. I didn't want to know.

By the time we got back to the truck, Holmes was shivering as he held his injured arm against his chest. His nipples were dark against his pale skin, stiff and pebbled with cold.

"If you could help me with what remains of my shirt," he said, "and with the buckles on the overalls."

Instead, I dug around in the back seat and came up with a Dodgers hoodie I'd left back there at some point. We eased his injured arm through one sleeve, then the other. "Leave the overalls," I said. His shoulders were narrower than mine, and I liked my hoodies big. I liked how it looked on him—how he looked in something that was mine. I yanked the zipper up. "You look more thug that way."

He gave me that tiny, amused huff. It would have been easy to accept the lie his face was telling: that everything was under control, that he was fine. But I helped him up into the truck anyway, and his body was stiff with the pain he fought so hard to mask.

"You can rest on the way," I said.

A bitter smile twisted his lips. "That would be nice, wouldn't it?"

By the time we'd turned around, though, his eyes were closed, and his breathing had gone slow and deep.

"H," I said.

He made a sleepy noise.

"Thanks," I said.

Maybe he didn't hear me. But maybe he did, because he let me pull him across the bench, and he rested his head on my shoulder, and he was asleep before we reached the highway.

Chapter 9

Irrelevant

We drove down the long, halide tunnel of light that was I-15. In the distance, brighter than the amber confetti of homes and businesses, a few Mormon temples glowed white. There was no way to miss them. Celestial landing strips, maybe. I left the stereo off, and I thought. I wondered how I was supposed to stay mad at him when he couldn't take care of himself. I wondered what I was supposed to do about the way his breath changed when I touched him.

Getting to Sundance meant going up Provo Canyon, and the route was almost identical to the way back to the Walker School. The canyon walls sheared off the edges of the night sky. The spray of Bridal Veil Falls was phosphorescent, backlighting a mule deer. In the draws, the shadows were deepest, and I had a moment where I thought about what it might look like from above, the dark spine of road winding through mountains, the dark ribs of the draws, like a snake's skeleton. Holmes was still breathing evenly, rocking against me every time we went over an uneven patch. I had a hard time not feeling like this was September, and we were doing it all for the first time.

But instead of taking the turnoff that would lead us back to Walker, we went to Sundance. The main area of the resort was a compound of cedar-colored buildings with steel roofs, a mixture of log and board-and-batten and glass. This time of year, this time of night, the parking lot was mostly empty.

"H?" I whispered.

He woke with a quick intake of breath, and then there was the sound of someone trying not to drool, plus the smacking of lips. If I grinned, he'd take it the wrong way, so I made sure not to let it show on my face. Still, he gave me a long, suspicious look as he ran the back of his hand over his mouth, as though somehow I had tricked him.

"How'd you sleep?"

"Fine."

"How's your arm?"

"Fine."

"Right. Why would you make this easy? What's your pain level?"

"Six." No hesitation.

"H, a six is not fine."

"It's insignificant." He wiped his eyes and pointed with his good hand. "Follow that road. She always takes the same cabin."

I let the Dodge roll forward again. "What if someone else is using it when she comes to visit?"

"You don't know my sister," Holmes said, voice dry.

"Because you never told me about her."

"Why would I tell you about her?"

"I don't know, H. Because—" We were friends, I almost said. Instead, I managed, "It might have been important."

"If it had been important, I would have told you."

That was the kind of thing that made otherwise sane, healthy, happy teenage guys want to drive off a cliff, so I said, "Are you close? She seemed…nice."

Holmes huffed that amused little breath, but then he said nothing. I guessed that was my answer and kept driving up the hill, and we left the lodge's central compound behind us. Pine and spruce and cedar grew thickly here—planted and tended, part of the ski resort's landscaping—and even with the windows up, their perfume filtered into the cab. I'd almost forgotten the question by the time Holmes started speaking.

"Noneley and I are not close. Not in the sense I think you mean. She's four and a half years older, and once she left for school, we saw each other primarily at holidays." He was silent for a moment. "You enjoy using the word genius. Noneley is literally a genius. She is the single most intelligent person I've ever met."

A million different questions sprang up, but on the other side of the cab, Holmes's silence loomed like a shadow.

Then he sighed. "Very well, Jack. If you must."

"She said something about setting your dad's desk on fire."

That startled a laugh out of Holmes. "She and my father do not have what you would call a healthy relationship."

"Gee," I said.

Holmes shifted his weight. He didn't look at me, but his—what was it? Disapproval? Defensiveness—locked around him like armor.

"Did he do the same…stuff that he did to you? To her, I mean."

"Do you mean, did he train her?"

No, I wanted to say. I meant, did he fuck her up with games and riddles and the sadism he excused as training? Did he make her feel like she couldn't be herself? Did he try to break her like he did you?

"My father's approach with Noneley—as far as I know, anyway—has been different. He ignores her."

"He ignores her? He—all the shit he's done to you, and Noneley doesn't have to go through any of that?"

"Noneley does not require the additional support that I do."

"Oh my fucking God."

Holmes turned toward the passenger window.

"He tortures you—"

"I do not want to discuss this."

"Too bad; we're discussing it. He tortures you, and he—he does all these horrible things to you, and you defend him and say it's for your own good, and whatever, fine. But you can't sit here and tell me that Noneley gets a total pass and pretend like it's ok. Why? Because she's a girl? And I don't want that bullshit about 'she doesn't need the same help.' There's got to be a reason."

"Of course there is," Holmes snapped, his head whipping around. "If you'd use your brain for once and think, Jack. Does it not occur to you that this how he hurts Noneley the most?"

I stopped the truck.

Holmes pulled back slightly and set his jaw.

I threw open the door.

"Jack—"

The cold air met me, running fingers through my hair, pulling the scent of cedar into my lungs. I stalked to the edge of the road and screamed, and when I ran out of breath, the sound echoed back to me. It died slowly, and when it had faded away to nothing, I went back to the truck.

"You drive me fucking crazy," I said to Holmes as I dragged the seat belt into place. "Do you get that?"

Holmes still held himself with the same wary watchfulness, like I was a feral animal. "I'm sorry I said—"

I snapped my teeth at him.

Something eased in his expression, and the tension in his body slackened. He huffed that little breath.

"You want to give it a try?" I asked, hesitating as I pulled the door shut. "Might make you feel better."

"God," Holmes said in an unfamiliar tone. "If only it were that simple."

We drove the rest of the way in silence.

Almost.

"You're supposed to say you're sorry too," Holmes said as the Dodge carried us up the slope. "Because our fight is now over, and I apologized."

"Ok, I'm sorry too. And I still hate you."

We drove another hundred yards. The cones of the headlights swept back and forth as the truck trundled and bounced. He looked at me the whole time, and the feeling of his attention fully directed toward me was so physical that I reached over and pushed on his face, turning his head away.

"Will you truly never forgive me?" he asked so quietly that I barely heard him.

I sat with that question for a long time. What he was really asking was, would I ever let him get close enough to rip out my heart again?

"I don't know," I finally said, my voice scratchy. "Getting stabbed to protect me was a good start. Do that a few more times, and maybe we can call it even."

After a moment, he nodded.

"H, no. That was a joke."

"Of course."

"I won't forgive you if you get hurt trying to protect me. That's not how this works."

"I understand, Jack."

I groaned. "Please don't get stabbed again."

"I didn't get stabbed. I was cut."

"Oh my God. I want you to promise you won't put yourself in danger because you think I'll forgive you."

"I promise you that I won't put myself in danger because I believe you'll forgive me. This is her cabin."

I slowed, stopped. The cabin was an impression at the corner of my eye: log walls with thick gray chinking, a gabled roof, at least one side that was floor-to-ceiling glass. I focused on Holmes. "What's the catch?"

"What do you mean?"

"That was too easy. What did I miss? What's the trick or the loophole or the escape clause?"

"There is no loophole."

After a moment, he slid toward the door, but I caught his arm. I didn't know how to ask him again. I didn't know what magnetized the air between us. Our breaths took on a rhythm. In the silence, with the truck's engine off,

I thought I could hear his heartbeat. That was impossible, of course. But I thought it anyway.

With a shrug, Holmes said, "It's not a loophole. I meant what I said: I will not put myself at risk for you because I believe you will forgive me."

I felt it coming, a train that couldn't be stopped, the mingled dread and thrill of something tremendous rushing toward me out of the dark.

"Whether you forgive me or not is irrelevant, Jack. I will do it, if it becomes necessary, because you are the most important person in the world to me, and because I love you."

He broke my hold gently, slid out of the truck, and closed the door with a quiet click.

Chapter 10

Thinking Righteous Thoughts

It took me a couple of minutes before I could get out of the truck. My face was flushed and prickling. My eyes hot. What do you say to that, I wanted to know. What am I supposed to say? What do you want me to say? But what I was really asking was, How am I supposed to do this again? I barely survived the first time; what am I supposed to do when you leave me again?

I wiped my eyes—they were still dry—and checked myself in the mirror. I still looked like the biggest jackass on two legs, so I patted my face once again, just to be sure, and got out of the truck.

By the time I reached the cabin, Holmes stood on the porch, knocking. He didn't glance over at me. No awkwardness or uncertainty marred the lines of his body. He didn't look remotely like someone who had dropped a megaton of emotional devastation into my lap. When I'd first met him, I'd thought of him as a Holmes bot because he'd been so icily locked away, so controlled, so reserved. But this wasn't that, either. It would be nice, I thought, if someone would tell me what the fuck was going on.

The door opened, and Noneley stood there. She'd ditched the cheerleader uniform, thank God, and opted for a Trinity College sweatshirt and a tiny pair of shorts. The sweatshirt was what I'd heard Emma and Glo call boyfriend sized, which meant it was attractively baggy, and the shorts left her long, smooth legs visible. I couldn't help myself; I looked at Holmes, saw him in my hoodie that was too big for him in the chest and shoulders, and my face heated up like a furnace again.

Noneley, of course, didn't miss any of it. She took in Holmes, grinned at me, and said, "Hello, baby brother. Hello, Jack. You got here just in time; I'm going to murder this boy if he doesn't leave."

Without another word, she headed into the cabin. Holmes followed, and I went last, shutting the door behind me.

Inside, it looked like an interior designer's fantasy of a Western-style log cabin. Only a few lights were on, leaving much of the space in shadow — better, I thought, to appreciate the view from the floor-to-ceiling glass wall that looked south. But I could still make out the cathedral ceiling, the fieldstone hearth, the ladder to a loft. The furniture was all reclaimed wood and leather and copper touches. In case it wasn't John Wayne enough for you, a longhorn skull peered down from one wall.

Movement in a darkened doorway drew my eye, and now I noticed several knives—apparently part of a set I could see in the kitchen— embedded in the doorframe. A pale face swam in the darkness.

"Is that Tom?" I asked.

Noneley made a disgusted noise as she moved into the kitchen. "He's so boring. He showed up a few minutes ago, snooping around." She pulled a bottle of amber liquid from a cabinet and drew out a tumbler. As she splashed a few fingers' worth of scotch into the glass—the peaty smell reached me now—she said, "I'd suspect Father of sending him to vex me, only that's not possible."

"Why?" I asked.

"She was going to kill me," Tom said, his voice high and piping from the darkened doorway.

"Were you going to kill him?" Holmes asked.

"I honestly don't know," Noneley said with a laugh. "Brother, what are you wearing?"

"Wait, why isn't it possible that Blackfriar sent him?" I asked.

"Because the only reason he'd be here," Holmes said, "is if he lost my father. Most likely, my father shook him off his trail, and so he came here, hoping to infiltrate our family by a different approach. The real question is why my father allows him around us at all."

"No!" Tom's protest sounded a little too outraged. "He didn't lose me; I was conducting my own investigation. That's why I stopped following your father!"

"Goodness," Noneley muttered and put back the rest of the scotch.

"She threw knives at me!"

"Is that Jack's?" Noneley asked. "It must be. How scandalous; let me take a photo."

Hot circles appeared in Holmes's face, but before he could speak, I said, "Stop teasing him. He's hurt, and he wouldn't let me take him to a hospital. He needs help."

She turned slowly toward Holmes. "Brother?"

"It is minor—"

"Both of you stop trying to impress each other," I said. "It's annoying, and I'm tired, and I'm out of patience for Holmeses." Before Holmes could say whatever he wanted to say—probably nothing nice—I caught the front of the hoodie in one hand and worked the zipper down with the other. He shifted and squirmed as I helped him out of the hoodie.

"Is that it?" Noneley asked, inspecting his bandaged arm. "It can't be all that bad, can it?"

"I told Jack—" Holmes began.

I pointed a finger at her. "I said stop." Then I rounded on Holmes. "She's teasing you. Quit giving her what she wants."

Noneley smirked. Holmes let out a series of disgruntled noises that verged on swears.

"Every fucking Holmes," I said under my breath. "I swear to God."

"I can help," Tom said from his hiding spot. "I'm in med school."

With a laugh, Noneley started toward a doorway at the other end of the cabin. "Come along, brother. I've got my kit in the bathroom, and the light's better there. Jack, help yourself to a treat. There's alprazolam, diazepam, I believe I even have flunitrazepam. And, of course, the scotch."

"Do you want me to go with you?" I asked Holmes in a low voice.

He was hugging himself with his uninjured arm, obviously trying to cover himself as much as possible, but he shook his head.

I let him go. The clink of metal instruments came from the bathroom, and Noneley's murmured instructions, and Holmes's monosyllabic responses. I pushed my hands through my hair. Then I poured myself some scotch, tossed it back, and choked to death.

Noneley started laughing again in the bathroom.

Tom poked his head out of the darkened doorway and looked around. He was dressed in the same suit he'd been wearing at the Zodiac party, but now it was stained in places, and I wondered if he'd been telling the truth about his own investigation. Into what? Blackfriar? If so, that sounded like a good way to get himself killed.

"Come on, already," I said. "She's not going to do anything to you."

"You didn't see her," Tom said, but he slipped out into the cabin's main room. He touched one of the knives still embedded in the wood. "She's insane."

"We can hear you," Noneley sang out to us.

I poured myself more of the scotch. It had gone down my throat like fire, but now some of that fire puddled in my gut, and it felt kind of good. I nodded to the deck, on the other side of the wall of glass. Tom gave the bathroom a wary look. He went out onto the deck first, and I followed, shutting the door behind me.

The air felt colder than it had a few minutes before, cold enough I was surprised not to see my breath steaming. They must have replaced the deck recently, or done some sort of repair, because the smell of fresh lumber met me. The stars and moon gave the strange illusion of brightness: the canyon seemed clear and well lit until I started focusing on details, and then I realized how little I could actually see.

"All right," I said. "Who are you?"

He wrapped his arms around himself. "I'm Tom Watson. Who are you?"

"Look, you're making a big mistake. I don't think you are who you say you are. And if I'm suspicious, you'd better believe the Holmeses are too. They're fucking sharks. The first drop of blood in the water, and they're going to tear you apart. Especially Blackfriar. So, whatever your game is, it's time to pack it up and head home. You don't like Noneley throwing knives at you? Imagine how you're going to feel when Blackfriar gets bored with you."

Tom was silent for a long moment, and when he spoke, his voice was bitter. "And I suppose you're telling me this out of the goodness of your heart?"

"More or less, yeah."

He laughed, the sound short and breaking off into pieces. "I know who you are. You're not a Watson, not really. You're a nobody. Vestigial. Genetic information that's worthless but that continues to be perpetuated. The blood means nothing unless you were raised correctly. With the proper training. In the right family."

It was so bizarre that for a moment, I didn't know what to say. That didn't last long, of course—and that comment sounded a little like Holmes in my head. "That's some eugenics-level bullshit. Bloodlines? Genetics? Family? Jesus, you're as bad as they are."

He cocked his head at me. His posture loosened. "You don't believe in it?"

"It's nuts."

After a moment, Tom let out laugh. "Huh."

"So, who are you? Really, I mean."

"I'm Tom Watson." And then he smiled. It didn't touch his eyes. "Who are you?"

All I could do was stand there and stare back at him. The primitive part of my brain told me if I looked away, if I moved—what? Well, I didn't know. But it would be some *Animal Planet*-level fuckening, that was for sure.

On the other side of the tall windows, a flicker of movement pulled at my attention. I ignored it, but Tom's posture changed, and he glanced over. Holmes was fending off Noneley, who was obviously being solicitous for the sole purpose of annoying her brother. Tom threw me a final, dead-eyed look and went back inside the cabin.

I stood there for a moment, my cheeks stinging in the cool. I thought I saw something move—the red-orange glimmer of animal eyes, a silhouette of hundreds of pounds of muscle, the trees rippling as they accepted it, whatever it was, back among them. I saw Tom's eyes floating in the darkness. Then I shook it off and went inside.

Holmes was seated on the couch, trying to pull on my hoodie, while Tom did his best to keep the hoodie off—under the guise of helping. It involved a lot of "Let me—no, like this—you're so brave—here let me try—you poor baby—" and, all the while, his hands touching every inch of Holmes's exposed skin. Holmes was warding him off with even less success than he'd had with Noneley, who sat at the island counter that divided the kitchen from the living room. She was helping herself to the scotch again and raised a glance toward me, grinning, in salute. It took me a moment to remember I was still carrying my own drink, and I downed it, coughed up my remaining lung, and wiped my stinging eyes.

"But he looks so butch," Noneley was saying with what sounded like disappointment.

"He's quite stereotypically masculine," Holmes said, giving up on the hoodie yet again to remove one of Tom's hands, which was stroking Holmes's biceps under the guise of sliding the sleeve into place.

"Gee, thanks," I said.

"Unless it comes to self-defense."

"Hey!"

"Oh yes," Noneley murmured. "We're aware."

"Well, combat of any kind, really," Holmes said.

"I handle myself fine," I said.

"Obviously not," Tom said. "You let him get hurt!" His voice was different, and it took me a moment to spot it—under the poorly faked outrage, a hint of camp had snuck into the words. It was even more noticeable as he went back to petting Holmes's shoulder. "You poor baby. Are you ok?"

"Of course he's ok. He's sitting right there. You're practically drooling on his tits."

Noneley coughed on her scotch.

With a vexed noise, Holmes sat up and warded off another of Tom's wandering hands. He looked at me, frustration and confusion marring his face.

"He's flirting with you," I told him.

"I'm not flirting with him." Tom pouted, which until then, I'd actually thought was just a thing on TV. "I'm helping him. Which nobody else seems to care about. Do you realize he got hurt?"

"He did? Where?"

Tom threw me a furious look and went back to cooing over Holmes

"Jack," Holmes said, and his voice was tangled with discomfort and uncertainty, "tell him to stop."

"Tell him yourself."

"Tom, please do not—no, don't—"

Noneley was laughing openly now.

"Put him in a wrist lock," I told Holmes. "That's how you started flirting with me, remember?"

"I did not—" But Holmes cut himself off, those bright spots of color warming his cheeks again, and I realized, to my surprise, I'd hit home.

It was enough to make me take pity on him. A little, anyway. I moved into Tom's space, and his only choices were to let me grind up on him or get out of the way. He got out of the way. I knelt in front of Holmes and helped him into the hoodie again, and I zipped it up for him. He wasn't meeting my eyes. Noneley was still laughing, and Tom was huffing and shifting his weight and using all the body language at his command to tell everyone how upset he was.

"How's your arm?" I asked.

"Fine."

"Do better than that."

He cut his eyes toward me—a bit sulkily, which was weirdly gratifying—and said, "It took fourteen stitches, but it's shallow, and Noneley provided me with antibiotics."

"How often is he supposed to take them?" I asked.

"Every eight hours," Noneley said.

"I'm perfectly capable—" Holmes began.

"With food," Noneley said.

Holmes met me with a challenging look that lasted less than a moment before he broke and turned away.

"Uh huh," I said. "Thank you."

"You're quite welcome, Jack. But Holloway is being decidedly obstinate, and he refuses to tell me what the two of you have been up to. What kind of trouble did my baby brother drag you into?"

"We dragged each other into it, I think. That's kind of our thing."

"That means you're a bad influence," Tom said. "You should be helping him. If you were really a Watson, you'd be helping him. That's what Watsons do."

"Good Lord," Noneley said as she poured more scotch. "He's been like this for weeks, you know. It's unbearable, and Father eats it up."

"You should leave," Tom said. "If I have to, I'll make you leave."

I was getting ready to say something suitably—well, butch, which felt like it was proving Holmes's point. Before I could, though, Holmes said in a dead voice, "If you touch Jack, I will kill you. Do you understand?"

The silence had a sprung quality behind it. Then Tom gabbled, "I wouldn't—I wasn't going to hurt him!"

Holmes lifted those silver eyes long enough to stare at Tom, and even though I had a lot of reasons to imagine all sorts of fun things happening to Tom, things like getting thrown through a plate-glass window or taking a weed whacker to the face or getting eaten by that mountain lion prowling around outside, I honestly felt bad for him. A little. He backed up, his sun-bleached hair falling into his eyes, and fell over a chair.

"Weeks and weeks," Noneley said to no one in particular. "It has to be one of Father's jokes."

Tom righted himself, and he put the chair between himself and Holmes.

"I was going to say something butch," I told Holmes.

Holmes held himself very still for a moment. Then, his fingers trembling, he traced the back of my hand. He withdrew the touch a moment later, hugging his good arm around himself.

"Well, since no one is going to tell me what's going on, I'll have to figure it out myself, I suppose." Noneley cracked a look at me over the tumbler. "Let's see. Holloway, you've been suspiciously quiet for weeks now, and you didn't put in an appearance at the party—what little there was of it—even though Father expected his heir to be present. Meanwhile, Jack, you showed up uninvited and managed simultaneously to surprise Father and ruin his evening, which means I would have liked you even if my baby brother weren't desperately in love with you."

The color in Holmes's cheeks deepened. Tom let out one of those outraged breaths.

"Then you disappeared," Noneley continued, "and the power went out—I'm assuming that was you, brother; he's always been unbearably dramatic, Jack, so you must prepare yourself for that—and no one could find Father, and the bitch went berserk. I tried to follow her and lost her in the chaos, and now here the two of you are. So, what did you try to steal from the bitch, and what went wrong?"

"Does she mean Maggie?" I asked Holmes.

He rolled his eyes. "They go back ages. Noneley can't stand being outdone."

"The bitch stole my maths paper," Noneley said with a grin. "Forgive me if I prefer to call her by her proper name. Come on, Hol, tell me. It had to be something important to you—so important, in fact, that Daddy's perfect boy did something naughty and broke one of Daddy's rules—"

"Stop," Holmes said in a tight voice.

Where I knelt next to him gave me a direct line of sight to Noneley's face, so I couldn't miss the unfathomable look that transformed her expression. Then it was gone, and she was smirking again.

"Well, what did you need, then?" she asked. "Besides patching up— I'm assuming you did something perfectly swoonworthy to get yourself that little beauty. What was it, Jack? Did he throw himself in front of a knife for you?"

"Yes, actually."

"If you were properly trained—" Tom began, but when Holmes looked at him, he cut off and took another step back.

Noneley let out an *aww* and mussed Holmes's hair, and while he sputtered and tried to fix it with his good hand, I said, "We need to access a laptop and phone, but I can't tell you why. Not yet. Can you help us do that?"

"Can I? I imagine so. But why would I, Jack? Aside from my devotion to my baby brother and, by extension, to you."

"He's not even a proper Watson," Tom said.

"Let's go with devotion and all that," I said. "Plus, there's a significant chance it will fuck with Maggie."

"Well, I do love fucking with the bitch. Do you have the devices?"

I retrieved them from the truck, and Maggie looked them over.

"These are Zodiac company property."

"That's right."

"You're asking me to breach my own family's proprietary security."

"Good God, Non," Holmes muttered.

I grinned. "That's right."

"Why didn't you say so? Anything to ruin Father's day." She turned toward Tom. "You, come along. And don't speak unless spoken to."

Tom shot me a poisonous look—although why any of this was my fault was beyond me—and he trailed after Noneley into one of the bedrooms, and the door shut behind them. Then Holmes and I were alone, and the room became a vacuum, and everything that had taken place between us in the Dodge came rushing in to fill that emptiness.

He had said, *I love you.*

Present tense.

Meaning, right now.

He was also still trying to fix his hair.

The second scotch was sending curling tendrils of heat through me, reaching from my belly to my fingertips, to my toes, my body unknotting.

"Here," I said, and I finger-combed it into semi-respectability. Then I studied his face. "Did she give you anything for the pain?"

"I'm fine."

"You can do better than that, please."

"No. I do not require a topical analgesic for stitches."

"I swear to God, I could almost hear you say exoskeleton. Will you take some aspirin? For me? Since it looks like your jaw is about to break off?"

After a moment, he gave a short nod, and I rooted around in Noneley's kit, which looked hardcore enough to handle World War III, until I found Tylenol. Holmes took two, and I felt his forehead.

"I don't have a fever."

"Christ on a cracker, H, I know. You got stabbed keeping me safe, and I have no idea what to do. You're lucky I'm not rubbing Vicks on your chest."

Silence answered me. Then he huffed one of those little breaths and leaned into my touch, and I scratched his scalp. Somehow, he ended up with his head pressed against my thigh. My body still had a lot of hormones running through it, plus the second scotch, and I tried to think righteous thoughts.

"Thank you for the acetaminophen," he whispered.

I made a noise that I hoped was enough for an answer.

"I don't know if coming here was correct." The words sounded wrung from him. "Noneley's feelings about Maggie make her involvement...complicated."

"Meaning, she could have recruited Baca to break into Maggie's office, and she might be the killer."

"In so many words."

I didn't answer right away. His breathing had slowed, deepened. My hand followed the back of his head. I raked my nails lightly across his nape, and he shivered and let out the tiniest sound of pleasure. Not to be crass, but at that point, thinking righteous thoughts wasn't cutting it any longer.

He couldn't have missed my reaction. He was right there, so to speak, and he had an annoying tendency to notice things. But he didn't move, didn't pull away, didn't freak out.

I heard myself talking, heard myself like it was someone else saying all these sane, rational things, when the other ninety percent of my brain was thinking about the way he'd looked with the hoodie hanging open over his chest, about the delicious red lines my nails left on his pale skin, about the way his body had fit against mine that one night, months ago. Like now. Like this.

"We needed help," that rational, non-hormone-crazed part of me was saying out loud. "We didn't exactly have a lot of options. It was a calculated risk, and besides, she obviously cares about you."

Holmes let out that little huff again.

"She does," I said with a laugh. "She's psycho like the rest of your family, but she loves you."

Holmes said nothing, but after a moment, he made a deep noise that vibrated through his chest. It might have been agreement. It might have meant anything.

"You need sleep," I whispered.

He nodded. The movement brought him precariously close to my, uh, situation.

"Let's get you into one of the bedrooms."

His protest was small and squeaky, and it made me grin as I crouched to get an arm around him. His eyes opened when I urged him to his feet, and they were molten in the soft light.

"Come on."

"Can't sleep."

"We'll see about that."

His next noise was wordless, kittenish defiance.

"Uh huh," I said with a quiet laugh. "Tell me about it in the morning."

The bedroom was clearly not being used, so I fumbled with his clothes in the dark: the hoodie first, his skin warm under my hand, the ridges of muscles the same as I remembered and, yet, different. Harder. More defined. It wasn't doing anything to help my situation. I got him out of the shoes, which I only now noticed were an ancient pair of Vans, and I felt oddly flattered by that choice. Then I rolled the overalls down and slipped them off. He sprawled across the bedding, his body a delicate marblework anatomy. I left him his boxers because he'd freak the fuck out if I didn't.

By the time I got him under the covers, his breathing was soft and regular, and sounds of movement came from the cabin's main area. I eased the door shut behind me and saw Noneley pouring herself another scotch.

"Where's the fanboy?" I asked.

"I sent him back to his hotel." She made a face and gestured to the laptop and phone. "There's not much, but you're welcome to it."

I wanted to take the computer and phone back into the bedroom, but I was worried the light from the screens would wake Holmes—and, worse, that he'd insist on examining everything right then. So, even though I didn't want to stand there with Noneley not-so-figuratively breathing down my neck, I did. I checked Baca's laptop first: her emails, her browser history, her hard drive. I even checked the calendar and saw only a series of meetings, appointments, calls. A quick check, but everything looked like it was connected to Zodiac, the kind of thing you'd expect to find on a work laptop. Then I checked the phone and did everything again. More of the same. Nothing interesting.

Except for one message. It was in the trash, delivered six days before, with only a number—no name—and it was short and sweet: *We need to talk, luv.*

Now, who did I know who talked like that?

I copied the number into my phone and forwarded myself the message. "Do I need to leave these on? So they don't lock, I mean?" I asked Noneley.

She watched me. The smirk was gone, and her face was intent, her fingers tight around the tumbler. "I'd like to keep them, if I may. I might be able to find something useful."

I wanted to know what *useful* meant to her. I wanted to ask what she'd meant when she'd said, *Daddy's perfect boy.* I wanted to ask what she knew about her father. If she knew he was a killer. If she knew what he'd done to Sarah Watson. I wanted to ask if she was the one who'd sent me that invitation, and if this was all a game to her. I wanted to ask what Holmes had said about me.

But I didn't ask any of that. I closed the laptop and powered off the phone, and I nodded and started for the bedroom where I'd left Holmes.

"Jack," Noneley said.

Her voice hooked me, and I turned.

She didn't look like Holmes at first—their coloring was so different, and her face was so animated, so expressive, so mischievously playful that the fact that it was all an act only seemed to be part of the fun. But the intelligence behind those hazel eyes, their tremendous focus when she brought them to bear on me—that was pure Holmes, and in that moment, the similarity was so obvious that it felt shocking I hadn't seen it until now.

"I suppose I should say something big sisterly."

"You'll kill me if I hurt him," I said. "Got it."

"You've already hurt him, Jack. If he weren't so attached to you..." She trailed off. She shrugged. The shrug was Holmes too, like watching a sculpture move.

I waited for more, but nothing came. She was ice and bone and amber in the shadows, and when I moved again, retreating to the bedroom, her hazel eyes followed me, glinting like the mountain lion's.

In the room, I thought about putting a chair under the handle, then fought a laugh. That wouldn't stop a Holmes. Each one of them was crazier than the last. I left Baca's laptop and phone on the dresser, and then I texted Dad: *Can I sleep over at Rowe's? Please?*

His reply came through almost immediately, and I barely scanned it—just enough to know it was an affirmative.

Holmes's breathing was quiet and steady. I kicked off my jeans, hung Rowe's blazer on the bedpost, undid the buttons on my shirt with trembling fingers. I was going to be a perfect gentleman. There would be an extra blanket in the closet. I'd put a pillow on the floor. He was tired, God only knew how tired, and he needed all the sleep he could get. And anyway, I hated him, although the details of that were getting fuzzier by the minute.

When his head came up from the pillow, his hair was standing up on one side, and his voice was cottony. "Jack?"

"Go back to sleep."

He put his head down. His breathing was still so soft. And then he stretched out an arm, hand turned up, fingers open.

I might be butch and stereotypically masculine and whatever else they wanted to say, and I was most definitely, most seriously, fucked in the head. But I'm not made of stone.

When I got under the covers, he curled up against me, his cheek pressed to my ribs. I didn't want to do it, but I couldn't help myself: I let my arm cradle him, drew him closer, settled him into place. We had always fit together. Always. From the beginning.

"Did you find anything?" he mumbled.

"Go to sleep," I said.

He stirred, trying to lift his head.

"Knock it off," I said. And then, hoping it might settle him: "I think we need to talk to Paxton. Tomorrow. After you sleep. God knows how we'll find him, though."

"Easy," Holmes said, burrowing into my side again, his body already loosening again with sleep. The last words were barely more than a breath, and I thought, at first, I'd misheard him. "We live together."

Chapter 11

A Living Saint

I shifted into park too hard, and the truck lurched to a stop.

Shading his eyes against the mid-morning light, Holmes glanced at me. He looked remarkably better after a full night's sleep. I'd only had a couple of quick looks in the mirror, but I was pretty sure I looked remarkably worse.

"What?" I asked.

"You stopped abruptly." Which, in true Holmes fashion, was both a statement and the beginning of an inquisition.

"Huh," I said and got out and slammed the door.

For those of you who haven't experienced this yet, apparently finding out that the boy you don't care about—scratch that, the boy you hate—has been shacked up with his super hot, super confident, super, uh, endowed friend, who also happened to be his first love and basically was Holmes's idol because he was mature and sophisticated and perfectly at ease with all the other Holmeses—apparently finding out something like that can really fuck up your sleep.

We were in another of the north-Salt Lake residential neighborhoods, not far, actually, from Baca's condo. If I'd had reason to suspect Holmes of killing her, and if I hadn't personally seen him sleep off the ketamine from a dart gun, I might have wondered about the proximity. As it was, I was doing plenty of wondering about Holmes's new—or maybe not-so-new—roommate.

The sidewalk did steady traffic in white yoga mommy types, with their leggings and long-sleeve athletic tops and sporty vests. Some of them were pushing strollers. Some of them were waddling with a bump. Only a few of them were carrying coffee, but again, this was Salt Lake, and most Mormons would rather be boiled alive in a fiery lake of coffee than drink it. One pair strolled past me, an older woman explaining vigorously how this new essential oil company was not a pyramid scheme.

Holmes's building looked out of place on the block—new construction shimmed into place between redbrick walkups. It was too sleek, too modern, a jigsaw of stucco and glass that was undressed and tinted, so that it looked more like an office building or a hotel. The grounds were zeroscaped and minimalist and obviously expensive, in contrast to the little patches of vibrant green cultivated in front of the other buildings. I studied it, trying to keep my engine going, but it was hard to stay mad at him when he was so goddamn stupid sometimes.

"Let me guess," I said. "Paxton picked it."

"Well—" He darted a sidelong look at me. "—yes."

I sighed, rubbed my eyes, and fought a losing battle against shaking my head.

"What?" Holmes asked.

"I don't know, H. What do you think?" Then I added, "Are we checking the garage first?"

His hesitation was obvious, but he ended on "Yes. Jack, is something—"

I started toward the entrance to the parking garage. Holmes caught up quickly, of course, and he watched me out of the corner of his eye, probably thinking I wouldn't notice.

The garage was mostly empty, aside from a few minivans and crossover SUVs, and Holmes indicated a lone Prius that had its hatchback open. It was currently stuffed with boxes and suitcases, clothes crammed into every available crevice, some of the garments already falling out of the car. One t-shirt had spilled out of the back and lay on the concrete: black, with pink varsity letters that spelled BIG DICK ENERGY.

"Of course he drives a Prius," I said.

"What does that mean?" Holmes asked, and of course, he didn't ask it like a normal person would, but because he actually wanted me to explain it.

"You've lived with him for God knows how many years. You tell me."

"I don't understand your tone. You sound upset." He touched the tab of the zipper on his—my—hoodie. In a testing voice, he asked, "Are you upset?"

The fun, appropriate, mature, and responsible thing to do would have been to be a passive-aggressive little bitch for the foreseeable future. But, since this was Holmes, he would only get earnestly worried and sincerely concerned and continue to make polite inquiries and look for social cues.

So, instead, I said, "You're goddamn fucking right I'm upset!"

The words bounced back from the concrete around us, so maybe it was more of a shout, and maybe it wasn't all that hard to stay mad at him.

"Jack—"

"You've been living here for five months, H? Less than an hour away? With him?"

"At the time, I believed—"

I held up a finger and made a warning noise, and to my surprise, H cut off. "Do. Not. Lie to me."

The corner of his mouth trembled.

"He blackmailed Aston," I said.

"I do not condone—"

"He got Dawson killed."

Holmes set his jaw. "You know perfectly well—"

"I don't know anything, H. I don't know anything about you. Last night—" My voice broke, and it was thicker when I managed to speak again. "He kidnapped me, remember? Did you guys laugh about that while you were hanging out together? Was that something fun to talk about after you finished fucking?"

The hurt radiated through his face, and then chips of fire flared in his cheeks, and his voice became brittle and high. "Stop talking! I want you to stop talking."

"Too bad." His hands opened and closed at his sides. "What?" I asked. "You want to hit me? Are you going to beat me up so I'll do what you want?"

"I would like to."

"Then do it. You do whatever the fuck else you want, so just do it." His fists tightened, knuckles white. "Do it!"

"Don't shout at me!"

"I'll shout if I want!"

When the echoes died away, the sound of traffic from the street filtered in. Holmes's breathing was labored, and his eyes were glassy with tears. He wiped his face on his shoulder and, in a tightrope version of his normal voice, said, "Are we finished?"

"No." But I had to jerk myself back from that, and almost as quickly, I said, "Yes. I don't know."

He nodded as though that had somehow made sense. He dried his eyes again, and tears filled them immediately, but his voice was steady as he spoke. "Paxton is clearly in the process of leaving. It would be in our best interest to prevent him."

I managed to make a sound that passed for agreement.

"I will go to the condo. You wait here in case he slips past me."

"Are you going to warn him?" I asked. "Are you going to tell him to run?"

Hurt fractured his expression again, but this time, it vanished into cold passivity. He held out his keys. "If you don't trust me, then I will wait here."

I considered the offer. Then I shook my head.

A moment later, he was gone, the door to the building closing quietly behind him.

My phone buzzed with a message from Dad: *Where are you?*

Another text came through almost immediately: *Why does the parental app say you're in Salt Lake?*

I slid the phone back into my pocket.

I remembered the weight of Holmes's head on my chest, the smell of his hair, the peacefulness of his breathing.

Instead of doing that to myself, I went back to the truck and got out an ancient pipe wrench Dad kept under the back seat. It had a handle two feet long, and it was solid steel, and in theory, it was only for self-defense. Maybe *he'll try to kidnap me again,* I thought as I gave the wrench an experimental swing. As far as I was concerned, that made everything self-defense.

I found a spot between a Honda minivan and a tiny Toyota crossover, and I waited and watched. It didn't take long. Paxton came out of the building at a frantic walk, boxes loaded in his arms, throwing glances over his shoulder. You couldn't miss him: tall, athletic, dark hair in a faux hawk, almond-colored skin. When he reached the Prius, he started shoving things around in the hatchback, trying to make room for the next load. He was still working on it when I whapped him in the back of the leg with the wrench.

He screamed and fell, and he grabbed his leg and rolled on the oil-stained concrete. I felt a moment of pity, maybe even worry that I'd overdone it. Then I stepped on his neck.

Paxton choked, slapping and clawing at my leg. His eyes looked a little bulgy. He was trying to work something out of his pocket with one hand.

"Hi, Pax," I said. "Let me run something by you really quick, before you do something stupid. I'm guessing you've got a knife, and you're thinking you're going to stab me in the leg. Which would piss me off. A lot. And I'm already pretty pissed off, so that's saying something. So, before you do it, you need to consider one thing: a knife in the leg is going to hurt like a motherfucker, but it's not going to slow me down when I break your head open with this wrench."

He sputtered, and he clawed at my leg some more, but he gave up on his knife. Spittle flecked his cheeks, and his eyes were wide and definitely protruding now as his face turned a surprising shade. Puce, maybe. I feel like that's what Ms. Prinze would have called it in seventh-grade art.

I took my foot off his neck before he passed out. In case you needed proof that I'm a living saint.

He coughed and hacked and spat, and he did a lot of massaging his throat and trying to look pitiful. I stood there with my wrench and enjoyed visions of braining him.

"Oi," he finally managed. "What the bloody hell?"

"What are you doing, Paxton?"

"Jesus, Mary, and Joseph. You could have killed me."

"Could have. Might. Will. What are you doing, Paxton?"

"What am I doing? What are you doing? This is how you spend your days now? Hiding in car parks, waiting for innocent passersby to hit with your club?"

"Remember how I told you I'm pissed off?" I gestured chest-high with the wrench. "I started here." I moved the invisible line up a few inches. "Now I'm here."

Paxton stared at me. Then he mouthed what I took to be, "Bloody fucking hell."

We were both quiet for a minute. Tires squealed somewhere else in the garage. Paxton's breathing did sound raspy, even when he wasn't making a production out of it, and that made me feel a little bad.

I felt less bad when he asked, "Where's Hol?"

"Interesting question. You tell me."

"Come off it, bruv. You wouldn't be here if you weren't with him, so where is he?"

"How long have you and Holloway been together?"

Paxton blinked. "What?"

"Have you ever heard of something called statutory rape?"

"Jeez—hold on, hold on. He's my little mate is all. We get on. That's it."

"I've got this crazy belief," I said, hoisting the wrench, "that the modern-day criminal justice system is missing out on the potential of corporal punishment. So, why don't we start with me breaking your leg, and we'll go from there?"

"Bruv, bruv, bruv, hold on!" Paxton scooted back against the Prius and held up a hand. "He's a mate. That's all, innit?"

"No, I don't think so. In fact, I don't think you're his mate at all. I think, as usual, you want something. And you'll do whatever you have to do to get it. You'll be the big brother. You'll be the sexy but untouchable best friend. You'll be the fuck buddy, right? You did it once, and you broke his heart. H might not see you for what you are, but I do."

His expression changed. The wariness remained, but the emotional undercurrent changed, became something that ran swift and deep.

"I'm going to ask you again," I said. "What are you doing?"

"You see what they're like." His voice was darkly, richly bitter, all the playfulness skimmed away. "The Holmeses. The Moriartys. They're not even proper people, are they? They look at the rest of us, they see playthings, toys, tools. You've been around them a year. You've been a Watson even less than that." He sneered. "How does it feel, yapping at their heels, hoping they decide to pet you instead of a swift kick to the ribs?"

"H isn't like that."

Paxton rubbed his chin. "Hol—Hol is a good bloke. Too sweet for his own good. They'll eat him alive when they get bored playing with him."

Moments slipped past us. The cotton of my shirt was bunched under my arms, and the smell of my sweat mingled with the oiled steel of the wrench. I didn't know what to say to any of that, so I said, "You haven't answered my question."

"I wasn't going to hurt him."

"You've hurt him plenty already. He told me what you did. How you pretended to be his friend. How he needed you. And as soon as you got what you wanted, you abandoned him. You knew what his life was like, and you left him in that hellhole."

Paxton stared at me. Then he burst out laughing. "Is that what he thinks? Christ, for a smart lad, he's a proper dumbshit sometimes. I was allowed to stay until Blackfriar decided he wanted this proprietary whatsit, some little piece of code he had to have. So, he enrolled me at the college where a certain professor worked, and I got to bend over and take one for the glory of the Holmes family. Photos. Shock. Chagrin. And then a quiet resolution, everybody satisfied. And then it was the next job. And the next. And the next. I'm the best Blackfriar has, you know."

"That's supposed to be better?"

He rubbed his jaw again. "Do you know anything about the Adlers? About the family, I mean. Not me."

"Here we go. Woe is me. Mommy spanked me and Daddy didn't believe in my dreams."

"Maggie's father shot mine when I was six." He flashed a grin. "Spoze you feel like a bit of an arsehole, don't you?"

It took me a minute. "Uh, yeah, actually."

Paxton's grin faded. "Shot him in front of me. In the face. My mom never came back from that. And I still have to see Maggie's dad at parties, still have to see Maggie, still have to smile and play nice. I'm alive because the Holmeses kept me alive. Kept me in that big, empty house as a pet. Because Blackfriar wanted me, but he was done with my dad, done with my mom. Those toys weren't any fun. He wanted something new."

"Jesus."

"Hol doesn't know, of course. He'd go bonkers. He's as stupid as they come about things like that. But I learned the lesson fast enough: you're alive as long as they want you alive. That's a family lesson, by the way. Always have a reason for them to want you alive. The Adlers are, if nothing else, survivors. And every once in a while, we do manage to put one over on the Holmeses. We might not make it look pretty, but we're still here."

"Why don't you run? Why don't you go live somewhere else? Anything would be better than this. Being used? Having Maggie call you up when she wants you to blackmail a closeted kid like Aston? Doing the Holmeses' and the Moriartys' dirty work until they get tired of you?"

Paxton gave me a strange, unreadable smirk. "Got it all figured out, have you?"

"I can figure out that much."

"Well, that's the Adlers sorted then. 'Nuff said." But the smirk got bigger. "And what do you figure happened to all the Watsons?"

The door to the condo building slammed open, and Holmes emerged at a run. He skidded to a stop, crepe soles squeaking on the concrete, and stared at us. His eyes fastened on the wrench, and I offered him my most innocent look and moved it behind my leg.

"Jack—" And then, with a trace of bewilderment, "Paxton?"

"Watcher, Hol," Paxton said miserably.

His face was pale, his eyes hollowed, and he was favoring his arm again. I realized I'd forgotten, in my masterclass of petty bitchiness, that he was still hurt, and that one night's sleep didn't make up for the months that he'd been running on nothing but adrenaline.

He was also holding a shoe.

Following my gaze, Holmes held it up so I could see it better. It was one of his chukkas—the shoes he invariably wore unless he was in one of his disastrous disguises. And the bottom was black with what looked like oil. Memory flashed: the oily footprint in Baca's front room.

"A car that looked like my car," Holmes said, his voice hard as his eyes slid to Paxton and then to me again. "We saw it on the security footage. And now this. In my closet."

"Shit," I said. "Someone's trying to frame you."

Chapter 12

I Tied My Laces

"It wasn't me," Paxton said, and the words came so quickly and easily that they had to be automatic. "I didn't do it."

The silence that followed had the same cold, cavernous quality as the garage itself. I shivered and chafed my arms; it might have been May outside, but May in Utah felt pretty damn chilly when you were underground.

"Honest, luv," Paxton said, twisting to look up at Holmes. "You know it wasn't me."

"H, go back inside." I tapped the wrench against my side. "Let me talk to him."

Paxton burst out laughing and held out a hand. "Hol, be a sweetheart?"

Holmes glanced at me, his expression searching, and helped Paxton to his feet. When Holmes wasn't looking, Paxton shot me a smirk.

"Ok," I said. "You can stay if you want, but stand back. I don't want to get brains on my hoodie."

"A bit much, innit?" Paxton murmured to Holmes, and for some reason, that made Holmes huff his little amused breath. "At least he's cute."

Holmes suddenly found something very interesting to stare at on the ground.

"Did he hurt you, luv?" Paxton asked, his fingers brushing Holmes's arm.

Holmes snorted.

"Course he didn't." Paxton's hand came to rest at the small of Holmes's back. "Come on, then. Let's get you out of that thing and into some proper clothes."

Which meant I had to trail after them, holding the wrench like a jackass.

When we got into their condo, I had that same moment of disorientation that I'd felt when I'd seen the building. The walls were a neutral color somewhere between untreated plaster and oatmeal. The furniture—a chaise, a coffee table, a dinette set—were chrome and leather and glass, and everything looked hard and uncomfortable. Paintings hung on the walls, beige texture pieces, gloopy dabs of paint, one that looked like a kid had gotten into wet concrete with a stick. A hint of something that might have been cologne or a candle, something peppery and tobacco-y, with a trace of citrus, hung in the air. No way Holmes had chosen that.

Paxton was talking a stream of nonsense as he shepherded Holmes into a bedroom. I left the wrench by the door and followed. The room was a spare, utilitarian space, the way Holmes's residence had been at Walker: bare walls, simple bedding, no knickknacks on the dresser. I stayed in the doorway, watching as Paxton and Holmes slipped back into their routine from the last few months.

It was…not what I expected. Frankly, it was kind of shocking. Paxton was still an ass, of course, and every other thing he said was flirty, provocative, risqué. But the way he moved around Holmes was completely unsexual. The way he touched him. The way he hovered in Holmes's no-fly zone. It was gentle. Playful. Almost childlike. He was walking a line the two of them had negotiated years ago, and I realized I was seeing Paxton the big brother, whom maybe nobody else had seen. Some of the things he said glanced right off Holmes's armor. Others made him roll his eyes. A few made him blush, which only encouraged Paxton—one comment, whispered into Holmes's ear, made Holmes shoot a look at me, his whole face catching fire as Paxton burst out laughing.

"Off with it—easy, luv, easy," Paxton said as he slipped my hoodie off Holmes's shoulders. He sucked his teeth when he saw Noneley's bandage. "Need me to have a look at that?"

"It's been tended to."

"It's been tended to," Paxton said. "Sod you, you little bugger. Say thank you."

"Thank—" Holmes cut off with a totally un-Holmes-like squeak as Paxton pinched his nipple.

Holmes's eyes cut toward me again, and then he directed a savage kick at Paxton, who laughed and dodged easily. Coming after him, Holmes drove a sidekick at Paxton that probably would have broken a bone, but Paxton slipped away again, laughing even harder, his face wild and animated. Under Holmes's mask of embarrassment, I could see the rueful amusement there too. He was still trying to cover the pinched nipple. In spite of myself, I started laughing as well.

Paxton ended up behind me, arms around me, laughing and threatening and demanding at the same time. "Oi, stay back, you! I mean it! Jack'll defend me."

"You've chosen poorly, then," Holmes said as he advanced on us.

"H!" I objected. I was trying to get free of Paxton, but not too hard — the amusement was infectious, and a part of me was starting to understand what Paxton was doing: breaking the tension of those awful moments in the garage, giving each of us time to steady ourselves. That realization was a surprise at the back of my mind, an unexpected dimension to someone who had been, in my mind, a cardboard cut-out of a fuck boy up until now.

"The last time I saw him working a heavy bag," Holmes said, still advancing, "he managed to trip over his own feet, get his shirt caught in the bag's stand, and in the process, nearly hang himself."

"Of all the fuckery! That was bad luck! And you promised you weren't going to tell anyone!"

"This is who you've chosen for your defender."

"Right," Paxton said, arms tightening around me. "Then maybe he's my hostage."

The change in his tone was slight, but combined with the change in his body, it rang a warning bell in my head. I got more serious about breaking free, but Paxton pulled me back a step and lifted me until my toes were the only thing touching the floor. I'd seen him naked, knew he had muscle, but he was stronger than I'd expected, and my twisting and elbowing wasn't doing anything to loosen his hold.

"Go on then," Paxton stage-whispered to me. "Beat me up and put on a good show for Hol, show him what his man can do."

Holmes stopped his advance. His face shuttered, and he folded his arms. "That's enough, Paxton."

A smirk laced Paxton's voice as he continued, "Or maybe we should flip the script, bruv. Make him jealous." He kissed my cheek, and he smelled like sandalwood and that hint of tobacco, his stubble scraping my jaw. His voice was raspier when he added, "Look at him."

He wasn't wrong. Holmes was glaring at us, that dead-ice look locking his face. Against all odds, it made me smile. I patted Paxton's arm. "Let me down, big boy. It's not fun for him."

"He'll like it later, though," Paxton said, but he released me, and my heels hit the floor. "Get his blood up, and he'll be proper possessive when he gets you alone."

"You were in the process of leaving," Holmes said. "Don't let us stop you."

"He's teasing you," I said.

"I know perfectly well what he's doing. He never lets up; it's unbearable."

That made Paxton laugh. He breezed past Holmes and opened the closet, and he laid out a washed pink oxford and navy chinos. "Are you going commando, luv?"

"Get out!"

Paxton threw a crooked smile and turned toward the door, but I grabbed his arm. "Nice try." I pointed to the bed. "Sit."

"Worth a shot, innit? And he makes it so easy." But he sat and spread his legs, and the joggers didn't leave much to the imagination. He made a point of meeting my eyes as he adjusted himself. Then he winked. "Offers open. We could make him proper jealous."

I recalibrated. Apparently, a fuck boy with a dash of big brother was still, by and large, a fuck boy, and I wanted to know what that meant for the months they'd spent together. I tried to drag my focus back to more important things—at least, what other people would consider more important—and asked, "Want to tell us what's going on?"

He shook his head; the crooked smile was back. "Sorry, bruv. Don't know what you're talking about."

"I think you do."

He shrugged.

"Why did you need to talk to Lynnissa Baca?" Holmes asked.

"Who?"

He was so smooth he was like glass. If I hadn't already known he was lying, I would have believed him.

"Nice try," I said again. "You texted her a week ago and said you needed to talk. About what?"

"She a friend of yours? I haven't been back to that school since I left, mate. Hand to God—ask Hol."

"This is serious," Holmes said. "Lynnissa Baca was murdered after stealing something from Maggie. Someone killed her last night."

Paxton smoothed the bedding, shaking his head again. Then he muttered, "Shit."

"You didn't know that? You'd better get ready for more questions; we won't be the only ones who track that message back to you."

Paxton dry-washed his face.

"You know something," I said. "You texted her. You needed to talk to her. When we got here today, you were getting ready to run. What's going on? Did you hire her to steal that stuff from Maggie?"

"Sod off."

"Did you kill her?"

"Are you taking the piss?" He dropped his hands and looked at Holmes. "Is he taking the piss?"

"If you—"

"I was in that tech boy's bed last night," Paxton said, still speaking to Holmes. "The little one who wears the jumpers. You want proof? He likes making videos."

"Pax," Holmes said in a surprisingly soft voice, "what's going on?"

The hurt caved in Paxton's face. "Yeah. All right. You want to know what's going on? What's going on is some serious shit, and you ought to leave. Get away from here. The same reason I'm running: because I'm a dead man if I don't."

"Why did you send Baca that message?" I asked. "What did you need to talk to her about?"

"You got something wrong with your fucking ears?"

"Why did you send Baca that message? Why are you running? What's going on—"

He made a furious noise and started to stand, but I was faster, and I shoved him back onto the bed. He half-fell, the springs protesting under his weight, and he tensed. I could read it on his face: the internal debate, whether to attack and take his chances.

"You're not a punching bag," I said, "and I tied my laces today. So don't fucking try me."

The fight drained out of him, but he only shook his head.

"What's happening, Paxton?" Holmes asked. "You say run, but—"

"I say run, but you don't fucking listen, do you?" He sat up, elbows on knees. "And what the fuck is wrong with you? 'I tied my laces.' What the fuck kind of thing to say is that? Spoze I didn't care about your fucking laces?"

I decided to ignore that. Catching Paxton's eye, I said, "You think you can run. That's fine. But you know he won't. And I think you care about him, even if you are just a fuckstick on two legs. Someone's trying to frame him for this. Maybe they're even trying to kill him. If you care about H, you need to tell us what you know."

"What I know," Paxton said, an echo of a laugh trailing the word. "I don't know shit, bruv. That's the whole problem."

"The text to Baca."

"Fuck me." He was silent, and in the distance, the hum of a vacuum filtered in from the next unit. "I met her at a Zodiac party. One of those team-building things. The tech boys play their video games and eat nachos, and the lot of them smell like unwashed socks."

"Why were you at a team-building exercise?"

"I was keeping an eye on a bloke. I was interested."

"What does that mean?"

He gave himself a tug through the joggers and cocked a smile at me.

"You willingly chose to live with him?" I asked Holmes. "Again?"

"It's complicated," Holmes said, and he blushed when Paxton laughed. "He has some redeeming qualities."

"Ok, you're stalking your next hookup," I said. "You go to this Zodiac event. And then what?"

"I met Lynn. That's what she went by, so you know. She stood out. Didn't look like the rest of them. Didn't act like the rest of them."

"How so?"

"Confident. Assertive." He shrugged. "I went home with her instead of the bloke."

"And?"

"Do you know how it works with a girl? Same general idea, but—"

"Paxton," Holmes snapped.

He smoothed the bedding again. The vacuum cleaner droned on the other side of the wall. When he spoke, he struggled with the first few words. "I have—had—a client. Someone interested in a few Zodiac assets. Proprietary stuff."

It took a moment before Holmes asked, voice charged with his shock, "You were stealing?"

"Come on, luv. It's a big company. It would've been fine."

"You were stealing from my father's company? After everything he's done for you?"

Fury rippled under Paxton's easygoing mask—there and then gone.

"H," I said quietly.

"This is unbelievable," Holmes said. "My father practically raised you—"

"H," I said more forcefully. When Holmes glanced at me, I shook my head. "Not right now."

After a moment, Holmes nodded, his mouth compressing into a line.

"Go on," I told Paxton.

"The bloke, I thought he might be ready to flip. Why I went there in the first place, innit? Thought I could score with him, take it from there. But Lynn, Christ, she didn't need any warming up."

"What do you mean?"

"She was mad, wasn't she? Hated the Holmeses. Hated Maggie. Said Maggie had stolen her work. Kept talking about how she deserved compensation, that kind of thing. I don't know the details, if that's what you want to know. She worked with Maggie in the AI lab, and I got the feeling this was more of an excuse than anything. They had a whole history of arguments—she told me about them later, all the fights she had with Maggie. She kept saying she was going to quit. That's who you want, you know. Someone who's about to leave, someone with a chip on their shoulder. They'll take something because they think its owed them, and they'll sell it for cheap because they don't know what to do with it once they have it."

Holmes's expression tightened, and he opened his mouth, but when I made a gesture, he shut it again.

"Luv, it was a tiny thing. It was nothing. I wouldn't hurt you or your family."

"It was the AI lab," Holmes said. "The single most important program in Zodiac. Don't insult me, Paxton. And do not try to minimize this."

Paxton let out a breath and offered me a smile, one of those expressions like we were on the same side, and wasn't Holmes being unreasonable, all that.

I gave him nothing in return. "What happened with Baca?"

"We hit it off," he said. "Met up again for drinks. Met up a few times. I started laying out the pieces for her, and the more we talked around it, the more it seemed like she might be interested. She wasn't just talking about quitting; she was sure Maggie was going to fire her. We hadn't talked about it explicitly, but she kept saying she wanted a piece for herself, didn't she deserve it, they'd stolen from her. Everything you want to hear."

"When did you decide to use the anniversary party as cover?" Holmes asked.

Paxton held up empty hands. "We didn't. She disappeared. Wouldn't message me. Wouldn't take my calls. Didn't answer the door. I spotted her a few times, so I knew she was alive, but she didn't want anything to do with me."

"Why?" I asked.

"Someone got to her, didn't they? That's what it was. Had to be. Corporate security, maybe. If it was cold feet, she'd have told me. We were having fun; no reason to disappear unless someone told her to stay away from me."

"This asset you wanted her to steal," Holmes said. "What was it?"

"Got me, luv. An algorithm, I think. Something to do with the machine-learning side of AI. Couldn't tell you what it was, though. Honest."

"How was it to be delivered?"

"Huh?"

But I understood Holmes's question. "Was she supposed to retrieve a portable safe from Maggie's office? Is that what your client wanted?"

"A portable safe?"

"Answer the question."

Paxton frowned, though, and he was looking at me too intently for my liking. "Would have been a flash drive, wouldn't it? A bit of code, that's all. Nobody said anything about a portable safe."

Holmes let out a breath and glanced at me. I shrugged.

"What are you two on about?" Paxton asked.

But it hit me again: his reaction when we told him. "You didn't know Baca was dead."

"No," he said. "I already told you that."

"So why were you running?"

His hand stilled on the bedding. He made a face.

"Paxton, why were you running?"

For what felt like a long time, he held himself perfectly still. The vacuum cut off. The silence sounded like wind rushing in my ears.

"Got home from the jumper boy's place this morning," he said, his voice stiff. "He was already here. In your room. Leaving that, I suppose." He nodded at the oil-stained chukka, which Holmes had deposited near the closet. "He didn't hear me; it's the only reason I'm alive. I got out of here. I waited. When he left, I started grabbing everything I could. I'm sorry, Hol, I am. But I can't help you. Nobody can. That's why you need to run. Take him if you want—" He nodded at me. "—but run."

"Who did you see?" I asked. "Who was in here?"

But Holmes's face was pale, and the corner of his mouth trembled.

"Blackfriar," Paxton said with a weird, tight laugh. "Who else?"

Chapter 13

'K Great Thanks Bye

We let Paxton go because there was no point in keeping him. I locked the door behind him, and when I got back to Holmes's room, he was holding the oil-stained chukka, turning it in his hands.

"Later," I said, taking it from him.

He looked at me. His eyes were lusterless, the gray of scuffed concrete. He'd bitten his lip while I'd been out of the room. Once, I guessed. He'd only allowed himself to do it once. I thumbed away the blood, and he flinched at the touch.

"Shower," I said. "Clean clothes. Food."

"My father—"

"Later."

I walked him to the bathroom, got the water running in the shower, and tugged on the overalls until he slapped my hand. He looked down, and he made an unhappy noise that was supposed to be a laugh. I used one finger under his chin to tilt his head up. We were the same height, and we were so close his breathing wove together with mine. I waited until he met my eyes. It was our thing, or it had been, and I wanted to know—what? I didn't want to think about that too closely.

"Not now," he said softly. "Please not now."

I pretended to consider it. "Five minutes, bucko."

Then I went for the overalls again, and when he shoved me, I did a whole Three Stooges routine on my way out of the room.

Holmes lived for this stuff, I'm telling you.

I went to the kitchen next. A quick check of the cabinets and pantry and fridge made it look like no one lived there: paper plates, plastic forks, a roll of paper towels. The only thing that might pass for food in a court of law was the meal-replacement shakes lined up in perfect rows inside the fridge. It was easy to imagine Holmes living like this for months—absorbed in his work, forgetting to eat until Paxton wandered in from his latest hookup and forced him to drink a shake.

Well, I thought, fuck that.

My phone buzzed with a text from Rowe: *Dude, where are you?*

And then another: *Your dad is pissed.*

Back to the bathroom: the water was running, but it sounded like it was still coming out of the tub spout and not the shower head. I opened the door, already starting to speak, and froze.

Holmes sat on the side of the tub, back to the door, feet under the running water. I had forgotten, over the intervening months, how pale he was: his body like a winter sky, darkened by the storm clouds of bruises rolling in. So many bruises. And scars, too—a crescent moon, a lightning bolt, a dark seam like a second horizon low on his back He was lines in so many places: hard, beautiful, rigid lines that marked the limits of that pale perfection. A universe of order and straight paths and unbent trajectories, like Holmes himself. But when he moved, bending to hold his hand under the water, to splash it against his legs, he was the arc of his biceps, the knob of shoulder and vertebrae, the elliptic of that jack-in-the-box ass.

He started to turn, and I yanked the door shut.

"Jack?"

I counted to ten silently. I thumped my head against the jamb. I wondered if he'd be polite enough to help me drown myself after he finished his bath.

"Is everything all right?" Holmes called.

I opened the door an inch. "Yep. Great. Everything's great."

The water splashed, the sound of it changing as it filled the tub.

"Are you sure?"

I laughed. A lot. Way too much. "Everything's super." And since I was sure I'd never in my life said super about anything, I rushed to add, "I'm running out to pick up some food, so I'm taking your keys, and I'm locking the door behind me."

"I'm not hungry—"

"'k great thanks bye."

There have been a lot of embarrassing retreats in my life, but I think I had a new winner.

It wasn't far to Bruges—they had another location in Provo, plus food trucks, and Ariana had introduced me to them last year. I used the ride to listen to Nirvana turned all the way up. I figured if I popped my ear drums, I wouldn't have to answer any future questions from Holmes about why I had turned into such a raving weirdo. I kept seeing the cruciform of spine and shoulders, the flex and torsion of muscle as he bent. When I got to Bruges, I had to sit in the truck for a few minutes to wait for a certain predicament to, uh, go down.

By the time I got back to the condo, Holmes was dressed in a pair of turquoise trunks and the pink oxford Paxton had picked for him, trying to do the buttons. He wasn't doing too bad a job of it, but his face showed his frustration, so I dropped the food on the table and helped him.

When I'd done up the last button, I asked, "Ready?"

"As I told you—"

"Great." I met his eyes.

For a moment, he tried to squirrel away. Then his eyes came to mine. His mouth gentled at the corners, softened, bent.

"Grade A dork. Still."

The steel flashed down. "You are insufferable."

"I know. Let's eat."

I steered him toward the table by the shoulders, sat him in a chair, and began unpacking our takeout. Holmes inspected the bag.

"Have you had their stuff before?" I asked.

He shook his head.

"It's basically the best thing on the planet."

"For a teenage boy," Holmes said, "what does that mean? A hamburger stuffed with pixie sticks?"

"You're a teenage boy, bucko. Although actually, if you caramelized the pixie sticks first, that probably would be fucking delicious." I opened the first takeout container. "Waffles with pearl sugar. This one is their s'mores, so marshmallow, graham crackers, chocolate."

"I remember this recipe. It's called diabetes."

I tried to slap him upside the head, but Holmes was too fast for me.

"This one," I said as I opened the second, "is called Cinnamonster."

"It has cinnamon, I presume."

"And bananas and blueberries and—you know what? If you're going to make that face, I'm not going to explain."

"I'll never know the mysteries of a waffle called Cinnamonster."

I stopped. Fists on hips. Glaring. "This is because you've been gone for five months, you know. You think you're way too big for your britches. Paxton has let you get totally out of control."

He huffed his little breath.

"This," I said with exaggerated patience as I took out the next one, "is the Holy Grail. It's the reason for living. When we invented this, the human race achieved its pinnacle."

"Is it a hot dog?"

"It's not a—H! How fucking dare you?"

Something played at the corner of his mouth, and I bit the inside of my cheek to keep from grinning.

"This is the Machine Gun," I said as I opened the container.

"Dear God. Did they let a teenage boy name the food too?"

I chose to ignore that. "Merguez sausage. Frites. Andalouse sauce. All on the best baguette you're ever going to eat. This is humanity's purpose finally realized. This is what you've been waiting for your whole life."

"Soggy bread stuffed with french fries?"

"They're frites, dumbass. This is classy as fuck. And that one's yours, by the way. I got one for myself."

"Jack, I can't—"

"Pick your waffle."

"There's no way—"

"Great, I'll take s'mores."

Holmes stared at me helplessly.

"Start with the Machine Gun," I said. "Then the waffle is like dessert."

"Like dessert?" he muttered as he picked up the sandwich. "It's pure sugar."

"At this point, no more talking."

To his credit, for a skinny white boy who lived off shakes and air, Holmes did some serious damage to the Machine Gun. I didn't expect him to finish it, but he polished off three quarters of it, and it didn't take him long—after the first experimental bites, he was ravenous. I ate my Machine Gun too, and we didn't have to talk, and we didn't have to explain, and we didn't have to deal with the fact that Blackfriar Holmes was apparently trying to frame his son for murder.

So, I was totally unprepared when Holmes said, "He saved my life in Hong Kong."

I chewed. I swallowed. I wiped my mouth with the back of my hand and ignored the horror on Holmes's face. "What? Who?"

"Paxton." Holmes picked up a frite that had fallen out of his sandwich and trailed it through drips of andalouse sauce. "After I…left, I began trying to track down Watson's package. I traced the fake deputy, the one who searched your room, to a location in Seattle. I lost the trail for a while and picked it up in Hong Kong. It's how I found my way back to Maggie, actually. How I learned she had been behind all of it. But in Hong Kong, I allowed myself to become distracted." He said the words clearly, with merciless precision. "And I would have died—should have died. Only Paxton had come after me, and he saved my life."

Conversational life hack? Stuff your mouth full of food so all you have to say is "Oh."

Holmes huffed his little laugh. "I am not sexually or romantically involved with Paxton."

Another conversational life hack? Don't let the son of a bitch at the back of your head do the talking. "That's kind of hard to believe considering you were in love with him for most of your life, and you've spent the last half a year shacked up with him."

Straightening in his seat, Holmes set his jaw, face hardening. Then he stopped, and the corner of his mouth quirked, and he said, "Jack, are you jealous?"

"Of course I'm jealous. And I'm mad. And I still hate you. And we're supposed to be eating, not talking about—about whatever this is."

The quirk came again—this time, the amusement was unmistakable, even coupled with disbelief. But Holmes didn't press the point. He toyed with the Cinnamonster, picking off the fruit in delicate, birdlike bites. When I finished the s'mores waffle, I told him he was ruining it, and I liberated the waffle and helped myself to the rest of it.

I was up to my eyebrows in Cinnamonster when I finally said, "He didn't abandon you, you know. When you were still living at home, I mean. That story you told me; he didn't just leave."

Holmes blinked once. Then again. Color came into his cheeks.

"I guess you ought to know that. He—it's complicated. And he should be the one to tell you. But he left because he had to, not because he wanted to go to school, not because he'd gotten what he wanted out of you, not because he'd been using you."

Holmes didn't say anything. His breathing stayed the same. His chest rose and fell evenly. The only sign was his hands, twisting a paper towel.

"So, if you still, you know, have feelings, maybe you should give him a second chance—"

"Stop."

I did. I stuck a fork in what was left of the Cinnamonster. After a minute, I licked whipped cream from my thumb, got to my feet, and started collecting the trash in the takeout bag.

Holmes stood and left, and a moment later, the door to his room clicked shut.

Great. Fantastic. Super.

I went to the bathroom and stripped down, and it felt good to be free of the day-old clothes. The warm water on my skin felt even better. The fancy body gel and hair stuff had to be Paxton's. After the shower, I borrowed somebody's deodorant and decided once and for all to shave my head because my hair was a fucking lost cause.

I was dreading the next part, pulling on my dirty clothes, when Holmes said, "I've left you something clean to wear."

That was all. The way hotel staff might tell you they'd changed the towels.

I opened the door. No Holmes, but the clothes lay neatly folded on the floor. They weren't his—the black tee with ZADDY printed on it could only belong to one person, and I didn't think I'd ever seen Holmes in jeans, and certainly not a pair ripped in so many interesting ways. They were bikini briefs, by the way, and I was sure Holmes had chosen them on purpose because of the little pouch on the front. I had an idea what the clothes meant. I had an idea of what he was saying, even if he couldn't say it any other way. I was starting to think maybe I hadn't been as quiet as I'd thought, walking in on him in the bath. I was thinking, with Holloway Holmes, I needed to learn how to read smoke signals.

I carried them out into the living room, where Holmes was reading on his phone. He'd put on his chinos and chukkas, and he looked ready to go.

He gawked at me, flushed, and ducked his head. "What are you doing?"

"Getting dressed."

"You should get dressed in the bathroom."

I pulled on the briefs, which, now, felt like they were the size of a kleenex. "Don't want to."

"This is inappropriate."

I held up the shirt. Examined it.

"Jack!"

"Zaddy."

"You have to get dressed!"

"What do you think that means?"

Maybe that was too much; his chin came up, and he fixed me with a look. "You know what it means. Put on your clothes, or I'm leaving."

"You're not leaving."

"I will."

He readied himself to stand, so I said, "Don't get off that couch."

"You're making me uncomfortable—"

"Bullshit."

He stopped. Swallowed. Looked away, and then back again, his eyes raking me up and down. I blew him a kiss. Then he took his phone in both hands and dragged his attention back to the screen. He looked like he was praying.

Trying not to laugh, I pulled on the shirt. The jeans next. The whole muscle-boy fuck-toy look wasn't exactly my thing, and the clothes were Paxton's, so they were a little too big for me. But I didn't look too bad, if Holmes's reaction was any indication. I would have felt bad—the poor guy looked like he was on the brink of a stroke—but he'd started this.

"I'm decent," I said. "You can stop pretending."

"I was not—" But he stopped when he looked at me again, and there's nothing quite like that feeling, being seen like that, being devoured, wholly and completely, by someone you want. His voice was weaker when he finished, "—pretending."

"Uh huh. Are you still mad at me about Paxton?"

"I was not mad at you. I was—am—upset."

I waited. "Do you want to elaborate?"

"I don't know. I have many feelings about what you told me. Some of them are conflicting." He held himself tightly, the way someone might their first time on the high dive. "It does not change what I told you previously. My feelings for Paxton are irrelevant in that regard. I love you."

"Just not enough to, you know, let me know you were alive."

He swallowed, and he brushed his jaw with his knuckles, and I could see the tremor there. But he didn't say anything.

I sighed. "Are we ever going to talk about your dad?"

"If you wish."

"H, come on. I'm not trying to be a bad guy here, but you have to admit, it's pretty bad."

"Paxton's analysis was subjective. Did my father do anything to frighten him? No. Does he have any evidence that my father planted that footwear in order to frame me? No. Paxton gave us his assumptions."

"Like I did."

Holmes locked his phone, turned it in his hands, ran his thumb along the side.

"Like my assumptions," I said, "about your dad killing Watson."

"I'm not saying you're wrong," Holmes began carefully.

"No, you don't need to say it. I know you think I'm wrong. And because I'm stupid old Jack Moreno, I'm not even worth arguing with. You'll ignore me, or placate me, and do whatever you want in the end."

"That's not fair."

"Two people in your life, two people you claim are important, are telling you that your dad is scary and bad and—and that he might be trying to frame you for a murder he committed. And you're not willing to listen."

"My father is misunderstood by many people—"

"He beat you. He hurt you. For years."

"—but he has always had the singular goal of protecting his family—"

"That's rich. Protecting his family? God only knows all the ways he fucked with your head."

Holmes's jaw tightened. "—and while I understand that you have concerns—"

"The games. The tests. All those fucking trainings. Why can't you bite your lip?"

"—you do not understand—"

"Tell me why you're not allowed to bite your fucking lip. Tell me. What's so fucking important—"

"You do not understand."

"I understand that he treats you like you're a lab rat, and that's half the reason you don't understand how amazing you are—"

"Jack, for God's sake, shut up!" Holmes shot up from the sofa. "You don't know what you're talking about, and you're embarrassing yourself!"

In the silence that came after, I thought I could hear the traffic on the street below.

"Every family has their own dynamic," Holmes said in a softer voice, "and with our families, that is truer than most."

"But I don't understand because I wasn't raised a Watson."

Holmes let his eyes slide away.

"Real nice, H. Really fucking nice. You know who you sound like? That ass-gape Tom. Maybe I don't know how these fucked-up families do things. But that doesn't matter. Because nobody should do that to anybody. And the whole point, H, the whole fucking point, is that you're letting it get in the way of what's right in front of you. I told you about your dad. Now Paxton is telling you. Paxton ought to know, right? He grew up with the families. He knows how they do things. You told me he's everything your dad wanted in a son. And he's so scared of Blackfriar that he threw everything in a car and tried to drive away just because your dad came poking around. What's that tell you?"

Holmes was perfectly still. He rubbed his jaw again, where the light picked out the faint stubble—barely anything at all, nothing more than a flitter of gold.

"Then we will talk to my father."

I shook my head. "Jesus Christ."

"I don't know what you want me to say, Jack. You believe he killed Lynnissa Baca, stole Watson's portable safe, and then framed me for the crime. For the sake of our investigation, let's say you're correct. What is the next step?"

"Get the police."

"With what evidence? A conversation you had with him months ago? Paxton's groundless fears? If you believe my father is responsible for these events, let's prove it."

I shook my head again, but I didn't have anything left to say.

Holmes, however, didn't seem to have that problem. He met my eyes—rare for him—and spoke clearly and coldly. "My father is Blackfriar Holmes, son of Archangel Holmes, son of Sherlock Holmes. He did not do this."

In that moment, I had a glimpse of it, of who Blackfriar was to Holmes: a towering genius, a master of every art and craft, distant and harsh and unforgiving, maybe even terrifying, except for when he was doling out praise and pleasure sparingly. A little bit like God, I guess. It must have been intuition, because it wasn't something my conscious brain put together, but I understood Holmes a bit. It was part of growing up, learning your parents weren't who you thought they were, not entirely. They skipped their medication because they were trying to save money. They peed themselves because they seized. They forgot to worry about your homework because they were worrying about how to feed you dinner, and they forgot to worry about dinner because the migraine was so bad they had to lie in a dark room and whimper. And even if it didn't happen like that, it happened somehow. You learned they had fears, prejudices, shortcomings. They were human, in other words.

What was it like for people who had been abused?

The question was so startling, and my knee-jerk reaction so strong—*Holmes wasn't abused*—that for a moment, I was disoriented. It took me a moment to realize Holmes was staring at me, waiting for a response.

All I could come up with was a nod.

"I'd like to retrieve my car," Holmes said. "And then we can visit my father. It's a Saturday; he'll be home."

It didn't take long for us to get ready. Holmes grabbed one of his gear bags, and I laced up my Stan Smiths, and we drove south, back to Zodiac. I had one of Dad's CDs in the player, turned low because that's how Holmes preferred it, but I couldn't have told you if it was Smashing Pumpkins or Pearl Jam or what. I kept coming back to my own question, to my own automatic denial.

When we got to the Scorpio parking lot, Holmes directed me to a spot near the front doors. I'd known he was driving a black Bentley—I'd seen it on the security footage, after all. But it had been one thing to see the coupe on a screen, and another to see it in person. Holmes dropped out of the truck, and I killed the engine and joined him as he inspected the car.

"It hasn't been moved," he finally said. "Although I'd like to check the Zodiac security footage to be sure."

"Great," I said. "So, someone else has two hundred thousand dollars lying around to pick up a spare Bentley to frame you."

"Another thread to follow. If someone purchased or leased a similar vehicle, that may be one way to find the killer. Or they may have stolen it and, in the process, incriminated themselves somehow."

"I guess. Seems like a lot of work; why frame you at all? I mean whoever did this, they did a good job getting rid of Baca without leaving behind any evidence."

"Why not frame me?" Holmes asked, the words surprisingly bitter. "I am unstable, reactive, dangerous. I have a history of violence."

I didn't say what I was thinking: *Yeah, but he's your dad.*

Holmes must have heard it anyway. His expression closed off, and he shrugged the gear bag higher. For a long moment, he stared at me. Then he turned and marched toward the Scorpio building.

"H! Hey, what are you—goddamn it!"

I jogged after him. His face was a frozen mask when I caught up.

"I thought we were going to see your dad."

"Yes."

"I thought he was at home."

"Yes."

"So, want to tell me what's going on?"

"What's going on, Jack, is that in your haste to demonize my father, you've overlooked the one person with the strongest reason to want Lynnissa Baca dead."

"Hold on—"

I tried to catch his arm, but pain flashed across his face when I touched him, and I dropped my hand. He sped up, not looking back at me, and headed toward the building.

"It was Maggie who stole Watson's safe in the first place, Jack." The words drifted back to me. "Maggie who hired Paxton to blackmail Aston and distract us. Maggie who had her vault broken into."

"Yeah, but—"

"I'd like to know what she has to say about all this," Holmes said, the words crystalline and sparkling with sharp edges. "Wouldn't you?"

Chapter 14

How Stupid Are You?

"Yeah, actually," I said as I caught up to him in the Scorpio lobby. It was empty today except for the guard manning the security gates, and the sound of our steps ricocheted against concrete and glass. "I'd love to know what Maggie thinks. I'd prefer to do it without walking into a building where she has her own private army who tried to shoot us last night."

"Then wait in the truck," Holmes said.

I wanted to say something back to that, something that would hurt him just as much. Instead, I swallowed and kept pace with him.

When we got to the gate, the guard gave us a cursory glance. He was one of those chipmunk-cheeked white guys, hair thinning on top, and he immediately went back to his phone as Holmes produced an ID badge and tapped it to the sensor.

The gate buzzed, and the guard's head came up again.

Holmes tried the card again, and he got another buzz.

"Did you program it yourself or something?" I asked.

"Don't be ridiculous. I'm nominally employed by Zodiac; I have access to every facility. The gate is malfunctioning."

"Sir?" the guard called.

"The gate is malfunctioning," I said.

Holmes shot me a sidelong look and stepped to the next gate.

When this one buzzed too, the guard said, "Sir, may I help you?"

"Why have the gates been deactivated?" Holmes asked.

"Sorry about that, sir. If you'll join me at the desk, I can see what's wrong with your badge."

"Uh huh," I said in a low voice.

Holmes darted another look of suppressed fury at me. Then he stalked over to the security desk.

The guard accepted Holmes's ID badge, tapped it against a sensor on his desk, and read something on his computer screen. His face changed, and I knew that look—it was halfway between *oh shit* and *gotcha*.

I wrapped my hand around Holmes's wrist and whispered, "H."

H tried to shake me off.

"We have to go," I whispered. "Right now."

"Sorry about that, sir," the guard said with overbearing good humor. "Gotta reprogram it. Give me a minute."

For a single heartbeat, annoyance stained the glass indifference of Holmes's expression. Then the mask broke, and I saw the flurry of processing as he made sense of what I'd seen too: the gates that didn't respond; the guard's surprise; the bad lie, the weak excuse.

Holmes nodded to me, twisting his wrist to free himself. I took a step toward the front doors, angling my body so I could look past the gates; I wanted a good line of sight when the stormtroopers charged us.

That's why I was a beat too late with Holmes.

He used his good arm to hop up and sit on the counter, and for a moment, the pose, with his legs dangling over the side, made him look relaxed, almost like a kid.

"Sir, you can't sit—" the guard began.

"H, no!" I shouted.

Holmes spun, bringing his legs around to the guard's side of the desk, and kicked the man in the chest.

The force of the blow drove the man back. He stumbled into his chair, which rolled out from under him so that the guard landed on the floor. I couldn't see him, but he wheezed for air. I winced; I'd taken some kicks to the solar plexus from Holmes. One time, I swear I could taste my own lungs.

Holmes slid off the desk, landing where the guard had stood moments before. He slapped a button, and the closest gate opened.

"Are you out of your damn mind?" I shouted.

"Perhaps. Either come along or leave, Jack." He bent, and when he stood again, he was holding a gun. "I don't have time to chat."

From deeper in the building came the sound of heavy steps, and a moment later, two men in dark suits appeared at the far end of the lobby. They paused, taking in the scene: Holmes with a gun, the fallen guard, the open gate, and me, Jack Moreno, dumber than shit.

Holmes sprinted for the elevators, and an instant later, I raced after him.

Shouts came at us from the guards: "Stop!" and "Don't move!" and even "Halt!"

That kind of stuff didn't work on Holloway Holmes, and since I was apparently incapable of doing anything but following him like a dumbass, it didn't slow me down either. Steps hammered the lobby's concrete, moving quickly toward us. My blood pounded in my ears. But I'd done all that conditioning with Rowe, running until I puked, swimming until I puked, and then running and swimming some more. For the first time, I found myself not only keeping pace with Holmes, but outdistancing him. I even had to tap the brakes a little. I still reached the bank of elevators first, and I hit every button I could reach.

An elevator door dinged open, and I grabbed Holmes by the shirt and dragged him into the car with me. I smacked the button for the tenth floor, and nothing happened. Then I saw the badge sensor mounted below the buttons.

Holmes was already moving, though, pressing an ID badge against the sensor.

"It won't work—" I began.

But Holmes jabbed the button for ten, and it turned green.

"Mr. Holmes, stop right there!" The security guard's voice couldn't have been more than a few yards away, but the doors were already sliding closed. I had a glimpse of him—a big guy with a flushed face, hand outstretched to catch the doors—and then the doors shut, and the elevator car began to move.

I slumped against the wall, sucking in air, adrenaline making me feel like I was buzzing. Holmes knelt, face pressed against the metal paneling, shoulders heaving.

"H?"

He made a noise. When I carded his hair, he shivered, and then some of the tension in his body relaxed, and he slumped against me. He couldn't be that out of shape, could he? We'd run maybe a hundred yards, and while we'd done it at a full-out sprint, I'd seen Holmes burn a lot more energy than that and not be fazed. But then, how long could anyone do it? How long could anyone not eat, not sleep, not relax, not ever, not for a minute, because you had been trained to expect more of yourself? And how long could he do it now that he'd given up the addies? One night's decent sleep and a solid meal weren't going to repair months and years of pushing himself beyond human limits.

Holmes shivered again and, using his good arm on the grab bar, pushed himself to his feet.

I looked at him. He looked at me.

"Your badge didn't work," I said, which sounded so inane and stupid and pointless that I wished I could call it back.

"I took the guard's."

And then the rest of it caught up with me, and I said, "What the hell, H?"

He stiffened. He folded his good arm across his chest. "My actions may seem precipitous—"

"Precipitous? You attacked that guy! And you didn't tell me you were going to do it. You didn't tell me anything, H! You didn't even tell me you wanted to talk to Maggie, not until we got here."

The elevator car whispered as it rushed up the building. I could feel its speed in my knees, in my ankles.

"It seemed prudent to avoid an argument—"

"Oh no you don't. No. No fucking way."

"I knew how you would react."

"Too bad! You still have to talk to me! You still have to tell me, and I still get a chance to react, even if you think you already know what I was going to say. Maybe I was going to tell you it was a good idea. Maybe I was going to tell you I was thinking the same thing, you stupid, self-absorbed, candy-assed dummy!"

He was breathing hard, but he didn't say anything. I was breathing hard too. The elevator hummed around us.

"Would you have told me it was a good idea?" he asked quietly.

"No. It's a fucking terrible idea. But I still get to be involved. We still have to talk about things. This is about me, too, H. It's about me, it's about my mom. It's not just another fucking game you and your messed-up friends and family are playing. Even if it weren't about me, I still get to be involved because I care about you, dumbass!" At the end, my volume rose again before I could wrangle it. I had to stop and thump one of the metal panels, and it boomed hollowly under my fist.

When the sound faded, Holmes said in a small voice, "I thought you hated me."

"I do hate you. That doesn't mean I can't care about you too. God, H, how stupid are you?"

He looked up at me, meeting my eyes again, and I didn't know what I was reading in his face. I thought, maybe, it was a question. I thought maybe it was the question I'd been waiting for him to ask me for five months now.

Then the elevator slowed abruptly, and I stumbled, one arm going around Holmes to steady myself. We rocked in place as the elevator came to a halt. The doors slid open. Holmes adjusted the gun against his leg, but an empty hallway greeted us.

The doors began to close.

"Fuck," I said and shouldered them open again. "Quick. They're trying to recall it."

Holmes slipped under my arm, and I followed him. The doors shut behind me. On the display above the next set of elevator doors, the number was rising steadily.

"They're coming."

Holmes nodded. He checked the slide on the gun and started down the hall.

This was Maggie Moriarty's private kingdom, the AI lab, and even on my third visit, it was creepy as shit. The blank walls. The long stretches of corridor unbroken by doors or windows. We headed for Moriarty's office, the corner unit at the end of the hall. The only sound was our shoes scuffing the high-traffic carpet.

When we reached the door to her office, the lights were on. Holmes put his good shoulder to the door. His finger moved once, hovering inside the pistol's trigger guard before he moved it safely outside again. He checked my face, and I nodded.

Holmes threw the door open, and I darted inside.

And crashed into someone.

We both went down, and I rolled and twisted and tried to get free. The other person—a man, my brain registered—was almost as fast as I was, and he knew what he was doing. In less than a moment, he had my arm behind my back, my face planted in the carpet. I let out a muffled, "Get the fuck off!"

And then the pressure on me lifted, and I flopped over and stared up into the face of Detective Rivera of the Utah County Sheriff's Department, who squeezed his temples and said, "You have got to be kidding me."

Chapter 15

Everyone's Best Interest

"You've got to help us," I said as I scrambled to my feet.

Rivera looked like he always did: muscular and squat in a cheap gray suit, one cauliflower ear he'd earned as a wrestler, his skin a darker brown than mine. His partner, Detective Yazzie, wore the same boxy glasses she always did, had the same bob of red hair that came straight out of a box, still looked more like the lady who would show you "the master bedroom of your dreams" instead of a detective. They traded a look, and Rivera opened his mouth to say something.

Then the thunder of stormtrooper steps reached us.

"Please," I said.

To my surprise, Rivera shot Yazzie a look. She grimaced and said, "Holloway, get over here. And give me that."

Holmes surrendered the pistol as Yazzie shepherded him to the far side of the room. Rivera was less gentle, prodding and shoving me until I stood next to Holmes. Then the detectives made a wall in front of us. I had just long enough to take in the state of Moriarty's office. The black velvet chairs had been moved from where they normally stood. The glass desk was covered in fingerprint powder. The tray of acid and 'shrooms was gone, taken by some lucky deputy, I guessed. The skull vase had been emptied of its dead roses. The painting of a woman's hand in a slave bracelet had been taken down and now leaned against the wall. Everything was like that. What I couldn't tell—what I wanted to know—was if Rivera and Yazzie were the first to search it, or if someone else had been here first. But before I could think about it any further, the stormtroopers arrived.

The first two wore suits, and they were the ones from the lobby. Six more men crowded behind them, and these were dressed in tactical gear. Nobody was carrying anything bigger than a pistol, but I wanted to know what kind of gear they'd left in the break room.

Rivera, being Rivera, didn't miss an opportunity to be a hardass. "Took you long enough."

One of the guys in the suit, with a sunburned nose and on his way to jowly, said, "Detective Rivera—"

"This is the kind of security we're dealing with? Jesus Christ. No wonder this place keeps getting tossed." Rivera grabbed my arm and jostled me. "These little shits walked right in here, did you know that?"

"Detective—"

"What the fuck kind of hayseed operation are you running?"

By then, the jowly guy had marshalled himself, and he barked, "Detective Rivera, those boys are trespassing. My men will take custody of them now."

Holmes tensed next to me. I gave a tiny shake of my head.

"What'd you say to me?" Rivera said.

But Jowly didn't back down. He moved forward, breaching Rivera's space, and made a move to grab my arm. "These boys are trespassing on Zodiac property—"

Rivera didn't even pretend it was anything but what it was: he slapped the guard's hand away before he could reach me. Jowly flushed until his whole face was red and his sunburned nose looked like a signal flare.

"These boys," Rivera said, painstakingly slow, "broke into an active crime scene. My crime scene."

"Zodiac security—"

"Will what?" Rivera said. "Sit on their fucking thumbs? A bunch of fucking mall cops?"

Jowly's shoulders inched up. He was breathing through his mouth now.

"This is still Utah County, isn't it?" Yazzie said. "And as far as I know, Utah County still falls under the jurisdiction of the Utah County Sheriff's Department. So, here's how it's going to go. Detective Rivera and I are going to take the boys back to the station, and we're going to have a talk with them. If Zodiac wants to press charges, they can take that up with the county prosecutor."

"My orders are to hold the boys—"

"Unless the rest of that sentence is 'until law enforcement officers can arrive,'" Yazzie said, "then you're talking about false imprisonment. Do you want to finish that sentence?"

Jowly glanced at his men. The second guy in the suit had an unreadable look on his face. The six in the tactical gear looked—blank. The realization felt like a punch to the gut: these guys weren't afraid of a couple of cops. If

Jowly said the word, they'd try to kill us. And since there were eight of them and four of us, they'd probably succeed. Yazzie and Rivera didn't do anything like go for their guns, but Rivera's fingers bit into my arm, and he held himself with a kind of coiled energy.

"Mr. Holmes has asked that his son stay," Jowly finally said. "Would the Utah County Sheriff's Department consider a father's request false imprisonment?"

"I'll let the sheriff make that call," Yazzie said. "From the station. Get your men out of here; I deal with enough macho bullshit as it is, and I don't need them jamming up my scene."

In the lull, the HVAC system's whisper was the only sound.

"You heard her," Rivera barked. "Move!"

Jowly gestured, and the guards backed out of the room. He and his buddy in the suit followed. They disappeared from my field of view, and a moment later, the elevator dinged. I took a step toward the door to check, in case a couple of them had lingered.

Rivera yanked me back. "Are you out of your damn mind?"

Hand on her gun, Yazzie gave me a disgusted glance as she moved to the doorway.

Even Holmes was giving me a so-non-judgmental-it-was-painful look.

"I was just checking," I said.

"You put up with this?" Rivera asked. "You deal with this every day?"

"He has a great many strengths," Holmes said.

"For fuck's sake," Rivera muttered and rubbed his eyes with his free hand.

"Clear," Yazzie said from the doorway.

Rivera got me marching with a shove; he still hadn't let go of my arm. "C'mon. And no talking."

"Somebody had to check the hallway," I said. "Nobody told me it was going to be Yazzie."

"You didn't think maybe it should be the trained detective, dipshit? You didn't think maybe it should be somebody with a gun?"

"Holmes had a gun until Yazzie took it away."

"Detective Yazzie."

"Yazzie and I are friends. I can call her Yazzie."

"What the hell did I say about no talking?" He immediately turned to Holmes. "Are you kidding me with this?"

"He's had a trying few days," Holmes said in what sounded like an apology.

I decided not to talk to any of them. As punishment. The whole elevator ride.

Rivera's iron grip tightened as he goose-stepped me across the lobby. Jowly and his partner were standing off to the side, watching us—the partner was talking into a phone. Yazzie watched them, dead-eyed; she didn't have her hand on her gun, but you could tell from how she walked that she was ready. Holmes, of course, looked like nothing bothered him. He didn't even seem to notice the guard at the gates, who was massaging his chest where Holmes had kicked him and glaring at us.

When we stepped outside, the sun fell on my face, and the day was warm, and the air was sweet with spring clover and fescue. Where the Zodiac landscaping ended, buffalo grass and Russian thistles and tumbleweed grew in chest-high tangles. The sound of the highway reached us even here, the rush of tires on pavement. The only other noise was our steps.

"The truck's over there," I said.

"Great. Give me a minute to put your head through the windshield."

But he started walking me the other direction, and Holmes and Yazzie trailed after us.

"H's car is over there too. We parked right next to each other. Rivera, you're going the wrong way."

"Detective Rivera," he said grimly.

"What the hell? H, help! I'm being kidnapped."

We were approaching a Chevy Tahoe done up with the Utah County Sheriff's Department logo or seal or whatever you called it, and now Rivera released me, turning the movement into a shove that sent me stumbling toward the SUV.

"Is this funny to you?" Rivera snapped. "Is this a big joke?"

"Easy," Yazzie said.

I caught myself on the Tahoe, turned, couldn't meet Rivera's eyes.

"What the hell is wrong with you?" Rivera shouted.

"Take a walk," Yazzie said.

Rivera rounded on her like he might shout at her too, but she stared him down. Shaking his head, Rivera turned away. He stalked toward the far end of the parking lot, ranting to himself, the words too low for me to hear them.

"What's his problem?" I asked.

"Get in the back of the truck," Yazzie said, and she took out a fob, and the Tahoe beeped twice.

"Am I under arrest?"

"No, Jack, you're not under arrest. Get in the truck, please."

I looked at Holmes. He glanced back at the Scorpio building; Jowly and his partner had followed us outside. "I believe it would be best if we did what they said."

"Fine." I yanked open the Tahoe's back door. "Come on."

"Holloway's going to keep me company," Yazzie said, holding out a hand to stop Holmes.

"Are you for real?"

From the end of the lot came Rivera's strangled scream: "Get in the fucking truck!"

So, I got in the truck.

Yazzie walked Holmes toward the back of the lot. I could still see them if I craned my head, but then I couldn't keep an eye on the Zodiac security goons. I figured maybe that was the point. Inside the Tahoe, the air was too warm for comfort, so I kept the door open. The breeze came into the truck in cool little licks, but I still had sweat on my forehead by the time Rivera came back.

He climbed into the front seat, started the Tahoe, and cranked up the air. He'd loosened his tie and unbuttoned his collar. I wasn't sure how old he was—not too old, I didn't think—but he sure looked tired. You could see it in his bloodshot eyes, in the way he held his head.

"Close the door," he said.

I closed the door. It was better with the air on. Something was playing on the Tahoe's sound system, but it was too quiet for me to make it out.

When Rivera spoke again, his voice had a measured calm. "Do you want to tell me what's going on?"

"Ok, first of all, we didn't do anything. H has every right to be in that building. It's his dad's company, and—"

Rivera looked at me in the rearview mirror, and I stopped talking.

"I like you, Jack. Against my better judgment, actually. You're about as dumb as they come, and you fall ass over banana into trouble every time I turn around, but I think you're a good kid." He seemed to consider that statement and added, "More or less."

"Um, thanks?"

"Do you understand what happened up there?"

He held my gaze in the mirror, and I broke first. I nodded and mumbled, "I was saying dumb stuff because—I don't know. I was still freaking out a little."

"Fine. That's fine. I don't care about that. You say dumb stuff all the time; I'm used to it. I was...out of line. Adrenaline gets going, you know?"

His silence lasted until I nodded.

"So," Rivera said, "I'm sorry."

"Yeah." His eyes were waiting for me when I checked the mirror again, and I flushed as I added, "Me too."

"Here's the deal, Jack. I don't know what I stumbled into. I don't know why someone broke into Margaret Moriarty's office last night. I don't know who it was, although I'm starting to have some thoughts about that. I don't know why her car was abandoned up Provo Canyon—"

"Wait, what?"

"—but I just stood in a room with eight men who were thinking about killing me because they didn't want to let you and Holloway out of their hands, and I don't like that. I don't like not knowing what's going on. Not knowing what's going on gets you killed. And I would really, really like to see my kids graduate high school."

Whatever was playing on the sound system, it was soft and kind of nice. Rivera moved his hands on the steering wheel. He turned up the air even though it didn't need it.

"I didn't know you had kids."

He shrugged. "I don't, most of the time." He must have seen the question on my face because he said, "Divorced."

"I'm sorry."

"That's what happens. You let things get away from you. You get angry. You hold grudges."

"I'm really sorry."

"It wasn't my fault. I'm fucking perfect."

That startled a laugh out of me, and I was surprised by the quick grin in the mirror, the way it crinkled his eyes. I asked the question before I'd even considered it: "How many kids do you have?"

"Two. Girls."

"How old are they? Are they in high school?"

"What's that supposed to mean?"

"Nothing!"

"Are they in high school? Why? You want to date them? Jesus Christ, Moreno, what the hell is wrong with you?"

"I didn't—that's not what—" The grin didn't surface this time, but I could see it in those bloodshot eyes. "You are such an asshole!"

That flash of amusement again. "Seven and nine."

I sat with that. Rivera turned up the music. I didn't know who it was. I didn't even know what it was. It made me think of Renaissance Faires and girls with long hair who loved crystals. Finally, I asked, "What is this?"

"Enya." When I didn't say anything, Rivera added, a little defensively, "Yazzie says I need to listen to something for my blood pressure."

I smiled and covered it with both hands, but the smile faded quickly. "Why are you telling me this?"

"Because, Jack, I think you're a decent person, but I also think you're a teenager, which means your brain starts in your dick and ends in your balls. I'd like you to know that what I'm asking you, I'm asking you because I'm a real person. I've got a life. I've got two little girls who actually like me, believe it or not. I've got an ex-wife who burned me in effigy, I shit you not. And I want you to think about all that before you answer when I ask you to tell me what I walked into up there."

"That's why Yazzie took H. You think he won't tell you, and you think I won't tell you if he's here."

"I think it's good practice to separate witnesses." He waited a moment and added, "And suspects."

The A/C was too cold now, and I shivered as goose bumps broke out on my arms. I thought about what he'd said. I figured Rivera might be lying, trying to make me like him or feel sorry for him or think of him as a human being. He was probably telling the truth, though. I could see him with two little girls. They'd be crazy about him.

"What do the police think happened?"

Rivera rubbed his jaw, the stubble rasping under the heel of his hand. He must have considered the question for two or three minutes; one Enya song faded into another, this one with a million flutes. When he spoke, it was grudgingly. "The official story from Zodiac is that there was an attempted break-in, which included cutting off the power to the Scorpio building and disabling the backup generator."

"That's what I don't understand," I said, more to myself than to him.

"What don't you understand?"

I weighed my options. "What did Zodiac say was stolen? Officially, I mean."

"Nothing. They said the AI labs were targeted, but they weren't breached, and the thieves left when Zodiac security arrived on the scene."

"And tried to shoot us full of holes," I said under my breath.

"Want to try that again? A little louder, maybe. That sounded like it had legal implications."

I gave him the finger in the rearview mirror, but I said, "Do you know who Lynnissa Baca is?"

"That's an interesting question."

He didn't say anything else, so after a few more moments, I said, "Look her up."

"No, Jack. That's not how we're playing this. This isn't you and Holmes playing treehouse detectives at your private school for rich kids. This is the real world, and there are people involved, organizations involved, that have a lot of money and a lot of sway. You need to tell me whatever you know. And you need to tell me now."

This was why I needed Holmes. I didn't know if I should tell Rivera everything. I didn't know if I should tell him some of it, or none of it. He might be able to help us find who had killed Baca—and, in the process, recover Watson's portable safe. I wanted to know what was in that safe. I needed to know. But recruiting Rivera could have the opposite effect. I trusted Rivera, and I trusted Yazzie—but did I trust everybody in the sheriff's department? The Holmeses and the Moriartys had a lot of sway, as Rivera put it, and anything I told Rivera, I had to assume it would filter through the sheriff's department in reports, briefings, water-cooler gossip, and the like. Rivera and Yazzie might be cool, but I didn't believe the rest of the department was untouchable.

"Maggie's car," I said. "Did you really find it up Provo Canyon?"

Rivera sat there for a minute. He pushed against the steering wheel like it was holding him up. Then he said, "Nobody has seen Margaret Moriarty since the Zodiac anniversary party last night."

"What—"

"The official explanation is that she went hiking and got lost or hurt. Search and rescue teams are already looking for her."

"That's why you're here. You thought maybe the break-in was connected to her disappearance."

"Is it?"

"I don't know."

"Jesus, Jack."

"I'm telling you the truth! I don't know!" There were too many possibilities, too many options. Holmes wanted to believe that Maggie could be behind all of this—that she had tracked Baca down, killed her, and recovered the safe. I knew what he'd say when I told him about her abandoned car. He'd say it was a ruse, a decoy, a misdirection. But the truth was, he didn't want to accept what was right in front of him. He didn't want to face the fact that his father was a psycho, a monster, a murderer. The reality was that I needed help if I was going to prove that Blackfriar was behind Baca's death. And for the first time in my life, I couldn't count on Holmes.

"Ok," I said, "I'm going to tell you, but you can't tell anyone. Not even Yazzie."

"That's not—"

"Not even Yazzie!" I tried to lower my voice. "Or I'm not telling you anything."

"She's my partner. This isn't the Wild West; I'm in a functioning sheriff's department. I have responsibilities, procedures—"

"If you need to tell somebody, we can talk about it. Maybe. But not yet. Not right now."

I couldn't read his face in the mirror when he said, "Fine."

"Promise me."

"Jack—"

"Promise!"

"Good Christ. All right, I promise I won't tell anybody until you and I have a chance to talk it out."

I took a deep breath. "What do you know about Blackfriar Holmes?"

Rivera turned his head to look back at me. Then he froze.

A soft tap came at my window.

It was like a nightmare, one of those dreams when you can't run fast enough, when something behind you is always getting closer.

Blackfriar Holmes stood outside the Tahoe, staring in at me, the tarnished tin of his eyes glowing in the spring sun. He wore a sharkskin suit, and as he held up his phone, his mouth offered its rictus smile. "Detective Rivera," he said through the glass, but his eyes were on me, and he was speaking to me, and the rictus was for me. "I've just spoken to Jack's father. He's agreed that it's in everyone's best interest if I take my son and his friend home with me." The dead-man's smile grew. "Now."

Chapter 16

Training

Rivera talked to Dad on Blackfriar's phone. He stood out of earshot, his body rigid. When he came back, he handed the phone to me and looked me in the eye.

I put the phone to my ear.

"You're at a sleepover with Rowe," Dad said.

"Dad, wait—"

"I don't think so. We talked about this. We talked about the lying." His silence vibrated across the call. "I am so disappointed in you."

"Ok, I'm sorry, but—"

"You're going with Mr. Holmes. You're going to get in his car, and you're not going to give him any lip, Jack. And you're going to thank him. Do you understand?"

Blackfriar watched me from across the lot, a tin-snip gleam in his eyes.

"What did he tell you? What did he say?"

"He said you broke into his company!" The fury bumped Dad's voice up a notch. "He said you hurt someone! What the hell is wrong with you?"

"I didn't—"

"And instead of pressing charges, he's sticking his neck out so that you and Holloway don't get arrested."

"That's not what happened!"

I could almost hear Dad wrestling with himself on the other side of the call. Finally, he asked, "Then what happened?"

Rivera folded his arms and stared at me. Dad's breathing sounded labored, and I wondered if the stress had kicked off a migraine.

"Detective Rivera wants to talk to me. That's all."

"That's not what Mr. Holmes thinks. He thinks they're going to take you in for questioning, and then they're going to arrest you. And you know what? When I asked Detective Rivera, he danced around the question." The tension in his voice broke, and he sounded tired when he added, "Jesus, Jack, what is going on? I thought we were over this."

The wind soughed through the tall grasses. A thistle, with its bright purple blossom, bobbed and swayed.

"Fine," Dad said. "I'm coming up there."

"No." I glanced around for Holmes, but in the confusion, I'd lost him. Yazzie stood alone, hands on her hips, her expression flat. "No, I'll go."

After a long pause, Dad grunted. "You screwed up, buddy."

"I'm sorry."

It must have cost him not to yell, not to tell me how hard I was making his life, not to say any of the things he was probably thinking. "We'll talk about it when you get home."

"The truck—"

"Don't worry about the truck. You're not going to be driving anywhere, Jack. Not anytime soon."

When I disconnected, Rivera's dark eyes rested on me.

I shook my head.

"I can put you in the Tahoe," Rivera said. "He wouldn't try to take you."

But he didn't sound sure about that.

I shook my head again. "No, it's—it'll be all right."

Rivera was doing everything except look at Blackfriar. He stepped closer, and his next words barely reached me over the sound of the wind. "What is it?"

"Jack?" Blackfriar called.

For a moment, frustration marred Rivera's face. Then he nodded, cuffed me on the side of the head, and sent me over to Blackfriar.

It shouldn't have been a surprise that he drove a black Bentley. If anything, it made sense, but I still had a moment of numb disbelief. At his boldness, I guess. And that Holmes hadn't told me.

Holmes sat in the back seat, and when I slid in beside him, he didn't look over. I buckled myself in, and Blackfriar started the car, and we eased out of the lot.

"So, Jack," Blackfriar said, the engine purring beneath his words. "Tell me about school."

I glanced at Holmes, but his face was vacant, and I realized he wasn't going to be any help. So, after a moment, I said, "It's good."

"How are your classes? How's chemistry? My son tells me you're doing better."

We spent the drive like that, in a kind of grotesque farce of civilized conversation: Blackfriar asking questions that sounded perfectly normal, while beneath the surface, dark waters roiled and churned. And through it all, Holmes remained silent, his face blank. He had locked himself away, and I was on my own.

They didn't live far, thank God—in Draper, on the other side of Point of the Mountain. On a bluff, of course, looking out over the Salt Lake Valley. We had to stop at the gate, where a line of young oaks and a hedge hid the house from the street. Then we followed a long drive as the gate rolled shut behind us. The lawns were the vibrant green that only comes from gratuitous amounts of labor and chemicals, and every flower bed was exquisitely laid out. You could tell that the early bloomers—the crocuses, the tulips, the pansies, the hyacinths—they were part of a plan that would reveal itself over the seasons. To anybody who had lived in Utah, it was obvious this little paradise had been carved out of the mountain— everything artificially leveled and even. Controlled. That was the word. Everything in Blackfriar's world had been subdued, beaten into submission. Even the mountains. A Holmes must always be in control.

The house itself was a monstrosity—the kind of thing that was too big to be called charming. It might have been beautiful, but it was so overwhelming that even that didn't feel true. It was a mixture of stone and stucco with a slate roof, dormer windows, a carriage house, hell, an honest-to-God turret. There was even a Juliet balcony. From the side, I caught a glimpse of the deck at the back, where it cantilevered out over the steep drop of the bluff.

Blackfriar stopped the car, and we all got out. I touched Holmes's arm, and he looked at me, eyes dull, as though he weren't seeing me.

"Reichenbach Grange, our home sweet home," Blackfriar said. "It's pretentious, I know, naming a place, but I couldn't help myself. It seemed appropriate to remember the place where Sherlock Holmes was thought to have perished, only for him to return triumphantly from the land of the dead. What do you think, Jack?"

"Wowzer," I said, and Blackfriar chuckled.

He didn't give us noogies. He didn't squeeze the back of my neck. But he was doing it, the whole routine, like he was a favorite uncle or an old family friend. He stayed behind us, and the force of his presence sent me walking, against my better judgment, toward the front door.

Inside, the house was a contrast of light and dark: the white walls, the wide rooms, the desert brightness that flooded the house from so many windows; and then the dark beams framing the ceiling, making me think of the hull of a ship, and the graywashed, aggressively rustic furniture juxtaposed to plush, rounded sofas and curved armchairs upholstered in blacks and browns. Blackfriar herded us down the length of the house until we reached what must have been a family room, where more windows and a pair of French doors led out onto the deck. My skin began to crawl, and I tried to figure out why. Paintings and photographs hung on the walls—all of them minimalist, all of them abstract, all of them expensive. Other pieces of art were displayed on stands: a deerstalker cap covered in what I thought might be Greek writing, with what looked like a bullet hole in it; a cell phone that had been disassembled and wired together with what I thought was an old-fashioned syringe; a floral arrangement with each flower made out of pages of books—when I got closer, I saw Holmes and Watson on the pages. Ms. Prinze might have known what to call it, some modern or postmodern aesthetic, maybe even something new and cutting edge. Me, though? Well, cuckoo for Cocoa Puffs didn't exactly sound like an artistic movement, but it came close.

And then I figured out what was bothering me: there were no smells. No people smells. No food smells. Not even new smells—new furniture, new carpet, new paint. A chill ran up my spine, and I fought off a shiver.

Voices broke the silence. "—knew where he was, I'd tell you," Noneley said. A moment later, she emerged from a hallway. Today she was dressed in leggings and a chunky sweater, and she'd added strands of glitter to her hair. "If only to get rid of you."

Behind her, Tom trotted along, clutching the old black doctor's bag to his chest. He was in another of those ill-fitting but somehow expensive-looking suits, and for a moment, Noneley's back was to him, and he hadn't seen the rest of us yet. It only lasted an instant, but hatred made his face incandescent. Then he saw the rest of us, tripped over his own feet, and went headfirst into a pouf. Whatever he had in the doctor's bag, it clattered and clinked when it hit the floor.

Noneley didn't look back at the noise; she shook her head and said, "Thank God, Father. He followed me all the way from Sundance. Can't you put a leash on him or something?"

"Holloway," Blackfriar said, "go to your room."

"It's not my room." Holmes's voice was cold, uninflected, the way he spoke when every piece of armor was in place. "I no longer live here, in case you've forgotten."

Tom was picking himself up, the contents of the bag rattling and chiming, and now his glare was directed at me.

A hint of color infused Noneley's cheeks. "I had the most wonderful conversation with the governor, Father. I think I've convinced him to sue Zodiac." She smiled. "It's going to be a bloodbath."

"I'm going to have a chat with Jack," Blackfriar said as though no one had spoken.

Holmes's head came up. His eyes widened, caught the desert light.

The color in Noneley's face darkened. "What about your pet? I'm going to have to hang a bell on him; I swear I almost stepped on him last night."

"Jack—" Blackfriar said.

"My training."

The words were so disjointed that, for a moment, I didn't understand what Holmes had said. I glanced at him. A pinprick of blood marked the corner of his mouth where he'd bitten his lip, and the light turned his eyes into mirrors.

Blackfriar turned to face his son.

"We spoke about continuing my training," Holmes said.

The silence lasted almost a full minute. Then Blackfriar smiled, and it was the rictus again, a winter of teeth. "I recall you telling me, quite forcefully, that you considered your training complete."

Holmes's jaw worked twice before he managed to say, "I was wrong."

"I'm sorry?"

Holmes raised his head and said, more loudly, "I was wrong."

"Ah." Blackfriar clasped his hands behind his back. "I see."

"Father—" Noneley began.

Blackfriar shot her a look, and Noneley retreated a step, bumping into Tom, although neither of them seemed to notice it. When Blackfriar returned his gaze to Holmes, Holmes ducked his chin.

"Really, Holloway," Blackfriar said, "this inconstancy. You've made so many...pronouncements lately." His gaze flicked to me, although I didn't understand what he meant. Turning his attention back to Holmes, he continued, "How will anyone take you seriously if you change your mind so easily?"

The corner of Holmes's mouth trembled, but his voice was steady when he said, "I believe now would be a good time to resume my training."

"Do you? But we have a guest."

The tremor, this time, seemed to run through Holmes's whole body. "Jack does not mind. You don't, do you, Jack?"

Blackfriar cocked a look at me and broke into a soft laugh. "Good God, his face."

I knew I needed to say something. I just didn't know what.

"I believe now—" Holmes began.

"I heard you." Blackfriar considered his son again. "I hear you telling me, my son. I hear another pronouncement."

Holmes looked at me, his eyes silver, and for a moment, I thought they were full of tears. Then he turned his head, and the light changed, and I couldn't tell. Whatever resolve he'd clung to, it shattered now, and he bit his lip savagely. When he spoke again, his teeth were crimson with blood.

"Please." He stopped. Once again, I was witness as he brought that tremendous will to bear again. His body stilled. And then he seemed almost relaxed, his voice even as he asked, "Please, Father. Would you consider resuming my training?"

Blackfriar glanced at me. I couldn't read the look on his face. It was like looking into the eyes of a dead man. Then the rictus stretched his cheeks, and he nodded. Another shiver passed through Holmes.

"Of course. Jack, make yourself at home. The Watsons always do."

Holmes left first, heading down a hallway, and he didn't look back, didn't try for one last glance. Blackfriar followed, his posture loose, verging on jaunty. When the sound of their steps faded, Tom let out a shuddering breath. Noneley pressed her fingertips to her eyes, and for a moment, the way she stilled herself was so reminiscent of Holmes that another chill ran through me.

Then she dropped her hands, smiled brightly, and said, "Well, that was something. Want a drink?"

I stared at her as she moved across the room to a well-stocked bar. She found a can of hard seltzer, opened it, and looked an invitation at me. After a moment, she shrugged and took a sip.

"I'd like a drink," Tom said.

Noneley let out a vexed breath, waved at the bar, and drifted over to one of the plush, rounded chairs. She dropped into it, curling her legs underneath her, and fixed me with a look.

By then, I'd recovered that classic Jack Moreno poise and panache and said, "What the fuck was that?"

"Father and Holloway playing their games. Father knows Hol's making a play, of course, and Hol knows Father knows, of course. But then, it's a gambit, and it's Hol, so that's all standard. God, who even drinks hard seltzer? But I'm drinking it, so I guess someone does."

"What do you mean he's making a play? What do you mean a game? That was—" Fucked up sounded debonair, like Jack Moreno, so I said, "That was seriously fucked up. H was terrified—he was on the verge of a panic attack."

"Oh yes, I think so."

I wanted to say, *And you stood there and didn't do anything*. I wanted to say, *What the fuck is going on?* I wanted to say, *I'm supposed to help him, but I have no idea what to do*. The best I could actually put into words, though, was, "Where are they? Where'd they go?"

"One of the training rooms, I imagine."

"Where?" She didn't answer fast enough, so I asked, "Down that hall, right?"

"Why? You're not thinking of—Jack, for God's sake, don't do that."

"He's going to—" What? Hurt Holmes, yes, that much was obvious. Break him. Try to break him, the way he'd been trying all of Holmes's life. Again, words failed me. "He's going to do something to him!"

"Yes, of course. That's the whole point."

I took a step, and a half-full can of seltzer missed my head by about an inch. It hit the wall, spraying foam and filling the air with a fruity, alcoholic tang.

"You cannot be this stupid," Noneley said, "or my brother wouldn't bother with you. Use your head, Jack, and think."

I tried to think. I did. But all I could see was the way Holmes's lip had trembled, the way he had braced himself like a man reaching into the heart of a fire to grab a live coal.

"If you go," Noneley said with the deliberate delivery of someone trying to be insulting, "he will hurt Hol more. Do you understand?"

"Yes, I understand—"

"Hol does not want you to go. Hol does not want you to see this."

"But he's—I don't know what's happening, but it's bad, and—" He needs me, I almost said.

"And he's doing it for you, you stupid boy." And then, as though the words finished the conversation, she said with disgust, "For heaven's sake."

I stared at her. I stared at the hallway where Blackfriar had taken Holmes. I tried to listen, and I couldn't hear anything except my heartbeat.

That was when I realized Tom was gone. It was easier to focus on that than on the helplessness curling its claws in my belly.

"Where'd he go?"

"Who knows? He's always popping up, disappearing, scurrying around underfoot." Noneley rose and stretched, and as she retrieved another can of seltzer, added, "It's exhausting, really. Are you sure you don't want a drink? God, you aren't old enough, are you? Would you like to try a beer?"

I rubbed my face. A laugh was welling up in me, and I thought if I let it out, my brain would short-circuit, and that would be the end. But I couldn't stay here, with this bright-eyed girl who spoke so casually about her brother being tortured, with the spiky smell of the seltzer turning my stomach. "He's in there, and he's—he needs you, and you're sitting here acting like it's a joke—"

"It is a joke, Jack." The sharpness of her tone made me raise my head. "Everything is a joke. You and Holloway would do well to learn that."

Somewhere, someone was screaming. It took a moment to decode the sound as the shriek of a violin. Shaking my head, I turned, heading back the way we'd come through the house. Without looking back, I said, "I've got to...I don't know. Get some air. Pee."

She laughed. The sound, high and tinkling, chased me down the corridors. My brain kept churning images: Holmes biting his lip; Holmes flinching; Holmes's guards and barriers stripped away, his face naked with fear. The night terrors, I thought. I wanted to laugh again, and I swallowed the sound. No wonder Holmes didn't sleep; I didn't think I'd ever be able to shut my eyes again. *He's doing it for you, you stupid boy.*

Somehow, I got outside. The day was bright enough that I had to squint, and when I leaned against the wall, the stucco was rough through Paxton's borrowed shirt. They'd laid down fresh mulch, and it covered up the sweetness of the flowers. I took out my vape, put it between my lips, asked myself if this was the best I could do. He was in there, hurting, being hurt, for me. And I might as well have been jerking off, standing out here with my fucking vape, getting high so I wouldn't have to hurt. Well, Holmes didn't have that option, did he?

So, after that, I took the vape out of my mouth. I looked at it. I dropped it on the brick walkway, and I stomped on it until it was nothing but broken slivers of plastic. My foot hurt. My head hurt. My whole body hurt, and the smell of the cannabis oil mixed with the mulch burn, making my stomach flop. Then I picked it all up, every tiny piece of plastic, my fingers slick and stinking from the oil. If I didn't, they'd probably punish Holmes for that too. I didn't know what to do after that. Wait around. Maybe if I asked nice, they'd let my dad come pick me up, and I could go home and pretend I hadn't seen Holmes made to beg.

It took a little while—I'm tough like that—but eventually, even I got tired of feeling sorry for myself. I knew what it was like to feel helpless, to feel guilty, to know you were responsible for awful things happening to someone else. That had been the story of my life since the night I ran and left my mom to die in the accident. I could either stand here and have my one-man orgy of feeling like shit, or I could do something. Something important. Something that would make me feel one percent less awful. Something like prove Blackfriar murdered Lynnissa Baca.

I went inside, found a bathroom, and dumped the pieces of my broken vape. I waited what I thought was a believable amount of time and flushed the toilet. I washed my hands, and I made sure I closed the door loudly when I left.

Nobody had come to investigate. Nobody had come to check on me. Yet.

I started off down one of the high-ceilinged halls. I didn't know which way to go, so I picked a hallway at random, choosing one that led away from where I had left Noneley, away from where Blackfriar had taken Holmes. Thick carpet swallowed the sound of my steps, and the only sound was the occasional screech of the violin. Every time it came, it startled me, sent my pulse racing and a fresh flush of adrenaline running through my body. It would stop just as suddenly, and for a moment, I would think that someone was screaming. And then it would happen again. And again. And again.

I found another large, open room that must have been another kind of family room—with another bar. I found two bedrooms that were perfectly made up in the same neutral tones, looking like no human had ever set foot inside them. I found a bathroom, a linen closet, and what I was pretty sure would have been called the billiards room if I'd been playing a game of Clue.

I was coming out of what was clearly some sort of studio, filled with paint and canvas and scraps of fabric and tote bins full of pins and ribbons and sewing gear, when a voice said, "You shouldn't be here."

I started at the words. When I looked over, Tom stood down the hallway, back the way I had come, clutching that stupid doctor's bag to his chest.

"Hot damn. Do you do that to everyone?"

I started toward the next door, and a quick check showed me Tom was following me.

"You were supposed to wait with Noneley."

"Oh, right." The next door led to stairs, and I had zero intention of going anywhere near a (potentially haunted) Holmes basement, much less with Tom, who probably would have pushed me down the steps as soon as I gave him the chance. "I'll go right back."

As I continued down the hall, Tom trotted after me. He didn't come too close, and the jingle of—I wanted to say metal instruments, but I had no idea what was truly in that doctor's bag—helped me keep track of him.

"Mr. Holmes wanted to talk to you. Mr. Holmes wanted you to wait."

"What's your deal?" The next door revealed a library. It was…awesome. Like, *Beauty and the Beast*-level awesome. But it didn't look helpful for proving that the senior Holmes was a psychopath and a killer, so I shut the door. Leaning against it, I gave Tom another long look. "Is this an act?"

He tossed sun-streaked hair. "I don't have a deal."

"Really? All this stuff with the Holmeses? The suits? The doctor's bag?"

Those words made him clutch the bag closer, as though I might take it. All he said, though, was, "I'm a Watson. A proper Watson—"

"Jesus Christ. Nope, I can't do this. Not today."

As I resumed my search, he followed, a bit breathless as he continued, "—trained in a family of Watsons, so that I know my place."

"Let me guess: your place is to serve nutcases like Blackfriar Holmes."

"Watch your mouth!"

The shout made me stop and turn. Tom was still hugging his fucking bag, but his eyes looked, well, crazy. It's not a polite word, but I didn't have a better way of describing those eyes: huge, wild, looking through me. My skin pebbled at that look.

"Watch your dirty, trashy, gutter-boy mouth," Tom said in a quieter voice. Almost a whisper. He adjusted the bag against himself—clink, clink. "You shouldn't be here. You don't deserve to be here." The final words were full of a rage that threatened to tip the whisper over into more. "You're ruining everything!"

For a moment, I was wordless. Then, like the poet of our age, I came up with "Fuck off, man."

But he didn't fuck off. He came after me. And my brain started thinking about all the sharp, pointed, metal things that could go clink-clink in a doctor's bag. We were all alone in this fucking labyrinth of a house. If I screamed, no one would hear me. Cecilia was probably topping off her Valium, and Noneley was probably planning her next round of bubbly, attention-seeking arson. Hell, if either of them heard me screaming, they'd probably pop popcorn and pull up a chair to watch Tom finish me off.

I risked another look. Tom was still ten feet back, still lugging that stupid bag, but I thought, maybe, ten feet was closer than he'd been a moment before. His color wasn't good, and he was breathing harshly. I wasn't sure he even noticed me looking at him, but he stumbled as he came after me—more like he got tripped up by his own two feet than anything else, and it reminded me of how he'd taken a spill in the living room a little while before.

One of my new life goals, which I'd formed in the last fifteen seconds, was not to be stabbed by one of Blackfriar's groupies, so I started thinking about how I could make my dream a reality.

Two doors later, I was certain that Tom was closing the distance. Eight feet between us. Barely. He looked almost sick, his face bloodless, eyes ringed by greenish-black circles. If he wasn't planning on murdering me, he was definitely thinking about ralphing all over the carpet. I wasn't trying to keep my glances a secret anymore; if he noticed them, they didn't bother him, and I didn't care if they did. He was close enough now to rush me, and that meant keeping an eye on him.

The next door was another of those magazine-spread bedrooms: the perfectly fluffed duvet, the perfectly plumped pillow, the single Calla lily that had to be silk resting on the perfectly rustic dresser, all of it looking like you weren't supposed to get within six feet of it. I bumped the door open and, with a final look for Tom, said, "Stay here."

He didn't, of course. As I crossed the room toward the closet, he lurched through the doorway behind me, cracking the jamb with his hip, the bag jingling and rattling as he righted himself. By that point, we couldn't have been more than a couple of yards apart. He opened the bag, and he slid a hand inside. I kept him in my peripheral vision as I opened the closet door an inch.

Acting, Mrs. Babcock had told us in eighth-grade drama (between doing crossword puzzles and researching, on the smart board, "how to sell your screenplay"), was reacting. So, I reacted.

"Holy shit." I slammed the door and put my back to it. "Get Noneley. No, scratch that. Get Blackfriar."

Tom blinked. He drew his hand, still empty, from the bag and wiped the back of it across his mouth. "What is it?"

"What the hell didn't you understand? Go get him!"

Instead, of course, he slunk toward me, bag held tight.

"Are you listening to me? Hey, dumbass, did you hear—"

I let him elbow me aside. Shoulders tight, he opened the closet door—obviously, the thought of finding some unspeakable horror in a random Holmesian bedroom was not out of the realm of possibility for him—and then said, "What—"

I kicked him in the back of the knee, and he stumbled into the closet. I shut the door, planted one foot at the base, and reached for the bed. It had a nice, wide headboard, and I got a good grip and hauled it toward me. It wasn't even all that heavy—the bed, frame and all, slid across the carpet.

"Hey!" Tom hammered on the inside of the door. "Let me out! Hey!"

"Hay is for horses, shit for brains."

I got the bed in front of the closet door, and then I stepped back. Tom immediately shoved the door open, but it struck the headboard. He probably had a quarter inch of space to work with. He shut the door and tried again. The bed shifted slightly. He could get out. Probably. Eventually. But by that point, I'd be long gone.

"You can't do this!" He slammed the door into the headboard again. "You aren't allowed to do this!"

"Easy there, buddy," I said as I headed for the hall. "Blackfriar is particular about his property."

Something scraped his voice raw as he screamed after me, "Let me out! Let me out! Let me out!" And then, in a hysterical spill: "They're going to laugh at me!"

I shut the door behind me as I stepped out into the hall. His screams continued—they sounded unhinged, and the momentary pleasure of getting rid of the dickweed was quickly changing into feeling doubly shitty about myself. He's fine, I told myself as I hurried down the hall. He's perfectly safe and fine in that closet. He's just mad, that's all. Maybe it would have sounded more convincing from somebody else.

Blackfriar's office was located at the far end of the mansion, of course. I ought to have known. It was another of the spacious, high-ceilinged rooms, and it had the clutter and chaotic, ordered disorder that, from what I knew of the Holmeses historically, seemed more in keeping with them than my personal Holmes's preferences for all things neat and tidy. It held all kinds of shit: a massive, rosewood desk; glass-fronted bookcases lining the walls; a tsunami of paper, some of it looking ancient and brittle; a stuffed raven posed for takeoff; a slipper that looked Middle Eastern, mounted on a plaque on the wall; a burgundy smoking jacket draped over a chair. The smoking jacket, along with the lingering smell of cigar smoke, suggested that thing against the wall was a humidor and not, as I would have chosen, a mini fridge for my personal stash of Coke. A spiral staircase led up to a mezzanine level with leather club chairs, a chaise, more bookcases, more paper. One wall was completely glass, with a pair of French doors that led out onto the deck. The afternoon sun played across the rumpled, glass-sequin valley.

I felt like I had stepped back in time. There were modern touches, of course—a top-of-the-line laptop, for example, and the array of charging cables that snaked through the papers on his desk. But it felt like a room from a different era. I had a hard time imagining Holmes in this room. For a moment, I tried to imagine what he'd be like in ten years, twenty.

Blackfriar would die eventually—at least, that was my theory; I was afraid, though, he might be following the Darth Vader trajectory instead—and Holmes might, one day, be the one who sat behind that desk, smoked cigars, read bizarre, antiquated texts, looked out on the world he'd conquered. Maybe. But if he did, I wouldn't know that man, and the thought of it made me inexpressibly sad.

A sound at the door made me turn. Cecilia Holmes stood there, dressed in slacks and a crisp white button-up. She wore pearls, and a part of me wanted to laugh: pearls around her throat, pearls at her ears. Her hazel eyes tracked me, but I'd seen a lot of people on bennies; she was handling them better than most.

"Hello, Jack," she said as she pulled the door shut behind her. "Has anyone ever told you you look like your mother?"

Chapter 17

Baritsu

"Mrs. Holmes. Um. Hi."

Jack Moreno, everyone. A national treasure.

Cecilia stared at me.

And then my brain caught up with what she'd said. "Wait, you knew my mom?"

She walked across the room. She trailed a finger along the raven's wings. She cupped the toe of the slipper that had been mounted on a plaque. She stopped at the desk, stirred the papers, and the soft rustle of the pages whispered between us.

"Sit down," she said. "I've been wanting to talk to you."

I dropped into one of the chairs in front of the desk. She took the chair behind it—Blackfriar's chair. She looked at home there. The afternoon light poured over her like liquid gold. It lit the silver in her hair, drew a strong shadow along one side of her face. She looked like Holmes, or he looked like her. His features were more masculine, of course, but it was impossible to see her right now, to be this close to her, and not know where Holmes's beauty had come from. She clasped her hands on the desk, and she wasn't wearing a wedding ring.

I wanted to ask again, like maybe she hadn't heard me, but I could taste my own over-eagerness in that urge. I forced myself to sit. To wait. She studied me. And then, without looking, she plucked one of the pages from the desk, turned it over, and rooted around in a drawer until she came up with a pencil. "Your cheekbones," she said. "Your nose." The pencil flew over the blank paper. The soft scratch of the lead filled the spaces between her words. "Your father's features are a good complement. You're much prettier than she was; your mother verged on horsey."

Literally nothing in my life had prepared me for this conversation—let alone for someone telling me my mom had been horsey—so I clutched the arms of the chair, bracing myself against the unreality of the moment, and tried to remember to breathe.

A few moments later, Cecilia held out the sketch. It was beyond good — it was masterful, and she'd done it in a matter of moments, from memory. Mom looked younger than I remembered, but she was wearing one of her favorite necklaces, one that Dad had bought her on a family vacation. I remembered the drawing Holmes had given me before he'd left, the one he'd done of the two of us, in bed, the moment of that first kiss. Good looks weren't the only thing he'd inherited from his mother.

"How have I done?"

I nodded and took out my taped-up Superman wallet. I took out the picture of Mom and Dad from their ten-year anniversary; I'd found it in a box when we'd moved, and I'd taken it without asking Dad.

Cecilia examined it. "She was older then, of course. This is how I knew her."

She plucked a frame from the desk and held it out to me as I returned the photo to my wallet. Then I took the frame and studied its picture: two men with a woman between them. The woman was Mom, barely more than a girl, and she looked even more like Cecilia's drawing than I had expected. The man on her right, with his arm around her waist, had brown hair and a crooked smile, and I was pretty sure he was wearing a Baja hoodie. He looked like whatever you called hipsters back then — maybe just plain old hippies. The man on Mom's left could have been Holloway: hair the color of aspen leaves in the fall, the same nose and jaw, the same slender build, like a blade.

"Leopold," Cecilia said, indicating the hippy. "Moriarty." Then she pointed to the blond man. "And Fairfax." Amusement gave her voice an edge. "Holmes, obviously."

I spared him a second glance before my attention floated back to Mom. She looked so young; that was all I could think, over and over again. I forced myself to pass the picture back, and Cecilia returned it to its place.

"They're all gone now," she said softly. "He keeps it as a reminder."

Down in the valley, light shifted, sparked, spun — the sun on cars, glass, chrome.

"You may ask me."

I had to clear my throat. "How did you know her?"

Her smile was surprisingly sad. "She was a Watson." Then she slid the sketch toward me. "Keep it. Please."

Those words were a doorway onto a million more questions — about my mother, about what being a Watson had meant to her, about what her life had been like growing up, and if she'd been part of the web of the great families, and which Holmeses she'd known, and what she'd been like before my father, before me. And, of course, the bigger questions, the ones you couldn't ask because no one had the answers. Who was she? Why didn't she tell me?

"What do you want from my son?" Cecilia asked, her voice even, her tone measured.

It took me a moment to regroup. "What? Nothing."

"This is not the time for lies."

"I'm not lying. I don't want anything from H. He's my friend. Was my friend. It's—I don't know."

Behind the chemical fog in her hazel eyes, something kindled.

"I don't want his money, if that's what you mean. I'm not trying to use him or anything like that." She still hadn't moved; as far as I could tell, she hadn't even blinked. That conversational void pulled more words out of me. "I don't know what you want me to say."

"I want you to say that you will leave, that you will end all contact with my son, and that you will never return."

I stared at her for a moment.

"I am, of course, willing to compensate you."

The violin shrieked in the distance, but this time, I didn't startle. I burst out laughing.

"Jesus fucking Christ," I said. "You're as bad as he is."

Nothing crossed her face, but she set the pencil down and sat back, hands flat on the desk.

"What's the problem?" I asked. "What's such a big fucking deal that nobody can wait to get me out of the picture? I'm a bad influence? I'm corrupting Holmes by treating him like a human being? I'm a distraction? He can't focus on his mission while I'm hanging around? I'm an embarrassment to all Watsons, is that it? You, and Blackfriar, and Tom, and everybody else—what's the matter?"

"You are a vulnerability. And my son cannot afford to be vulnerable."

"See, that's what I'm talking about. That kind of crazy bullshit. I'm not a vulnerability for H. We make each other better. He told me that, you know. Not about me. Before he knew—he told me about the Holmeses and the Watsons, how they were at their best when they were together. And that's true; I've seen it. I'm living proof of it."

"My son is a child, and he indulges in childish fantasies." For the first time since I'd met Cecilia, color rose in her cheeks, and something seemed to burn off the chemical haze in her eyes. "The Holmeses are not better when they are with a Watson. They are more human."

"News flash: that's better. He's not a robot, and he's not a soldier, and he's not a famous detective from a hundred years ago. He's a sixteen-year-old boy who's been brainwashed, and yeah, he's a genius, and yeah, he's special, but he needs someone who cares about him. Someone who reminds him he's human."

Cecilia leaned forward, her mouth opening. Then she seemed to change her mind and shut it again. She reached for the laptop on the desk, pulled it closer, tapped the touchpad. It woke immediately, without a password, and she navigated through a series of pages until the screen changed again, and a video began to play. When she turned it toward me, I saw Holmes.

He was standing on something that reminded me of a wrestling mat, and he favored one side, as though he couldn't quite straighten up. The camera angle didn't show the walls of the room, so it was hard to tell how big the space was—or, for that matter, where he was. His hair was disheveled, and although it was hard to tell through the footage, one cheek looked red, as though he'd been struck. It took me a moment to realize he was wearing the pink oxford that Paxton had picked out for him.

"What is this?" I asked, head coming up, but Cecilia's face was carved ivory. "Is this right now?"

"It is called baritsu."

"What does that mean? What's he doing to H?"

She didn't answer, and movement on the screen made me turn my attention back to Holmes. He was circling, moving in that loose, liquid fighting stance that I recognized from all the hours we'd spent sparring. The pose was different, though; with every step, it was obvious that not only was he favoring his right side, but he looked exhausted. He was slower, choppier, the familiar grace of his body marred and fractured. It was like someone had taken my Holmes and made a video of him and played it back at a quarter of the normal speed.

I didn't realize there was audio until Blackfriar spoke: "Again."

Holmes moved forward, and Blackfriar moved into view. He was still dressed in the sharkskin suit, and his movements were the same as ever: oil and well-machined gears and clockwork ballet. As I watched, Holmes closed with his father, and for a moment, he moved like my Holmes again: the boy who was a whirlwind, a rushing river, a shooting star.

Blackfriar was faster. He slid away from Holmes's blows, and he made it look like he wasn't even trying. Then, somehow, he had moved behind Holmes, and I saw that Blackfriar carried a cane in one hand. He lashed out with it now, the thin length of black wood a blur on the video feed, and the air cracked as it connected with Holmes.

"No son of mine is so slow," Blackfriar said.

Stumbling, Holmes cried out. It sounded more like a sob. He righted himself, regrouped, faced his father. But it was clear from the way he held himself that the blow had done something to him. His arm—the arm where he'd been cut—hung at his side, and blood soaked the sleeve of his shirt.

I scrambled out of my chair. "Where are they?"

"Sit down."

"He needs me!" My shout rang out in the study.

Cecilia's face remained untouched. It didn't matter; I didn't need her. I'd find Holmes on my own. I started to turn. Then I saw the gun in her hand. Small. Tiny. A nickel-plated revolver. And pointed right at me.

"Sit down," she said.

"You're his mother, for fuck's sake." On the screen, Holmes was staggering, trying to keep himself upright. It looked like so much blood. My face prickled. My eyes were hot and wet. "He needs you. How can you let this happen?"

"Sit and watch. And then tell me, Jack, that human is better."

"Say the word, my son," Blackfriar was saying on the screen. "Tell me you're done, and you can rest, and I will…speak with Jack."

Holmes wavered on his feet. It was hard to tell, but he must have shook his head because Blackfriar let out a small, disgusted noise and started to turn.

The assault was lumbering, almost comically bad, as if Holmes were doing a poor impersonation of himself. He charged Blackfriar, and Blackfriar moved like a snake. The cane connected once with Holmes's knee, and then again across his back, and Holmes fell. He caught himself on one knee. His whole body shook as he struggled for breath. I watched him try to push himself up. Watched, and did nothing, as Holmes brought that tremendous will to bear, one more time, for me.

Then he sagged back down, his body trembling, hands spasming against the mat.

"Why," Blackfriar asked in a tone of mild disappointment, "must you always choose the harder path?"

It was like somebody had wiped my mind clean. A white haze haloed the edges of my vision. Bells were ringing inside my head. I moved, and Cecilia said something, the revolver jabbing toward me.

I couldn't parse the words, but I heard myself saying from a long way off, "Then shoot me, you fucking bitch."

I ran.

The bells were louder, filling my head. My haloed vision collapsed into a tunnel. I knew the hallway they'd taken; I'd start there, and I'd kick down every goddamn door in this place until I found him. I shouldn't have left him. The thought kept time with my feet hitting the floor. I shouldn't have let him go.

When I passed through the vaulted entry hall, though, Noneley had the front door open, and Rivera and Yazzie were standing there. Not bells in my head, a voice said, because I'd been stupid again. Literal bells. The doorbell. Rivera went to say something and then clocked me again, his face changing into something like fury.

"Your father—" Yazzie said, the words barely audible through the rush of blood in my ears.

"What is the meaning of this?" Blackfriar strode through the hall. He didn't look at me, didn't even glance. I was a zero, a cipher, in his universe. The only thing that kept me from launching myself at him, from trying to kill him right then, even though I knew he would kill me first, was Holmes.

He was trying to hold himself up, limping as he came toward the gathering near the front door, his face bloodless. Maybe that was because of all the blood soaking his sleeve. I ran to him, and I got an arm around him as he started to fall.

Hissing, Holmes pried at my hand. "My ribs."

"I'm sorry," I said, adjusting my grip, pulling him against me by the hips. "I'm sorry, H. I'm sorry. I didn't know. I'm so fucking sorry."

He must have hated it, this moment of weakness. He was trembling, and his legs couldn't support him any longer; it was all I could do to keep both of us upright. When I pulled him against me again, he pressed his face into my shoulder, and he shook once, hard. I cupped the back of his head with my free hand and held him.

"What's going on here?" Rivera barked in his cop voice.

"What's going on, Detective," Blackfriar answered, "is that this is bordering on harassment. I told you that I had no interest in pressing charges, and I told you that I would deal with the boys."

"I can see you're dealing with them," Rivera said, and his voice verged on a shout. "I can see exactly how you're dealing with them!"

"I'd like you to leave, Detective, and you can be sure that I will be speaking to the sheriff—"

"Mr. Holmes," Yazzie said, holding out a packet of paper, "we're here to execute a search warrant. We'll need you and your family to vacate the premises for the duration of the search."

"That's ridiculous. A search warrant?" He snatched the papers. "For what?"

"For evidence connecting you to the death of Lynnissa Baca," Rivera said, but his gaze moved past Blackfriar again, coming to rest on me and Holmes. "Jack, what the hell is going on over there?"

Holmes trembled against me, and I held him tighter. For a moment, rage ate up all the oxygen in my lungs, and I couldn't say anything.

Before I could recover, Blackfriar turned away from the detectives. He tossed the paperwork on the floor and strolled toward the hallway he had come from. "This is a joke. There will be no search of this property until my lawyers see that paperwork. You can wait outside until they arrive."

Rivera started after him, shaking off Yazzie as she tried to catch his arm. "Mr. Holmes, you're under arrest for the murder of Lynnissa Baca."

"Don't be ridiculous," Blackfriar said. He was still walking toward us, and he still hadn't looked at me, not once. "On what evidence, Detective? You haven't even conducted this farce of a search."

When Rivera caught Blackfriar's arm, for a moment, the senior Holmes was charged with potential violence, a kind of living darkness that threatened to coil, strike. Then I watched Blackfriar suppress it, the way I'd seen Holmes do so many times before.

"I don't need a search warrant to look in the windows of your Bentley," Rivera said as he snapped the first cuff into place.

A smile creased Blackfriar's face. "Good Lord, Detective, you're going to lose your job for this."

"We'll see about that," Rivera said as he locked the second cuff around Blackfriar's wrist. "Meanwhile, a word of advice for the future: if you kill a woman, don't leave her jewelry lying on the seat of your car."

I might have been the only one to see Blackfriar's face as Rivera delivered those words. Blackfriar's back was to the door, where Noneley and Yazzie were standing, and Holmes's face was buried in my shoulder. But I was looking straight at the son of a bitch, and I saw the moment, the instant, the flicker.

Shock. Then fear. Then the nothing of pure control.

But I had seen it: Blackfriar Holmes was afraid.

Chapter 18

Family

I watched from the front door of the Holmeses' manor as Blackfriar was packed into the Tahoe and Rivera drove away. Yazzie watched, her expression sour, gripping the search warrant packet so tightly that the pages folded. Noneley didn't move.

"What is going on?" Cecilia asked, emerging into the entry hall. Tom trailed after her, which meant either he'd gotten free on his own, or she'd heard him crying for help. He stared murder at me and then turned his attention back to the conversation. Cecilia's gaze settled on Yazzie. "What's happening?"

Yazzie told her, and after a moment, Cecilia indicated they should step outside, and she shut the door behind them. That left me, Holmes, Noneley, and Tom.

Noneley turned a huge, wide-eyed smile on us. A laugh bubbled up. "Oh my God, did you see his face?"

"A little help, please?" I said and tilted my head at Holmes.

"He's going to be furious," she said with another laugh, tipping her head back so the sound carried up to the high ceiling. "Arrested. By a local cop. God, he's never going to live this down."

"Noneley, some help?"

She shook her head, pressed her hands to her cheeks, as though fighting the grin spread there. Then she started off down the hall, and her laughter floated back to us.

I adjusted Holmes's weight against me and tried to speak so only he would hear. "H, I'm going to help you lie down. I need to call an Uber, and then we're going to get you to a doctor." Holmes shook his head against me. "Yes, sir. No arguments."

Tom watched us. He was still clutching the black doctor's bag, but he let go of it with one hand long enough to push back sun-streaked hair. Then he took a nervous step toward us.

"Stay where you are," I told him.

"Don't be ridiculous," Tom said. "He needs help, and you can't carry him yourself."

"I can carry him," I said. But I stayed where I was, holding Holmes to me, because the honest truth was that I could barely keep him upright. I might be able to get him over my shoulder, do a fireman's carry, but with Holmes's ribs injured, I had no idea what that might do to him. Finally, I ground out, "Fine. Leave the fucking bag over there and show me your hands."

Tom looked frozen for a moment. Then he set the bag down, and he held out his open hands. I nodded, and he came over to us. Between us, we managed to get Holmes into the living room, and we stretched him out on one of the plush, rounded sofas.

"No doctor," Holmes said.

"Why not?" I asked as I stuffed a pillow under his head. "Would it be bad press if everybody found out your dad beat the shit out of you?"

Holmes's fingers bit into my wrist. "No. Doctor."

"Yeah, no, no fucking way—"

"I can take a look," Tom said, the words tentative, his gaze moving from Holmes to me. "I have training."

"You're in med school, Speed Racer," I said. "You're not a doctor."

"I wasn't referring to medical school. Watsons are trained to handle a range of emergency situations."

What I wanted to say was something along the lines of *I am so sick of hearing about the fucking Watsons*. But if I tried to take Holmes to a doctor, he'd fight me every step of the way, and even if Tom was a potentially murderous psychopath, right then, he was offering to help.

Finally, I settled on "Let's see how bad it is."

Tom retrieved his bag from the hall, and I started unbuttoning Holmes's shirt. He tried to tear my hand away, moaning and protesting and being, as per usual, a little shit about everything, but it was like wrestling with a puppy.

"Knock it off," I told him as I yanked the shirt open. "Or I'll drag your pasty ass to the ER."

He mumbled something petulant and outraged, but when I took his hand, he let me. It was a shock, again, seeing the perfectly defined musculature of his torso: everything hard and strong, a topography of work and sacrifice and power. The little patch of silky gold hair between his pecs still took me by surprise, even though I knew it was there. Where the shirt was rucked back far enough, hints of darker gold suggested the hair under his arms.

The clink of metal came as Tom set down the doctor's bag. He opened it, and I said, "Think about what you're going to do next," I said. "And think about doing it slowly and carefully."

Tom's face was grim, but he nodded. He drew items out one by one, slowly, like I'd suggested. Sterilized packets with needles and sutures. A hypodermic needle and syringe with a small prescription bottle. A brown prescription vial, where pills rattled. Sterilized bandages. Scissors. Antiseptic wipes. He cleaned his hands thoroughly, professionally, and some of the awkwardness that clung to him evaporated as his movements became controlled, clinical, skilled.

"I'm going to remove his sleeve." Tom picked up the scissors. "Unless you'd rather help him out of the shirt."

I made a face, mostly because I wanted to fight with Tom about everything, but I said, "It'd be murder on him to get him out of the shirt. Go ahead and cut it off."

Tom snipped the shirt off Holmes in precise, economical movements. I helped him get rid of the fabric. Holmes's chest and arms pebbled with the cold, and he made a faint noise of distress, blinked his eyes, tried to sit up. With my free hand on his shoulder, I pressed him back and murmured, "Easy, easy. Stay still."

"The shot will numb his arm—" Tom said as he reached for the syringe.

"Let me see that." I took the prescription bottle.

"Lidocaine," Tom said. His expression was unreadable when I glanced up. "Does that meet with your approval?"

For lack of anything better, I grunted and held out the bottle. Tom administered the injection the way he'd done everything else while attending to Holmes, with a smoothness I hadn't seen from him over the previous days. Holmes made another sound, but some of the strain in his face eased. I smoothed hair back from his forehead.

"Is he going to be ok?" I asked. It was a dumb question, I know, but I couldn't help myself.

"Fine," Holmes said and started trying to sit up.

"Cut it out." He let me press him back down, his eyes half-closed. How hard had he pushed himself, I wondered, to end up like this? How much of that seemingly limitless reserve of energy had he burned through in the last few days, only to find himself drawing on it again today? He wasn't a machine. He wasn't even really a Holmes bot. He was a boy, and his shoulder was like spun glass under my hand, and for me, he had asked himself, one more time, to do the impossible.

What had I done for him over the last few days? Told him over and over again that I hated him.

"He'll be fine," Tom said as he prepared the needle and suture. "A few torn stitches. It's exhaustion more than anything else, I think."

I kept brushing Holmes's hair back. I couldn't stop myself. "He doesn't sleep. I tell him he needs more sleep, but he doesn't."

Tom gave me a look I couldn't read.

"He doesn't eat, either. He's like one of those air plants. Only one of those air plants that doesn't sleep."

"Jack," Tom said slowly, "maybe you'd like to step outside."

"No." I clutched Holmes's hand hard enough that he stirred, and I had to force myself to relax. "No, I'll stop being weird."

Tom frowned at that, but he bent and went to work. He was done with the sutures in a matter of minutes, and then he cleaned Holmes's wound and bandaged it again. Holmes's eyes were still slitted, but I thought he was tracking me as I followed Tom's movements. I squeezed his hand lightly.

"I have some pills," Tom said. "For the pain. Let me get him a glass of water."

"No, I'll do it. I'm not totally useless." I started to stand, but Holmes protested wordlessly, and he made it hard to let go of his hand. "H, don't you want some water? I'll be right back."

Finally, I got free of him. I checked the bar, but all they had was tonic water.

"That way," Tom said.

I hurried in the direction he'd pointed, and it only took me two wrong turns to find the kitchen. It was about what you'd expect: acres of marble and maple, a pantry the size of a war room, a fridge that might technically have qualified as a studio apartment. I got a bottle of water and hurried back.

As I returned to the living room, Holmes made a noise that was an unmistakable mix of fury and frustration. Tom had taken my place on the couch next to him, and he was running his hands over Holmes's side, where the red marks of blows were unmistakable against his fair skin. He did something, and it was like someone had flipped a switch: Holmes's eyes snapped open. I couldn't imagine what kind of resolve it took, but Holmes forced himself to sit up, and he caught Tom's arm.

"Ow!" Tom said, trying to twist free.

"Do not touch me!" Holmes shouted.

"H, hey—" I began.

"Your ribs—" Tom said, still trying to break Holmes's hold.

"I have told you I do not want you to touch me!"

By that point, I'd reached the couch. I touched Holmes's arm, and he flinched and turned on me. For a moment, nothing registered in his face. Then recognition filtered in.

"Easy," I said, rubbing his arm, working my way toward his fingers. I pried them loose from around Tom's wrist. "How about you let Tom go?"

Holmes swallowed. He looked lost inside those starlight eyes, but he let me peel his hand away.

"Tom," he said like it was a question.

"He was helping you." I grabbed some of the cushions and shifted them around to prop Holmes up, keeping one hand on his arm the whole time. Tom scooted backward, reached the edge of the couch, and fell off. Which, to be fair, seemed kind of consistent for him.

After a few more deep breaths, Holmes seemed more aware, more awake. He rubbed his face and, in a low voice, said, "I have told him—"

By that point, Tom was on his feet again. A flush filled his cheeks, and he shook the sun-streaked hair out of his eyes.

"Sorry about that—" I began.

"I was trying to help!"

"I know. H knows too, but he got confused—"

"That's what Watsons do. They help their Holmeses."

"Tom, I'm sorry. H is sorry. Seriously."

Tom began shoving the suture kit, the bandages, the syringe and needle, the prescription bottle, everything, back into the doctor's bag.

"Thank you—"

"Everything was fine—" He yanked the bag from the table and clutched it to his chest. He sounded like he was about to cry. "—until you came back."

He ran out of the room. In the process, because he was Tom, he managed to crash into one of the walls. It wasn't even a little crash. It was a head-first, full-speed, total collision. He scrambled to his feet and sprinted away, and he left one shoe behind.

"If that's the kind of help the Holmeses have been getting," I said, "maybe it's time to start hiring out."

Holmes huffed his little breath.

When I turned back to him, his arms were folded across his chest, a futile attempt at hiding the marks that in the next day or two would turn him into a mass of green and purple bruises. His eyes were half-closed again, and he rocked slightly from side to side, unable to hold himself upright.

I touched his shoulder, and he shivered. "Let's get you to your room, ok? Do you have a room? If you don't, I found a million guest rooms. You need to sleep. Then eat. Then sleep. In between, I'll allow some light pooping. Oh Christ, and when did you take your antibiotics?"

But he didn't answer, not even that little huff of breath. He was shivering harder, uncontrollably. His face had become a fortress, that place of unbreachable walls, how he kept all his demons out. And, in the process, kept himself alone.

"H," I whispered, and I ran my fingers through hair the color of aspens, followed the line of his neck, found the warm curve of his nape. I stopped because I didn't know what to say. I couldn't say, *I saw.* I couldn't say, *I know what you did for me.* Because Noneley was right; he wouldn't want me to know, might never forgive me for seeing him like that. I couldn't even say, *I'm sorry.* The best I could come up with was "Are you ok?"

He shook his head, and a tear slipped out.

I sat still. I breathed through my nose. Blackfriar was in police custody, which meant murdering him was going to be more difficult, but I still thought I had a shot. Red pinpricks clustered at the edge of my vision. I was vaguely aware that I was clutching the couch cushion hard enough that my fingers ached.

And then, brick by brick, Holmes finished putting up his walls. He blinked his eyes clear. He looked at me. He still couldn't pass for anything but exhausted, but the cold control was back. His voice even came close to normal as he said, "I'm sorry, Jack. I was disoriented; I took a bad fall, that's all. I'm fine."

I couldn't help it: a wet laugh escaped me, and I wiped my eyes.

"I am, truly." Holmes moved into my line of sight. For a moment, our gazes matched. Then his mouth quirked into a smile. Not the full one. Not the great, big dorky one. But real enough. Because he was worried about me, I realized. Because he knew he could give this to me.

I snuffled, and it threatened to turn into a full-out sob.

"Jack—"

"Are you finished?" Noneley asked, and I had to scrub at my face again before I could look at her. She stood in the hallway, grinning at us. "Whatever happened to your shirt, Hol?"

He scowled at her and folded his arms more tightly over his chest.

"Come along, then," she said. "Family council and all that. Sorry, Jack, no Watsons allowed."

Holmes hesitated. Then he rose. If you didn't know him, it would have looked a little stiff, a little slow. If you'd seen him move before, though, it was a rusty, creaking imitation of Holloway Holmes.

"You need to rest—" I began.

"I will, Jack. I promise. But this comes first."

"This?" I shot up from the couch. "Them? After what just happened? They—" I stopped myself in time, barely. *They knew*, I wanted to say. *They knew what he was doing to you, and they let it happen.*

But Holmes must have heard some of it because his spine stiffened, his shoulders straightened, and he sounded a little posher when he said, "They are my family."

"Yeah, I know, but—"

"Have I ever interfered with your relationship with your father?"

"That's not the same—"

"When you planned on running away last year, when you were determined never to talk to him again, did I intervene?"

"As a matter of fact, you couldn't stop telling me it was such a bad idea." My volume slipped, and the words were louder than I'd intended. "You're hurt, and I'm not going to let you—"

"You're not going to let me," Holmes said.

I stopped. My voice was tight, buckled down, when I said, "I didn't mean—"

"Enough."

A shimmering sound filled my ears.

"Go home, Jack. This is a family matter now; I will handle it with my family." He stepped back, watching my face, and turned. A moment later, he and Noneley had disappeared down the hall. I couldn't even hear them because, of course, they were fucking Holmeses.

I started walking because it was either move or kick something, and I figured if I kicked something, I'd break it, and I'd spend the next forty years trying to earn enough money to replace it. I did a couple of laps around the room, my breathing getting faster and faster, and then I charged toward the French doors. Outside, the air was warmer than I expected, the sun dazzling me for the first few steps, my steps ringing out against the deck. I went all the way to the rail, leaned over it, and screamed down into the valley. I did that until I ran out of air, and then I sagged across the rail, staring down at the drop. There wasn't even a dramatic echo.

Noise behind me made me turn, and for a moment, I thought Tom had come back. Maybe he was going to help me out, push me over the rail, get it over with. But instead, it was Yazzie. She watched me for a moment, took off her glasses, cleaned them on her shirttail.

"Save it," I said. "Whatever it is, I don't want to hear it."

She seemed to think about that for a while. She put the glasses back on, shrugged, and said, "You can't be here, not while we're executing the warrant."

"Fine."

"Do you want a ride?"

"I said fine."

She straightened her jacket. The wind pushed through my hair.

"Sorry," I mumbled.

"Let's get you a ride home."

That meant Deputy Utley, he of the pouchy eyes and the plastic fork stuck behind his ear. I didn't understand why he did that. Maybe in case of emergency. Maybe all of a sudden, he'd need to eat something with a fork, so he had to be prepared. Instead of having him take me home, though, I asked him to drive me back to Zodiac. The truck was still there, and Utley was nice enough to wait while I made sure it started. Then he rolled out of the lot, and I drove home.

Home, because this was a family matter now, and for Holmes, family didn't include me.

I tried not to think about it. I tried to think about anything else. Spring in Utah is beautiful. I mean, I guess I'm biased, but it really is. The valley and the canyons and the sides of the mountain all turn green. The peaks are still furry with snow. The sky, a perfect blue, goes on forever. Spring can't do anything about how junky I-15 looks—the car dealerships and the light industrial zoning and the commercial lots and the low-rent apartments crowding the freeway, so much concrete and asphalt and bare, whitish-brown earth. But it's still better than I-15 in the winter.

Across Orem, up the canyon.

The Provo was running high with snowmelt, and a trout jumped and broke the water like the slice of a knife. Early, I thought. He must be a go-getter. The bald faces of granite contrasted with the dense vegetation that bloomed wherever water ran: the green of cottonwood leaves, the purple of lupine, the red of Indian paintbrush.

When I got back to campus, I waffled. Instead of taking the turn to go back to the cottage, I let the truck go straight. Maybe I'd do a quick tour of campus before I went home to face the music. Maybe I'd get lucky and find a serial killer who specialized in guys who can never get their hair to look right and who constantly, with the best of intentions, manage to fuck everything up with the most important people in their lives. Hell, maybe I'd find a cliff and drive off it.

Instead, I ended up at the boathouse. My dealing days were done, so I hadn't been here in the last few months except for the occasional odd job — sweeping down the spider webs, opening things up for spring, a complaint about stiff hinges. But I'd spent a lot of time here before. A lot of quiet nights, waiting, listening to the water. I let the truck die and rolled down the window and listened now.

It wasn't just the water, though. There was laughter. There was the wind in the grass. A group of kids emerged, and two boys started playing frisbee while a cluster of girls sat and talked and pretended not to watch. It took all of five minutes for the boys' shirts to fall off. The rest of us didn't mind: muscles moved pleasantly under smooth skin, everything easy, natural looking. Before Holmes, I would have said they were graceful.

I thought of the bruises on his body, the angry red marks of violence, what he'd borne for me to keep me safe—even knowing it was only temporary, that eventually, he would fail, and his father would have me. It had been stupid, I wanted to tell him. It had been a waste. He wouldn't have hurt me, not physically. Well, he might have killed me. But not today. Not right then. You could have let him scare me or shout at me or threaten me, whatever it was, and spared yourself the pain and the humiliation and, what I knew had cost Holmes the most, the failure. To be pushed to the end of his strength, cornered, pressed to his limits. And to find, in the end, it wasn't enough. For Holmes, who expected the impossible of himself, it was worse than any blow from a cane, worse than torn stitches, worse than bruised ribs. You could have saved yourself all of that, and it would have been the smart thing to do.

But he hadn't.

And then, when I thought I knew why, when I realized how stupid I'd been for months and months, he'd told me to go home. Because this was a family matter.

My phone buzzed in my lap. Figuring it was Dad wanting to chew my ass, I reached to silence it. But it was from Rowe. One of the dozens of messages he'd been sending me all day. There were a lot of *Where are you?* And *Your dad is pissed.* And *Jack, everybody's worried.* And then there were the other ones—the ones I thought of as authentic Rowe texts. *I found a chair in the dumpster behind Butters. It looks lonely.* And *Are ass cramps a thing? Not like diarrhea. On the outside of your ass.* And *Dude, remember that fluffy toilet paper I was telling you about? It's back.*

This most recent one was a fist bump and a heart, and I wanted to send a petition to the universe to explain Rowe because I just couldn't.

I sent the text before I had time to consider what I was doing: *Almost back. Where are you guys?*

Approximately a million texts came back: a surprised face emoji, a dog emoji, a fireworks emoji, a Bitmoji Rowe who was eating shrimp cocktail. Mixed in were the pertinent details like *Library* and *Dude, are you ok?*

I drove to the library and parked in one of the service spots behind it, and I let myself in through the back door—not normally open to students—with one of the spare Walker keys I'd kept. Hand to God, I only kept them now so I wouldn't have to bother Dad when I helped cover a shift.

Mostly.

Inside, the library was cool, and it smelled like recycled air and old paper and the carpet that Dad and I were going to rip out over the summer. My eyes adjusted to the dim lighting as I moved along the stacks. I hadn't spent much time here, not even since I'd become a student at Walker. I had this weird thing about someone almost trying to kill me, and it made me avoid the library if I wasn't doing something for Dad. But I knew the layout, and I figured Rowe wouldn't be in the main area of the library. Trying to keep Rowe from talking was like trying to stop the Provo with your bare hands. They'd be in one of the study rooms with the door closed.

The first room I checked had Danny Cabell in it, his frizzy mop of hair bent over his phone, and he was definitely watching porn. He turned bright red when he looked up, and I smiled an apology and yanked the door shut. The second room I checked had Alonna Flores, who was studying like always. She was three years into her four-year plan to crush every academic record at Walker, and she glared at me for the interruption. This time, I was the one who turned red as I backed out of the room.

Rowe, Emma, Glo, and Ariana were in the third room, and they were laughing when I stepped inside. Ariana and I locked eyes for a moment, and she broke our gaze first, laughing harder. It was still awkward seeing her— we'd broken up a few months ago, for a lot of reasons. She still looked great: dark brown skin, great curves, hair spilling to the small of her back. She'd ditched the coppery highlights, and it made her look more mature. She and Emma and Glo had hit it off when I'd brought Ariana to a party in December, and they'd stayed friends in spite of the breakup.

"Jack," Rowe said—well, it was Rowe, so it was almost a shout, library be damned. "Holy shit, man, that's hilarious!"

I got as far as "What's hil—" before Emma and Glo spotted me and dissolved into fresh gales of laughter.

The girls were a study in contrasts: Emma tall, dark, an umber cast to her skin. She wore cat-eye glasses, and she moved like an athlete. Glo was petite, with golden skin, and she almost always had a book. Today looked like no exception, although the book was facedown, so I couldn't see the cover. Rowe, Emma, and Glo were—well, not exactly a throuple, but something like that. They loved each other fiercely, and while Rowe and Glo were romantically involved, I hardly ever saw them without Emma.

Even Ariana had glanced back at me, eyes widening.

Then I remembered the ripped jeans, the shirt that said ZADDY.

"It's not a joke," Glo squealed as she laughed harder. "Oh my God, he was serious."

"They're not mine," I said.

"Look at his face," Emma said before collapsing against Glo. She was laughing so hard she was crying.

"I had to borrow—no, you know what? I'm not going to defend myself." I finished moving into the study room and shut the door behind me. "Could you dumbasses keep it down? We're in a library."

"It's ok, dude," Rowe said, stretching his arm out for a fist bump. I obliged because Rowe was an exception to my general rule against fist bumps. "You look hot."

"You look like a SoundCloud rapper," Ariana said with a grin.

I couldn't help the betrayed "Ariana!" that escaped me.

She shrugged, and her grin got bigger.

"And his hair," Glo was saying to Emma, both of them laughing harder.

I fixed my hair. Tried to fix it. Couldn't remember what it looked like and reached for my phone to check. Ariana was hiding her amusement behind one hand. Rowe, on the other hand, was staring at me with that earnest devotion people commonly associate with puppies.

"Your hair is fire, dude. Don't listen to them."

"Oh my God," I said under my breath.

"His little spikes," Emma was saying. She looked like she and Glo were about to laugh themselves under the table.

"Never mind," I said. "I'm leaving. You jackasses can fuck around without me."

"He's very sensitive," Ariana said. "You're hurting his feelings."

"Don't go," Emma said through her laughter.

"We'll stop," Glo said, but she spoiled it by giggling and wiping her eyes.

"Please don't be mad, Zaddy," Rowe said, and the little shit's expression of pure, trusting, innocent dedication didn't waver for a moment, not even a tiny bit.

"I hate all of you," I said. "I have no friends. You're dead to me."

But they were starting to pull themselves back together by that point, and I let them convince me to stay, although I grumped about it and made them work a little harder than usual before I sat at the table.

"And I do not look like a SoundCloud rapper," I snapped at Ariana. "Whatever that means."

She met me with a flat look. "You know exactly what it means."

I had to bite the inside of my mouth not to grin because, as usual, she was exactly right.

"Dude," Rowe asked, lowering his voice to slightly-lower-than-deafening—a Rowe whisper, in other words. "Is he back?"

"That's all we've been talking about," Emma said as she took Glo's hand.

"Holloway," Glo said. "That's why you disappeared again, right?"

Ariana stood. She was wearing this cute crop top with booty shorts, and her dad would have killed her if he'd seen it, and her mom would have had a stroke. I looked; sue me, we used to do a lot more than looking, and it was hard to break old habits.

"I've got to go," she said as she grabbed her phone.

"No, wait—" Glo said.

Emma shushed her, and Glo subsided unhappily.

"You don't have to go," I said. "It's not—that wasn't why—"

"I've got work," Ariana said, and she squeezed my nape as she passed behind me. "Bye, SoundCloud."

She shut the door quietly behind her.

The three of them shared an unhappy silence. It was Rowe, of course, who broke it, shaking those messy bangs as he leaned toward me. "But dude, for real: is he back?"

I nodded.

"Holy crap, man. That's—" He checked me. "That's good, right?"

I saw the skepticism on Emma's and Glo's faces. They'd been there for me in the months after Holmes had disappeared. They'd seen what it had done to me.

"I don't know," I said.

"Do you want to talk about it?" Glo asked.

I thought the answer was no. But then I started talking, and it all spilled out. Not the scary stuff. Not the whole truth. But enough. The outline.

"He's in love with you," Rowe said. "And he's sorry, and he's trying to make things right."

"Maybe," Glo said.

"What do you mean, maybe? He told Jack straight out. And he stood up to his dad for Jack. And you know H; he's not good at talking about his feelings, so you know he's, like, making this extra effort for Jack."

"I don't think any of us know Holloway," Emma said quietly.

"I mean," Glo said to Rowe, "not everything adds up. He's been back in Utah for how long? We don't know. Long enough to be living in a condo with an older guy. He didn't contact Jack. He didn't tell Jack he was here. Jack never would have known if they hadn't bumped into each other at that party."

"Ok, but maybe H was embarrassed." Rowe sat up straighter, glancing at me for confirmation. "Maybe he didn't know how to have that conversation, but he wanted to, and then they bumped into each other."

"But we don't know that. We don't know anything about why he didn't contact Jack."

"Dude," Rowe said to me, "help me out."

"I don't know," I said. "What H has said, the way he's acted—what he went through for me today, I mean, I don't want to tell you the details, but it was awful. And there are these moments when I know, or I think I know, what he's feeling."

"But," Glo prompted.

"But you're right. Why didn't he call me? Why didn't he tell me he was back?"

"Why did he leave?" Glo said softly.

I shrugged. My face felt hot, and I looked down at the table. Chair legs whispered against the carpet, and a moment later, Rowe was squeezing onto my chair, wrapping an arm around me. I didn't cry. But I did have to blink a lot. He smelled like warm teenage boy and deodorant, and it was nice.

"It's ok, dude. It's going to be ok."

I shrugged again because I didn't have anything better to do. By degrees, I realized Emma was not-looking at me so intently that it had become a kind of presence. Rowe and Glo both seemed aware of it too. I forced myself to look at Emma, but she still didn't meet my gaze, so I asked, "What do you think?"

"I don't think I'm the right person to ask."

"You're my friend."

"But I'm not—I don't, you know, want—" Finally she blurted, "I'm ace."

"Maybe that's better," Glo said. "Maybe you've got a different insight than the rest of us."

Emma sat still for a moment. Then she raised her head, and behind the cat-eye glasses, her eyes were wet. "Jack, I've never seen somebody hurting the way you were after Holloway left. I don't want that to happen to you again."

I nodded.

"You—you were pretty hard on yourself right now, telling us all the good things he did for you, telling us how you feel when you're around him, and how you told him you hate him, and how that makes you a shitty person. But I think maybe part of you does hate him, a little. Still." She seemed to hear herself and rushed to add, "I don't know. I shouldn't have said that. But I thought you were going to die, Jack, and we love you, and—and you deserve to be happy."

My throat was scratchy. I dredged up a watery smile. "So, one yes, one maybe, one no."

"We're not voting, dude," Rowe said, squeezing me. Somehow, amazingly, no ribs popped out of my chest. "Whatever you do, we'll support you. Em's right: we love you."

Glo was clutching *Seriously MOUSE-taken: A Friendly Feline Mystery* to her chest, and her dark eyes shimmered. "Of course we love you. We want you to be happy, that's all."

And all three of them had said it, so I had to duck my head and mumble, "I love you guys too," and Glo and Emma both made those noises people make at babies, and Rowe turned the hug into some kind of shambling, unstoppable wrestling move that carried me out of my seat and pinned me against the table, and all I could do was laugh and beat on his shoulders until he had finally hugged me to death and released me.

"You're insane," I told him as he straightened his shirt. "He's a lunatic," I told the girls. "You realize that?"

"Sorry, Zaddy," Rowe said with a smirk.

"It's because he's still using that salt spray," Emma said. "That's why his hair looks like that."

Glo shook her head "I'm telling you, I know he says he doesn't, but I think he's using curling ribbons."

"I'm done," I said, and I would have left right then only thanks to Rowe, I didn't have any feeling in my legs. "I'm never talking to you again."

But we did talk. Not about Holmes, not after that conversation. Just about stuff. They were starting to make plans for the summer, and because they were my friends, they invited me. But they were talking about Cancun and London, and Glo kept insisting on Bali, and it never occurred to them that we'd had to cut our grocery bill so that I could keep my phone, and that vacation meant maybe a night camping at Bear Lake if Dad's health stayed good.

Still, I would have stayed longer, but my phone buzzed with a message from Dad: *How's everything going?*

It took me a moment to remember that, as far as Dad knew, I might still be facing trespassing charges, and that I'd pissed off one of the most powerful families in the world, and, even worse, lied to him. I texted back: *Fine. No charges, so everything's ok. I'll probably get a ride home soon.*

The delay between messages felt like a silence that grew and grew.

A ride from the library? Dad asked.

"Shit," I said.

"What happened?" Rowe asked.

Emma sat up from where she was reclining against Glo. "What's wrong?"

"My dad. These stupid parental tracking apps."

Rowe shifted in his seat, and he couldn't quite meet my eyes as he said, "Uh, Jack, like, about that."

I glanced at him as I got up from the table.

"So, um, your dad is a little, like, intense, when he gets mad, so, um, maybe don't, you know, use my name if you're going to lie to him." He sounded almost apologetic when he added, "You know, if you can help it."

It was as close as Rowe had ever come to telling me I was a piece of shit.

I shook my head. "I'm sorry, Rowe."

"No, dude, it's, like—"

"No, that was shitty of me. I'm really sorry. I'll make it up to you, and I won't do it again."

Some of the tightness left his expression, and his usual broad, generous smile rolled out again. "It's cool, dude."

We said goodbye, and I left. It was one of those perfect spring evenings, the shadows long and cool, the sides of the mountain purple. The temperature had dropped enough for me to shiver and chafe my arms as I turned toward the truck. Then I stopped.

Ariana was sitting there in the little green deathtrap she called a car. The Geo was silent, and she had her head down, looking at her phone. I thought about getting in the truck and leaving. Instead, I approached, and she must have seen the movement because she looked up, and her eyes fastened on me. She opened the door of the car, but she didn't get out.

"I thought you were leaving," I said.

She held the phone in her lap, both hands tight around it.

"If you were waiting for me to leave—" I stopped. "If it's too weird, we can figure something out—"

"No, Jack. I did leave. And I came back." Her hands flexed and closed around the phone again, and she looked out the windshield, I guess so she wouldn't have to look at me. "I've never asked you—Emma and Glo told me a little, even though it's none of my business—even when we were dating, I wondered."

I thought of a million, magical ways that I could get out of this conversation. The frontrunners were alien abduction or killed by frozen poop discharged from an airplane. But since I was, technically, supposed to be a man, I dug down deep, looked for a pair of balls, and finally managed to say, "I wasn't lying when I told you there was nobody else. But I'd be lying if I told you that I didn't start, you know, having feelings for him while we were dating." I waited, but she was better at it, and I heard myself say, "There were a lot of reasons we broke up."

"I know. I didn't—that's not what this is about. That's not what I wanted to talk about. Or I don't think it is, anyway. I came back because—" She did this weird little laugh. And then she looked at me, and whatever she saw, it made her smile, and her body loosened, and she shook her head. "God, Jack, are you doing it all over again?"

She didn't have to say what it was. It was fucking everything up. Being Jack Moreno, and finding my own particular brand of screw-ups to ruin a good thing.

"I don't know. I don't want to. I'm trying not to." And then, channeling the ultimate expression of dudes who know jack shit and have the emotional IQ of boot leather, "It's complicated."

She laughed again. "Oh my God."

Somehow, that made it easier. I found myself smiling. "Come on, you honestly didn't expect me to do better than that, did you?"

"No, Jack. I did not." She was doing it again, her hands opening and closing around the phone. Then she said, "I saw how you looked at him. And I saw how he looked at you. I don't know what else you're waiting for."

I rolled one shoulder.

"God, Jack, don't screw it up."

I thought about saying *I so solemnly swear*, but my throat wasn't working, and anyway, I figured I didn't want Ariana to kick my newly discovered balls back up into my body.

"I'm going now," Ariana said, her voice thick. She set her phone between her legs and reached for the door. "I'm going to go."

The Geo sounded like a lawnmower as she pulled away.

My phone buzzed again.

Dad: *Get your ass home.*

And then, on the heels of that text, another: *This boy is driving me out of my goddamn mind.*

Chapter 19

Baseball Bat Beats Knife

I drove home. The cottage glowed against the dusk, light seeping out from around the blinds, warm and yellow and pushing back the gloom—even if it was only by a few inches. I thought I could make out Dad's silhouette through one of the windows. No sign of Holmes, but that had to be who Dad meant. My heart was beating so fast I thought I was going to be sick.

For my birthday, in some bizarre attempt at kindness, Holmes had bought me a truck. He'd ordered it, paid for it, had it delivered. He hadn't shown up in person of course. And it wasn't just any truck—it was a fully loaded 2019 Ford F-150. Black. I didn't exactly have a truck fetish, but if I had, in theory, this truck would have produced spontaneous orgasm. And so, because I'd been firmly committed to hating Holmes with all my heart, I'd given it to Dad, and that's why I was driving the Dodge.

All that is a long way of saying the Ford was parked under the carport, so I had to use one of the staff spots in the lot and walk the rest of the way. I spent the time focusing on not projectile vomiting, *Exorcism* style.

When I got to the cottage, the porch boards creaked underfoot. The front door opened easily. We never kept it locked, not living all the way up here. The smell of red sauce and cheese and carbs met me, and my stomach grumbled. I wasn't sure the last time I'd eaten, and although fifteen seconds before, I would have sworn I wasn't hungry, my stomach now decided to turn itself inside out.

Dad was in the kitchen, standing sentry over a pan of lasagna. Holmes sat on the couch, the stiffness of his body badly disguising his injuries. He'd found a crisp white oxford (of course he had, this was Holmes), and it only made him look more washed out. Dad narrowed his eyes when he saw me. Holmes's head came up, his face transparent with relief.

"Outside," Dad said.

"I just got here."

"Jack—" Holmes began to rise.

"Outside," Dad said again.

"Don't get up, H. I'll be right back."

Holmes sank back onto the couch; even that short attempt seemed to have exhausted him, his face bluish in its pallor.

Dad bulldozed me out onto the porch and pulled the door shut. The light by the door threw a yellow cast over half his face, picking out the lines and wrinkles. The other half lay in darkness.

"We haven't had lasagna in a while."

Folding his arms, Dad seemed to wrestle internally for a moment. His voice was surprisingly even when he said, "Do you want to try that again?"

Crickets chirped in the night. Leaves whispered against each other with the perpetual restlessness of the canyon.

"I'm sorry," I said, inspecting my Stan Smiths because it was easier than looking him in the eye.

The wind died. The trees held their breath. I risked a look up, where Dad's face was still half a canvas of that waxy light. At the edge of my vision, between the porch and trees, stars glimmered.

"We've talked about this. About lying."

"Dad—"

"You lied to me about Rowe."

"Hold on."

"You kept lying. You were gone almost twenty-four hours, and I still don't have any idea where you went. I wouldn't know anything, in fact, if you hadn't gotten yourself arrested by the police!"

The last words surged into a shout, and I dropped my eyes again. When I shifted my weight, one of the old boards protested. "I didn't get arrested—"

"Don't talk back to me."

I felt so shitty about it, I did the only natural thing: I brought my head up and said, "I wouldn't have to lie to you if you treated me like an adult." Dad tightened his arms across his chest, and I blurted, "And I can say my opinion too. It's not talking back. I get to say something too."

There might have been silence. Or there might have been fireworks going off. Or there might have been one of the background special effects, a sad trombone. I wouldn't know because my heart was pounding so hard I couldn't hear anything.

But I heard Dad fine when he said, "All right. Explain."

I opened my mouth. Then, after a moment, I shut it again.

"You lied about Rowe," Dad said quietly, and I was surprised, even as I tried to stay afloat in the flood of emotion, that he no longer sounded angry. "You trespassed on private property. You would have gotten arrested if Mr. Holmes hadn't intervened. And you lied to me again, Jack. Tonight."

"I didn't want you to worry—"

Dad gave a tiny shake of his head, and I stopped. I was breathing hard. My face felt puffy, and I was blinking as fast as I could.

"I thought we were done with this," Dad said, voice gentle. "I thought we were done with the lying, Jack."

I had to gulp air, fight to keep my voice steady. "It's not his fault."

"What am I supposed to think? Holloway reappears, Jack—comes out of thin air, as far as I can tell—and we're right back where we started."

"That's not how it was." Although a part of me realized that yes, that's exactly how it was. "Dad, he didn't do anything. I fucked up."

"Watch your mouth."

"I messed up. I shouldn't have lied. I know that, and I know you worry, and you're right. But it's not H's fault."

"Were you going to tell me?"

I stared down at the Stan Smiths again.

"Were you going to tell me," Dad asked again, more slowly this time, "Holloway was back?"

It took me a beat too long. "Yes."

Dad shook his head. He stared off to the side, and the rest of his face was swallowed up by shadow.

"I was," I said. "It all happened so fast."

"Jack, what he did to you—"

"He didn't—he wasn't trying to hurt me. He was doing what he thought was right. He would never hurt anyone, especially not me, ok? He—"

Dad didn't raise his voice. Lost in shadow, he didn't even seem to move. The words were flat and dead and still somehow hard as a slap. "I need you to stop talking now."

I stopped.

"What's going to happen if I tell you not to see him?" Dad asked in that same awful voice. "Are you going to keep lying to me? Are you going to ignore me? Are you going to refuse?"

Goose bumps chased themselves up and down my arms. The smell of the new leaves came, and it made me think of dark places under trees, and being very small, and very far away, and very alone.

"I asked you a question, son."

I wiped my eyes.

Dad let out a slow breath and nodded. "Go to your room."

I let myself into the house. H tried to sit up again, but his movements were uncoordinated, and he looked like maybe he'd been dozing. "H," I said, and I had to keep it short or I was going to fall apart completely. "I can't—you've got to go home."

A question settled on his face, but before he could ask it, I plunged down the hallway. I was already coming undone, my chest hitching, my body pins and needles everywhere. When I got to my door, it was stuck, which it did sometimes, so I bumped it with my hip.

Several facts registered in a row:

My lamp was on.

My door hadn't been stuck; it had been locked, but the flimsy latch popped right out of the frame.

A man dressed in black was searching my room.

He was kneeling, frozen in the process of sliding out one of the desk drawers, his head turned toward me. He wore one of those balaclava things, but it did nothing to hide his surprise and frustration.

All of my helplessness, all of my shame, all of my rage crystallized. I shouted, "Hey!"

Then I launched myself at him.

All things considered it was one of my better fights. I closed with him while he was still getting to his feet, and I threw a nasty kick that should have caught him in the face and broken nose, teeth, and if I were lucky, his jaw.

Instead, I got one foot tangled in a pair of discarded boxers. I tried to keep going, but as I brought my weight down, I found something that was definitely not the floor. There was a moment of resistance, as whatever it was tried to support my weight. And then it gave way suddenly. The floor turned slick, and I slipped. My kick caught the intruder on the side of the head instead of full in the face, and he staggered and crashed against the desk.

Gushers, my brain told me. You stepped on a pack of Gushers that someone had apparently at some point lost in the mess of clothes. I had enough clarity for a single, horrified thought: If I survived, Holmes would never, ever let me live it down.

By then my momentum was carrying my foot out from under me, and I was falling backward. I landed hard on my ass. The intruder loomed over me a moment later, stomping down toward my face. It was an ugly, effective street-fighting move, which meant Holmes had tried to use it on me every time we sparred. I rolled, and the intruder missed me.

I kept rolling until I hit the wall, and then I scrambled upright, bracing myself to take the blows that I knew were already coming for me.

Only, they never came.

A pained grunt pulled my attention to where Holmes stood. He was fighting one-handed, keeping his injured arm close to his side. Once again, I could see the contrast between the Holmes I knew and the one who stood in front of me. His blows were ragged, almost clumsy. He looked slow, although I knew he still had to be faster than me. The intruder had a knife by then, and he lunged twice, bringing it up in the kind of underhand blow meant to slide the blade under the ribcage and be instantly fatal. Holmes dodged both times, but the movements were stumbling, graceless. He chopped down, catching the intruder on the wrist with the blade of his hand, and the knife tumbled free. The intruder spun into the movement, hooked Holmes's leg, and sent Holmes crashing to the floor.

A feat, by the way, I'd never once managed.

I was halfway to my feet when the intruder spun and clubbed me on the head, and I went down.

Blinking to clear my vision, I tried to make sense of the scrambled data making it to my brain. I was on the floor. Holmes lay in the doorway. The intruder gave each of us a considering look and bent to retrieve the knife.

He was still standing up when Dad came through the door with the baseball bat.

It turns out, baseball bat beats knife.

The intruder was still bent over when Dad came through the doorway, and the first—and only—blow caught him at the base of the skull. The intruder dropped and lay still.

Dad was breathing so hard he sounded like he was hyperventilating. He swung the bat again—a wild, aimless blow—and then caught himself on the wall. He glanced around, but I got the feeling he wasn't seeing anything. Somehow, I managed to get onto my hands and knees, and Dad's head swiveled to bring me into focus. I had a moment long enough to think, Why didn't he get the gun?

He let out a frayed sound that might have been a laugh and leaned more heavily on the wall. "Jack, what the fuck is going on?"

Chapter 20

His Heart

Dad hadn't killed him, which was kind of impressive in itself, since he'd clearly been channeling his inner Cody Bellinger. We tied the intruder up with an extension cord, and I took a moment to study him as Dad called the police. I put the guy at my height, maybe a little shorter, but carrying an extra hundred pounds, and all of it muscle. He was white, the kind where they've got a blue tone to their skin—on him, it was most noticeable around his deep-socketed eyes. He couldn't have been more than thirty. Black shirt, black tactical pants, black boots; the suggestion of ink on his arm, maybe a triangle. He looked like he could have been one of the background baddies from take your pick of *Die Hard* movies. On the phone, a dispatcher was telling Dad that a cruiser was headed our way. Dad called campus security next, and while he was on the phone, I checked on Holmes.

"For the last time, Jack," Holmes said, catching my hand and pushing it away from his arm. "I'm fine." A bit of the posh slipped into his voice. "Utterly incompetent and totally worthless, but fine."

"If you fell on the stitches—"

He caught my hand again, but this time, he squeezed my fingers once and kept his hold. His eyes found mine, the gray shaded by the fullness of his pupils. "I am fine," he said quietly. "I assure you."

His hands were rougher than I remembered. The knobby knuckle was still knobby, though, and I focused on that, anchored myself to it. His thumb was trembling when it brushed the back of my hand.

"Your head," he said in that same quiet voice. Meant only for me, I realized, as Dad talked in the background.

"Fine."

"You may be concussed."

"I'm not. I don't think so, anyway."

"Where else did he hit you?" Holmes asked.

"Just my head."

"How many blows?"

"H, you saw him hit me."

"Yes, but when I entered the room, you were already on the floor."

"Oh. Right."

Holmes's eyes narrowed.

"He hit me in the 'nads."

"No, he did not."

"He did. They're super swollen; if you don't believe me, you can check for yourself."

Holmes got those delightful red circles, but he said, "He didn't hit you at all."

"Ok, I fell."

But his eyes narrowed some more. And then they got wide, and his mouth opened, and if you've never seen a Holmes gaping at you like a trout, you really should treat yourself sometime.

"Jack!"

"It was an accident!"

"A preventable accident."

"It could have happened to anyone."

"Anyone who uses a sock on the floor as a Pop-Tart sleeve."

"Ha! You think you're so smart. For your information, it wasn't a sock, it was a pair of boxers, and it wasn't a Pop-Tart, it was a pack of Gushers."

The horror in Holmes's face told me I hadn't made the point I thought I had.

Fortunately, at that point, Dad came back, phone held low at his side. He was trembling, and he kept wiping his mouth.

"Dad, maybe you should sit down," I said.

He dropped into the chair at my desk. His eyes drifted over to the bound intruder, and then he yanked them back again. "They're sending over the night watchman," he finally said. "What's he going to do? Give him detention."

"Dad, it's ok—"

"It's not ok, Jack. He was in our house. He tried to kill you!" Dad fought visibly to control himself, and his voice was a little closer to normal when he said, "What's going on? Do you know something about this?"

"I may be able to explain some of it," Holmes said. He released my hand and wobbled, but when I reached for him, he shook his head. Easing himself down next to the unconscious intruder, Holmes tugged up each sleeve, and I saw something familiar.

"I've seen that before," I said. "That tattoo."

Holmes shot me a look.

"A triangle inside a circle. That guy at the condo building, he had one."

"One of you better tell me what's going on," Dad said. "Right now."

"I don't know what's going on," I said. "But I've seen that tattoo before."

"It's a mark they give themselves," Holmes said, releasing the man's collar as he stood. "It's the mark of the organization to which they belong. A brotherhood."

"What brotherhood?"

Dad's response was even more succinct: a bewildered "What?"

"The Moriartys' criminal machine," Holmes said. "One that, supposedly, was eradicated over a hundred years ago."

"Obviously they weren't eradicated enough," I said. "Hold on, you're telling me the Moriartys have, like, their own personal mafia?"

"The Moriartys' enterprise, when it was at its height, made the mafia look like neighborhood bullies. There's no adequate comparison for the international scope and scale of their organization."

"But you know about them."

"As I told you, I spent several months tracking the operatives who stole Watson's safe. With Paxton's help, I traced them back to Maggie. This merely confirms my suspicions that she has been behind the events of the last year. I imagine she has been orchestrating these things for much, much longer."

"Jack," Dad snapped.

I shook my head. "Right. Sorry. It's a lot to take in, that's all." I gave my dad a long look. His face was drawn, his eyes hollow, his hand still trembling, even locked around his phone. "You're not going to like it."

He nodded.

So, I told him. Not everything. I held back the parts that I could spare him, the ones where I'd been in the most danger, the things I knew that would upset him the most. But I told him enough. About Sarah Watson's death and my belief that Blackfriar had been behind it. Holmes didn't argue, but the set of his jaw told me he still didn't buy it. About Sarah's contingency plan: the family tree, the portable safe, everything that had been sent to Holmes. About Paxton, who had distracted us while Maggie stole the safe. And about the invitation to the Zodiac anniversary party that had gotten me tangled up in this mess again.

"What do you mean, the truth about your mother?" That was the first thing Dad asked. "What's that supposed to mean?"

"I don't know," I said. I looked at Holmes, but he shook his head. "I still think Maggie was the one who tried to kill me that night in the canyon. The man who ran us off the road. He'd been waiting to catch me alone, without H. It was—Dad, the similarities to the crash that killed Mom, it was almost identical."

Dad nodded, but he said, "But what's the secret, Jack? You know your mother was a Watson, although I've got no clue why that matters. And you know you're a descendant of the Watsons, but again, I have no idea why anybody cares about a blood connection so distant. Let's say you're right about everything. Let's say you're right about the accident—that it wasn't an accident, that someone was trying to kill your mother. What's left?"

"The proof," Holmes said.

Dad sagged in the chair and shook his head.

"H is right," I said. "What if there's proof that Moriarty killed Mom? What if that's what Sarah sent H? And that's why I'm the only one who can open it?"

"I want you to stop," Dad said. "You've got to stop. I want you to tell me you'll stop."

I stared at him.

He sat up straighter, shaking his head again. "You're done, Jack. This is over. Holloway, I understand that—hell, I don't understand anything, and I don't know what to say to you except I want this to stop. Do you hear me?"

"Mr. Moreno—" Holmes began.

"Someone is trying to kill my son," Dad said over him, his gaze fixed on Holmes. "You told me—you promised me—that you'd keep him safe. I want your word, right now. No more. It ends here."

"Hold on," I said. "I'm right here. I get a say in this."

"You gave me your word, Holloway."

"Hey! What the hell?"

Holmes gave me a long, considering look.

"Don't even think about it, H," I said. "It's my decision."

"If we are to keep Jack safe—" Holmes said, turning to my dad.

"No."

"—he must be removed from the area."

"Dipshit, I said no."

"Perhaps from the country. My sister could help—"

"Are you fucking listening to me?"

Dad slapped the desk. "Jack, for God's sake be quiet!"

The stillness that came after made my skin itch.

"Stop talking about me like I'm not here," I said, surprised at how even my voice was. "This is about Mom. My mom. That means it's my choice."

Dad and Holmes traded a look.

I opened my mouth to tell them what they could do with that look, but before I could, a knock came at the front door. A man's voice called from the front of the cottage, "Campus security. Mr. Moreno, are you there?"

Dad gave me a final, considering appraisal as he rose to his feet. He had to stop and steady himself on the desk, and when he started toward the front door, it was more of a lurch. He trailed one hand along the wall. He'd been worried all day, and he'd worked his full shift and probably some extra, and all the medicine and PT in the world couldn't fix everything.

"Mr. Moreno," Holmes said, and Dad glanced back. "If you want to keep Jack safe, you must say nothing of this to the police. We don't know who this man is. We don't know why he came. He attacked us and had a knife. Knowing Jack's history, any self-respecting law enforcement officer will assume Jack is dealing drugs again and that this man was attempting to hit his stash."

"Hey!" When Holmes glanced at me, I said, "Rude."

"But true."

For a heartbeat, Dad stared at us. Then he shuffled down the hall, head bent, and the whisper of his hand sliding along the wall came back to us.

After that, I didn't have a good opportunity to tell Holmes he could go fuck himself, in no uncertain terms, if he thought I was going anywhere. I wanted to tell Dad the same thing in what I hoped would be slightly more respectful terms. I didn't know this night watchmen—ever since Olin Campbell, our last head of security, had been murdered in his office, we'd had a hard time keeping regular staff. This guy was one of those old white men with a flat-top and the kind of boiled-down jawline that made me think he spent lots of time being grimly, efficiently athletic. He didn't say much; he just stood in my bedroom, a hand on his gun, and told us to wait for the deputies.

They came next, a couple of deputies named Werner and Stanton, and they separated us and started taking statements. I stuck to the details Holmes had given me, and Werner, who was a fiftyish Latina with a lazy eye, seemed satisfied.

It didn't go quite as smoothly when Rivera and Yazzie showed up.

Rivera came in like someone had fired him out of a cannon. He took one look, marched straight across the living room toward me, and grabbed me by the arm. He was wearing a Provo Angels tee and drop-crotch joggers with an admittedly sweet pair of Jordans, and the whole thing was so surreal, like catching your uncle wearing his baseball cap backward, that I grinned before I could help myself.

"Maybe I should—" Yazzie said.

Rivera hit the carport door and yanked me out of the cottage before she could finish.

I stumbled down the steps behind him, and when he released me, I stumbled and fetched up against the F-150. "Watch out," I said, straightening my ZADDY shirt. "This is new."

"What's going on?"

"You busted in here like you've got a rocket up your chute—"

Rivera clapped his hands in my face. "Cut the crap. I want to know what's going on. You think you can lead me around by the nose, make me look stupid? What the hell is wrong with you, Jack? I'm on your side. What did I ever do to make you decide it was your personal mission to fuck up my life?"

The chorus of insects swelled again. Then the carport door rattled open, and Dad stuck his head out. The look he fixed on Rivera was unmistakably a warning, then he glanced at me.

"We're ok," I said. "I'm just telling him about the attempted burglary."

"My son is a minor," Dad said.

"This is a chat, Mr. Moreno." Rivera's voice was tight, and it was obvious he was keeping it professional only by sheer force of will. "If I take a statement from your son, I'll inform you."

Dad shook his head.

"It's fine, Dad," I said. "We'll be inside in a minute."

"I'm leaving the door open," he said, with another of those warning looks at Rivera and then a glance at me, to make sure I understood.

I nodded, and Dad disappeared back into the cottage.

Rivera folded his arms across his chest. He had some solid biceps, and if you swapped the drop-crotch joggers for something that didn't look like it was from 2007, he actually would have looked dope. Except for the fact that he looked like he could bite through the wheel well of the Ford right at that moment.

"What do you mean?" I asked. "About me fucking up your life?"

"Blackfriar Holmes." When I didn't say anything, Rivera turned his head and spat. "I was told to go home, Jack. After that little stunt with the photo blew up in my face."

"What do you mean? Wait, is that why you're dressed like Vanilla Ice?"

"I'm not dressed like Vanilla Ice, you little jagweed. You don't even know who Vanilla Ice is."

When I grinned, Rivera blew out a breath. Some of the tension in his chest and shoulders eased, and he shook his head like he was working it out of his system.

"What photo?" I asked. "I don't know what you're talking about."

"The photo. The one you sent me." I shook my head, and Rivera said, "Of Blackfriar Holmes walking into that dead woman's building."

"I didn't send you a photo."

"But you sat there in the truck, and you told me—" Rivera made a furious noise and took out his phone. After a few taps, he held it out to me. On the screen, a photo showed Blackfriar walking into Lynnissa Baca's condo building. I shook my head, and Rivera said under his breath, "You've got to be shitting me."

"I've never seen that before," I said. "Where'd you get it?"

"An anonymous package." He stuffed the phone back into his pocket. "Delivered to the sheriff's department. Which I assumed was from you, since the Treehouse Detectives seemed convinced-slash-terrified that the senior Holmes was involved in this. It was enough to get a warrant, and we found the woman's jewelry in his car. God damn it, you were there for that." He squeezed his eyes shut, rubbed them with one hand.

"You seem, uh, tired," I said.

"Ha."

"Rivera, I promise. I didn't send that picture. And I wouldn't try to fuck up your life. I mean, maybe if I had free time."

But that didn't earn a smile. Rivera dropped his hand and opened his eyes and considered me. "Well, someone did. The photo's gone."

"What do you mean it's gone?"

"It disappeared, Jack. And now Holmes's lawyers are claiming the picture I took of it, as backup, is photoshopped, and they want to drag in experts, all of which would have been nice to know before I made an ass of myself by arresting Blackfriar Holmes. I'm lucky all the sheriff did was send me home. Hell, he still might fire me."

One part of the statement overrode everything else. "It's gone?"

"Poof."

"How?" Then I shook my head. "And you think H and I did it somehow."

Rivera grunted. "I thought—I don't know what I thought. Maybe you knew something. It's hard to think straight when you've got a team of fancy lawyers screaming in your face about false arrest and wrongful imprisonment and police brutality. Christ Almighty, it's a shit show."

"What about the jewelry?"

"His lawyers haven't outright said we planted it, but you can tell they want to. Right now, they're floating all sorts of possibilities. One is that he gave Baca a ride in his car, and she left the jewelry there." He snorted. "Like it fell off her. I'm starting to think he could leave DNA evidence at a scene and walk away from it."

I didn't know where the photo had come from. But I knew the last time I'd seen Baca's jewelry, it had been in her condo. After she'd been murdered. Which meant someone had been back. Someone had taken it off her body, and then used it to frame Blackfriar.

"What?" Rivera said, his attention sharpening on me. "You got something to tell me?"

I shook my head. He watched me for another minute, which is a long time to stand in the dark with crickets chirping and the breeze keening. Finally, I said, "Is he out of jail?"

"He never went to jail, Jack. He had my ass on a platter before we were halfway to the station. The county attorney tore me a new asshole—I've never heard the words 'insufficient evidence' more times in my life."

"He's free. He's been free this whole time."

"What does that mean?"

I barely heard him. I was trying to think. If Blackfriar were being framed, did that mean he was innocent? Or was it just another layer, another complication, part of the game?

"Jack," Rivera prompted.

"I don't know. Sorry. I just—I don't know."

Rivera seemed to consider this. Finally, he said, "Jack, if there's something about Blackfriar Holmes, you've got to tell me."

"No."

"Jack."

"No, I promise." I met Rivera's eyes, and then I had to look away again. It was harder this time to say, "I promise."

"Jack—"

"We should go back inside," I said. "My dad'll be worried."

I didn't miss the way Rivera looked at me, but when I started toward the cottage, he didn't stop me.

We gave our statements. A pair of deputies took the intruder away. Eventually, Rivera and Yazzie let us sit together again in the living room. I had a headache—it had started small, barely noticeable in the adrenaline rush after the fight, but it had gotten steadily worse as the minutes dragged into hours. Holmes could barely keep himself upright. He kept yawning, slumping against me, and then jerking himself up into a sitting position again. Dad didn't look much better. He had that tightness around his eyes that said he was getting a migraine, and he probably thought I wouldn't notice, but he was clutching the leg of his jeans the way he did when the pain was bad.

When Rivera started in again on the sequence of events, I said over him, "Can we go? Because we're exhausted, and we've already talked about this, and we didn't do anything wrong."

"Nobody's saying you did anything wrong," Yazzie said. She was wearing a plaid shirt with pearl-snap buttons, and some of her hair was sticking up behind one ear. "But this is serious, Jack, and we want to make sure we get everything right."

"But we went over this." I met her gaze. "Please? We can finish it tomorrow."

"Too bad," Rivera said. "We've got work to do, and the techs are still processing your room—"

"Then they can keep processing it."

"Jack," Dad said in that worn-out voice that said he was really not well.

"They can keep processing it, and we can go to a hotel or something. Come on, we've got to look like shit. We feel like shit. Please?"

Yazzie flicked a look at Rivera. He grunted, but apparently that meant something because Yazzie said, "We can finish this tomorrow. If you'd like police protection—"

"No," I said, shooting up from the couch. "We're good. Thanks, Yaz. Thank you. You're amazing."

She rolled her eyes, but she smiled and got a little pink. Rivera rolled his eyes too, so I gave him the finger.

It wasn't quite that easy, of course. I had to pack a bag for me and another for Dad, including his meds. He tried to help, but he kept stumbling and catching himself on the wall until I sent him back to the recliner. The techs processing my room let me grab some clothes for me, and I added some for Holmes just in case.

By the time we were out of the house, it was almost two in the morning.

"The closest hotel—" Holmes began, looking at his phone.

"We're not going to a hotel," I said and pushed his phone down. I got an arm around Dad's waist, and he leaned harder into me than I expected. "There's a couple of guest houses for visiting faculty, that kind of thing. Just on the other side of the Toqueah." I hoisted the duffel and adjusted my grip on Dad. "Here we go."

I made it about five feet before I had to stop, lower the duffel, readjust Dad.

"Jack," Holmes said, "I can help."

Dad was doing that funny breathing he did before he got sick, so I tried to shift his weight again, make it easier on him. When he was settled, I reached for the duffel again. "I've got it."

Holmes's hand was cool when it closed around my wrist, and when I looked up, gray eyes held mine. "Jack, you do not always have to do everything yourself."

"You're hurt—"

"One arm," Holmes said, and then he gave that little amused huff. "I am perfectly capable of carrying this bag."

"But you're tired—"

He cocked his head. He didn't smile, but the moonlight caught the amusement in his face, and after a moment, the corner of my mouth quirked against my best efforts.

"Fine," I said and dropped the duffel.

"So gracious," Holmes murmured as he picked up the bag.

"Thank you. I am gracious. And strong. And butch. And manly. And I can do everything myself, and I don't need anyone, and I'm stone faced and stoic and repress all my feelings because I'm a guy. But mostly butch. Did I mention butch?"

"Many times," Holmes said in that same underbreath. "If anyone doubts it, they can examine the holes in your underwear."

I tried not to laugh, but it was definitely harder to keep Dad upright when I was fighting the giggles.

The faculty housing was built behind Walker Hall, hidden from view by a windbreak of scrub oak and pine, and the air smelled like resin and thawing earth and sego lilies in bloom. Dad was barely conscious by the time I got the guest house unlocked, and my shoulder was aching from half-carrying him across campus. Inside, it was cool, and the air had a hint of mustiness, but the lights came on when I hit the switch. I sat Dad on the couch, found the linen closet, and started making up one of the beds.

A moment later, I heard the furnace crank, and then the vents began to pop and groan.

When Holmes popped his head into the bedroom, I said, "Thank you."

He didn't say anything, but he joined me at the bed, and he helped me finish the sheets. We laid out a blanket, and then I got Dad into the room. After working off his shoes, I dug around in the duffel and came up with one of his prescriptions.

"I'm all right, buddy," he mumbled.

"Trazodone," I said as I pressed the pill into his hand. "One. Because you need to sleep."

Holmes appeared with a glass of water, and Dad took the pill. He got under the blanket, and his breathing had evened out by the time I turned off the light.

"Would you like to—" Holmes began.

"You should—" I said at the same time.

He stopped and let out that little huff of breath.

"Go shower," I told him. "I brought stuff in that bag, plus some clothes for you to sleep in."

"I'll help you make up the beds."

"H, when we train, you practically run to the showers after we're done. It's been—I don't know how long. Twelve hours since you worked out? You're probably ready to claw your way out of your skin."

Indecision made a war of his perfect features.

"Go," I said and laughed, and I gave him a push. "And take your antibiotics."

"You do not have to take care of everyone," he said. "You do not have to do everything yourself."

"I'm not doing everything myself. You are one hundred percent in charge of showering. You're a big boy now, and I'm definitely not going to scrub your balls for you."

Color rose in his face, but he cocked his head. "Why does that make you defensive?"

"Could you please get in the shower?" Without waiting for an answer, I made my way to the linen closet. "Now, H."

I didn't linger, and as I carried the bedding into the second bedroom, his steps whispered behind me. Moments later, the bathroom door clicked shut, and the water began to run.

I made up the beds. There were two of them. That was good; he'd be more comfortable that way, and anyhow, we weren't—I mean, it wasn't like we had even talked about—I mean, the night at Noneley's had been a necessity. The linens smelled faintly of detergent, and the house was warming up. I kicked off my Stan Smiths, and that felt like pure heaven. When I stretched out on the bed, that was even better.

The water shut off. I felt myself dozing, but a sound roused me. I listened, and it came again. Holmes, in the bathroom, a mixture of pain and frustration.

Anybody with some brains would have stayed where he was.

Jack Moreno rolled his dumb ass off the bed and padded toward the bathroom.

Tapping on the door, I called, "I'm coming in, so make sure you put away Mr. Squishy."

I couldn't hear anything, but the silence on the other side of the door had an unfamiliar quality, and when Holmes spoke, he packed a lot of dry amusement into the one word: "Enter."

The air was warm and humid and smelled like the Dial soap I'd brought, and there was a hint in the air of him, the smell of his skin. He stood in front of the fogged mirror. He was wearing a pair of my boxers—clean, thank you very much—that were printed with otters, and he was trying to get himself into the Abercrombie hoodie Dad had bought me (since my favorite Dodgers hoodie had been abandoned back at his condo). His skin was prettily pink from the heat of the shower, and his hair was a darker gold, almost bronze, where it still held water.

Without speaking, I took the hoodie and helped him slide his injured arm in first. We got his other arm in place, and I zipped it up. The ridged definition of his abs was insane, the muscle compact and defined under the back of my hand as I worked the zipper. When I looked up, he was watching me, his pupils dilated.

I crouched and shook out the joggers still neatly folded on the floor. They were lightweight and soft from being washed so many times—they weren't the booty shorts I knew he liked to sleep in, but I hadn't been sure how warm the cabin would be, so I'd gone for the non-booty-length option.

"I can do that," Holmes said.

I swatted the back of his calf, and he obediently raised his leg. We repeated the process, and I pulled the joggers up. I thought I saw something happening behind the otters, but the joggers were loose, and then I wasn't sure. There was definitely something happening behind my otters, which isn't an expression, but it should be.

I stayed there, sitting on my heels, my hands on his hips. I trailed them down his thighs, settling the joggers, feeling the compact strength of quads and glutes. A lesser man might have called it groping.

My voice was husky when I said, "Guess you'll have to find somebody else to do this once you get rid of me."

Water dripped in the shower. Holmes brushed a hand through my hair. "I am sorry I told you to go home, Jack. I was exhausted, not thinking clearly, and my family was in a state of crisis."

I cleared my throat, but it didn't help because I sounded the same. "That's not what I'm talking about. You know that's not what I'm talking about."

Plonk. Plink. His fingers scratched lightly across my crown.

I pulled my head away and got to my feet. "Send me away, H? Really?"

"It is the only —"

"What the fuck is wrong with you?"

The words bounced back from the paneling, the mirror, the fiberglass.

"Your father is sleeping," Holmes said.

"I don't get you." I rubbed my face. "I really don't, H. Because one minute, you're—" I almost said, *Letting your dad torture you.* Instead, I managed to say, "—throwing yourself in front of a knife to protect me, and the next minute, you can't wait to get rid of me."

"I don't want to get rid of you."

"What the fuck right do you have to say that kind of thing to my dad? He'll do it, H. He'll put me in a fucking shipping container if he thinks it'll keep me safe."

"Your volume."

"That's not your choice, do you get that?"

"Your safety —"

"You don't have any right to say that to him —"

"Your safety, Jack —"

"—or to talk about me like I'm a toy you can put on a shelf because you don't want anybody to mess with your things —"

"Let me speak!" His voice cracked. Chest heaving, he stared at me, seconds ticking past. And then, voice at the breaking point, he said, "I want you to be safe."

"I don't want to be safe! I want to be with you!"

As our shouts faded away, I waited for the creak of springs, the slap of steps. But nothing came; between the trazodone and outright exhaustion, Dad probably could have slept through Armageddon. Silence settled into every nook and cranny of the cabin. It felt like an infection, like a heat multiplying and spreading and making me itch.

"Two months ago," Holmes said, "I was admitted to the emergency department."

"What? Why? Why didn't you—"

He held up a hand, and I stopped. It took him a while before he spoke again. "I had been…rash. Overenthusiastic. And, combined with my abrupt cessation of Adderall, dealing with the symptoms of withdrawal." A tiny slant hardened his mouth. "Inadequately, as it turns out."

"What happened?"

"I collapsed." He rolled one shoulder, the way you might if you said you had a headache. "Paxton took me to the hospital. He thought it was a heart attack—"

"Jesus Christ."

"—which it was not, Jack. I'm fine."

But I thought about how slow he'd been, relatively speaking. How he'd trembled and dropped to his knees after our sprint to the elevator.

"You're not fine," I said.

"My capacities are reduced."

"What did they say?"

"It is a temporary setback."

"What did they tell you?"

"With adequate rest and continued training—"

"Tell me what they said!"

The resolve in his face yielded, and he suddenly looked sixteen and tired and alone. "They believe there may be damage to my heart. Further testing is required."

"God damn it."

"Jack—"

"God fucking damn it." I tried to blink my eyes clear, and I turned away from him, moving in a circle. "This is my fault."

"This is why I didn't tell you."

I punched the wall. I hadn't even planned on doing it, and the pain of the impact drove up my arm. "This is my fucking fault. I never should have sold you that shit. I kept telling myself it was ok. I kept telling myself that you'd just buy it from someone else."

"You are correct. I was not prepared to stop using that medication—"

A wild noise escaped me, because I had done this to him, and I couldn't take it back, couldn't undo it. His heart. I swung again, vaguely aware that I was going to break my hand this time.

Only, instead, H caught my arm.

"Jack, please."

I tried to breathe through my nose, but it was getting snotty, so I had to suck air through my mouth.

Holmes rubbed my arm. "I would not have told you—"

"You should have told me first fucking thing!"

"Jack, enough." Poshness slid into his voice with each word. "I will not have you taking responsibility for my choices. Continue to behave like this, and I will become cross."

I snuffled into my sleeve. I wiped my eyes.

"I would still be using the drug if it were not for you," Holmes said in a softer voice, although the accent was still there, and we both knew why he was doing it. His hand slid down my arm until his fingers tangled loosely with mine. "I only tell you this so that you understand: I cannot be trusted to keep you safe. I thought that, even with these limitations, I would be adequate to the task. I am not; events have proved that. I told you once that I will never want you to leave, but for the time being, the only safe option—"

"Nowhere is safe, H. Don't you get that? I could get hit by a bus. I could get food poisoning. I could have a brain aneurysm, and my brain could be a ticking time bomb."

"That's specious reasoning—"

Tugging on his hand, I started toward the door, and Holmes followed. We moved into the bedroom, and I sat him on the bed. Then I stood in front of him, opened my phone, and found the list I'd been keeping.

"James Watson," I said. "Died 1933. Fishing accident."

Holmes's eyes narrowed.

"David Watson. Died 1938. He was twenty years old, and they finally called it a stroke."

"What is this?"

"You know what this is. Florrie Sheahan, née Watson. Died 1946. Hunting accident."

"Where did you get this list?"

"Carolyn Clayton, née Watson. Died 1981. Car accident."

"Who gave this to you?"

"June Watson. Died 1989. Car accident."

"Jack, these names—"

"Brian Roe, son of Deborah Bly, née Watson. Died 1996. Car accident." I looked up from the phone. "I can keep going."

"Your assumption—"

"Don't," I said. "This one time, H, give me a little credit. No family has that many accidents. Did you honestly think I wouldn't do some research? Someone is killing Watsons, and you knew." My voice trembled. "Someone killed my mom, and you didn't tell me."

"Jack—" Helplessness bloomed in his face. "We simply don't know. We don't know if someone is doing it. We don't know why. It may be another of those strange twists of genetics, that the Watsons are inclined to sudden, violent death the same way they're inclined to find a Holmes."

"Someone is doing it."

"We don't know—"

"H, someone is doing it. That night in December, that night we got run off the road. Someone was trying to kill me."

"There have always been theories," he finally said. "Among the Holmeses. The most popular is that the Moriartys have been killing Watsons for generations, trying to eradicate them. A Holmes is always at his best when he is with a Watson, so it would be logical to attempt to remove the more vulnerable element and, in the process, weaken the Holmes family."

"Maggie Moriarty killed my mom."

"We don't know that."

"She did. And she tried to kill me." A strange thought hit me. "Why didn't she try to kill Sarah?"

Holmes shrugged. "Perhaps she did. You suggested that someone else arranged for Sarah to meet her killer the night she died; perhaps that was Maggie."

I stared at him.

"I know what you believe, Jack," he said without meeting my eyes. "But I'm unwilling to believe that my father would murder a girl simply to safeguard corporate profits. Even to keep family secrets, as you suggested, I don't think he would go so far."

All I could come up with was "Why?"

"Because he's never had to resort to those measures before," Holmes said. "My father has handled a great many threats to our family, including various attempts at blackmail, and he has never had to resort to murder. If he had wanted to silence Sarah, he could have done so through other means. Besides, the current focus of our investigation is Maggie. She murdered Lynnissa Baca, and then she attempted to frame me, and when that did not succeed, she framed my father. Do you agree or disagree?"

"Maybe."

Holmes set his jaw. "Explain."

"I don't know, H. I'm just saying maybe. Maggie disappeared, right? That's suspicious too."

"Fact: Lynnissa Baca worked with Maggie. Fact: she had a history of confrontations with Maggie. Fact: she stole valuable property from Maggie. Fact: A Moriarty agent attacked us at Baca's condo. Fact: Lynnissa Baca's jewelry, which we saw was still in the condo after her death, was later planted to frame my father. Fact: we were attacked and almost killed tonight by another agent of the Moriartys, who was searching your room, doubtless under the impression that I had attempted to hide Watson's portable safe there again."

"But that's what doesn't make any sense," I said. "If Maggie killed Baca, why didn't she take the jewelry then? Why would she send her agent here to look for the safe?"

"Because her first attempt was to frame me. When we were too quick and managed to remove the incriminating evidence, she had to compensate. Please try to keep up, Jack."

My cheeks stung, and I looked him in the eye.

Holmes broke first, looking away and mumbling, "I did not mean—"

"I know what you meant."

"Jack, please."

"You're right. You're always right; you're Holloway Holmes. So, if you say it's Maggie, then I guess it's Maggie."

"That's not what I meant—"

"But you don't have to be such a fucking bully about it." I grabbed the duffel and headed for the door. "I'm going to sleep on the couch."

Chapter 21

What Do You Want?

Sleeping on the couch, though, was not as easy as I'd hoped. I found a spare set of sheets, and I made up the couch as best I could, and then I turned off the lights and lay down and promised myself I'd brush my teeth for an extra thirty seconds in the morning. The cabin was silent, and a moment later, when the light in the bedroom switched off, everything was dark. A faint dusting of light came in behind the curtains, but it was hardly anything — up here, with only the moon and stars, it was barely enough for a scraping of gray under the windows.

For what felt like a long time, I played the conversation in my head over and over again. I came up with a million better things to say. Things like *I'm not saying it's not Maggie, but you've got to admit there are some pieces that don't add up,* and *I saw your dad that day in my bedroom, and I'm the only one who knows what he looked like and how he acted, and I'm telling you, he killed Sarah,* and *Why are you being such a condescending, self-righteous, arrogant prick?* Smart stuff like that.

The scuff of a bare sole on the floorboards made me lift my head. An even darker outline stood against the darkness. Holmes's familiar breathing, a little accelerated, a little distressed.

"Go away. I'm mad at you."

Instead, he knelt next to the sofa, and a moment later, his hand found mine. No fumbling around in the blackout, which is what I would have done. One moment nothing, and the next, his hand was there, closed around mine.

"We're fighting," I said and yanked my hand away. "Go back to the bedroom so we can have a decent fight."

His voice sounded more upset than I'd expected, and I flopped onto my side, trying to make out his face in the dark. "I do not want to fight with you. I never want to fight with you."

The house creaked and settled. The forever wind of the canyon rushed through the aspens, teased the windows, carried on into the dark. A part of it rushed through me too.

"I do not believe you're correct," Holmes said, and the dilemma in his voice was even stronger. "But I do not want to fight with you."

I flopped around some more. Finally, I ended up on my side again, propped up on one elbow. He was still only a shape in the darkness.

"In the first place," I said, "even if you think I'm stupid, you can't talk to me that way."

"I don't think you're stupid. I think you're one of the smartest people I've ever met."

I snorted. "Don't lie to me either."

"I'm not lying."

"We don't have to agree on everything, although I swear to Christ, if you ever talk bad about Bagel Bites again, we are going to have a real fight, like, a major one."

He let out his little amused huff, but he sounded closer to crying.

"It's ok, H. I'm—well, I was going to say I'm not mad at you, but I still kind of am. I might be wrong; that's fine. I'm wrong all the time. Look at my chemistry homework. I don't care about being wrong. I care about you treating me, you know, like you respect me. Even if you're a million times smarter and better at everything. If we're going to be friends, you have to do that. That's the minimum."

"I should not have said what I did," Holmes said. His breathing became more labored, and I thought maybe now he was crying. "I'm sorry."

I reached out, and he found my hand again instantly in the dark. Always. He would always find me, I thought. Even in the dark. "I'm sorry too."

Some of the strain in his body eased. A million things ran through my head, things to say, stupid things. *Get up on this couch* was the best of them, and that should tell you something.

But what came out of my mouth was "I love you." A little caw of a laugh escaped me. "Still. So much that it hurts. So much I don't know what to do sometimes."

His hand tightened around mine. It felt like a long time before he said, "I did not think—I mean, I assumed your feelings had changed. Because of what I did."

"Oh my God, H. For real?"

That got me a real laugh, one that was rich and deep and surprisingly mature, and I had a glimpse of what it would be like, a future with him, a full-grown Holmes to wrangle every day. "I love you, Jack. Of course I love you. More than anything in the world."

"Well," I said, "good."

He adjusted his hand around mine. He seemed closer in the dark.

"Maybe you should kiss me," I said.

"I—I don't know if that's a good idea."

"Won't know until you try."

He bent, and his dry lips scraped across mine, and his breath, when he pulled away, was hot against my cheek.

My heartbeat slowed, and my body felt loose and heavy, and I probably looked like a huge doofus. "You can do better than that."

He gave his tiny, amused breath, but it had a little note of panic too. When he dipped his head again, his lips found mine, and I caught a handful of his hair.

That, ladies and gentlemen, was a serious kiss.

I don't know how long it went on, but when I finally had to let Holmes up for air, his chest was heaving, and my lips were chafed raw. I could feel the pulse of blood in my joints. It took me a moment to realize my face was wet, and another one to understand that Holmes was crying.

Propping myself up on an elbow, I tried to scan his face in the dark. "Hey, what—are you ok? What happened? If you didn't want to do that—"

"Of course I wanted to do it." His voice was a jangle of emotions I couldn't separate. "Good God, Jack."

"Ok." A flush moved through me, low and slow and creeping, like a banked fire. "Did I do something wrong?"

His laugh sounded like a sob.

"H, what's going on?"

"This," he said. "This is exactly what I promised myself I wouldn't do. I swore I wouldn't let this happen. And here we are, and I—I cannot help myself, Jack. I know what is right, and still I cannot help myself."

Because I had only a glimmer of what was going on, I tried for lighthearted. "Maybe it's like you said: Holmeses and Watsons finding each other."

"No. No, it is not that. It is you."

In the dark, I couldn't tell if his aggravated breathing meant more tears or not, but I reached out a hand, and I found his hair, and I stroked it. He was shaking again.

"Do you want to lie down?" I asked.

He shook his head.

"Is this because you're afraid I'm going to get hurt?"

Another shake of his head. But he said, "Yes."

The truth had come first, though. I remembered him telling me why he was so frightened of—well, of all of this. Of the emotions. Of the way his body reacted. Of how it affected his judgment.

"A Holmes must always be in control," I said, and I couldn't keep the barb out of my voice.

I recognized the sound of him bringing himself under control: the sudden symmetry of his breaths, the stillness of his body. After a moment, he said, "Yes."

"I told you, nobody expects that of you. Nobody sane, anyway. You're a person, a human being. And you're not even an adult yet. I mean, neither of us is."

He didn't answer.

The light dusting the window didn't reach him, and I wanted to yank the curtains off the rod, find a light switch, burn down an orphanage—anything so I could see his face. I tried to take a few deep breaths myself, and when I thought I could, I said, "I love you because of you. Because of who you are, I mean. Holloway Harrowgate Holmes. And I want to be with you. I don't care who your family is, and I don't care about Holmeses and Watsons. It doesn't matter who my mom was, or who her mom was, or any of it. What matters is us, you and me."

He shifted on his knees. His voice was rough and raspy when he said, "It is not that simple."

"It is. I think it is."

He shook his head; that much I could see in the dark. "Jack."

I found him. I kissed him. His mouth was soft, and he tasted the way I remembered, and his hand found my nape. I could feel the knobby knuckle of that hand, the one I was obsessed with. The kiss said, I'm yours. And it said, You're mine. And it said what I didn't know how to put into words, something like, You're safe, and something like, Let go. Maybe it came close to the feeling I had when the sun hit him right and gave his eyelashes a golden nimbus: a prism of light flowering in my chest.

But Holmes pulled back first. His breathing was hectic, like a fever against my face. I thought he was crying again. "I can't."

"What do you want? Quit worrying about your parents and family legacies and keeping me safe; stop thinking about all of that for five seconds, and tell me what you want, just you, Holloway Holmes."

He had said it before; I should have expected it. "When has it ever mattered what I want?"

"Now, H. It matters right now. To me. It's the only thing that matters."

He was silent for a long time. He bowed his head, and his answer was a whisper that still managed to be surprisingly firm. "I am sorry, Jack. I cannot give you what you want."

The banked flush of embers stirred to life, and sweat prickled under my arms. I was still stretched out on the couch, propped up on an elbow, and I had to look like a million kinds of dumbass. I sat up, and Holmes moved, his head coming up, watching me. Wary. I wanted to laugh. *Do you think I'm going to hurt you?* I thought about asking. That was a nice thought, and it made me want to cry. How the fuck was I supposed to do that?

I got off the couch, found the duffel, carried it into the bathroom, shut the door. When the lights came on, my eyes had a hard time adjusting, and I was a brown smear in the mirror. I ditched my clothes in a heap by the door and started the shower. Holmes had left the soap in its little dish, of course. My skin prickled as the heat and humidity opened my pores. Good water pressure, I thought. The spray sounded loud against the fiberglass. That's good, I thought. Real good. I'll be able to cry as hard as I want.

When the water warmed, I got in the shower. I stood there for what felt like a long time.

I don't know when I noticed him. I hadn't heard the door open, hadn't heard steps. If he'd called, I hadn't heard his voice. But he was standing there, staring at me through the frosted glass of the shower door. There was nobody else it could be, but I still had a moment of disorientation, because this was so unlike Holmes. The boy who loved secrets, who protected his own more closely than anything else, was surprisingly shy when it came to—well, pretty much everything.

He still hadn't said anything, hadn't moved. He was just standing there, being a creep. I had no idea how puffy my face was, how red my eyes were, but I was past caring, so I slid the door open a few inches and looked out at him.

He'd been crying too; his face was a mess, and the perfect Ivy League part had come apart into a wild cloud. You could see every one of the thousand shades of gold in that hair. It looked like he'd been pulling at it.

"What?" I asked.

He stared back at me.

It felt like someone was stitching a line down the center of my chest, down my belly, between my legs. I thought of his condo, and now here we were, our positions reversed. Maybe this was payback. Maybe he wanted to humiliate me. Unlike Holmes, though, that kind of stuff had never been a big deal for me. When he still didn't say anything, I gave the door another nudge, opening it a few more inches, so he could look all he wanted. Fuck him if he thought it would scare me or freak me out or teach me a lesson, whatever he wanted. I turned into the water and soaped up.

A soft thump made me glance over, and I was surprised to see the Abercrombie hoodie lying on the floor. I couldn't help myself: a quick look at all that smooth, pale skin, the dark gold fire of the hair under his arms, that little patch at the center of his chest. Every muscle defined and perfect. I dragged my eyes back to his face, but I couldn't read anything there, and I have no idea why the words that came out of my mouth were "I just got you dressed. If you think I'm doing it again, you're out of your damn mind."

Holmes met my eyes. He tucked his thumbs under the waistband of the joggers. Then he stopped. The tension made the muscles in his shoulders and arms pop, some invisible struggle playing out in the dynamic strength of his body.

"What are you doing?" I asked.

He was still looking at me, and it felt like a challenge, but it was also a request, the way he'd looked at me so many times. Asking for help.

The shower seemed much louder now. I said, "Knock it off."

His hands tightened around the elastic waistband of the joggers.

I turned off the shower, but the hiss of white noise didn't go away. "Come on, stop it."

Still nothing. He was still breathing those slow, even breaths, and watching him, watching his chest expand and contract, was hypnotic.

"You don't have to do that," I said. "I'm not mad. Well, not that mad." I grabbed a towel, ran it over my head and face, and wrapped it around my waist. "What's going on? You look like you're about to blow a gasket."

He slid the joggers down, stepped out of them with the grace I remembered, every pause a pose that some sculptor should have been there to capture. Then he stood there in nothing but my old otter boxers. He was taking deep breaths, deep enough that I could see the slight swell of his belly.

"Stop," I said, and it was hard to be mad at him any longer. I stepped out of the shower. I picked up the hoodie. When I straightened, he had his thumbs under the waistband of the shorts, and I could see that same battle playing out across his body again. I dropped the hoodie and caught his wrists in my hands. "H, stop. I don't—that's not what this is about. I don't want you to do something because I lost my temper. I don't want you to do anything you don't want to do. I don't want you to rush into anything. I don't ever want you to feel like you have to do something because I'm mad—"

He broke my hold with his usual ease, and before I could react, he captured my hands in his own. His touch was light. He felt cool, my body still warm from the shower. He turned my hands in his, raised them, brought them to his face. We had known each other almost a year, and in all that time, I had touched him so little. He adjusted my hands, pressed them into place, holding them there, my thumbs at the corners of his mouth.

I had seen, this spring, jacaranda blossoms so pale they were almost blue, trembling with the breath of the mountains. I had seen, when I'd been twelve, a foil of goldfinches flocking against the crushed dusk. I had seen a shooting star once, thinning across the sky like combed silver. And I had seen Holloway Holmes smile.

He smiled now.

His face changed, and his body stilled. Not the rigid control I associated with Holmes, but something different, something deeper. A calm I wasn't sure I'd ever seen before. His smile grew until it was so dorky and generous and beautiful that I felt it cleave me, and everything before this was before, and everything after would be different.

He nodded, and somehow he was the one reassuring me now, and he said one thing, one thing only, barely more than a breath.

"Jack."

Chapter 22

Everything After

It's called fade to black for a reason, motherfuckers, but I will say this: I was right. Everything before was before, and everything after would be different.

A hand brushing my hair woke me, and for a moment, I didn't know where I was. The unfamiliar ceiling, the strange walls, light that wasn't the morning light of my bedroom. Then Holmes's face moved into view, and I groaned, "What time is it?"

"Time to be up, Jack. Time to go."

"That's a suspiciously vague answer."

He hesitated, uncertainty in his features, so I tapped my lips. Holmes huffed that little breath and kissed me. Then he went back to bossy: "Up, Jack. Quickly."

He was already dressed in the joggers, which was disappointing, and he was holding the hoodie, obviously waiting to be helped. I bundled him into it and zipped it up, and then I stumbled off to the bathroom to try to become a human being operating on what I suspected was a criminally short amount of sleep.

But a quarter of an hour later, we were in the truck, driving out of the canyon in the purple dawn.

"Where are we going?" I finally asked. "And why?"

"Maggie's."

"She's missing, remember? She's not going to be home."

"I imagine that's exactly where she'll be. This home is…private, I suppose you might say. No official paperwork ties her to it. The police would have no reason to investigate."

"Oh my Christ, we're going to her lair?"

"Don't be ridiculous."

"It's her secret hideout, right?"

"There's no easily traced connection."

"And let me guess: she'll have some serious defense system, maybe even guards."

"We should assume top-of-the-line security measures."

"Sorry to break it to you, H, but that's a lair."

Holmes refused to talk to me until we got to the other side of Heber.

We followed the state highway north. Morning spilled into the valley, turning the fields and hills gold, painting its way up the back of Timp in broad strokes. A deer was picking its way through a fallow field, stopping now and then to eat, and its shadow tamped down the wet grass.

When Holmes told me to turn, I said, "You realize Park City is, like, basically one-hundred percent villains and lairs and that kind of shit."

"No more talking," Holmes said and got out his phone.

His instructions took me up one of the canyons, and we turned down an unmarked road and crossed a bridge that didn't have guard rails. It was maybe a five-foot drop to the creek below, but I still didn't like it. Then we wound our way through lodgepole pines on a dirt road, the Dodge thumping and rocking and humping its way over a foothill.

On the other side, in a small, timbered bowl, was Moriarty's lair.

It was a glass cube, and in the deep morning shadows, untouched by light, it looked like the shell of some sort of insect. I realized, in that way, it reminded me of the Scorpio building. We followed the dirt road down into the bowl until we were halfway to the house, and then Holmes made me stop in a pullout, and I killed the engine.

The trees seemed thicker as we proceeded on foot, and I lost sight of the house almost immediately. Aside from our steps, the only sound was the occasional rustle of leaves and branches as wildlife fled from us. It was a shock when we came over a rise and the house sprang into view again: dark glass, a box of shadows. We watched it for a moment, but nothing moved inside. Nothing we could see, anyway. I was about to take a step when Holmes caught my arm. Then I heard it: something buzzing at the edge of my hearing.

"Is it a trap?" I asked. "Is it lasers?"

"Is it lasers," Holmes said with undisguised disgust and let go of my arm.

He started walking to the house.

"Hey! That was a legitimate question!"

He didn't stop, so I had to hurry to catch up to him.

Up close, it was obvious that the house was more than glass. Dark wood accented the structure, and the roof was metal—not steel, but I couldn't say what. Off to the right, the sound of a pump came, and running water, and I glimpsed what I thought was a swimming pool.

When we reached the front door, it stood ajar. The noise Holmes had drawn my attention to came again, and now I recognized it as words, but I couldn't make them out.

"We should have guns," I said. "We definitely need to buy some guns."

Holmes snorted softly.

"Excuse me?"

"Stay behind me."

I didn't argue the point because it was so stupid it didn't deserve an argument. I followed Holmes into the house. He moved slowly, his gaze roving, and I tried to see what he was seeing. Inside, the house looked just as modern as you'd expect from the glass cube design. Wood and stone competed for space, with the occasional touch of enameled metal to break things up. Parquet floors, shiplap walls, plank ceilings, all the wood ultraprocessed until nothing wild or natural remained. I imagined this was what it would feel like if one of those Scandinavian furniture catalogues ate you alive.

A voice came out of nowhere, the words loud enough to make me jump: "Maggie? Hello, Maggie, are you there?"

"A virtual assistant," Holmes said, pointing to a speaker in the ceiling.

"Jesus Christ."

He offered me a look, his mouth crooked with amusement.

I gave him the finger.

"Hello, Maggie?" the virtual assistant repeated. "Are you there?"

Holmes cocked his head.

It might have been ten seconds later when the voice said again, "Maggie? Maggie? Maggie?"

"That's creepy as fuck," I said.

"It's software," Holmes said.

"H, the door was open, and we've got some sort of femme-bot version of HAL on a loop—"

"Not a bot," Holmes said. "A virtual assistant."

"—and something is definitely wrong. And seriously? You had to interrupt me for that?"

A hint of color came into his cheeks, and he started moving again.

Our progress through the house was slow. Holmes considered every step, and although it seemed crazy, I figured out pretty quickly that he was checking for traps. The layout of the house also slowed us—it was made up, we discovered, of nesting layers of rooms, and while the outermost layer was composed of long, open spaces to take advantage of the floor-to-ceiling windows and the beautiful views, each progressive section of rooms seemed more convoluted, with unnecessary doors and doglegged hallways that dead-ended in linen closets or a single, ancient portrait of some grim-faced Moriarty ancestor, or simply nothing at all.

And part of what slowed us was the simple fact that the house was a batshit clusterfuck. Every room had something that suggested, at best, a sick sense of humor, and at worst, wear-your-face-as-a-mask insanity. A sprawling octopus of a sofa, for example, its legs curling across the room to make any direct route impossible, its upholstery printed with illustrations of men and women being disemboweled, or having limbs amputated, or being castrated. In another room, a grand piano was shaped—in part, anyway—like an elephant, so that the keys looked like its tusks. In another, Moriarty had hung photos everywhere. It took me a moment to understand what I was seeing, and when I did, my gorge rose. Wounds. Lacerations, tears, cuts, incisions. Infected ones. Ones crawling with maggots. Ones that were strangely pallid, and I couldn't help but think the people in question had been dead. She had hung mirrors between the photos, cleverly painted, so that you'd turn, and for a moment, you'd think someone had flayed the skin from your face. My shirt was damp with sweat, and I caught myself breathing through my mouth.

As we worked our way from room to room, the voice of the virtual assistant followed us, with its queries of "Hello?" and "Maggie?" and "Are you there?"

When we found her office, Maggie Moriarty was sitting in front of a chessboard, and she was dead.

I knew it the way I'd known when I'd seen Lynnissa Baca: the too-still body, her pallor, the way she slumped in her seat. The animal part of my brain knew before the rest of me caught up. Moriarty was dressed in her usual getup: a studded leather jacket, black leather pants, black combat books that laced up to her knees. Her eyes were closed.

"Stay back," Holmes said.

I scanned the office—a teak desk, a leather chaise, built-in bookcases that had been staged with trinkets, a pair of cabinets on the wall with one of the doors ajar. A glass door led out onto a tiny, enclosed patio, I guess in case she needed a moment of fresh air without having to navigate that maze. No samurai swords or antique pistols, not even a nice modern battle axe, but she had a good-sized stapler on her desk, so I grabbed that and nodded to Holmes.

He approached her slowly. The lines of his shoulders hardened; his back was tight. He waited, and after what felt like an eternity, he checked her carotid for a pulse. After another eternity, he peeled back one eyelid. I glimpsed a dark, fixed pupil and pulled my gaze away. On the chessboard, a game was in progress. Moriarty had been playing black, and although I didn't know much about chess, I thought it looked like she'd been winning. Except she'd lost her queen, I saw after another moment. The black queen still lay on the board, tipped over after she'd been taken by a white bishop. I could hear myself breathing too fast.

When Holmes joined me, he was scrubbing his hands on the joggers. "She's dead."

"Fuck that," I said. "How the fuck can she be dead?"

"Maggie," the virtual assistant said overhead, "you've failed to respond for over an hour now, so I'm contacting emergency services. I hope everything's ok."

Holmes pointed to a wine glass, and I thought of Lynnissa Baca again. "She was poisoned." He moved behind the desk. "Jack, if you prefer to keep watch—"

I managed to shake my head. "No. No, I can help."

"We don't have much time. It might be better if you brought the truck to the front door."

That was enough to draw me out of my shock. I shook my head again, cleared my throat, and said, "I can do this."

I checked the bookcases, but while the trinkets looked valuable, they didn't look particularly interesting or important, and so I moved on. I tried the door to the patio, and it opened, and air smelling like wet stone and metal and a hint of pine met me, cool and refreshing. Nothing out there either. I worked my way around the room, looking for what I thought Holmes would look for—although God only knew what that was; maybe footprints? I stopped at the cabinets on the wall and opened them.

They held a whiteboard. I'd seen this at school, whiteboards and bulletin boards with doors that could be closed and, if necessary, locked. On the whiteboard, someone had taped pictures. Hundreds of pictures. I stared at them, trying to make sense of what I was seeing. Many of the pictures were old—black and white, for the most part, and depicting people with dated clothes and old-fashioned hair. Beneath them were written names.

Timothy Watson.

Daniel Watson.

Carey Watson Roper.

Myron Watson.

Romeo Shakespeare Watson.

Aurelia Watson Jefferson.

My mother: Camilla Catherine Sixsmith.

On and on like that. And as I scanned the names, I recognized many of them. Watsons who had died young. Watsons who had, I was sure, been killed.

"Jack," Holmes said, and his voice was a whip. "Get away from there."

I stepped back. And then I saw it.

They weren't just photos. They weren't just a random assemblage of black-and-white. I'd seen this before, when hundreds of little photos made a bigger picture, one that you could see if you looked at them all together. There was a word for it we'd learned in art. Ms. Prinze had taught it to us. A photo mosaic.

And now I saw it.

I heard Holmes moving. Felt him take my arm. But I couldn't look away.

Me. It was me. A photo mosaic of my face, a candid, when I was smiling and looking away from the camera. And someone had made it out of dead Watsons.

Chapter 23

Impossible Things

I couldn't walk right. My legs were stiff, and although I didn't fall, I kept feeling like I was about to—like my legs would lock on the next step, and I'd tip over. Holmes kept a hand on my arm, steering me through the labyrinth of nightmares, until fresh air met my face again. Outside, my brain registered pine duff, sage, a hint of wood smoke. Hands pressed me down, and my ass found cold concrete.

"Put your head between your knees." Holmes's voice came from a long way off. "Breathe. Do you remember you taught me a special way to breathe? Show me again, Jack."

I breathed. Holmes's hand shifted on my neck, his fingers playing lightly with my hair. I counted my breaths and breathed some more. Holmes stayed with me, his hand on my nape an anchor to reality. After a while, I said, "Ok."

His fingers traced a question on my skin.

"I'm ok," I said with a little more conviction, and when I tried to sit up, Holmes let me. He studied me, and I pushed on his face, turning him away from me. "Don't be a goober."

The bowl of the canyon was quiet. I blinked a few times, rolled my head on my neck. A wave of nausea crashed over me, but it faded as soon as it came, almost a memory. Above me, a red-tailed hawk floated in the sky. It looked motionless, like someone had pinned it there, but that was impossible.

"If I had known" Holmes began.

"Stop." When I looked again, the hawk was gone. That was the deal with impossible things, I guess. The only thing I could think to say was "So, now we know who's been killing Watsons."

Holmes shifted, and it was a long time before he said, "Perhaps."

I rolled my head on my neck again. "If I'm wrong, tell me why I'm wrong."

"I don't know, Jack." He turned back to me, and if anything, the worry in his face was even more intense. "Are you all right?"

"Sure. Yeah. I mean, why the fuck not?"

He pulled his knees to his chest. He must have found something super interesting about my sneakers.

With a sigh, I peeled one of his hands free and squeezed it. "I'm freaked out."

When Holmes looked up, his eyes were liquid, and he said, "As am I."

I nodded. He squeezed back.

Something moved off in the brush, the sound of fast, frantic movement, and it broke the moment. "We should go, right?" I asked as I got to my feet. I gave Holmes a tug, and he let me help him up. "Get out of here before the police arrive?"

Holmes nodded. "If you'd like to get the truck, I will make a quick pass—"

"No," I said.

"Jack, it's only reasonable—"

"No."

"In any similar operation, having a driver on standby—"

When I touched his jaw, he flinched. He almost covered it, but I hadn't missed it. I kept my hold loose, playful, as I shook his head back and forth. "N. O. I know you're trying to protect me, and I appreciate it, but I will go out of my skull if you leave me alone right now." I wagged his head in a nod, and in my best English accent said, "Quite right, Jack. Jolly good."

"That is not how I sound."

"You sound much sexier."

He twisted free, scowling. "This is a tactical mistake."

"So, I'm shit at tactics. Add it to the list. And say, 'Jolly good,' just once, so I can get it right next time."

"You are an idiot," he said and stalked away.

I went after him. We followed the house. It was built onto a section of land that had been leveled out of the bowl, which meant that on three sides, it was easy to follow the perimeter of the building. The walls of windows allowed anyone to look inside.

"Do you think someone was spying on her?" I asked.

Holmes shushed me.

"Do you think the killer, like, ambushed her?"

"I don't know, Jack. Please be quiet."

"Do you think there's a clue or something?"

He rounded on me. "I think there's a possibility the killer is still in the area, and so I would like you to be quiet." He shook himself and chuffed and folded his arms across his chest. "Please."

I tried not to, but I couldn't help myself. I grinned. Then I mimed zipping my lips.

"Imbecile," Holmes muttered as he turned and started forward again.

I don't know why it helped to be a jackass. I guess it was either that or—or fall into that black place again. Seeing Moriarty hadn't hit me as hard as seeing Baca, but it had still been, well, a lot. Especially combined with the photo mosaic, all those dead Watsons, and the ass-busting creepiness of seeing my own face staring back at me. Moriarty—or whoever it had been—hadn't been so crass as to paint a target on me, but I thought the message was pretty clear. So, I could either think about that, about how somebody was trying to kill me the way they'd tried to kill everybody else in my family tree, or I could jackass around and drive Holmes to the brink of justified homicide. The latter seemed like the better option.

I was so caught up in trying not to think about the photo mosaic that when Holmes stopped, I noticed too late and crashed into him. A swear slipped out of his mouth, and he clutched me, and for a moment, we both wavered. I glimpsed the drop-off in front of Holmes, and I wrapped an arm around him and grabbed the rail of Moriarty's deck, which was directly above us. Holmes's muscles were taut, and he smelled like Dial soap and the particular smell of his hair and like the store-brand detergent Dad and I used. Like home, I guess, if I had to put a label on it. For a dozen heartbeats, I held him against me, and the adrenaline rush of almost falling faded by degrees. Holmes wrapped a hand around my wrist, and after another few heartbeats, I let him go.

"As I thought," Holmes said. "An approach from this side would be difficult, perhaps impossible, and it would offer no advantage, considering—" He stopped. Without even seeming to think about it, he grabbed my arm and leaned out over the drop.

I clutched his forearm, and I tightened my grip on the rail. Holmes was using me more for stability than anything else, but one thing you learn when you spend time in the mountains is that any drop-off can give way at any moment—nothing is ever as solid as it looks, and sometimes, the ground just gives way.

For close to a minute, Holmes did nothing but stare.

"What?" I finally asked. "What is it?"

He pulled back from the ledge and said, "See for yourself."

We had to improvise, since we couldn't trust his bad arm to hold our weight, so while Holmes held onto the deck railing, I gripped the waistband of his joggers. If I fell, a naked Holmes would have to explain how I died, which was probably a fate worse than death for him, so I figured it would pretty much square us.

For a moment, I couldn't see what Holmes had noticed down among the scree and scrubby trees and brush. And then I spotted it: something definitely not natural—black and oblong and half-hidden by a scraggly maple.

"What's that?" I asked.

"Let's find out."

We had to backtrack to the front of the house so that we could come down the slope without breaking our necks. In the back of my head, a timer was running—I wasn't sure how much time I'd wasted freaking out, but emergency services, if they were coming, couldn't be far. Moriarty's hideout was remote, but it wasn't that remote. Hell, I was surprised nobody had flown in with a helicopter yet.

Making our way down the bowl was harder than it had looked. The ground was crumbly and gave easily underfoot, which meant we both slipped and skidded a lot (although, of course, I slipped and skidded more than Holmes, who even managed to make almost falling on his ass look like he was doing ballet). Twisted junipers dotted the side of the hill, making the air wintery with their smell, and the bark on one ripped up my palm when I started an uncontrolled slide and had to grab it to stop myself. There were clumps of blue spruce and yellow-brown shrubs that were coming back to life. We were halfway down when a fat hare burst out from where it had been hiding under a log and sprinted off into the tree line.

When I glanced over at Holmes, he was grinning like a little kid. The death and madness of Moriarty's house seemed like it had been years ago, and here we were, the two of us, looking like a pair of morons as we stumbled and slipped and half-fell down the slope, and the sun was rising, warm whenever it touched me, and the air was sweet, and we were together.

When we reached the bottom, I got there first, and Holmes came down at a controlled fall-slash-run, so I caught him and steadied him, and he put his good arm around my neck and breathed silent laughter against my cheek. And I could have stayed there forever, like that, just the two of us.

It was easy to pick a path over the scree and around the stunted oaks and maples and pines that were trying to grow in the tumble of rocks. And it was easy, when we got closer, to see what had caught Holmes's attention from above.

I only knew one person who carried a black leather doctor's bag.

"What the hell?" I asked.

Holmes shook his head as he crouched next to the bag. He studied it for a moment, and then he looked up the sheer wall of the outcropping, up to where Moriarty's house perched above us. The sun made it glitter now, and it was almost too bright to look at.

"Either someone planted this," he said, "in an attempt to frame and perhaps discredit Tom—"

"Or option B," I said, "he's a psycho killer who's obsessed with the Holmeses and decided to take matters into his own hands."

Holmes let out an unhappy breath, but he didn't argue. He opened the bag slowly, and he began to take out items. Prescription bottles, like the ones Tom had used to administer the local anesthetic before stitching up Holmes's arm. A couple of them had miraculously survived the fall, and the tinkle of glass suggested what had happened to the rest. Prescription vials, the brown plastic kind, with pills that rattled as Holmes set them aside. I inspected some of these. Dealing to the Walker kids meant I knew my bennies, and Tom had been packing a lot. A lot of opioids, too, for a med student who couldn't write his own scrips.

Then Holmes's body changed—like a ripple passing through water, there and then gone. He drew out something else. Photos, a packet of them, the paper glued together where they'd gotten wet. Holmes considered them. His face was blank. And then he showed me.

In the photo, Blackfriar Holmes was walking through Lynnissa Baca's condo garage, holding a light in one hand to blind the security cameras.

Chapter 24

What No Watson Has Done Before

I got Holmes back to the truck, and we drove out of the canyon.

On the way, an ambulance passed us in the opposite direction, siren wailing. Emergency services. I kept my gaze forward and tried to pretend everything was normal. Then I thought maybe a normal person would look, because it's hard to ignore an ambulance under the best of circumstances. I glanced over as they drew even with us, just for a moment. I caught a glimpse of the driver: blond, twentyish, familiar. And then the ambulance was racing up the canyon. Maybe on an app, I thought. Maybe that's why I thought I'd seen him before.

For lack of a better option, I routed us home. Holmes sat in the seat next to me, clutching the doctor's bag in both hands. He'd returned everything to the bag, to avoid leaving additional evidence at the scene. I wasn't sure what to make of that—it seemed like the police had a right to know that Tom had been blundering around Moriarty's house before she died, especially since he'd been in such a hurry to leave that he hadn't stopped for his precious bag. Another possibility occurred to me.

Holmes said, "Yes, he may be dead."

"Jesus."

"It's a possibility we must consider."

"Do you think he's dead?"

"I don't know."

"Do you think he killed Maggie?"

"I don't know."

"He couldn't have killed Maggie, right? I mean, you've seen him. The guy's a klutz. He trips over his own feet, walks into walls. He couldn't have killed her."

"He might have."

"H, come on. Maggie's, like—well, she's like you, and your family. She's on a whole other level. There's no way Tom sat down with her to play chess and tricked her into drinking poison."

"As I said: he might have." I opened my mouth, and Holmes said, "Jack, you are under the assumption that I, my family, the Moriartys, perhaps even the Adlers, that we are somehow different. I would think that your exposure to me would have convinced you that Holmeses are equally subject to frailties, sicknesses of mind and body, mistakes in judgment, etcetera."

"I know you're not Superman if that's what you mean. But you are different, H. In a good way. You're amazing. And even though Maggie was evil and sadistic, she was like that too. I'm sorry, but I can't imagine Tom Watson getting the better of her."

"Then you must work on your imagination. The Holmeses, the Moriartys, the Adlers—we are all human beings. No one is immortal, and even a genius, to borrow one of your favorite words, cannot predict or prevent every possibility. For all of us, there is always luck or fate or catastrophe, call it what you will."

"Fine. Maybe Tom could have killed her. Maybe he discovered the one possibility she hadn't counted on, and he got her. But honestly, H, do you think he could make it look like a suicide?"

Holmes didn't respond, but he clutched the bag tighter and looked out the window, and that felt like answer enough.

This early, this far out, the drive was quiet and green and peaceful. A few people still ran cattle up here, and we passed a ranch where a herd of black-and-white cows were standing in a field, munching their breakfast. The sun had cleared the mountains, and I felt like I could see to the end of the world.

We hadn't even made it to Park City before Holmes's phone buzzed. He drew it out of the joggers and spoke quietly for several moments. When he disconnected, he said, "I need to return to Reichenbach."

"What?"

"Noneley is...missing."

"Wait, are you serious? When? How?"

"Sometime last night."

"You didn't ask when?"

"I asked. The answer seems to be...contested."

The tires thrummed against the asphalt before I said, "What the hell does that mean?"

"If you can't take me, then I'll get an Uber or rent a car. Park City—"

"Knock it off; you know I'll take you. H, what's going on?"

"A family council. There are matters to be discussed. One of us must be dispatched to recover Noneley; God only knows what she's gotten herself into."

"What about Maggie's murder?"

"I will tell them."

"If they don't already know."

He turned a look on me.

"Come on," I said. "Your dad was released from police custody last night. This morning, we find Maggie dead. She's dead the exact same way Lynnissa Baca died; don't tell me you didn't notice that. And Tom, who's obsessed with your dad and follows him everywhere, somehow dropped his bag right outside Maggie's house."

In a voice like ice, Holmes said, "I assume you mean something by all this."

"Are you kidding me? H, what about the photos?"

"What about them?"

I risked a look. His face was marble—composed, chiseled, unyielding.

"Fine," I said. "You don't think it means something, that we've got photographic proof of your father breaking into Baca's building, blinding the security cameras so nobody would know he'd been there?"

"It may mean many things."

The laugh tore its way out, leaving my throat raw. I shook my head and settled my hands on the steering wheel.

"Something about this amuses you?"

"No. None of it's fucking amusing. It's sad, that's what it is."

Air hissed from the vents in the dash. My eyes were dry and gummy.

"Park City will be far enough," Holmes finally said and settled back in the seat as though we'd decided the matter.

"No. No fucking way." And the universe was kind and open to me making dramatic statements in that moment, because the on-ramp was right there, so I merged onto the highway headed back to Salt Lake.

"I said—"

"I heard you. What are you going to do? Throw yourself out of the truck? You already used that threat on me, remember?"

"And it worked," Holmes said coldly.

"God damn, H, what is going on with you?"

"I'm sorry, I have an aversion to being treated like an idiot, especially by—"

"By a Watson? By a brown kid who's poor and can't finish his chemistry homework?"

"I was going to say by my boyfriend," Holmes said sharply.

A horn blared, and I jerked the truck back into our lane.

"But I did not say it," Holmes said in a more level voice. "Because it is not something we have talked about, and I realize it would have been precipitous."

I opened my mouth to say—what? Yes, obviously. But I wanted a way that didn't sound quite so desperate.

Before I could, Holmes said, "You believe my father killed Baca. And now you believe he killed Maggie. And you tell me that he all but admitted to killing Sarah, and I cannot believe, Jack—cannot believe—that you didn't tell me sooner."

"I didn't tell you because he was going to take you away. He was going to find another prison, H, a worse one than Walker, and he was going to stuff you there. I didn't tell you because I didn't want to lose you."

His throat moved once, reflexively, but when he spoke, his voice was unchanged. "Regardless, you are wrong. My father is many things, but he is not a killer. If nothing else, for the simple reason that there are more expedient, and less legally complicated, ways of resolving problems."

We drove a quarter mile, and I could feel my heartbeat in my face. "All right," I said. "You explain it."

"Explain what?"

"I don't know. The photos in Tom's bag for a start."

"I can't explain them."

The laugh ripped free of me again.

"What do you want me to say?" Holmes asked. "I have no idea why he was there or what he was doing. It seems likely that he broke into Baca's house. Fine, I will give you that. But he didn't kill her, Jack."

"How can you say that? You're the smartest person I know, and I don't understand how you can sit there, defending him, while all this evidence piles up."

"Because he is a great man!" Holmes shout echoed in the tiny space of the cabin. He had twisted in his seat to face me, and out of the corner of my eye, I could see the fury contorting his features, the corner of his mouth trembling because he wanted so badly to bite his lip. "There is no one else like him in the world, and because people do not understand him, they are frightened of him, and because they are frightened of him, they are quick to believe the worst. I did not think you would be the same."

I nodded. I wondered if he knew who he was talking about, if he knew he wasn't talking about Blackfriar, not really. The truck rocked when we went over a slight irregularity in the road. My cheeks, my forehead, my mouth—they felt numb and buzzing, like I'd stuck my head in a swarm of bees. "He hurts you."

Holmes went still.

"You think I don't know," I said, and my tongue was thick too, thick with those invisible beestings. "But I know. He hurts you in so many ways. He's filled your head with—with batshit stuff like 'A Holmes must always be in control,' like telling you not to bite your lip, like all the tests and games, all the things he's taken away from you because he thought they'd be a weak spot or a distraction."

When Holmes spoke, his voice was stiff. "You have no idea what you're talking about—"

"Give me a break."

"—and so I'll ask you this once never to speak of it again—"

"Can you even hear yourself? Can you hear what you sound like?"

"Did you hear me?" The shout hammered at me, the force of it something physical, like I ought to be pressed against the car door. "Do not speak of this again."

I shook my head. I blinked my eyes, and then blinking wasn't enough, and I had to peel one hand off the steering wheel to wipe my cheeks.

"Jack," Holmes said, his voice broken and confused and hurting. When I looked over, blood stained the corner of his mouth; he'd bitten down too hard because he'd held himself back too long. "I don't mean to—" He drew a breath. "Yes, my father is a difficult man. He is a hard man. But he is also a great man. He is hard and difficult because he is great. I understand that you do not agree, but in this matter, I do not need you to agree or approve, not when it comes to my relationship with my father."

"You wanted to stop," I said, and I could hear the tears in my voice. "Let's stop."

"Who would I be without him, Jack? What would I be? Tell me, please. All the things you prize about me, I owe them to him. To his training. Yes, even to the games. You say you love me; then be grateful that he made me who I am."

You'd be happy, I wanted to say, but my throat had closed up. That's what you'd be without him: happy.

Holmes said, "I understand your concerns, and I'm not passing judgment on you for drawing the conclusions you have. But it is a mistake to theorize without all the data—"

Unable to help myself, I mumbled, "It's not the data that's the problem."

"Excuse me?"

I drew a deep, shaky breath and rewrapped my hands around the wheel. The vinyl squeaked.

"You had something to say," Holmes said.

I shook my head, but more words tumbled out. "What's it going to take, H? A bottle of pills with his fingerprints on them? A video recording of him dosing Baca's wine? Even that wouldn't be enough. You'd have to see him, standing there, with your own eyes, and I bet you'd still tie yourself up in knots finding a way to tell me he's not a bad guy." I knew I needed to stop. I knew I needed to hit the conversational brakes. But a dam had broken inside me, and the words spilled out now, a seething flood that had been building for the last nine months. "You know what I think, H? I think you can't let him be bad. I think that's what this is about. Because if he's a bad guy, then what he did to you is bad, and that's too much for you. And I'm sorry for what he did to you. I am, H. It breaks my heart, and I'd take it away from you if I could. But pretending it didn't happen, pretending what he did to you is ok—that's not helping you either. Nobody should have done those things to you, least of all your father. Anybody who tells you otherwise is full of shit."

Silence avalanched down. We drove, and when I looked over, he was biting his lip, his eyes full of tears. He seemed to register me a moment later. He pried his jaw open—it looked like it cost him—and he blinked. Tears rolled down his cheeks. I have no idea what effort it took for him to speak, but for Holmes, effort was never the question. His will rose again, and his voice sounded close to steady.

"Anything I have suffered in my training has been my fault."

I shook my head.

"Yes, Jack. Because I was too slow. Because I was too weak. Because I was stupid."

"I can't do this. If this is what you want to do, then let's stop, because I can't."

"He blames himself, did you know that? My father is harder on himself than anyone else could ever be. He hates the demands that my weakness places on him. Do you think he likes it? My failures take their toll on him more than anyone else."

I can't, I thought. I can't. But I heard myself saying, "None of this is your fault. How do you not realize that?"

His voice quickened, annealing into something harder. "Of course it is."

"H, it's not. You need somebody to tell you that, and I love you, so I'll tell you. None of that was your fault. Nothing he's done to you has been your fault. You're not responsible for any of it."

His breath came in short, broken bursts. He savaged his lip. When he spoke, his teeth were red with blood. "You were correct. I am done talking about it. It seems you will never understand—"

My own anger surprised me, almost strangling me. "What the fuck do I have to understand about watching him beat the shit out of you?"

Color drained from Holmes's face. He swayed, and he put a hand on the dash to hold himself upright.

"I saw him!" It was like an infection being drained, the words rushing out of me, taking the anger with them, so that with every syllable I felt smaller, meaner, emptier. "Your mom made me watch that fucking camera footage as he tortured you! And you did it for me, H, and I am never, ever going to stop feeling like I want to die when I think about that. Don't sit there and tell me he does it because he's helping you. Don't tell me it takes its toll. He loved it. He enjoyed it. I watched him, and he relished every fucking minute of it."

Holmes stared at me for what felt like a long time. Then he turned forward, resting his cheek against the glass. He drew his knees up and held himself like that, making himself into a ball. The way animals do when they're defending themselves, I thought. Or when they're hurt.

"H," I said. My throat burned. I wasn't sure, I realized, if I'd been shouting.

His breathing was rhythmic, so even and perfectly measured it almost sounded mechanical.

"I'm sorry," I said. "I didn't mean to say any of that. I'm really sorry. You're right: it's none of my business, and I—I take it back, ok? We don't have to go to your parents' house. We can go back to the cottage. We can go back to Walker and find a place for us, and we can just—" Tears threatened to sink me. I didn't know what we could have. I didn't know anything right then.

For a moment, his head came up from the glass, and I thought, yes, anything, I'll take anything, every hateful, hurtful thing you've ever wanted to say—give it to me now, but don't be silent. But all he did was pull up his hood, hiding his face from my view, and then his head lowered to the glass again.

I had never seen him like this, so completely shut down. Before, his rage had always been white hot, a wildfire burning through his usual control. This was so much worse. I couldn't even tell if it was anger or if it was grief or shame or pain. Maybe Holmes didn't know either. Maybe it was a little bit of everything.

And so, because I didn't know what else to do, I drove to Reichenbach Grange.

When I pulled up in front of the mansion, the police cars were gone. The search was over. Or perhaps it had been canceled, the same way Blackfriar had been released. I'd thought I'd known how much power the Holmes family had, but I was starting to realize that it extended further than I'd ever imagined. Blackfriar had been arrested for murder, with serious evidence against him, and he'd still walked away without being charged. He'd killed Sarah. He'd killed Baca. He'd killed Maggie. What would he do when he got tired of me interfering with his son?

Holmes opened the door and slid out of the truck. He reached back for the doctor's bag, and I said, "Maybe you should leave that here."

He barked a laugh and yanked open the bag. "Worried I'm going to turn over all the incriminating evidence to my murderous father?"

I tried to look at his face. Behind him, the bluff dropped away sharply, and clouds floated over the valley.

"Good heavens, Jack," he said with another of those laughs. He pulled the packet of stuck-together photos from the bag and tossed them onto the seat where he'd been sitting. "Happy?"

"Why can't you forget I said anything?" I asked. "Why can't we go back to the way things were? You were right: it's none of my business. I'm sorry I opened my mouth."

Holmes shook his head. He was still so pale, shadows smudging his eyes. "If you believe my father killed all those people, Jack, then may I make a suggestion?"

I tried to swallow, but something was caught in my throat.

"Do what no Watson has done before," Holmes said. "Solve it yourself."

Then he slammed the door and went inside.

Chapter 25

A Balanced Breakfast

I sat there for a couple of minutes, in their expensive driveway in front of their incredible mansion, hating the Holmeses. Every one of them. Then I started the car and drove off their property; it'd be a shame if the butler had to toss me out, or whatever the procedure was.

I ended up parked at a Sinclair, pounding a bag of mini-Reese's and drinking a Coke. It was a balanced breakfast because it was cherry Coke, so there was fruit involved. My head started hurting, and I gave up on the Reese's and put on my sunglasses because now it was too bright in the valley. I looked around, considered my options. The Sinclair was pretty nice, and I didn't know this area well, but there had to be someone around here who could help me get high.

My phone buzzed with a call from Dad, and I saw that I'd missed several others from him already. I waited for this one to go to voicemail, and then I texted him that I was ok. I couldn't bring myself to read the dozen or so messages that he'd sent over the course of the morning. I already knew the gist of them: he was upset, and how dare I, etc. As soon as I'd finished my message, Dad called again. I put the phone face-down on the seat and drank some more Coke.

Getting high sounded wonderful. Getting high sounded like a guaranteed way to stop feeling like this. Or, at least, to keep feeling like this, but under a nice, cloudy layer of cannabis. But the problem with getting high was that it was giving Blackfriar—and, by extension, Holmes—exactly what he wanted. I was a Watson, which apparently meant, dumb as shit, clueless as hell, and the kind of wonder-fuck whose only purpose in existence is to trot around at the heels of the Holmeses and write down all the important, brilliant, savvy things they do and say. Like Tom, I thought. Glued to Blackfriar's ass.

For a few minutes, I played around with the idea of tracking down Tom, but there were at least two problems with that: first, I had no idea where Tom was staying, whether he was at the Grange or in a hotel or sleeping in his car; and second, even if I did know, the odds were that Tom would be halfway up Blackfriar's butt. If that were the case, then I wouldn't be able to ask Tom any of my really good questions like *How did your doctor's bag end up at Maggie's house?* And *Did you kill Maggie Moriarty?* And even better *Did you see Blackfriar murder her?*

So, for the moment, Tom would have to wait.

I wasn't sure what my next step should be. By this point, the police would have overrun Moriarty's house; there was no way someone that famous could end up dead under suspicious circumstances and not get the full treatment. My headache was worse, and now my stomach was doing something funny, because apparently mini-Reese's do not mix well with cherry Coke. The smell of gasoline came in through my open windows, and sunlight flashed on windshields and chrome. My phone buzzed again, and I silenced it. Maybe, I thought, if a long-haul trucker came by, he'd be nice enough to let me stick my head under his tires.

My eyes fell on the photos of Blackfriar. They were unmistakably him, and I thought of what Rivera had told me: the photo sent anonymously to the Utah County Sheriff's Department, the one that had been part of the case Rivera had been building against Blackfriar. I thought about taking these photos to Rivera; he'd know what to do with them. But the same thing might happen again. If one photo could miraculously disappear, it could happen to several. Things like that happened, sometimes. One of the perils of dealing with lots and lots of physical evidence in departments that were perpetually understaffed and underfunded. Things slipped through the cracks, or they got misplaced. Hell, maybe that first photo would show up in a day or two, or in a month, or in twenty years. That'd be a laugh, wouldn't it?

But for the time being, it wasn't so funny. Without the photo, nothing put Blackfriar at the scene of Baca's murder. And there could be explanations for everything else, like her jewelry, which they'd found in his car. An affair, that was the simplest one. Or, as Rivera said, he'd given her a ride.

I picked up the photos and studied them. They had a time stamp, and it looked like the whole stack of them had been taken some time between 8:37 and 8:38 PM—after the blackout at Zodiac, while Holmes was passed out in the Dodge and we were hiding in last year's corn maze. That confirmed what we'd already known: whoever had killed Baca, they'd done so shortly after she'd arrived home.

There were so many strange things about that scenario. Why would Baca go home, when she had to assume that Moriarty, at least, would mark her as a potential suspect? Maybe going home was the best way to avoid suspicion, but if it had been me—speaking as someone who, by the ripe old age of seventeen, had learned the hard way the dangers of keeping your stash in the house—I wouldn't have taken the stolen property directly back to my home. I would have found somewhere to hide it until I was ready to make the handoff.

And maybe she had. That made me sit up a little straighter, push the sunglasses up onto my head, study the pictures more closely. If that chain of reasoning were correct, then Baca might have stopped somewhere on her way home and hidden the portable safe. But if so, where had she hidden it? Salt Lake was a big city, and she could have stopped anywhere in the valley on her way home. It made me itch to get another look at her phone and laptop, but since those were currently in Noneley's possession, I figured that wasn't an option. Not right now, anyway.

The other possibility for why Baca had gone home directly after the burglary was that she was meeting someone. And that meant Blackfriar showing up the way he did, while his company's anniversary party was still in chaos, while his security team would have been freaking out, while his wife and daughter were still in the middle of the madness, well, that made it even more interesting.

I spent a little longer with the photos, trying to peel them apart, but when a couple of them tore, I gave up and put them in the glovebox. I started up the truck and rolled out of the lot. It was time to do a little driving.

Chapter 26

A Certifiable Non-Genius

I didn't start my search on the Zodiac campus only because I didn't have life aspirations of making toilet wine while Rivera gloated. Instead, I started on the road that passed in front of Scorpio, where Holmes and I had done some impromptu off-roading to escape the jammed parking lot. You could still see where the Dodge's tires had torn up turf and tumbleweeds with equal abandon. The Scorpio building itself was a sheet of white fire in the spring sunlight.

I followed the road to I-15, and I drove north toward Salt Lake. As I drove, I kept the voice memo app on my phone open, and I listed exits, along with any obvious places to stop: gas stations, restaurants, shopping malls, big-box stores. The whole point was to generate a list of possibilities, because the reality was that Lynnissa Baca couldn't have hidden the portable safe anywhere. Her options had actually been fairly limited; she'd been on a tight timeline, and in order to get back to her condo before Blackfriar arrived, she would have had to limit any side trips. That meant wherever she'd stored the safe, it had to be relatively close to her route home. A part of me protested that it wouldn't have taken all that long to get off the highway, drive a block or two, and get back on I-15 a few minutes later. But the reality of that expanded my search into a kind of impossibility, and so, for the present, I stuck with what had the best chance of working.

The clouds had moved out. The sky was clear and blue, and everywhere, trees were leafing out and flowers were shooting up, and apparently everybody loved tulips because I could see beds full of them, even from the highway. I wanted to put on music. I wanted something to scream to. Stone Temple Pilots sounded good. "Big Empty." I wanted to sing that line where Scott Weiland tells you about driving faster. Where he tells you conversations kill.

Instead, I rattled off every fast-food joint I saw for twenty miles, and I wondered if everything the Watsons did was destined to be much less glamorous than the Holmeses.

By the time I'd gotten to Baca's condo, my throat was dry. I swigged some cherry Coke, which only made my head start pounding again, and I sat and considered the building. I only had a vague impression of it from that night—cut me some slack; I'd just had my best friend come back from the dead, and we'd spent the earlier part of our evening being chased by guys with guns—but by daylight, it wasn't anything particularly impressive: tall, skinny, crammed onto the block. The kind of place that was expensive, but only because of location.

I stuffed the photos and a pair of disposable gloves in my pocket—part of the gear I kept in the truck, since I still got called out to help Dad on random occasions. Then I walked down into the parking garage. The smell of cold concrete and motor oil met me, and I checked the photos as I worked my way through the garage. Baca's car was gone—presumably, impounded by the police, although I figured somebody else could have taken it, perhaps the same person who had stolen her jewelry. As I got closer to the door that led into the condo building, I noticed something I hadn't spotted before. In at least one of the photos, I could see Lynnissa Baca's parking spot in the background behind Blackfriar. But in the photo, like today, the car was missing. Which meant Blackfriar had arrived before Baca had gotten home. That seemed important, although I wasn't sure what it told me.

I put on the gloves and used my Albertson's card to get past the locked door, and I rode the elevator up to the fourth floor. Someone had taken the tape off all the security cameras, so I was being recorded for posterity. I waved to the one in the elevator. Maybe it would make Yazzie smile when she inevitably arrested me for this.

As I made my way down the hall to Baca's condo, one of the neighboring doors opened on a chain, and an eye looked out at me. I had a moment to gather an impression: white, old, short. Then the door slammed shut.

Maybe I'd tell Yazzie I was looking for a place of my own. Maybe I'd tell her how good I was with the neighbors.

I wasn't sure that my card trick would work on Baca's door, but when I tried the handle, it was unlocked. Police tape still crisscrossed the doorway, and I figured whoever had been here before, they hadn't been worried about the police knowing they'd visited. I stepped between the strands of police tape, and then I was officially breaking and entering and disturbing a crime scene and whatever else Rivera had dreamed about slapping me with over the last year.

The apartment was in shambles. From my last visit, I had the impression of a clean, orderly space, every piece of furniture carefully chosen, every little decorative piece deliberated over. Now, fingerprint powder covered everything, and the expensive furniture had been overturned, cut open, in some cases—like the coffee table—disassembled. The accent table near the front door had its doors and drawer open, and the mail that had been neatly stacked on top now spilled in a white stream across the floor.

I made myself look at the chair where Baca had died. There might have been a stain. Or it might have been a shadow, or a trick of the imagination. But otherwise, it was just a chair. I realized I was breathing through my mouth, and my pulse hammered in my throat.

When I took a deep breath through my nose, something foul met me. It made me think of wet garbage and overheated motors. I picked my way across the room, stepping around an overturned chair, an eviscerated cushion, and made my way into the connecting kitchen. Whoever had done this—and it hadn't been the police—they had done the same kind of damage to the kitchen. Drawers lay around the room like they'd been hurled, and a dent in one wall suggested the fury behind the search. Their contents were spilled across the floor—measuring cups, silverware, the random bits that collected in drawers like markers and free stationery and Scotch tape. Someone had dumped out the flour and sugar and rice. Cabinet doors had been ripped off their hinges, and from the darkened cavities, pots tumbled out like steel tongues. The fridge was open and silent, and I guessed the motor had burned itself out. The rotting produce smell made me gag.

I winced. Somebody—probably somebody like me and Dad—was going to have to clean up this shit. Psycho billionaires and royal bloodlines of famous detectives didn't worry about that kind of stuff.

The rest of the apartment was in the same condition. Baca's dresser had been destroyed. Her mattress had been slit, springs and foam exploding out like intestines. Her desk lay on its side, and one searcher had gone through the apartment, systematically kicking a hole in every interior door. Part of the search, I wondered. Or spite? Or nothing more than the childish love of destruction?

By the time I got back to the living room, I knew I was in over my head. The police had already searched Baca's residence for clues to who had killed her. Blackfriar had made sure that there wasn't any evidence; like Moriarty's death, it could—and eventually might—be written off as a suicide: the empty wineglass, the residue of prescription painkillers, with no hard proof that anything else had happened. The only positive note was how thoroughly this place had been tossed. It told me something important — people were still looking for the safe. Maggie had been looking for it. Blackfriar, I thought, was still searching. I couldn't help the grin that started as I realized how it must feel to be a genius and to be a Holmes and to be the walking embodiment of an evil overlord, and still have somebody outsmart you.

Which didn't bode well for me, but hey, maybe there was an advantage to being a certifiable non-genius. Like, maybe you thought about people like people, instead of like chess pieces or tools or toys.

And Lynnissa Baca had been a person. She hadn't been perfect. She'd been combative, from what Paxton had told us, and she'd been open to the idea of stealing from her employer and selling what she stole to the highest bidder. She'd been a thief. And, I was starting to suspect, she'd been manipulated by Blackfriar into stealing Watson's portable safe, probably without even realizing Blackfriar was orchestrating events. She'd paid for it with her life.

But that didn't make her any less of a person. She'd had a home, a life, people who cared about her.

And if she was a person, that meant she had patterns, routines, certain things she liked to do, certain ways she liked to do them. If I was going to figure out anything that the Holmeses and Moriartys couldn't figure out, it was because I was a normal human being, and not — well, whatever they were.

So, I told myself, keep going.

I'd documented possibilities on the drive to Baca's condo. Now, I ran through the sequence of events in my head. She parked in the garage — plenty of hiding places there. She came upstairs. The elevator, maybe, or perhaps even the elevator shaft could be additional hiding places. She came down the hallway. I thought of the suspicious neighbor who had watched me? Would she have entrusted somebody else with the safe? Or left it in an empty apartment? Or maybe someone who was out of town, and she was watering their plants?

The options seemed limitless, but more and more, I was convinced of one thing: Lynnissa Baca had known, before she'd even made it out of the Scorpio building at Zodiac, that her plans had gone horribly wrong. Holmes had interrupted her when she'd been rifling Maggie's vault. I'd run into her in the hallway, creating a possible witness. Security had responded to the alarm. Even if my suspicions were right, even if Baca had been planning on meeting Blackfriar that night, she would have been thrown off-balance. If she hadn't planned initially on hiding the safe, there was a high chance she would have done something to get rid of it before anything else could go wrong.

And then, of course, Blackfriar had killed her.

I turned for the door; I'd go back down to the garage, and I'd work my way back up more slowly, taking time to note anywhere Baca might have potentially used as a hiding spot—

My Stan Smith slipped on an envelope.

It wasn't enough to make me fall. I caught myself, stepped free of the fallen piece of mail, reached for the door.

And stopped again because all the Christmas lights in my brain went on.

Why was Baca's mail here, lying on the floor? The obvious answer was the search, but that wasn't correct. Baca's mail had been piled on the teak accent table the night Holmes and I had found her dead. And that didn't fit with anything else in Baca's condo. It didn't fit with the coffee table free of magazines, or with the desktop clean of paperwork, or the dresser without a single Taco John's receipt, even though you were only keeping them because you told Holmes that taquito was so bad you deserved a refund. In other words, no clutter in the condo. Not anywhere. So, what were the odds that, of all things, the mail was left in a pile by the door?

Not high, I guessed, and a heatwave rushed through me. Not unless you'd stopped for the mail on the way up, and you were surprised by a supervillain waiting for you inside your condo.

Why stop for your mail? If you're on the run, if you've burgled one of the most powerful people in the state—maybe even in the country—and everything went wrong, why stop to see if you'd gotten the Kroger ad?

I reached for the door and stopped again.

Mailbox key. I needed the mailbox key.

The one Baca had used would have been taken with the rest of her personal belongings, I guessed—or, worst-case scenario, had been taken by Blackfriar. There was a chance that he'd come to the same conclusion I had. But still, I had to see. Baca would have had a spare key to the mailbox. She might have kept it in the office, or in the kitchen junk drawer, or in some random place I wouldn't normally think of. I looked at the chaos in front of me. It would take hours to find something in this mess. It might take days.

Unless, a part of my brain said—and it sounded a little like Holmes— unless she kept it where she leaves the mail.

The drawer of the accent table was open, and when I glanced inside, I saw nothing. But I gave the table a shake, and something rattled inside. I pulled the drawer out, and a small, silver key slid into view.

Bingo.

I don't really remember going downstairs. I took the stairs; I remember that, because the elevators took too long. And I remember the sound of movement behind the neighbor's door, the realization that I was dealing with a Grade-A snoop. But after that, it's a blur of movement, me taking the steps three at a time, the relative darkness of the stairwell, the sound of my sneakers squeaking against the concrete.

I found the mailroom in the lobby. The tile and the high ceiling echoed every sound, and it sounded like there was someone else with me, somebody else coming with me. And there should have been. Holmes should have been. The hurt of that was a kind of counterpoint to the daze of this moment. Because he had said, *Solve it yourself.* And I was about to do just that.

The little key fit neatly into the lock of Baca's mailbox. I turned, opened the door, and the rush left me lightheaded.

Because there it was, small and oblong and black.

Watson's safe.

Chapter 27

Watson's Safe

For lack of anywhere better, I carried the safe to the truck and sat there and stared at it.

It was black, and although the outer material felt like plastic, the weight suggested there was metal involved in the construction. It was somewhere in size between a glasses case and a dopp kit—big enough for a phone, your wallet, keys, maybe a nice, fat watch. When I held it in both hands, it seemed so small. People had died for this. Even more people had been hurt for this. It wasn't like Scrooge McDuck's swimming pool-size vault. The safe was trembling, and a distant part of me recognized that no, I was the one shaking.

I thought about calling Holmes.

Then I opened the cover plate to expose the combination lock, and I set to work.

Holmes had told me (it felt like years ago, although it had only been a day or two) that Watson's original message had said the safe was meant for me. Which meant, in theory, I should be able to open it. The key part of that sentence was *in theory*, because I'd never gotten any secret communication from Watson, and there weren't any family secrets about a four-digit number, and I'd never owned a decoder ring or any cool shit like that.

So, because I'm a Boy Genius, I tried my birthday.

Nothing.

I tried again, because my hands were shaking, and I thought maybe the tumblers hadn't set quite right.

Still nothing.

Ok, I thought. I tried my birth year.

Nope.

I tried Mom's birthday, Mom's birth year.

I tried the date of the accident.

I sat back and stared at the safe. I told it, "You're making me look stupid."

Holmes wouldn't have said anything, but I could imagine the look on his face.

Part of me understood that if it had been something as simple as my birthday, a Holmes or a Moriarty would have had this safe open in seconds. They were all geniuses; a four-digit combination should have been child's play. I grinned reluctantly as I rolled the tumblers back and forth, the stamped metal rough under the pads of my fingers. That must have driven them crazy. I bet Holmes could do the math in his head, tell you how many possible combinations there were. I wondered if Maggie had tried it that way, running through each possibility, scratching them off some giant cheat sheet.

I tried Dad's birthday. I tried his birth year. I didn't know when my grandparents had been born—I'd only known my Dad's parents, and they'd died when I'd been little. Ok, I thought, and I did a mental knuckle-crack. I multiplied my birthday by Mom's (and yes, I had to use my phone and, in the process, ignore the missed calls from Holmes and Dad and Rowe and Emma and Glo). There were too many digits, so I tried adding them together. Then I tried subtracting them. Then I had a stroke of genius. Dad's birthday plus Mom's birthday equals me, right? I mean, kind of. So, I tried that.

When it didn't work, I was glad I hadn't shared that stroke of genius out loud.

For a while, I stared at the safe again. The last of my nervous energy burned itself out, and the shakes left me. My neck and shoulders ached from hunching over, so I forced myself to lean back, rest my head on the seat. Holmes and I had only gotten a couple of hours of sleep last night. We'd been…busy, and then Holmes had wanted to leave at the ass crack of dawn, and although I was sure I'd slept the night before, I was having trouble remembering where and how much. Noneley's cabin, I thought. And the way Holmes had tucked himself into me.

My head came up with a start, and my neck hurt in a new way, and my eyes were all gummy. I most definitely had not drooled on my shirt.

The safe had not miraculously opened itself while I'd been, uh, thinking.

It was stupid. That thought came to me as I stared at the black box. The whole thing was stupid. This was a stupid way to live your life. People were supposed to have jobs and go to school and fall in love and find meaningful things to do with their lives. You weren't supposed to get caught in these elaborate games that the three families played—

My hands moved across the surface of the safe.

The three families.

But not the Watsons.

I was doing it wrong. That was the problem. I was going at this the wrong way. I was trying to play this game like a Holmes, trying to be as smart as them, trying to be as clever. But that was a mistake, because I wasn't all that smart (Exhibit A: my chemistry grades) and I wasn't all that clever (Exhibit B: Dad busting me the first time I got high because I 'hid' my vape at the back of my underwear drawer). I wasn't a Holmes. I wasn't much of a Watson, either, I guess, because the Watsons didn't traditionally pick fights with the Holmeses and ruin any chance they had, even though they were desperately in love. I mean, not historically, anyway. But I was still a Watson. And a Watson had sent it to me. And she'd done it because she'd believed I could open it, even though we'd known each other only briefly, even though she hadn't given me a single clue about any of this.

So, start there, I told myself. It's got to be easy. Whatever it is, it's got to be something you can figure out. I'd tried birthdays, and those hadn't worked. What else?

Well, hell, I thought, a smile pulling at the corner of my mouth.

I tried 1-2-3-4.

Nothing.

I thought about it and tried 4-3-2-1.

Nada.

And then it hit me, and I laughed out loud.

2-2-1-2.

The final two was a substitution, because B was the second letter of the alphabet. Holmes and Watson's London address.

The lock clicked open.

I tried to take deep breaths, but I couldn't seem to slow myself down. My hands were shaking again. I lifted the lid and found four envelopes tucked inside the safe. White, business-sized, the kind you'd pick up at Walmart for cheap. Their corners were bent from sliding around inside the safe. I opened the first one, and a flash drive fell into my hand. I opened the second and found another flash drive. The third held four small plastic baggies that held hair—two blond, two brown. I remembered what Rivera had said, about DNA evidence, and I wondered if that had been Sarah's plan as well, a way to frame the Holmeses if she needed to. I opened the fourth envelope, and a silver chain slithered out.

For a moment, I couldn't even breathe. I stared at the chain. My fingers wanted to close around it, but they didn't move. I knew that chain. It was a necklace, with a little artsy geometric pendant. Dad had bought it for Mom when we'd gone to this mining town thing, with all its Old West vibes, and a million tourist attractions like 'local' artists. Mom had liked it anyway; she'd worn it all the time.

I was shaking harder now. I turned the safe upside down. I shook it. Nothing fell out. This was it. All that death and pain for this.

The last year had taught me to be cautious, so even though I wanted to clutch Mom's necklace, even though I didn't want to let it out of my sight again, I returned it to the envelope. I closed it in the safe with the hair samples and scrambled the tumblers, and then I considered the flash drives. It would take me over an hour to drive back to Walker, and even there, there was no guarantee I'd have a chance to look at the contents of the drives. Dad was going to skin me alive and hang me from the flagpole as a warning to other teenagers. I'd be lucky if he let me out of my room again before I turned thirty. I could drive back and use one of the computers in the library, but that meant no privacy. Maybe the computer lab, later, if I waited until campus closed for the day—

Then I shook my head, opened the door, and climbed down from the truck.

Dumbass, I told myself, but the thought felt distant, padded by a layer of shock, and I was still shaking.

The safe bumped against my thigh as I jogged back to Baca's condo building. I let myself in through the garage again, rode the elevator up to the lobby, and found the condo office. It was closed, of course; it was a weekend—although I'd lost track of whether it was Saturday or Sunday by this point—and the strip under the door was dark. My Albertson's card let me in, and I shut the door quietly behind me. I kept the lights off as I moved across the office, rounded the L-shaped desk, and made my way to the computer.

It seemed to take an eternity to power up. Holmes had told me the password, and it let me through the lock screen. I took a deep breath and set the safe on the desk. When I inserted the first flash drive, I got the usual message about whatever whatever, and then a moment later, I could see the files. Or better said, file. One. A video.

I clicked on it, and it began to play.

For a moment, the angle and the dark were so disorienting that I didn't know what I was seeing. Then my brain reconfigured, and I understood: I was looking down a steep slope. The footage was grainy, probably because whoever was recording this had used the zoom feature gratuitously, but I could still make out a surprising amount of detail. At the base of the hill sat a Lexus, and the car looked like it had been through hell: headlights smashed, windows shattered, a tire blown. The roof had a slightly crunched look. A numb part of me thought, That's what happens when you roll.

My breaths were short and shallow and fast. Dizziness pulled at me, and I grabbed the desk.

The Lexus. That thought was clear, at least. And then, a little clearer: Mom's Lexus.

A man entered the frame, stumbling on the uneven ground, something held low against his side. I let out a breath and leaned closer. I knew this guy. The colors were washed out in the dark, but I knew he had a peach-colored face. I knew the way he walked. I knew how he held a gun low against his thigh. I knew he had a scar now, one that I'd given him. This was the same guy who had tried to kill me a few months before, when he'd run me off the road. And now I was seeing it happen again, only it wasn't again—it was before.

They had told me he was trying to help, a distant, childlike voice said. They had told me he was carrying a tool.

But I wasn't fifteen and hurt and disoriented from a car crash. I wasn't heartbroken and traumatized in a hospital room. I was here, now, watching an indisputable video recording of the man carrying a gun. I watched as, in the video, the younger me threw open the back door and ran. I looked so much smaller, part of me observed. I had been smaller. I had been a child.

The peach-faced man stopped to glance into the car, and then he continued walking. Coming after me. To kill me. Waves of hot and cold electrified me. I felt like every hair on my body was standing on end.

And then a second man entered the frame. This one, I knew from the first instant: the oily grace, the unnatural smoothness. Like a bead of mercury. Like smoke and shadow.

Blackfriar Holmes approached the Lexus. He looked through the driver's window, and then he reached inside. He yanked, the movement of one arm savage, his body telegraphing the fury behind the motion. And then he turned and walked away. Something hung from his hand. Something thin, something that would have been invisible on a camera at that distance, except that the silver caught in the headlights and glittered.

Mom's necklace.

The one Cecilia Holmes had included when she'd done her sketch of Mom.

When Blackfriar exited the frame, the video ended. There had been no audio, but in the crushing emptiness of the office, silence rushed in on me. My ears rang with it. My breathing was still so fast, so light, like stones skipping over water. My hands ached around the edge of the desk.

Questions fragmented inside my head: Where? How? Why? And one word, again and again: No.

Displaced air alerted me a moment too late. I started to turn. Holmes had already made his way around the desk. His face was ashen, and he looked, if anything, more exhausted than ever: the dark hollows around his eyes, the sag of his shoulders, the way his injured arm hung at his side.

"Jack." He sounded hoarse. "Thank God. I tried calling."

"My phone was silent—" I furrowed my eyebrows. "H, how did you find me—"

He streaked toward me with a speed I thought he'd lost. I was still turning, trying to bring myself around to face him, my body slowed by the one-two combo of surprises: first, the video; and second, now, the impossibility of Holmes being here, of him darting toward me with that strange look on his face.

I didn't realize he was holding a needle until I felt the prick in my neck.

It was like someone started blowing up a balloon inside my body—not a sense of pressure, but of everything swelling, distorting. I tried to say, "What the hell?" but the sounds that came out didn't match the words in my head. I stumbled and threw an arm out. I wasn't sure if I was trying to punch him or grab on to him. The office tilted. When I reached for the desk, it slid out from under my hand.

Then Holmes's good arm was around me, the woodsy heat of him filling my chest, and he was saying something, although I couldn't make out what. The words, like the world, got bigger and bigger, inflated by whatever Holmes had jabbed me with. I was on the floor now, staring up at Holmes, only his face was wrong, like I was looking at him in a funhouse mirror. He rolled my head, touched my neck, combed back my hair. He floated above me like the moon, while that balloon in my head got bigger and bigger.

And then it popped.

Chapter 28

Little Brushes

A man was talking.

I jerked upright, choked on my spit, and hacked to clear my airways.

"Easy," the man said. His voice was neutral but hard. A cop voice. "Stay there for a minute."

But I rolled onto my hands and knees, still coughing. My head felt like it was packed with clouds. My body ached. Exhaustion tried to drag me under again, and for a moment, when I closed my eyes, I felt myself slipping. I forced my eyes open again and struggled to get to my feet.

"I said stay right there," the cop-voice said.

"Kid," a second man said, "stay down."

Holmes. The thought was a beacon fire, burning through the fog of my thoughts. Holmes had been here. Holmes had—

The needle. The world swelling up. The fall.

When I moved too fast, the world lagged a half-second behind, but I managed to find the desk. I was still in the condo office. The computer was there, but the flash drives were gone, and so was the safe. I craned my head. I'd been right about the cops; they wore blue uniforms with patches and badges and radios, all the stuff cops lug around, and one of them was shining a flashlight at me even though—well, I didn't know what time it was, but I could tell it was still day.

No Holmes.

"Something wrong with your hearing, son?"

"You feeling all right?" The one without a flashlight crouched to look me in the eye. "You were out cold. Kind of scary. Want to tell us what you took?"

I shook my head. Words felt just beyond my fingertips.

"You live here?" the one with the flashlight said. He angled it, and I held up a hand to block the beam. "Hey, I asked you a question."

"Some of that street stuff can kill you. If you took something, you ought to tell us." The second cop tapped his badge and said, "How about we start with our names?"

I shook my head again and got to my feet. The world whirled, steadied, slipped. My hip caught the desk, and I pressed the heels of my hands to my eyes. When I pulled them down, the flashlight caught me dead on, and I had to shield my face again.

"Sit down," the one with the flashlight said. "I want to get a look at your eyes."

Holmes had come after me. He had followed me; it was the only explanation. I built the chain of thoughts like one of those Lego Star Wars monstrosities, trying to fit a million tiny pieces into place. He had followed me, and I had found the safe, and then the video, and Blackfriar. Mom. And then Holmes had drugged me. My neck stung when I found where the needle had gone in. And he'd taken the proof: the flash drive and the safe—and with it, Mom's necklace. The one Blackfriar had taken from her as she'd been dying.

"Kid." The one without the flashlight stood, and he held out his hands like he was playing defense. "Take it easy. You don't look good, and you definitely shouldn't be on your feet. Why don't we figure out—"

Shaking my head, I started toward the door.

"Hey," the one with the flashlight barked. "We're talking to you!"

When he grabbed my arm, it was like somebody set off fireworks inside my head. I turned and swung a great big hook. It was the kind of blow that would have disgusted Holmes: sloppy, with no power behind it, and telegraphed from a mile away. Somehow, it still caught the cop on the jaw. He made a little bleating noise and stumbled back. Then he reached for his gun.

The second cop already had me, though, forcing me to the floor. My chin bounced off the boards, and a moment later, the cold steel of cuffs snapped shut around my wrists.

"You're under arrest," that cop said. When he read me my rights, he didn't sound nearly as friendly as before.

They put me in their cruiser and drove me around for a while. It was stuffy in the back of the car, and the heat and the rocking motion of the car and the lingering effects of whatever Holmes had put in my system made me droop, my head bouncing against the glass. I stumbled when they hauled me out of the car, and the one I hadn't punched had to march me into the station to keep me from falling.

Processing seemed to go on for a long time. They wanted to ask me questions. They took my Superman wallet, keys, and phone. They took my Stan Smiths and my belt. They wouldn't let me close my eyes. Once, when they were shouting at me to turn, I lost my balance and cracked my head against the wall, and the cop I'd punched burst out laughing.

Eventually, they put me in a holding cell by myself, maybe because I was a kid. There was a bench and a stainless-steel toilet, and I used the latter and then the former. It didn't feel like sleep, because the little movie theater in my head kept playing the worst parts of the last few days: watching Holmes be beaten by Blackfriar; the footage of the accident, where I saw myself run; the ghost of Holmes's face behind me, and the prick of the needle. I woke up, and my face was wet, and I had to ball myself up to keep from sobbing.

I don't know how long I slept, but I'd been awake a few hours before footsteps came down the hallway—a harsh, brisk clip that suggested somebody who was pissed the hell off. Voices murmured outside the cell, and a moment later, a buzzer went off, and the door opened.

Rivera stepped into the cell. He was dressed in jeans and a Hogle Zoo t-shirt, and his dark features were crumpled. He stared at me for a moment. Then he hurled the Superman wallet. It struck me in the chest, followed a moment later by the keys, then my phone, and then one Stan Smith after the other. Glaring at me, Rivera stood there, breathing hard. Then he turned and stalked out.

When I poked my head into the hall, Yazzie was leaning against the wall. She was in jeans and a pink blouse, and she pushed up her glasses when she saw me and shook her head.

I pulled on one Stan Smith. Then the other. She held out my belt, and I took it as I stuffed my wallet and keys into my pockets.

"Come on," she said, and I didn't have a mom, not anymore, but I knew what mom-level disappointment sounded like.

Dad was waiting in the processing area. When he saw me, his face transformed. There was this lightning stroke of rage, and then it was just black clouds again as he clenched his jaw. He caught my upper arm and hauled me toward the door.

We drove south on I-15 in silence. The Ford was a lot more comfortable than the Dodge—new suspension, leather seats, good tires. The engine had that nice rumble. The clock said it was barely three in the afternoon, and outside, sunlight glittered on glass, tines of light raking the valley. We passed Point of the Mountain, and I tried to see if I could find the Grange up on the bluff, but I couldn't.

An hour of silence is a long hour.

When we got to the cottage, Dad parked under the carport, and we went inside. He turned, and I almost ran into him. He held out his hand.

I gave him the keys.

"Phone," he said.

I winced and gave him the phone.

"Wallet."

"What am I going to do, order a pizza—"

He slapped me. It caught me on the side of the head, and it wasn't hard; he'd cuffed me harder than that goofing around. But the shock of it made me rock sideways, raise a hand to my head, stare. Dad was shaking, his breath coming in huge gasps, tears running down his cheeks. He held out his hand again.

I gave him my wallet.

"Go to your room."

Which was hard, because he was taking up the tiny walkway that led between the living room furniture. I shuffled sideways, trying to get around the coffee table.

"They found you passed out on the floor," Dad said, and I thought maybe his teeth were chattering. "Passed out, Jack. In the office of a condo building that you broke into—"

"I was—"

"—after fucking around in a crime scene!" The swear more than the shout made me flinch and draw back. "After you lied to me! Again! After you disappeared! Again! For fuck's sake, Jack, we were attacked last night in our home! By a man who tried to kill you! And the next thing I know, you're gone. I thought someone had found you last night."

"There was something important—"

"I thought you'd been killed!" It wasn't a shout; it was a scream, tearing his throat on its way out. The last of the color had bled out of his face. "And you couldn't be bothered to answer your fucking phone!"

"I told you I was—"

"Stop talking!" He grabbed me by the shirt and hauled me up onto my toes and shook me. His face was a stranger's: pale, sweating, contorted. And then he let out a sound like a sob, and he shoved me away from him as he let me fall. He grabbed me again and yanked me across the living room, and then he shoved me toward the hall. When I stumbled, he came after me and shoved me again. My shoulder checked the wall, and I slid, and Dad shoved me again. I would have fallen, but he caught my shirt, dragged me upright and shoved me some more.

The next thing I knew, I was tumbling through the doorway to my room. I got tangled in a pair of joggers and went down and landed hard on my ass.

Dad filled the doorway. He was still trembling, and he clutched the doorway to keep himself upright. The tears glistened like brush marks on his cheeks. We'd used little brushes; Ms. Prinze had only ever let us use little ones. He opened his mouth like he was going to say something, and then he closed it again and slammed the door.

Chapter 29

The Morenos

I didn't sleep. I didn't know if that was called poetic justice or irony or the universe being a bitch; Dad had my phone, so I couldn't look it up. I stayed where I was, on the floor. My ear stung where he'd hit me, and my face got that sunburn-tingly feeling, and I put my arm over my eyes. But I didn't cry. I guess I was all cried out. I guess you run out eventually.

I needed a plan. All of this had started because I'd wanted to know the truth about Mom. Because someone—I still had no idea who—had sent me a message. And now I knew the truth: Blackfriar Holmes had killed my mom, had hurt my dad, had tried to kill me. On more than one occasion, it turned out. I'd had the evidence in my hands—not just the video, but physical evidence. Mom's necklace, with Blackfriar's fingerprints on it. I'd had everything I'd needed to get justice. And Holmes had betrayed me, taken it, and left me with nothing.

But every time I tried to come up with my next step, I hit a wall. What would I do? Show up at the Grange and demand that Holmes give me back the safe? The Holmeses were rich and powerful; they could laugh in my face, shut the door, and live the rest of their lives without being worried about me. Holmes had already shown where his loyalty lay. He had told me, over and over again, that I didn't understand his relationship with his father. He had warned me. He had tried to tell me.

I'd read about abuse after meeting Holmes. It wasn't something I'd thought about before I knew him. I mean, I knew it happened, and I knew it was bad, in that distant sort of way you know things are bad when that particular evil hasn't touched you yet. But after meeting him, after seeing him try not to bite his lip, after noticing that knobby knuckle on his left hand, after learning about Blackfriar—after all of that, I had started reading. And the thing about kids who were abused, according to Wikipedia, is that they blamed themselves. They found every possible reason to excuse their abuser. And part of me was so angry about that, angry with Holmes that he could be so stupid when he was so smart otherwise, angry that he couldn't see that he was doing what every other abused kid did, and that he didn't need to make excuses for a piece of shit like Blackfriar. But I touched my puffy ear, and it was hard to hold on to the anger because we all want our parents' love.

A crash came from the kitchen: several thuds, as well as glass breaking, and a heavy, familiar sound—Dad hitting the floor. I sat up. Silence. Then glass broke again, a smaller sound this time. More silence.

I crawled over to the door. My voice was clotted, rough when I called, "Dad?"

My blood pulsed in my ears.

I opened the door; at least the hinges didn't squeak. "Dad, I'm not coming out, but are you ok?"

The refrigerator clicked, and the compressor whirred.

I padded down the hall and stopped. Dad lay in front of the refrigerator, seizing. It was almost over; his body was relaxing again. But several broken bottles of beer lay on the floor, along with a can of chili that, thank God, he hadn't opened yet. He'd kicked over one of the stools when he'd fallen, and one foot was tangled in the rungs.

After putting Dad on his side and making sure he was breathing, I got his foot free and set the stool upright. I grabbed paper towels and threw some down on the beer and glass.

Dad mumbled, "Buddy?"

"Hey," I said, crouching next to him. "You're ok. You just seized is all."

His breathing was soft and slow. Finally, he said, "I wanted a beer."

"Yeah, I guess you kind of earned one."

His voice was a little clearer when he said, "No, I broke all the bottles. I wanted a beer. God damn it. What a fucking day."

That startled a laugh out of me, and a little crook of a smile tugged at the corner of Dad's mouth.

"Want to sit up?" I asked.

He started trying, so I helped him.

"Chair?" I asked.

Dad grunted, and together, we got him in his chair. I grabbed some towels, and put them around him, although he'd actually escaped most of the beer, and I didn't smell any pee, which meant maybe Dad was finally getting some wins. He sagged back against the seat, eyes closed, his breathing still deep and relaxed. I cleaned up the beer and glass, and I put the chili in a pot and started warming it on low.

"Need anything?" I asked.

Dad gave a miniscule shake of his head.

"I'll go back to my room."

A tiny nod.

I started to turn, but Dad held out one hand. He didn't open his eyes. He didn't say anything. He had calluses and thick fingers, a workman's hand. He was waiting.

I took his hand and wiped my eyes on my shoulder.

For a while, that was it. Dad sat there, breathing. He adjusted his hand around mine once, but he didn't squeeze or clutch or grip me. I cried harder and harder because it turned out, you can't run out. There are always more tears; that's one of the laws of the universe, I guess.

After a while, Dad started to shush me. His eyes came open a little, and he looked half-asleep.

"He killed her," I said through the tears. "Blackfriar. Mr. Holmes. He killed Mom."

Nothing changed in Dad's face. His eyes were still mostly closed. His breathing stayed smooth and regular. When he spoke, his voice was gentle. Firm, but gentle. "Tell me everything."

So, I did. All of it this time. I talked until I was hoarse, but I told him all of it: from the first time I'd found Blackfriar in our house, through the course of the investigation into Baca's murder, everything up to Watson's portable safe. When I finished describing the video and told him about Mom's necklace and Holmes's betrayal, Dad's hand tightened around mine once, crushingly tight. He released me almost at once, but his face showed the effort.

"I know I should have told you—"

"Yes, you should have." Dad was struggling to sit up. "But that ship has sailed."

"I didn't have any proof. We didn't know anything, not for certain."

"Jack, that's done. We'll talk about it later. Right now—" He grunted, straining to rise, and I got a hand around one arm and helped him to his feet. Once he was standing, he patted my hand, and I let him go. "Right now, we need to talk to Detective Rivera."

"Dad—"

"It'll be fine, Jack. I don't think there are criminal charges in it for you— well, let's hope nothing comes out of today, anyway."

"I'm not worried about criminal charges. Dad, you can't call Detective Rivera."

"We can trust him. You should have seen him at the jail; he went after those guys with his teeth when he thought they were going to hold on to you."

"It's not about trusting him." Dad had his phone out, and I put my hand over it. "Dad, stop. Detective Rivera can't do anything."

"He's a detective, Jack. Even if it's not his jurisdiction, he'll know who to call, who to talk to—"

"It's not that simple!"

"You're telling me there's proof that man killed your mother! I'd say it's pretty goddamn simple!"

We stared at each other, our shouts clashing like thunderheads. In the silence that came after, I realized, with a kind of distant discomfort, I was taller than my dad. I forced myself to level my voice. "The police can't do anything."

"This is America, Jack. If that man killed your mother—if he's killed all the people you think he has—then he's going to prison for the rest of his life. It doesn't matter how rich he is."

"The Holmeses and Moriartys get away with everything. Didn't you hear what I told you? This has been going on for—for generations. Rivera arrested Blackfriar today, yesterday, whenever it was, and Blackfriar walked away from it. Rivera can't do anything. The police can't do anything."

Dad set his jaw. I recognized the look on his face; I'd seen it on my own a time or two. "All right. Let's say you're right. Let's say he can buy his way out of this. What you're talking about, a video and a necklace, that's not going to prove he killed her. It puts him at the accident, Jack. That's all. Worst-case scenario, he gets a slap on the wrist for not helping someone in need—a Good Samaritan law. And that's if Utah even has something like that."

I scrubbed my eyes and nodded. I'd known that, sort of, in the back of my head. But hearing it out loud was different. It was a video of Blackfriar walking up to a car. Something glinted in his hand. It could have been a trick of the camera. It could have been anything. There would be a million stories for how his fingerprints came to be on Mom's necklace.

"Hey," Dad said, his voice softening. He put his phone away and rubbed my shoulder. "Hey, come on. We'll figure it out."

I shook my head. "I thought—I don't know, I thought if people saw that video, if they understood. He did it, Dad. I know he did it. He killed Mom, and he's going to walk away from it, the way he walks away from everything." I shut my mouth, but a moment later, I was speaking again. "I thought—" I thought I was special. That's what I wanted to say. I thought, because I was a Watson, because I had Holmes, the good guys would win. But that sounded like little kid stuff. I dried my eyes on my shoulder again and didn't finish.

Dad found my arm, squeezed it, looked me in the face until I finally shook my head and shrugged. "We're a country of law and order," he said. "We'll talk to Detective Rivera, and we'll start there. One way or another, Jack, we'll get that son of a bitch." He hesitated. "Jack, I don't know why Holloway did what he did—"

"Because he's been fucking brainwashed by his fucking psycho father!"

Dad waited in the wake of my words, the silence drawing out like a tide. I had to dry my eyes again. He squeezed my arm once more, ran his hand through my hair, and said, "Sit down. I want you to eat something."

I shook my head.

"When's the last time you ate?"

"I don't know. I ate a million mini-Reese's at a gas station."

For some reason that made Dad laugh, and he pressed me down onto the sofa. "Let's get some real food into you."

"I hate Reese's. I'm never eating Reese's again."

He riffled my hair again, ignoring my glower as I tried to fix it, and shuffled toward the kitchen.

"I'll get it," I said. "You should be resting."

"I'm going nice and slow. Lay back and close your eyes."

I thought about watching TV, but my eyes were itchy from all that crying, and closing them sounded good. From the kitchen came the clink and clank and clatter of Dad doctoring up the canned chili, his uncertain steps, the rattle of the compressor. As the chili warmed, the smell reached me: tomatoes and cumin and beef and other deliciousness. The rustle of plastic suggested this might be my lucky day, and we were having haystacks.

That was my last clear thought before an undertow pulled me down. In my dreams, Holmes was there. Holmes practicing that ridiculous smile. Holmes helping me up after I'd fallen while we'd been training. Holmes pressing my hands to his cheek, his face radiant, when he'd come to me the night before. When I'd thought I'd understood. When I'd believed what I'd wanted to believe, what he'd let me believe: that I mattered to him the way he mattered to me.

I woke to Dad thumbing tears from my cheek, his fingers scritching pleasantly through the hair above my ear. He made shushing noises and urged me to sit up. Sleep dragged at me. I wanted to sleep. Forever sounded like a reasonable amount of time, if it meant I could dream about Holmes in those moments when the lie had been perfect, when I'd known, in a way that seemed subatomic, coded into the physics of my existence, that we belonged to each other.

"You're going to feel better," Dad said as he wiped my cheek again. "He hurt you before, and you survived, and you're going to survive this."

I nodded.

He wrapped my hands around the bowl with my haystack: Fritos, then chili, then cheese. Heat seeped through the ceramic and warmed my fingers.

"I'm not hungry, Dad."

"I want you to take ten bites."

"Five," I said automatically.

His grin flashed out. "Nine."

"Six."

"Eight."

"Seven."

"Eight." I opened my mouth, and he said, "Eight, Jack."

I'd smashed half the bowl before I realized what he'd done. By that point, I was shocked to discover I felt partially human again; I wasn't sure when I'd last eaten a full meal, and although Dad had doctored the chili to mouth-blisteringly hot, that only made it better.

"I don't know what to do," I said as I picked out a Frito and ate it, and then I hit a couple of more spoonfuls of chili. The haystack was disappearing at an alarming rate. "I'm a Watson. I'm supposed to, I don't know, solve crimes. Or help solve them. But Dad, I don't have any freaking clue what to do next."

"You don't have to do anything, Jack." He sat on the arm of the recliner; it was one of the things he did when he was tired, the way he always was after seizing, but didn't want to let himself sleep yet. If he was going to force himself to get up and do something, when all he was supposed to do was sleep. "This isn't a story; this is real life, and you're a teenager, and you've done more than anyone could reasonably expect of you. We'll get the police involved, and we'll do everything we can to make sure he pays for what he did."

"How can you be so calm?" I mumbled. Exhaustion gathered itself again, pounced, bore me down. "He killed Mom. How can you sit there?"

"I'm not calm. I'm furious. But your mother is dead, and you're alive. My job is to keep you safe, Jack. That's what matters right now."

I opened my mouth to say something, but a yawn came out. The bowl slipped from my fingers and clattered to the floor. I was barely conscious enough to be grateful that somebody had finished the haystack.

A part of me was aware that something was wrong, and I tried to ask what was happening, but instead of a question, all I could manage was a soft noise.

Dad heaved himself up from the arm of the recliner. He combed his fingers through my hair, and past him, on the counter, I saw one of his prescription vials sitting out on the counter, next to the spices, where he'd been fixing the chili. That seemed important, like I needed to run a thread from point A to point B, but I couldn't do it, not with all that weight dragging me down.

Dad's voice was strange and hard and unfamiliar, at odds with the gentleness of his touch as he helped me stretch out on the couch. "I don't know anything about Holmeses and Moriartys, Jack. I don't know anything about Watsons. I wish your mom were here to tell you about that; if it meant something to her, she never told me. But I know this: you're not only a Watson. You're my son. You're Jack Moreno. And the Morenos don't run away from their problems."

Then sleep rushed in like the blackness between the stars, and I was gone.

Chapter 30

Watch Out, World

The sleep was deep and dreamless. Or, if there were dreams, they were the kind that crumbled into sand by morning, and it was a mercy not to remember them.

On the same trip to that old mining town where Dad had bought Mom's necklace, one of the "fun" "activities" (notice my generous use of quotes) I'd been required to participate in was taffy-pulling. In case you've never done it, it's exactly what it sounds like. You pull taffy. Forever. Or, at least, it feels like forever. And it's hot at first, and your hands are covered in oil, and you pull. And pull. And pull. The taffy resists, and then it loosens up, and every other pull it tries to slip out of your hands. But after a while, it's got a sheen to it, and they say it looks satiny. Which, I guess, it kind of does.

Which is a long way to say that waking up was a bitch.

I knew I needed to wake up. And I kept trying. But it was like pulling taffy: consciousness kept slipping away, and the harder I pulled, the looser and slipperier it became, and I'd fall back into nothing.

And then, one time, it worked, and I lay there, and everything had a soft sheen in the morning light.

My first thought was that I'd passed out on the couch. I'd fallen asleep on the couch enough times to recognize the signs: my head on a pillow, a blanket tucked around me, all Dad's work. He said I was too big for him to carry to bed now.

My second thought was that Dad would kill me if he saw me hungover like this.

It wasn't a regular hangover, with the headache and the need to vomit and the unrelenting determination that dying was the only solution. And it wasn't exactly the way I felt when I smoked too much, and I still hadn't come down properly, although it was closer to that. My body ached, and my head felt weirdly tight, like skin stretched across the mouth of a drum. My mouth was dry, which was weird, because some passerby had drooled a fuck-ton on the pillow while I was innocently sleeping.

I stumbled to the bathroom, peed, drank water from cupped hands, and pawed through the medicine cabinet until I found the Tylenol. Then I started the shower and sat under the water until I felt human enough to stand and clean myself up.

As my brain kicked into second gear, a few thoughts worked their way to the top. Bits and pieces of the day before began to come together. Snatches of the fight with Dad. His fall. The—

The chili.

"Motherfucker," I said and got a mouthful of shower spray.

Wiping my eyes, I rinsed off and dried myself.

He'd drugged me. My own father. I scowled in the mirror as I ran the towel over my chest. Bad enough to be treated like a kid in general, but to have him put me to sleep, literally, the way he and Mom joked about using cough syrup when I'd been little. He was as bad as—

Oh, I thought as one tired little synapse fired. Shit.

I forgot the towel and ran, buck-ass, toward the front of the cottage. Dad's keys were gone from the hook near the door. So were my keys; I vaguely remembered surrendering them after Dad had brought me home from jail. Dad's shoes were gone. There was a scrap of paper on the kitchen counter, but that could wait. I sprinted down the hall, the cottage's old boards thundering under my bare feet, and threw open Dad's door. His room was always neat. I dropped onto my knees, pulled out the gun safe, and knew. It was open. And the gun was gone.

"God damn it," I said and ran back to the kitchen.

The note had Dad's handwriting, and it was a single sentence: *Under no circumstances are you allowed to leave the cottage. Love, Dad.*

I stared at the note. Then I laid it on the counter again and put my head in my hands. He'd gone to take care of it himself. Of course he had. He'd as much as told me the night before. He was furious about Mom. He was determined to keep me safe. His last words, before the chemical haze had scrubbed away memory, came back to me: *The Morenos don't run away from their problems.*

And he'd bought a fucking gun.

The first thing to do was call Rivera, and I spent five minutes going through my room, throwing everything I owned in a hundred different directions, until I remembered I'd given up my phone last night too.

"You have got to be kidding me," I told the face in the mirror.

I took a few panicked breaths. Then I forced myself to take deeper ones. Ok, I thought. Ok. He's gone. He's gone to do something. And whatever it is, it's bad, because he doesn't know what he's going up against, not really, and because he's sick, and if he seizes or if he gets a migraine or if he stumbles because his balance still isn't a hundred percent, Blackfriar will destroy him.

For a moment, the panic actually seemed to stop my heart. I'd heard about panic attacks, about how they felt like a heart attack, how they felt like dying. I wasn't sure if this was one—maybe it was a baby one, or maybe it was only the Jack Moreno Special Edition Freak-out™. But whatever it was, I felt like my heart had locked up in my chest, and my lungs weren't working, and all I could do was sag against the desk and struggle to hold on.

When it was over and my body was mine again, my face got hot, and my eyes stung, and I dropped into the chair. But I didn't let myself cry. If I started crying, I might have another panic attack, and if I had another one, I might legit die. Even if I didn't, I wasn't any use to Dad like this. He needed me.

And that thought was a lifeline. He needed me, and I could help him. I had to help him.

I glanced down at my dangly bits. I had to help him. And I couldn't do it while I was free balling.

Jazz hoodie. Joggers. The Cortez because Mom had given them to me and I was going to kick some ass in her name today. The next step was to steal a car. I was pretty sure it was Monday. Or maybe it was Tuesday. It would have been nice to know, but I didn't have my phone. Either way, classes were in session, which meant a lot of staff would be in classroom buildings, and the staff housing would be mostly empty. I could take a custodial cart for cover, and I could get into any of the staff houses with a screwdriver—if anybody even bothered with the locks.

My plan worked, and ten minutes later, I was headed down the canyon in Ms. Albrecht's 2009 gray Hyundai Elantra, which had the incredible distinction of being so bland that it was practically invisible. I figured she'd understand it was an emergency. Or, if she didn't, I'd tell her it had to do with colonialism. She'd eat that up.

Dad might have taken my wallet, but the last year and change had taught me a few important lessons. The first was that you can never have enough cash, because you don't know what kind of emergency you're going to have, and bill collectors can't take your money if they can't find it. So, by the time I hit I-15, I'd made a stop, and I now had a burner phone with plenty of minutes.

I drove north and called Dad. When he didn't pick up, I left a message, asking him to call me back. I tried again, just in case, but he didn't pick up that call either. I left another message.

I tried Holmes next, with the same results. Big surprise. I left a message anyway.

My first thought was to drive straight to Reichenbach Grange. I had a good plan that went something like this: charge in there, and if anything gets in your way, plow through it. There was even something in there, a vague, half-formed vision, about kicking down a door.

But as the Elantra purred up I-15, reality started picking apart the Boy Genius's plan. If Dad had gone to the Grange, how was I going to reach him? I couldn't kick down a door—hell, I don't even know if I could have shot out a lock, and for that matter, I didn't have a gun. And what if Dad hadn't gone to the Grange? If I showed up at the Holmeses' mansion and charged in and Dad wasn't there, I'd have given myself away, and my only advantage—if it could be considered an advantage—was the element of surprise. Once that was gone, I had nothing.

On the other hand, the Grange was the only place where I did have a chance to rescue Dad. If Dad had gone to confront Blackfriar at Zodiac, I didn't have a shot. There were twelve buildings on the Zodiac campus, each of them big enough for hundreds of people, each with plenty of spots to hide Dad. And that's not to mention the Zodiac security team. Or what if Dad had gone somewhere else? What if he'd called Blackfriar, and they'd arranged a meeting?

The possibilities multiplied and branched, and frustration made my eyes tear up again. I tried, again, to bring myself back from the edge. Think, I told myself. Think. You're not a Holmes, and you're not a Moriarty, but you're not stupid either. You've done hard things before. The hard thing right now is to keep your shit together and help Dad, so think!

Maybe yelling at myself was genuinely a good motivational strategy. Maybe I needed to start using it for chemistry. Or maybe I was lucky, or bouncing along in the Elantra jarred something loose, or the universe decided to be merciful for once. Whatever the reason, an idea came to me.

Tom.

We'd found Tom's bag at Moriarty's house. He'd been there the night she died. Or someone had wanted us to think he'd been there the night she died. Either possibility raised some interesting prospects. And now that I knew Blackfriar had killed my mom, now that I had reason to believe that

Blackfriar had been killing Watsons for decades, a question crystallized in my head—something that had been bothering me since the night I met Tom Watson: why did Blackfriar put up with him?

Because now I knew that Blackfriar wasn't above murder. And I knew that Blackfriar wanted the Watsons dead. As Cecilia had shown me—painfully, irrefutably—the Watsons did make the Holmeses better. Not better detectives. Not better warriors. Better people. More human. More complex and intricate and fully realized and wonderful, the way all people become when their lives intertwine. Blackfriar didn't want that—not for himself, and most certainly not for his son. So, why had he allowed Tom to follow him around? Why, for that matter, had he allowed Tom to stay alive?

Because he had to. That was one answer. Or because he needed to. That was the other.

Either Blackfriar needed Tom for something, and his usefulness made Blackfriar willing to put up with a puppy dog Watson trailing him everywhere. Or, for some reason, Blackfriar couldn't get rid of Tom. And that made me think of another Watson who had tried to get leverage over the Holmes family. Holmes—my Holmes—had told me from the beginning that the Watsons were notorious for getting close to the Holmes, for learning their secrets, for profiting from the details of their lives.

What did Tom know that Blackfriar wanted to keep secret?

I didn't have any proof that Tom knew something. I didn't have anything but an inconsistency, the nagging certainty that Blackfriar's behavior was wrong, out of character, and that, therefore, some other force held him in check. There was a possibility, yes, that Tom was an instrument, and that Blackfriar was keeping him alive for some purpose. But I didn't think that was the case. Blackfriar was always trying to slip away from Tom, avoid him, escape. That was what had bothered me: the subtle imbalance of power between them.

And the next thought was logical, cool, controlled: if I knew that secret, I could make Blackfriar leave us alone. If he had Dad, he'd have to let him go. He wouldn't ever bother us again.

And a smaller, darker part of me thought, If I knew that secret, Holmes would have to come back to me.

I crushed that thought out and tried to focus. The next step was to find Tom. That night at Sundance, Noneley had said something to him about getting back to his hotel. So, which hotel? There were hundreds of them in Salt Lake. Even more if you extended the range to include Utah Valley or Park City or, say, Sundance. Needle, meet haystack.

But that wasn't quite true, was it? Because people picked the kind of places they wanted to stay based on a lot of factors, and some of those factors, you could predict. Before Mom died, when we'd traveled, Dad and Mom had gotten into—well, they weren't arguments, but they were definitely disagreements about where to stay when we went to Disney, when we went to watch the Dodgers play, when we went to that old mining town. Mom liked upscale. Mom liked boutique. Mom liked expensive. Dad liked anywhere you could accumulate (and then pay with) points.

What did I know about Tom Watson? Not much. But he'd glued himself to the Holmeses, and that said something about his character. And he'd done so by blackmailing Blackfriar (at least, that was my theory), and that said something about his stupidity. When I'd trapped him in the closet, he'd sounded hysterical, something about being laughed at. So, somebody who wants connection, somebody who wants attention, but, at the same time, is afraid of it. Somebody not too bright. Tom would want somewhere fancy, I figured. Especially if Blackfriar was footing the bill. Somewhere with a reputation—not a boutique. Tom would want the recognition, the name power. And he'd want somewhere big, somewhere with lots of room, because the other thing about Tom Watson was that sometimes he wanted to disappear.

I grabbed the burner phone and, after a few fumbling minutes, pulled off the highway and sat in the parking lot of an Olive Garden. I wish I could say it was because I'm safety conscious and all that, but the reality was that the phone was an Android, and I couldn't find the damn browser. Once I could give the phone my full attention, it wasn't hard, and I got a list of five-star hotels. I started by limiting my search to Salt Lake; Tom would want to be close to the action. With the list pulled up on my phone, I backed out of the parking stall. A cute girl in waitstaff black waited for me to pass. She must have been about to start her shift, maybe the early lunch crowd, and she looked at me long enough for it to be one of those kinds of looks, and I grinned, and she smiled back.

Jack Moreno, Sex God and Boy Genius. Watch out, world.

I hit the curb on the way out of the parking lot, but only because the Elantra was the size of a tuna can and didn't turn like the truck. I didn't look back in case the girl was still watching.

When I asked for Tom Watson's room at the Apollonia, I got a long hold, and then a regretful, "We have nobody registered here by that name, sir."

When I called the Hotel Monaco, I got a snippy guy who, I decided, had a raging case of hemorrhoids.

No Tom at the Hotel Monaco either

At the Grand America, though, I hit the jackpot.

"I'll put you through to his room, sir."

The phone rang and rang and rang and bounced back to the front desk.

I hung up, accelerated—well, in an Elantra, it's more like pedaling with your feet, Flintstones style—and headed for the Grand America.

Chapter 31

This Wasn't a Sherlock Holmes Story

The Grand America was a spear of pale stone against the spring sky. You could tell before you even got to the door the kind of place it was: perfectly trimmed boxwood (God knows it looked better than how the Walker boxwoods turned out when I did them); annuals popping with pinks and reds and blues; pavers for the driveway instead of poured concrete, with a long, covered loading and unloading zone at the front door. In case you missed all the other signs, the letters spelling out the name of the place were done in gold.

I drove around a couple of times and finally left the Elantra in what I figured—based on the number of tiny domestic sedans—was the staff lot. On a cement pad, a heavyset woman in a maroon uniform was smoking, while a second woman with Raggedy Ann hair talked loudly and picked at her nail polish. A bucket of sand was studded with cigarette butts, and a landscaping rock held a plain metal door open.

"—if he doesn't like a finger up there, fine, I told him, but a lot of guys do—" Raggedy Ann was saying.

The heavyset woman pulled her cigarette away long enough to give a derisive snort.

"—but there's no call blaming me," Raggedy Ann continued. "You ever seen when they unplug those inflatable things, the ones waving around at the car dealership? It was like that."

I jogged toward the door and gave them a casual smile, a little wave.

Their eyes followed me as I headed inside.

Behind me, the smoker said, "Did you try plugging him back in?"

That cracked both of them up.

I stood at the bottom of a stairwell. Another fire door, this one painted the same beige gray as the walls, opened easily and revealed a long service hallway. Nobody came to the Grand America to stay on the ground floor; I figured these had to be offices, along with the kitchen, storage rooms, that kind of thing. I started down the hallway, checking doors. The first was locked. The next opened onto a small room that held towels. Another met me with a blast of hot, humid air, the fragrance of seared meat, and a welter of voices. I glimpsed kitchen whites and let the door fall shut. It was nice to be right sometimes.

The problem with a fancy place like the Grand America was that they were all about making rich people happy—or, at least, making sure rich people didn't complain. I didn't think I could slip the front desk staff twenty bucks and get Tom's room number. I definitely couldn't get a key to Tom's room, not like that. What I'd probably get was arrested, and while it'd be nice to give Rivera another early Christmas present, spending the next few days in jail wouldn't do anything to help Dad.

A kernel of an idea took shape, and I moved more quickly down the hall. I checked doors, finding more custodial closets, an empty conference room, and what looked like a break room where a girl in a maroon uniform was bent over a microwave, watching something cook. Dad used to say that would make your eyes fall out, but I figured now might not be the time to tell her.

The first office I came to said SECURITY, and that one was locked. The next said EVENTS AND CATERING, and when it opened, a woman was speaking on the phone. She cut off, so I pulled the door shut, and before it had closed, she'd already started speaking again. The door marked MANAGER opened, and I risked a look.

Lights on. Computer on, but locked with a password. The smell of cheesy-dog farts, explained by the half-eaten cheesy dog lying in its foil wrapper on the desk. It was an office: desk, chairs, filing cabinets. Most importantly, phone. I stepped inside and shut the door.

When I picked up the phone, I made a gamble and pressed zero. A moment later, a chipper guy said, "Good morning, Mr. Valenzuela. How may I help you?"

I checked the clock; it was technically still morning, but only by a few minutes. That seemed impossible. "A young man named Tom Watson grabbed me in the hall a few minutes ago. He's locked out of his room, and he's having a meltdown because he says nobody at the front desk will help him."

The pause was one of those silent, frozen gulps that people everywhere have been making ever since asshole managers came into existence. "Mr. Valenzuela, I assure you, no one—"

"Get somebody up to his room and open it for him. Now."

"Yes, Mr. Valenzuela. Right away, Mr. Valenzuela."

"What room is he in?"

"2210, Mr. Valenzuela."

"I'm going to call him in five minutes and apologize for my front desk staff," I said, "so he'd better be in his room."

I dropped the phone back into place, cutting off the final, squawking, "Yes, Mr. Valenzuela."

As I took a step toward the door, it opened, and a man stepped into the room. He was about my height, his hair clearly dyed, and I pegged him for one of those European looking Latin guys. I was also fairly sure he was wearing shoulder pads in a suit that was already too big for him. He fixed me with a cold look and said, "This is a private office."

Time at Walker had been beneficial for a lot of reasons. Among them, it had exposed me to an entirely new altitude of teenage assholery.

"My dad said I could use it," I said, channeling my inner Walker boy. "Because I have to print my stupid homework, because I have to redo it because Ms. Parrish is a bitch because Britt and I only did half of it together."

Struggle played itself out in Mr. Valenzuela's face. I knew guys like him, guys like Mr. Taylor at Walker. On the one hand, this was his tiny kingdom, and he wanted to let me know who was in charge. It was why the chipper little front desk boy had sounded like he was about to pee his pants. On the other hand, I was a teenage boy wandering around his expensive hotel, claiming "Dad" had told me I could, and it wouldn't do to upset a paying guest.

"Let me show you to our business center," he finally managed to say, although he sounded like he choked on it a bit. So, he walked me to the business center, and he gave me this fixed smile like he had wooden teeth, and then he left. But not before saying, with a little edge to his voice, "In the future, for your own safety, please pay attention to signs that indicate areas meant only for our staff."

"That office sucked anyway," I said, jiggling a mouse, no longer looking at him. The Walker boy trick of being the center of the universe. "It smelled like farts."

Mr. Valenzuela stalked off, practically vibrating with pent-up rage, and I felt a little bad. Not for him, but for whoever was about to get their ass chewed.

As soon as he was gone, I crossed the lobby, which was all wood paneling and natural stone and thick rugs. Voices bounced back from the high ceiling as a party of rich—and clearly already drunk—white ladies tried to check in. A table centered in the middle of the room held a bouquet of flowers the size of a Smart car, filling the air with their perfume. The heavyset lady I'd seen smoking was behind a concierge desk now. She stared at me as I passed, so I gave her another smile.

I took the elevator up to the twenty-second floor. An anxious-looking white girl in a housekeeping uniform was waiting outside 2210, and as soon as she saw me, she used her key to open the door. "Sorry about that, Mr. Watson," she said. "We're really, really, really sorry for the inconvenience."

Ok, I felt bad about that too, but I was still in my Walker boy mode, so I stepped past her without saying anything and let the door fall shut. Her steps padded away on the thick carpet.

I leaned against the door, breathing deeply to slow my heart. It had been a gamble, coming up here like that. Tom might have been in the room. He might have raised hell. But it had worked. So far.

It wasn't technically a room; that was my first realization. It was a suite, and I stood in the living room / sitting area / whatever you wanted to call it, which had a couch and a coffee table and a TV, and a lot of hotel literature that looked like it'd never been read. The carpet was a green and gold arabesque, and the walls were the same green. Sea foam, I decided to call it. That's what I would have looked for in the paint store, anyway. The furniture was all cherry wood, the curtains were gold, the slider led out onto a balcony. All the pieces straddled nicely the divide between comfort and Grandmother's sofa you weren't allowed to sit on. The dominant smell was corn chips, but it had notes of wet towel and dirty laundry too.

The bouquet was explained in part by the trash covering the coffee table: empty bottles of wine, dirty glasses, cans of Coke and beer, bags of chips with their tops rolled closed, half-empty boxes of movie theater candy spilling Mike and Ikes and Butterfinger bites and those mini-Charleston Chews across the polished wood. I wasn't sure what it told me, aside from the fact that Tom's idea of living it up apparently included hitting the Dollar General. It was interesting nobody had cleaned it up. If he'd told housekeeping to stay out, that was even more interesting.

I moved into the bedroom. An enormous bed, with rumpled bedding pushed to the foot. The obligatory chair and desk. A dresser. Another TV. A door that led to the bathroom. The closet. The window here, like the one in the living room, looked out over the dusty gray-and-brown cityscape of Salt Lake.

I checked the closet first. It was stuffed with clothes, all of them looking new, some of them still with the tags on. Expensive stuff, too. No suitcase. Maybe at a fancy place like the Grand America, they were willing to store your suitcase somewhere else, but I thought maybe something else was happening here.

The dresser was next. More clothes. Every drawer, full of them. More shirts and pants. There was some casual stuff in there, jeans and tees, but much of it was button-ups and chinos. It reminded me of Holmes, a little. I didn't think that was a coincidence. He liked low-cut briefs, apparently. And he liked them in a lot of bright colors. Under all that fancy underwear, I found a box that said Speer Gold-Dot Personal Protection Short Barrel, and in the corner, 38 SPL +P, 135 GR. I knew enough to know it meant bullets, and when I opened the box, brass cartridges winked in the light. Not a full box, though. Some of them were missing.

I shut the box, slid the drawer closed, and checked the bathroom. On the counter, toiletries were laid out: new toothbrush, new floss, new razor, a bottle of shaving cream that was full when I checked. A few different lotions and creams that looked hella pricey. The good stuff was right out in plain sight: prescription vials of brown plastic, each one with scraps of paper and adhesive that suggested where labels had been torn off. I uncapped each vial in turn and took a quick look. Bennies, I figured, although that was strictly a guess. But maybe something more interesting. And with the labels torn off, which meant Tom was a bad boy.

I went back to the living room and found the fridge hidden inside a cherry wood console. I helped myself to a Dr. Pepper because the Cokes were all gone. There were some cans of Escape to Colorado, which was Epic's IPA. Joslyn had dated a guy who worked at the brewery, and a few times he'd brought their stuff to parties. I thought about that and still went with the soda. Mr. Responsible.

I sat. I drank Dr. Pepper. I picked at the Charleston Chews.

I had a problem. I had a bunch of problems, actually. One of those problems was this room, and what it told me about Tom. It gave me an outline of who Tom Watson was—maybe not the full picture, but enough. He was clumsy, awkward, uncomfortable in his own skin. I'd known that already because he tripped over his own feet. He was nervous, temperamental, high-strung. I'd known that too, the way he'd freaked when I'd locked him in the closet. He was dangerous. I didn't know that for a fact, but I knew my scary meter had gone off the charts when he'd started following me through the Grange.

And one of my problems was that the stuff in this room didn't line up with who I thought Tom Watson was. A med school student, he'd said. With his sun-streaked hair and his name and his clothes, I'd been sure he was like everybody else I seemed to meet these days: from a stable home, growing up comfortably (maybe even with wealth), and devoted to Blackfriar Holmes the way only a true Watson could be.

But what I saw here was somebody who had clearly come into a lot of money and didn't know what to do with it besides buy gas station snacks and shop for clothes at the mall and try to obliterate any evidence of who he'd been before. I mean come on, I thought as I popped some Mike and Ikes. He'd even gotten rid of the suitcase. So, one of my problems was that I didn't know who Tom Watson had been before, and that meant I didn't know who he was, not really.

On the other hand, all the evidence suggested I'd been right: Tom had some kind of hold over Blackfriar, and he was using it not only to stay close to the family, to glue himself to the Holmeses with a kind of frenetic determination, but to get money. And that was basically the real-life equivalent of grabbing the tiger by the tail, because how stupid did you have to be to try to blackmail Blackfriar Holmes. Better Watsons have tried before, I wanted to tell him.

My other problem—my bigger problem—was that I didn't even know what I was looking for. The problem was that this wasn't a Sherlock Holmes story. It wasn't as simple as sniffing corks or weighing cigar ash or knowing about a secret indigenous poison because you read about it in some weird British scientific journal. The Royal Society, my brain supplied a moment later. This was real life. With real people. And it wasn't about a clockwork puzzle of evidence and logic and reasoning. It was about all the stuff that made people people, the stuff that wasn't logical or rational, the stuff sometimes you didn't know, not even about yourself. The kind of stuff that explained why a boy could hate his father and fear him and know, beyond a shadow of a doubt, that his father was guilty of murder and worse, and still, at the same time, want his love and approval and affection. Even though a part of him knew he'd never get those things. Even though all the years were proof of it. It was about how a man could treat his only son the way Blackfriar treated Holmes. No, the problem wasn't evidence, although I still didn't know how we were going to prove Blackfriar had killed my mom and Lynnissa Baca and Moriarty. The problem was I didn't know what to do about Holmes, my Holmes. I didn't know how to help him. And without him, it didn't matter what I did; I'd already lost.

But that was a dark road to go down, and so I forced myself to concentrate. The problem, in other words, was that I didn't know what I was looking for, and I didn't know what good it would be if I found it.

By then, I'd finished the Dr. Pepper, so I did a jump shot, three points, and started searching the place for real. This time, I hit all the spots I would have used if I were trying to hide something. It was depressingly easy. I mean, I know I'm a boy genius and all, but Tom really needed to up his game.

My first score came with the dresser. I'd pulled out the drawers on one side, and in the hollow space at the back, someone—presumably Tom—had taped a plastic bag. I reached for it, had a brainstorm of Holmes losing his mind because, well, fingerprints, and hurried into the bathroom. The Grand America might have been a five-star hotel, but it didn't provide even a single pair of disposable plastic gloves. I'd have to let Mr. Valenzuela know, maybe by spamming their Google ratings page. In the meantime, I made do with the complimentary shower cap.

Back at the dresser, I drew out the plastic bag. On closer inspection, it was from Harmons, the kind they automatically use to bag your groceries unless you tell them not to. The top was tied shut in a granny knot, and I wiggled one end loose.

Inside lay a pair of disposable plastic gloves, exactly the kind that I was going to tell Mr. Valenzuela to start stocking. They looked like they'd been worn and pulled off—stretched and crumpled and turned halfway inside out—and a few dark hairs were caught on the nitrile. Parting the top of the bag, I leaned closer for a better look. I thought I could see fine granules of powder on the gloves as well. Lynnissa Baca had dark hair. And there had been something in her drink—something crushed up and added to the wine, leaving a residue on the glass. Maggie Moriarty had dark hair too, and her killer had used the same method.

Had Tom killed them? Or one of them? The idea was compelling; Tom certainly seemed capable of murder. This might be some kind of grotesque trophy. But while Tom seemed capable of killing to get people out of his way (namely, me), I didn't think he'd kill to impress Blackfriar. Blackfriar had plenty of people who would kill for him, and none of them walked into walls because they got flustered.

The other possibility was that I'd found the blackmail I was looking for. But that didn't seem quite right either. When Sarah had tried to blackmail Blackfriar, he had worked quickly and ruthlessly to find whatever material she had and destroy it. The only reason it had taken him as long as it had was because Holmes had interfered, hiding Sarah's laptop before Blackfriar could reach it. Tom hadn't hidden this blackmail material—if that's what it was—particularly well; it had taken me less than five minutes to find it. If Tom was holding this over Blackfriar's head, the only question was why he hadn't ended up in a shallow grave in the desert already.

I retied the plastic bag and set it near the bedroom door.

I made my next hit literally thirty seconds later: the book was between the mattress and the box spring. My first thought was that it was old, because it was a hardback and the cover was stained, and when I flipped through it, the type was cramped and, for lack of a better word, cheap looking. But then I decided it wasn't old. There wasn't any of the usual stuff you see at the beginning of a book, so I couldn't check the copyright date, but there was a kind of introduction. It was a genealogy of the Holmes family written by amateur historian Benjamin Baxter, who'd published it himself in 1997. A hundred copies had been printed. That's what the introductory note said. And out of those hundred copies, one of them had ended up here, hidden in Tom Watson's room.

I flipped through the book again. Genealogical charts and tables were interspersed with long—and I mean long—sections of text. Apparently, this guy had thought it important for everyone to know exactly how diligent he'd been in his research. It was the kind of thing that made you think there was a reason why, for a long time, people who wrote books were the same people who insisted it was a good thing to be a virgin.

A section of the book caught my eye, and I slowed. The pages were dogeared and worn. Dirt, specks of what might have been food and drink, smudged ink—these things all suggested that this portion of the book had been read and re-read and thumbed through time and again. It was near the end of the book, where the most recent generation of Holmeses was listed. I stopped at the chart with Blackfriar's name. He was listed as married to Cecilia Norton, with no children. Cousins from Blackfriar's generation appeared off to the side: Susan Holmes, Donagh Kennedy, Richard Holmes, Fairfax Holmes, Evelyn Ross, more. On several of the names, someone—perhaps Tom—had penciled in death dates. I turned back a page and immediately got lost in the web of relations, so I returned to the end of the Holmes family tree. Blackfriar and Cecilia.

Holmes had been born in October of 2004, and Noneley was only a few years older. The book had been published in 1997, so it didn't mean anything that the children weren't listed. They didn't exist in 1997.

Why had someone torn the pages from the Holmeses' copy of the book?

A sound made me turn.

Tom stood in the doorway that connected the bedroom and the living room. He held a revolver, and it was pointed at me. I shifted, and he made a warning noise.

"That's mine," he said. "Put it down, please."

It was only a .38; I knew that because I'd seen the box of cartridges under his fancy underwear. But the barrel of the gun looked like a tunnel from where I knelt on the floor. I laid the book on top of the bed.

Without breaking his gaze, Tom nudged the Harmons bag where I'd left it by the door. The plastic crinkled and rustled. "You've been busy."

"Did you kill Lynnissa Baca and Maggie Moriarty?"

Tom shook his head, and I couldn't tell if it was a no or if he was just trying to get that sun-streaked hair out of his eyes. He studied me. His hand flexed restlessly around the butt of the revolver, his finger snaking inside the trigger guard until he fumbled it out again. This was the same guy who couldn't cross a room without slipping on banana peels; all it would take was for him to flinch at the wrong time.

"Could you put that down?" I asked. "You're making me nervous."

"You think you're so much better than me."

I shook my head.

"You do. You think—" He shuddered, a convulsion working its way down his body in slow motion. I waited for the spasm that would depress the trigger. They called it trigger pull weight. They measured it in pounds. Another afternoon lost on Wikipedia after Dad bought that stupid gun. But then Tom steadied, seemed to gain control of himself. "You think you're special. But you don't understand: no one is special, and nothing changes. The Holmeses, the Moriartys, the Adlers, the Watsons."

"I don't think I'm better than you." Well, I did, a little, but only because I'd never held a gun on somebody. "Tom, did you kill them for Blackfriar? Because if he made you do it—"

"You're so stupid." He crowed a little laugh, and his smile was ugly and sneering. "Get up. It's time to go."

"Did Blackfriar kill them?"

"Get up."

"Did you follow him? Is that what happened? You're always following him. Did you watch him kill them?"

"Stand up!"

I got to my feet, hands in the air, but I stayed by the bed. "You never went to med school, did you?"

"Of course I did." Another of those twisting contortions clutched him, and the gun wavered. "Stop talking."

"You never had the chance, I bet. You wanted to go. You're definitely smart enough to go. You know a lot about taking care of people. You're good at it. You know what I think?"

"Stop talking."

"I think someone in your life got sick, and I think you stayed to take care of them. Because you're a good person. Instead of going off to college, you stayed and helped. And you learned all these important skills."

"Where is the bag? My bag. I want my bag."

"Did you drop it? Did Blackfriar startle you when you followed him to Maggie's, and you had to leave it?" He flinched, and I knew the answer. "Who was it, Tom? Who got sick? Your dad? Your mom?"

His breathing was high and labored.

"Your mom," I said softly.

"She ruined everything." He stopped, breathed shrilly, twitched. For a moment, the raw chaos underneath the mask appeared, and I wanted to step back, move away from what I saw in his face. And then he stitched himself back together again, and the look he turned on me was cold, dispassionate— a skin of ice over the madness roiling underneath. "She wouldn't be reasonable. She didn't want anything to do with the Holmeses, wouldn't even ask, wouldn't let me ask. And so I sat in that shitty house when she got sick. She wanted me to sell his bag, and I wouldn't, and she—she laughed at me. But I wouldn't sell it. Then we lost the house, so I sat in that shitty apartment. I waited for her to die, with her shots and her pills and her screaming. She wouldn't even pick up the phone. She would have rather lain there, pissing herself, always screaming." He put his free hand to his face, covering one eye while the other fluttered uncontrollably. "We have to—" He pressed down hard on his eyes. The gun trembled. "We have to go."

"You were smart, though," I said. "You've always been smart. You figured out something. Something that would make the Holmeses help you."

"I told her that's what the Watsons have always done, but she wouldn't listen. That's what we've always done. They pretend they don't like it, but they need us too. They want the world to know how special they are, and we're the ones who tell the world. It was the same, I told her; it was the exact same thing. We get close to them. We know them in a way nobody else does, that's what Watsons do. We see the human under—" He giggled, and he dropped his hand, but he looked blind, like he wasn't seeing me at all. "— under the deerstalker cap. And they hate it, that they're still human, and that we can sniff it out. But they need it too. Even when they don't know they need it. Mr. Holmes didn't even want to see me at first. He needed some…encouragement."

"What is it?" I asked softly. "What did you figure out?"

"We have to go," he said, and I could hear the effort in the words, the attempt at concentration as Tom tried to drag himself back together. "You shouldn't be talking—we have to go."

"What was it? What did you figure out?"

"Stop talking!" He fought against another of those ripples that contorted his body. Then, chest heaving, he dropped his hand to his side. "We're going. We're going right now. And don't—don't try anything. You wouldn't want your dad to get hurt. If you try anything, he's going to get hurt."

I stared at him. I pressed my hands against my thighs.

Tom gave me that sneering smile again. "You don't want that, do you? Come on."

"You're lying."

He laughed. Then he pulled out his phone, tapped the screen a few times, and held it out toward me. On the screen was a photo of Dad. He glared into the camera with a fuck-around look I'd never seen on his face before, but it was definitely Dad.

"You think you're so much better, but you're not, are you?"

I stared at the photo. The screen timed out.

"Are you?" Tom shouted.

I shook my head.

"Say it."

"I'm not better than you."

"You're not a Watson."

His pause was a prompt, so I said, "I'm not a Watson."

"You're—you're a stupid little kid."

It was, in its own way, easier to deal with this than to think about what was happening to Dad; Tom had me on the verge of rolling my eyes. "I'm a stupid little kid."

"Yeah," Tom whispered. "You are. So, don't try anything. Understand?"

I nodded.

That seemed to satisfy him. "Let's go."

Chapter 32

The Game Is Over

We went to the Grange, of course.

Tom was driving a black Bentley; apparently the Holmeses had a type. The gates opened as we approached, and then the mansion appeared, the mixture of stone and stucco, the raven's wing of the slate roof, the turret, the carriage house. Tom parked in front of the door, and the smell of fresh mulch and flowers met me when I got out of the car.

He herded me through the house, taking me down the maze of corridors that led to Blackfriar's study. When we reached the room, though, it was empty, and Tom chivvied me toward the French doors. We stepped onto the deck outside, and I understood why.

Blackfriar sat in a wicker chair, typing on a laptop. There was a whole patio set of wicker furniture arranged around a firepit where, even though the day was pleasantly warm, a low flame burned. Gas, not wood. And the firepit itself had decorative glass that glinted and sparkled. The valley spread out below us, and the air smelled like dust and open sky and the cedar boards underfoot. Then Blackfriar raised his head, the tarnished tin of his eyes settling on me, and I caught a whiff of fish oil.

"Hello, Jack."

"Where's my dad?"

"Have a seat."

"I want to see my dad."

Blackfriar sighed and set the laptop aside. "Sit down."

"Kidnapping," I said. "False imprisonment. Assault. Those three are freebies, just off the top of my head. Detective Rivera can come up with a lot more; he gets a boner thinking about all the stuff he likes to charge people with."

Shaking his head, Blackfriar stood. He waved Tom off as he approached me, and Tom retreated a few steps, the gun dipping. I set myself. Blackfriar's fancy shoes clipped the boards.

"Take a seat, Jack."

"If you hurt—"

The blow was like lightning. I'd been preparing myself for it. I'd been ready, or so I'd thought. But when it came, I didn't even see it. There was the sense of impact against the side of my head, and then a pain that I'd felt once before—a concussive wave inside my skull, like my eardrum had burst. The world tilted, and I found myself on the deck, propped up on my arms, trying not to be sick.

"I've told you politely several times," Blackfriar said as he grabbed my hair and began dragging me toward the patio furniture, "to have a seat."

I screamed and scrambled after him, but I was disoriented, my balance disrupted. Holmes had used that move on me before, and it did something to the inner ear. The best I could manage was a kind of quasi-coordinated tumble in Blackfriar's general direction. When we reached the seating, I screamed again as Blackfriar hauled me upright. I did my best to move with him, which probably saved my scalp, and a moment later, I found myself hurled into a chair.

"There," Blackfriar said as he returned to his seat. "Isn't that much more civilized?"

The world was still spinning: the sun seemed to move over the valley and then jerk itself back into place. I closed my eyes and counted to ten, and a wave of nausea passed. When I opened them again, Blackfriar's face was doing the same trick, drifting, ghosting, and then snapping back to its original position.

He smiled. "Hello, Jack. You have something that belongs to me."

My words sounded slurred when I finally said, "Where's my dad?"

For a moment, Blackfriar's smile froze. Then it widened. He let out a quiet laugh. "Do you know, Jack, I think I might understand it, what my son sees in you. A certain resilience. A certain bravura. It has its appeal. No common sense, of course, but that's to be expected with a Watson. If circumstances were different, I dare say I might even...approve."

Tom made a choked noise from the French doors.

"You're worried about your father," Blackfriar said.

My vision was steadying. The little flame hissed in the firepit. I could smell it now, the hint of gas floating underneath the fish oil stink.

Finally, I said, "Yes."

"Then you understand that I feel the same way, Jack. I am possessive. I do not like people touching my things. You have something of mine, and I want it back."

"Watson's safe."

"Where is it?"

"Don't have it."

"But I think you do, Jack. You separated from my son, which is unusual. You were arrested at Lynnissa Baca's condo, which raises further questions. Yes, I know about that. So, I believe you found Watson's safe."

"Nope."

Blackfriar bared his teeth. "Lying is a filthy habit."

"I want to see my dad."

"Jack, you're testing my patience."

"I want my dad."

Blackfriar sat back and let out a disappointed breath.

"I want my dad," I said again.

"I'll tell you what—"

"I want my dad right fucking now!"

He sat forward so quickly that I shot backward in my seat, but Blackfriar didn't stand. He reached down and picked up something. It was a wiffle bat—long, plastic, hollow. He held it up for display, and with one hand, he crimped the yellow plastic. I'd already known the bat was soft; we'd had a wiffle ball set in Salt Lake. I wriggled farther back in my seat.

"No, Jack," he said with another laugh. "Not you. When I hurt you, I will enjoy doing it with my own two hands. Let me ask you a question, Jack." He gave an easy swing of the wiffle bat, and it whistled as it carved the air. "How many times do you think I'll have to hit your father with this before his brain begins to bleed?"

My breathing was harsh in my ears, and then the wind picked up, and all I could hear was its scream.

"How many times," Blackfriar said, and he paused to give another of those lazy, smiling swings. "Before it begins to swell? The bleeding is bad enough, you understand, but when the brain begins to swell, that's the real problem. See, there's nowhere for the brain to go." He tapped himself lightly on the head with the bat and grinned like we were just goofing around. "The skull offers no flexibility. So, when the brain swells, what happens?"

I couldn't swallow. All I could do was follow the bat with my eyes as he gave another of those warm-up swings.

"Jack," he said softly. Then the yellow plastic was under my chin, pressing against my throat—threatening to make me choke and make me puke and make me suffocate, all at the same time. Blackfriar forced my head up. The tarnish of his eyes held mine.

"Pressure," I said and gagged as the bat dug into my throat. "It's called cerebral edema."

"Yes," Blackfriar said.

The pressure against my throat increased once more, and I gagged again. Then the bat was gone, and I leaned over the arm of the chair, heaving and trying not to let anything come up.

In a quiet voice, Blackfriar said, "Shall I let you watch, Jack? You can keep count."

I squeezed my eyes shut. Memories flickered in the dark, the jitter of an old projector, like the ones at the dollar theater. Mom with a Super Soaker, a summer night, the smell of the grill. Dad in the garage, oil on his hands, ignoring my bitching as he made me learn how to change the oil in the Dodge. Holmes. The stupid, ridiculous smile. The look on his face when he said my name.

I sat up. Found Blackfriar's face. And I said, "You hired Baca to steal the safe from Maggie. Why?"

"Why does one hire anyone to do anything, Jack?"

That was an answer, I decided. Of a kind. "You tried to frame H for Baca's murder."

"Tried to frame," Blackfriar said in disgust. "I needed to keep the two of you busy. And, of course, I hoped the police would tie you up, occupy your time. I should have realized that you deserved my full attention."

"That's why you told the security guards to hold on to us."

"And that went wonderfully as well, didn't it? Believe me, Jack, this streak of bad luck is unusual."

"You tried to kill me."

Nothing changed in his expression. Not even a flicker. "You'll have to be more specific."

"And you killed my mom."

For a moment, he went completely still. I'd seen that move on Holmes, the total blankness of body, meant to give nothing away. And then, carefully, Blackfriar laid down the bat.

"Yeah," I said. "I opened the safe. Bet that makes you fucking nuts, doesn't it?"

"Where is it?"

"Outsmarted by not one but two Watsons. Christ, does that chap your ass or what?"

"Where is it, Jack? I will not ask again."

"You killed her. I have proof, and you're going to prison. You're going to pay for what you did to my mom. To all the other people you've hurt." I wanted to say something about Holmes, but my vision got blurry, and my voice turned thick. "I know you think—"

"You know." The words were low and ferocious. "You know. What do you know? Nothing. You don't know anything, you stupid little boy. Just like your mother. Pretentious, presumptuous, arrogant. Nosy and meddling. Killed her? I stepped on her, the way you'd step on a bug. Do you know what it's like? Do you know what we've had to put up with? Generations of Watsons sniveling, moralizing, temporizing. A parade of mediocrity across lifetimes. Everywhere we go, a Watson is there interposing, interjecting, interfering. Even here. I was so sure I could finally escape. So sure that I had broken the chain. And then here she was, sticking her nose where it didn't belong, always so self-righteous."

"You killed my mom."

"Yes, Jack, I did. What are you going to do about it?"

"I'm going to destroy you."

He studied me for a moment. The sun caught the gray of his eyes and turned them to fire. Then he burst out laughing. "You misunderstand your situation. I'm willing to make you a deal: Return what is mine, and I will release your father."

I'd spent enough time around Holmes to hear the hook hidden in the proposal. "And what about me?"

Blackfriar sat back, out of the sun, extinguishing the fire in his face. He smiled. "You, Jack. When I'm finished with you, you'll go to jail. And when you leave jail, you'll go to prison. Breaking into the Zodiac offices. Breaking into Tom's hotel room. Assault with a deadly weapon. The list will go on and on. And then, Jack, there will be more…incidents. You've been a very bad boy; I have no doubt you will continue to be a bad boy, which means years will be tacked on to your sentence, and then more years, and then more. And if I choose to let you out, it will be when you are old and grey, and the world will have left you behind. That is the price of—" For a moment, fury twisted his voice like shrieking metal. "—touching my things."

An arrowhead of birds drifted across the sky. Pelicans. Their dark geometry marked their course—back to the Great Salt Lake, I guessed. They were late this year. Maybe they'd gotten lost. Maybe they'd forgotten, for a while, home.

When I brought my gaze back to Blackfriar, he was still smiling. I said, "You won't get away with this."

"Jack, I already have gotten away with it. This is the natural order of things, the way the world is meant to be: the supremacy of mind and will and excellence, without the shackles of bad conscience."

I thought of the way Holmes, my Holmes, moved through the world: an origami of light and purity and grace. I shook my head. I didn't want to put it into words, to tell Blackfriar how wrong he was, or what he had missed, or what he had hacked and slashed and burned in a sacrifice for power. I didn't know if I could put it into words, what it meant to touch the edge of something vast and wonderful like Holloway Holmes. And even if I could, it would have been wasted on him.

"Do you know," Blackfriar said, his lips peeling back to expose more teeth, "the video really doesn't do it justice. There's nothing quite like the experience, is there? I remember the little boy who ran away and left his parents to die. I remember the sound of his weeping. I've enjoyed that memory. Now here you are, and time has brought us full circle. I think I would like to see that terror on your face once more. Before I break you, Jack, shall I tell you what your mother looked like at the end? The noises she made before she died?"

I launched myself out of the seat and hurdled the firepit. A wave of heat rolled up from under me, and then I was clear, landing on the other side. As I came down, I threw the first punch. Hit hard, hit fast, hit first —

My fist caught air. I was still moving, carried forward by my own momentum, and the resistance I'd expected didn't come. Blackfriar was gone, a ghost, and then a blow caught me in the solar plexus. A second blow caught me on the back — a hot line that ran from shoulder to shoulder. I crashed into Blackfriar's now empty chair, and it flipped, spilling me onto the deck. I rolled and tried to come up, but weight landed on my back, a knee pressing between my shoulder blades.

"I got him," Tom said, and I wanted to groan. "I got him, Mr. Holmes!"

"I tripped over a chair, dumbass," I wheezed, face pressed into the boards. "You didn't get anything."

Blackfriar laughed softly. Then something hard dug into my cheek. I rolled my eyes, trying to see. The slender, polished length of a cane ran up to Blackfriar's hand. He leaned on the wood, and the ferrule bit into my flesh. I had a mental flash: the metal tip going through my cheek, breaking teeth, spearing my tongue. Panic rose like static.

Maybe that was why I didn't hear footsteps. Maybe that was why I didn't hear anything until Blackfriar let out a frustrated breath.

Then, behind me, Holmes said, "Enough, Father. The game is over."

Chapter 33

Miscalculated

Nobody moved. Tom's weight still bore me down against the deck. Blackfriar dug the cane's ferrule into my cheek. I couldn't turn my head. I could barely breathe.

"This no longer concerns you," Blackfriar said. "Leave, now, and you will not be punished."

The silence was the kind that came after thunder, when you knew it hadn't finished, maybe it was only getting started. Tom's breathing had turned shaky, and part of me didn't blame him. I felt it too, the energy charging the air until the hair on my arms wanted to stand up.

"The game is over," Holmes said again. And then, after another of those vibrating silences, "I am sorry, Father."

"I will not tell you again."

Holmes sighed. "Tom, to the extent that it is still possible for you to avoid criminal charges, I suggest you remove yourself. You may also wish to prepare an explanation of your behavior over the last few weeks and, at the earliest opportunity, contact an attorney for your defense."

Tom shifted.

"Stay where you are," Blackfriar snapped. His voice had lost its control, and the edges were frayed and snarled now. When he spoke again, some of the smoothness came back, but not all of it. "You've made a gambit, my son. A poor one, one that will not succeed, but nonetheless, I am impressed. I told you once that we had found something to inspire you; it seems I was correct that by appearing to threaten this boy —"

"Please," Holmes said, and the word was so gentle that it broke something inside me. "Please," he said again, "do not do this. Do not make this harder than it must be."

Blackfriar's silence was a black hole.

Holmes let out another of those long, slow breaths. "The police have been contacted. They have evidence that you were involved in the death of Camilla Catherine Sixsmith."

Barking a laugh, Blackfriar twisted the cane, and the ferrule sliced open my cheek. Blood, hot and stinking, ran down the side of my face. "Is that all? The video? Good God, Holloway, this wasn't a gambit. This was a suicide run. What were you thinking?"

"Not only the video, Father. The necklace. With your fingerprints. The one you took from her the night you killed her."

"Nonsense. She was a family friend; she'd shown me the necklace on a number of occasions, and at various times I'd handled it. Of course my fingerprints would appear on it. My behavior on the video is strange only because I was in shock. I intended to contact the authorities as soon as I regained control of myself."

The words had a rote, mechanical quality that sent up a chill up my spine. I could hear him saying them in court. I could hear how he'd make them sound—sad and confused and believable. He was right; in all likelihood, it wouldn't ever make it to court. Maybe there'd be some buzz, maybe some bad press. Maybe he'd step out of the limelight for a while. And my mom would still be dead, and Blackfriar would be free.

For a moment, the injustice of it overwhelmed me. Sarah Watson had died for what was in that safe. Lynnissa Baca had died for it. Maggie Moriarty had died for it. And their deaths meant nothing. Blackfriar would use their bodies like steppingstones without a second thought.

"Perhaps," Holmes said. "But I think the prosecutors will be less inclined to believe your version of events, especially after you're convicted of two other homicides."

A beat. Then, the single word crisp: "Explain."

"You didn't know? Your pet Watson has been keeping secrets, Father. The powder will, I'm sure, match the opioids that killed Lynnissa Baca and Maggie. And the hair will confirm the link to at least one victim. But it's the DNA evidence on the inside of the gloves, Father, that will put you in prison for the rest of your life. You ought to have burned them, rather than taking them with you. But then, you always favored—what did you call it? Bravura?"

Blackfriar's gaze settled on Tom, and Tom shrank back. "I didn't—I was trying to—" In a squeaking cry, he finished, "Someone might have found them!"

"Perhaps this will only make things worse, Father," Holmes said in that cool, crystalline voice. "But Jack was the one to find the gloves. I simply recovered them and turned them over to the police. I thought you should know. I imagine he thought sending that photo to the sheriff's department would incentivize you."

For a long moment, Blackfriar was still. Then he exhaled, a long, hissing breath.

"Mr. Holmes," Tom babbled, "I never would have—"

The ferrule left my cheek, and Blackfriar gave a vicious swipe. Tom screamed and fell back, and I took advantage of the opportunity to roll out from under him. I caught a glimpse of Tom with a hand pressed to his face, blood running down his cheek, and then movement pulled my attention back to Blackfriar. The cane whipped down at me.

And then Holmes was there, turning the blow aside. The ferrule cut into the cedar boards of the deck, scoring a line across them. I scrambled backward, trying to get to my feet, and that damn chair caught me again. I tried to shake myself free as the two Holmeses faced off.

I still don't know who moved first, but Holmes flowed like silk, and Blackfriar's cane whipped empty air. For a moment, shock covered Blackfriar's face. And then Holmes caught him with a heel strike, and the crack of Blackfriar's nose breaking was the sound of storm clouds opening. He stumbled back, staring at Holmes, his face white behind rivulets of blood. For a moment came fury, the rage of a star being born. And then all that fire went into the machine, and he attacked with a kind of clockwork madness.

I'd finally managed to defeat my only real attacker so far, the chair, and was about to help Holmes—I had big plans of kicking Blackfriar in the knee and, if I were lucky, crippling him for life—when Tom body-slammed me. We both went down and hit the deck hard. I rolled, trying to get free, but Tom clung to me. He whaled at my face and head, using his fists like clubs, and when I tried to crawl away, he clawed at me and dragged me back. In the first, frenzied moments of the fight, all I could do was be an animal, and let the animal instincts take over, telling me to cover my face, draw my legs up, protect eyes and organs.

But then a different part of me woke up. I wasn't an animal. I was Jack Moreno, and I was a Watson, and Holloway Holmes had trained me. Well, he'd tried to, anyway. We'd never covered assault by patio furniture, but I had the basics down. Kind of.

Tom's attack was wild and uncoordinated, and when the opening came, I took it. He reared back, trying to get more leverage as he hammered at me with his fists, and I bucked him. He toppled sideways, giving me room to get my legs free, and I kneed him in the chest. I kicked him again, and he moaned and rolled away from me, and I started getting to my feet. I had a glimpse of Holmes and Blackfriar, the blur of movements, the grunt of blows that connected, the whistle of air. Holmes's injured arm hung at his side, and blood stained the sleeve of his white oxford.

Looking was a distraction, and it cost me. Tom sprang at me again, and I barely caught the motion in time. I avoided a blow to the head, but he still bore me back down to the boards of the deck. We thrashed together, sending patio furniture skittering away from us. Something heavy clunked as we knocked over a table—Blackfriar's laptop, I realized. And then my back connected with something hard, and the faint smell of gas reached me, and my brain decoded this as the firepit.

That thought lasted only a second before Tom got hold of my hair and slammed my head against the stones of the firepit.

The world scrambled. When I came back to myself, Tom was standing over me, dragging me up by the hair. The heat of the flame pressed against the side of my face.

"You ruined everything!" Tom was screaming into my face. "You ruined everything! It was all going to be fine, and you had to ruin everything!"

He forced my head toward the flame, and the heat became pain. The smell of burning hair came to me, and I screamed as the fire burned me. I kicked at Tom's legs, beat at his hands, clawed at his fingers. I could smell my skin blistering, and I was still screaming. Maybe it was training. Maybe it was panic. I don't know, and Holmes has never asked, so I'm going to give myself the benefit of the doubt. Whatever it was, I caught hold of Tom's pinky and snapped it.

Now he was the one who screamed.

He released me for a moment, and his face was more outrage than pain—disbelief that I would dare to hurt him. I lunged away from him, trying to escape, but he grabbed me with his good hand, dragging me back toward the fire. I cast about for something, anything.

And saw the laptop.

With its matte aluminum case.

With its glorious fourteen inches and four and a half pounds.

My fingers were greasy with sweat and fear, and they slipped along the metal. But I caught it, and I brought it up and around in a long arc as Tom screamed and pulled me toward the flame.

The corner of the laptop caught him above the ear. The force of the blow tore the laptop from my hand, and distantly, it clattered to the deck. Tom's eyes went blank, and he wobbled and fell into the fire.

I scrambled to my feet, kicking Tom free of the flame. He lay unmoving. Dead, maybe. I wasn't sure. Panic clutched me, and I couldn't spare time to check.

During my scuffle with Tom, the tide of the battle had clearly turned. Holmes was favoring his side again, and his movements were slow and disjointed, telegraphed so that even I could read them. Blackfriar's face was a mess of gore, and the way he moved suggested that Holmes had damaged his hip or leg, but it was clear that he had the upper hand. Holmes spun out a flurry of blows, and Blackfriar sidestepped them without even appearing to try, and the cane cracked across Holmes's back hard enough to open a weal—I knew because a ribbon of blood unscrolled across the oxford, low, just above his waist.

I moved, trying to circle behind Blackfriar, but he angled himself to keep both Holmes and me in his view. Holmes was breathing hard, sagging against the deck railing, and I didn't think he could raise his injured arm. For a moment, none of us moved.

"You lost," I told Blackfriar. "Let us go, and you can try to run."

"Lost?" Blackfriar said, and he smiled blood at me. "We haven't even finished playing."

Holmes pushed himself from the rail, wavered, and fell back. Exhaustion hollowed out his features, and he looked gray with it. His heart, I thought. The doctors were worried about his heart.

"We're leaving," I tried again. "H, come on. We're going right now."

He gave a tiny, weary shake of his head.

"H!"

"No, Jack." He set his jaw, and with that same tremendous power of will I'd seen from him before, he forced himself away from the rail and stood. "He must be stopped."

"Yes, Holloway," Blackfriar said. "Stop me. Show me that my time and effort in correcting you have not been in vain."

Holmes struck like a viper, faster than I believed possible, but somehow Blackfriar dodged. He slapped Holmes, an easy, openhanded blow that sent Holmes reeling back against the rail again.

I took a step, and then I retreated as the cane sliced the air where my face had been. "H, don't do this. This is what he wants. You're giving him what he wants."

All I got was another stubborn, dazed shake of the head. He stumbled—lumbered was a better word, shaggy, enervated movements— and swiped at Blackfriar. Blackfriar leaned back, and this time, he delivered two slaps. Holmes's cheeks were red as he fell back again. He was biting his lip, and he looked so young. And lost. He looked lost.

"Pathetic," Blackfriar said. "I taught you better than this."

"H, stop! You're giving him what he wants—this is what he wants." I didn't know why he wanted it, but I knew it—could read it in Blackfriar's face, in the mixture of pleasure and satisfaction and amusement that limned his features. "He's never going to love you."

Tom moaned and stirred, and I inched toward him, but I kept my gaze on Holmes. His face was bloodless, his eyes unfocused, his whole body shaking with the effort of staying upright. And for a moment, pain twisted his face. Pain that I had caused.

The words kept coming. "He's never going to respect you. He's never going to give you what you want, what you deserve, but he'll let you think that he might. He'll show you the possibility. Because that's how he gets what he wants. That's how he controls you."

Fury lit coals in Blackfriar's cheeks. He took a step toward Holmes and barked, "This is the kind of friend you've chosen. Do you hear him? Do you hear him presume to speak about you as if he knew you? Do you hear him dare to speak as if he understood you?"

With another of those muzzy noises, Tom rolled onto his side. I forced him face down and pinned him to the deck, never taking my gaze away from the Holmeses.

"He is my friend," Holmes murmured.

"He is nothing," Blackfriar said. "And you—you are a fool. You are a failure. You are weak. And you are a disgrace to our house. To think that I called you my son."

Tom squawked a half-conscious laugh.

And everything tumbled into place. The photo in the study. The hair samples in the safe. The genealogical book that Tom had pored over, and the death dates that he'd penciled in. The secret he'd held over Blackfriar Holmes's head. What I'd been asking myself since I met Blackfriar. The way Blackfriar had said, *No son of mine.*

For a moment, the enormity of it staggered me. All I could do was watch as Blackfriar stepped forward, as he closed the distance with Holmes, as he said, "Ask me for my forgiveness." Holmes bit his lip, and Blackfriar made a disgusted sound. Seizing Holmes by the jaw, fingers biting into Holmes's flesh so hard that they left white marks in the already pale skin, Blackfriar said, "I thought we had broken you of that. Perhaps a reminder is in order."

It might kill him, a small voice in my head told me. If you tell him, it might destroy him.

But no one had told him the truth, not once, in his whole life. It had always been games and tricks and webs of deceit.

"He's not your dad."

The wind picked up. The pelicans moved like charcoal over the clean canvas of the sky. Holmes went still in Blackfriar's grip, and Blackfriar's body coiled like a spring.

When the wind died, I said, "Blackfriar. He's not your father. Not your biological one."

"He's lying—" Blackfriar began.

"You don't look alike," I said. "Your hair, your face. Maybe your eyes, but even those aren't quite the same. And you don't act the same. You move the same, but that's because he's trained you. And he's never once been kind to you, H. I kept wondering—everyone kept wondering—how he could treat you like that, how he could do those things to his own son. But that's the point: he didn't."

Holmes looked at me, and I saw the light go out of his eyes. Because he knew. Or he believed me, and it was the same thing. He looked smaller, like something vital had been bled from him and left less.

"That's what Sarah figured out," I said. "The hair samples in the safe. They weren't so she could frame the Holmeses and blackmail them. She did a paternity test. Tom figured it out too; he had that genealogy book, and something in there must have tipped him off. That's what he was using to get close to your family. That's the secret he was holding over Blackfriar's head. When I found the gloves at the hotel, I thought maybe that's how he was blackmailing him, but that didn't make sense, because Tom had already gotten a hold over Blackfriar before he killed Baca."

"This is ridiculous," Blackfriar said.

In one smooth movement, Holmes broke Blackfriar's hold. Livid impressions rose on his jawline where Blackfriar's fingers had bit in. Holmes flung Blackfriar's hand away and, his voice thick and posh, said, "You are never to touch me again."

For a moment, rage ran through Blackfriar's face: mindless, sweeping, untrammeled. It was like a forest fire in thick woods that were old and overgrown, where the blaze burns out of control. Reason and control ashed away, and what remained was a kind of insane fury.

His voice was frayed, slipping out of his control as he said, "Perhaps it is better this way. You were always a tremendous disappointment."

The knife appeared in his hand like magic, and he drove the blade toward Holmes's side. Holmes pivoted, but the attack had been a feint, and Blackfriar had already changed direction. He buried the knife in Holmes's chest.

Shock wiped Holmes's features clean. He wobbled from the force of the blow. His eyes roved, as though he were searching, and he found me.

"H," I said. And then, "H!"

A grin pulled savagely at the corner of Blackfriar's mouth as he released the blade. He turned, already dismissing Holmes from his reality, and looked at me. "Now, Jack. Let's play a game."

"No more games," Holmes choked. And then Holmes grabbed him by the collar.

Blackfriar startled, and as the collar pulled tight around his throat, he choked. Holmes set himself against the rail. The knife still stuck out of his chest. Why isn't he bleeding, a part of me thought. And then another part of me saw the way he had tensed himself, the last strength of his body summoned by that indomitable will, and I thought, No, please no. I screamed it. "No!"

Holmes pushed off with his feet, and he made the move look graceful as he rolled over the railing and fell. His grip was like iron, and he pulled Blackfriar with him. For a moment, they were a blur of movement, tumbling out of sight, and then they were gone.

I sprinted toward the rail, unable to stop myself.

And then I saw it, the hand I knew, the hand I had held, Holmes's impossibly strong hand, wrapped around the base of one of the balusters. His knuckles were blanched from the force of his grip.

I grabbed his wrist, muscle and tendons tight and warm under my hand, and I felt, rather than heard, the relief that rolled through him.

Then, voice still shaded with posh, he said, "I have miscalculated, Jack. Blackfriar is holding on to my leg. I shall need you to help me back up."

Chapter 34

I Want to See H

The police came. The ambulances. More police. Rivera and Yazzie, of course.

But not right away. Between the two of us, Holmes and I managed to get both him and Blackfriar back onto the deck. I borrowed Tom's gun, since he didn't need it anymore, and that went a long way toward keeping Blackfriar under control until Holmes could cuff him to a baluster. Baritsu was all well and good, and yes, frankly, it was fucking terrifying, but a lot of terrifying things are less terrifying from behind a .38.

Holmes warded off my attempts to, you know, get the knife out of his chest and perform lifesaving first aid.

"A covert stab vest, Jack," he finally said, and he indicated the outline, barely visible under his clothes. Then he winced. His bloody arm still hung to one side, but with the good one, he probed at the laceration on his back. "Although this model did not cover me sufficiently."

After that, he didn't want to talk, which was good, because I didn't have any idea what to say.

The responding officers didn't have any better ideas than putting us all in cuffs, which didn't seem particularly fair, but at least they ignored Blackfriar's commands that they free him immediately. As higher-ups responded, and responsibility ran up the paygrade, the situation stabilized, and eventually, they took all of us to the hospital.

Since there wasn't anything seriously wrong with me, once I'd had the burns and cut tended to, I got to sit in an ER cubicle while a bored uniformed officer from the Draper police scrolled on his phone. I thought that was a great idea, but they'd taken away my burner, along with everything else, so all I could do was lie there. They had some medical pamphlets on the countertop against the wall, but I decided to pass on *Leaking? Burning? What to Know about Your Discharge.*

Some super-spy must have flooded the hospital with sleeping gas or something because the next thing I knew, someone was shaking me awake. I decided it was probably the superspy, and I figured whoever they were, they were doing all right without me, and I could probably sleep for a couple of years. Then somebody like Rivera said, "Stop faking."

"Oh," I said and opened my eyes. "Hey."

He was back in the same cheap gray suit, or a clone of it, and he was rubbing his cauliflower ear. "What did I ever do to you?"

"Hi, Rivera."

"I've always been fair. I've stuck my neck out for you."

"I missed you."

His jaw sagged.

"Did you miss me?" I asked.

"Perfect," Yazzie said from the doorway. She was cleaning her glasses. "We're in a hospital, so they can treat the stroke right away."

After Rivera recovered, he and Yazzie interviewed me. It was an interesting technique. It mostly consisted of Yazzie asking questions and Rivera shouting, "You could have been killed, dumbass." Sometimes he changed it up. Sometimes he asked me if I was stupid, or how stupid I was, or if I knew how stupid that particular decision had been. It was a surprisingly effective technique; I told them everything.

At some point during the interview, Dad came into the cubicle, and I stopped talking so I could half-fall off the exam table and crash into him. He staggered back, and we got tangled in the privacy curtain. The curtain rings shimmied and chimed along the rod, and Dad grunted and laughed and squeezed me back, and Yazzie had to help both of us before we fell and took the curtain with us.

"Where were you?" I asked, questions spilling out faster than Dad could answer them. "What happened? Did he hurt you?"

And at the same time, Dad was asking, "Are you ok? What happened? Why didn't you stay in the cottage?"

The short version seemed to be that Dad was fine, albeit embarrassed about having to explain how he'd shown up at the Grange, immediately been disarmed and taken hostage, and then rescued hours later by police. I did my own quick recap, and I tried to ignore the fear and worry in Dad's eyes.

Dad sat while we finished the interview, but it didn't take much longer.

"Was Holloway telling the truth?" I asked. "Did he really turn over all that evidence to the police?"

Yazzie nodded.

"That's good, right? That means you've got everything you need to charge him with murder."

Rivera rubbed his eyes. Yazzie looked away.

"What?" I asked.

"Jack," Rivera said.

"You've got to be shitting me," I said. Ok, maybe a little louder than normal, because a nurse pulled back the curtain and raised his eyebrows.

Dad waved the nurse off, drew the curtain shut, and said, "Jack."

"Ok, fine," I said in a lower voice, "but you've got to be shitting me. He's going to walk?"

"Nobody said he's going to walk," Rivera said. He dropped his hands. His eyes were bloodshot. "Jack, the gloves, the hair, the powder—that's solid stuff. They've got amazing stuff now, and they did the preliminary tests, I'm talking ninety minutes to get an answer, and they rushed them through. It's Blackfriar's DNA on the inside of the gloves. And the hair belonged to Lynnissa Baca. So, we'll nail him on that."

"Especially since that boy is about to flip," Yazzie said, and I figured she meant Tom.

"What about Maggie?"

"That's a problem," Rivera said. "We need to coordinate with Park City, or whoever's handling it. There's no record of emergency services responding to a call to the location you described. No record of Margaret Moriarty being found—dead or alive. As far as anyone official is concerned, she's still in the air."

I tried to think about what to say to that, but I kept seeing, in my head, the driver of the ambulance we had passed. He had looked familiar; that's what I'd thought at the time. But from where?

"That doesn't necessarily mean anything," Rivera continued. "If Tom flips—and I think Yazzie's right; he's on the edge already—he might be able to give us Blackfriar for that one too."

"Ok, so what's the problem?" I said. And then it hit me, and I said, "Are you serious? He killed my mom."

"Jack," Dad said softly.

"You've got to be fucking kidding me."

"Hey," Dad said, a little louder this time. "Knock it off."

"He killed her. You've got it on video, and what? You're not going to do anything."

"Of course we're going to do something," Rivera snapped.

"It's complicated," Yazzie said. "The video doesn't show the accident itself. We don't know who that man is, the one accompanying Blackfriar."

"He's the same guy who tried to kill me in December. He's the same fucking guy!"

"Yeah?" Rivera asked. "Do you have a name? An address? How about a Social Security number?"

"Fuck you! What the fuck do you think your job is?"

"Jack!" Dad barked.

"You've got his fingerprints on her necklace. You can see him in the video. You can see he took something; you can see he's carrying it."

"Nothing is final yet," Yazzie said, "but we already know the prosecutor won't bring anything against the Holmes family that isn't airtight. The accident happened almost two years ago, Jack. And there's just not enough."

My face felt tingly and numb and puffy all at the same time. I lay back on the exam table and closed my eyes.

"Yet," Rivera said. "There's not enough yet."

I knew he was trying, so I nodded.

They talked quietly to Dad for a couple of minutes. Then they left.

A chair squeaked as it was pulled across the linoleum, and then Dad breathed out as he lowered himself to sit. After a few seconds, he rubbed my leg.

I shook my head and screwed my eyes shut tighter.

"It's ok, buddy. You did good. You did so good. Your mom would be so proud of you."

I shook my head again and put my hands over my face.

"Hey," Dad said. "Hey, come on. We know, and that's something. And Detective Rivera and Detective Yazzie know, and they're going to work on it. And he's going to prison, Jack. He'll spend the rest of his life there. It doesn't matter why."

But I didn't say anything to that because we both knew it wasn't true.

Finally, I sat up. "I want to see H."

Dad looked at some spot in the middle distance. His hand paused on my leg, and then, after a moment, resumed rubbing my shin again.

"What?" I asked.

"Buddy."

"Is he ok?"

"He's fine."

"Are you sure? Did you talk to his doctor? Because sometimes H acts like everything's ok, and then you find out he's been shot with a dart full of ketamine or he tore his stitches open or—" I slid across the exam table, the paper rustling underneath me. "If he's asleep, I won't wake him—"

"Buddy, he doesn't want to see you." Dad seemed to hear that, how it sounded, and he said quickly, "I mean, he asked them not to let you into his room. He—he wants some privacy right now."

But I hurt him. Those were the first words that came to my head, mile high and neon. But I told him the worst thing in the world. I ripped the foundation of his universe out from under him. And I had to do it, and I want him to know that I only did it because I had to, but that doesn't change how much it hurt him, or that I was the one to do it. And I need to know he's ok.

What came out was, "But I need to see him."

"I know, buddy. He's ok. We'll see him tomorrow, when he's feeling better."

I couldn't help myself. The tears came faster than I could blink them away.

Dad shushed me. He rubbed the small of my back.

It was everything: physical and emotional and mental exhaustion, and the backwash that came after all the adrenaline had poured out of me, and the disappointment of learning that Blackfriar would skate on Mom's murder—and the murder of God only knew how many other Watsons. But most of all it was this. The knowledge that I had hurt Holmes so badly that he didn't want to see me.

With a grunt, Dad got up from the chair. He got up on the exam table next to me, and he pulled me against his shoulder, and he let me cry.

Chapter 35

What an Interesting Question

I didn't see Holmes the next day. Dad and I drove up to the U of U hospital again, and we spent hours struggling with a web of bureaucracy, first being shuffled from one person to another, and then waiting, and then being shuffled around some more, until finally a gray-faced old man told us, apologetically, that he couldn't even confirm that Holloway was still in the hospital.

"Patients have a right to privacy," he said. "You understand."

Dad had to drag me out of the hospital. And I mean drag, literally.

The next day, I found where Dad had hidden my keys, and I tried the hospital again. By myself.

Dad had to bail me out of the security office. It probably would have been worse—I'd punched one of the guards—but I had the feeling someone had called someone who had called Rivera, and that was the only reason I wasn't cooling off in a cell.

When we got home, Dad sat me on the couch and stood over me. "That boy has a right to be left alone," he said, his voice quiet and even. "I know you care about him—"

"I need to see him."

Dad sat on the coffee table, which was hard for him because his mobility was still impaired. He waited until I finally looked him in the eye, and he waited some more until I broke and looked away.

"He cares about you too, Jack. But he needs some time."

"What if he doesn't?" I asked, and I pulled up my shirt to wipe my nose. "What if he's gone again? What if it's like last time?"

"It's not like last time," Dad said.

"I just need to see him for, like, five minutes."

"Buddy," Dad said, and then paused. "Jack."

I ran my sleeve over my eyes. I looked at him.

"You're being selfish," Dad said, and he stood, and he hugged me against him, and he said, "It's going to be ok."

Then he made me give him the keys to the truck, and he sent me to my room.

I was vaguely aware that finals were happening, that school was ending, that kids were going home. I'd been excused from my finals, I guess. Or maybe I'd failed all my classes. I didn't know, and I didn't care.

It took me longer, the next day, to find where Dad had hidden the keys. But the nice part about being worried out of your skull, like, so worried you might be legally insane, is that you're motivated and you have a lot of free time on your hands. So, I found them, and I drove to the Grange.

It looked the same as ever—it hadn't burned down to a smoldering ruin, and there wasn't any visible sign of stormtroopers, and if any ghosts were haunting it, they weren't working the day shift. The windows glinted in the late morning light, and the only sound was the truck's tires rumbling up the driveway.

When I knocked, no one came to the door. I tried the bell. Nothing. That thing about being crazy applied here, too; the door opened easily, and I stepped inside. The smell of smoke met me—foul, clinging, making my gorge rise. It wasn't the smell of a campfire or a grill; this was half-burned textiles and blistered paint and man-made chemicals heated until they vaporized. But the house itself looked the same as always: the white walls, the dark timbers, the inverted ship's hull of the tall ceilings. The shape of it now made a cavity in my mind, and I thought, instead of a ship's hull, of the curve of a skull. Nothing looked like it had been touched by flame, but as I moved deeper into the house, the reek followed me.

I ended up in the living room where Holmes had brought me on that first visit, and I stopped and stared. All the furniture had been pushed to the edges of the room: the sofa, the chair, the occasional tables, the sculptures and the mixed-media pieces of art.

In their place, someone had laid shards of glass. Hundreds of them. The shape was roughly circular, and most of the glass was smoked and dark, so that at the right angle, it looked black and opaque. Around the rim of the circle, though, was a thin ring of fragments of glass that had been stained gold. I stared at the arrangement for a while. I moved around it. The sun was at the wrong angle to come in from the windows, but I imagined what the installation would look like when light hit it, when you could watch the beams rake their way across it over the course of a day. Like a star being born, maybe. Or the sun collapsing in on itself.

"Do you like it?" Cecilia Holmes stepped into the room. She had her blond hair up in a complicated braid, and she was wearing a brown skirt and a man's chambray shirt, and it looked simultaneously chic and wholesome, like she'd just stepped in from milking the cows. "Hello, Jack."

"What is it?"

She cocked her head. "That's a dangerous question to ask an artist." When she reached the circle of shattered glass, she stopped and trailed a finger over one of the golden pieces. "Among other things, these are infused with honey from the ancestral estates on the Sussex Downs; there are a few aunts and uncles who still keep the hives there." She flipped over one of the smoked pieces. "For these, I used ash. There was a photo I was ready to let go." Standing, she offered me an unreadable smile. "When that wasn't enough, I burned my husband's study."

My laugh was more startled than amused, but Cecilia didn't smile, and I swallowed the rest of the noise.

"Would you like to sit?" she asked.

"I want to see H."

She nodded.

"Where is he?"

"Sit down, Jack."

"Fine. I'll find him myself."

"He's not here, you stubborn boy. Now sit down."

I sat on a chair pushed into the corner. Cecilia brought another chair over and sat, looking at me. Outside, a cloud moved in front of the sun, and the whole valley dimmed like it was on a switch.

"I'm not going to apologize," I said. "I hope he stays in prison the rest of his life. I hope he dies there."

Her hazel eyes were steady on me. "I did not expect an apology from you, Jack. Allow me to apologize, though, for his actions. It is not enough to tell you I am sorry for your mother's death; she was an interesting, impressive, and challenging woman. The world is less without her."

"You let him do it."

She touched the placket of her shirt, flattened it against her belly.

"Why didn't he kill me that night? He could have found me; it wouldn't have been hard."

"Because he wanted you alive. Because he is a Holmes, and although he is fully capable of going against his nature, there is still a part of him that…values the Watsons."

I wiped my eyes; I hadn't felt the tears until then. "Until they become a problem. Until they're inconvenient."

"Yes."

"That's why he tried to kill me once he knew I was involved with H. And that's why the attacks stopped once H was gone. Because I wasn't a problem."

For a moment, I thought I saw compassion in her face. But it might have been the light. Or it might have been a shadow.

"Is H ok?" I asked.

I wasn't sure what changed in her face; nothing I could put my finger on. But it softened a little, and she said, "Of course not."

"Where is he? He needs me. I don't understand how nobody gets that." Another moment passed, and she didn't even seem to be breathing, so I shifted to the edge of my seat. "I don't know what you want. You tell me to sit, and then you don't say anything, and H is hurting really bad right now. If you won't tell me where he is, I'll find him myself."

Her face was like deep snow.

"You know what I don't get," I said. "I don't get how you could let it happen."

"If you're referring to recent events, I was otherwise occupied freeing my daughter. A paramilitary organization. Something to do with her government work, I believe. It was all quite…patriotic."

"No, I know about that. Enough, anyway. I know it was Blackfriar. I know that's how he got both of you out of the way. I'm talking about all of it. All these years of it. H was a child, and you let Blackfriar do that to him. You knew what it was, you knew it wasn't training. You knew it was all of Blackfriar's rage, that he hated H because H wasn't his son, that he was punishing him for being who he was, and that it wasn't H's fault. And you let it happen. You're as bad as he."

She nodded slowly. "And yet, my son is alive. And he is strong. And I am alive, Jack. And while it may not seem like an important thing to you, to me, it matters a great deal. I learned early in our marriage what my husband was capable of. I could either give my children a mother, with whatever small influence I still held. Or I could be the sacrificial lamb."

"Why didn't he kill H?" I asked. "If he knew the truth, why did he keep him alive, hurting him like that, spending all those years trying to break him?"

She cocked her head, as though looking for the trick in the question. "Because he enjoyed it, of course."

I couldn't say anything to that.

The clouds moved on. The lights in the valley went back up. There'd been an accident on I-15, a bad one, and the cars were piling up and sparking like quartz, and greasy black smoke plumed up into the sky.

"You know what I've been thinking about?" I asked. "I've been thinking about the fact that somebody framed Blackfriar with Lynnissa Baca's jewelry. I was at her condo after he killed her. I saw that jewelry; it was still there. So, somebody went to her condo, picked up a few distinctive pieces, and put them in the Bentley. And I don't think it was Maggie; she was too busy trying to find the safe."

"My daughter has always had a sense of humor."

I nodded. "And somebody had to send me that invitation, telling me to come to the Zodiac anniversary party."

"I thought you might help my son. As you told me once, the Holmeses are better with a Watson."

"But then you tried to pay me off. You tried to scare me into leaving."

"Goodness, Jack." She laughed softly. "You should have seen yourself: the outraged dignity, the sheer stubbornness."

"Yeah, it worked. After that, I wouldn't have walked away from H for anything. That was smart. Reverse psychology; I bet it works on the Watsons every time." I sat back and ran a hand through my hair. "You know what I don't get? I still don't know why Sarah sent that stuff to H. And I don't know why she made it so that I'd have to open the safe. But the thing I keep coming back to is that somebody had to give Sarah what was in that safe: the hair samples, the video of the accident, the necklace."

For a long time, Cecilia said nothing, and I thought she wouldn't say anything, and her pulse fluttered in her throat. When she did speak, the sound startled me, spiking my pulse. "Who says Sarah Watson sent anyone anything?"

"But—" I began. And then I stopped. What had been in the package that Holmes had received? A printed family tree of the Watsons. The safe. Instructions. Had they been in Sarah's handwriting? Had she signed anything? Holmes might have investigated the return address, found the lawyer, drawn the conclusion that Sarah had left the package as a backup or a contingency. But that was an inference. An abduction. And lawyers could be paid.

Cecilia's eyes were cool and deep, and they made me think of trackless forests and earth that never saw the sun.

"What was on the other flash drive?" I finally managed to ask. "One of them had the accident, but what about the second one?"

"I don't know, Jack. But you have an active imagination; I'm sure you can guess what my husband feared Sarah had."

I didn't need to imagine or guess; I knew, because Blackfriar had told me. He'd thought Sarah had evidence. Videos. Proof of Blackfriar trying to break Holmes, trying to turn him into a sociopath. Like what I'd seen of Holmes's training. Worse.

Nodding, I said, "You know what else I keep coming back to? That video, the one of the accident. I keep coming back to the coincidence that someone happened to be standing there, at that moment, taking a video on a random stretch of highway."

"A tourist, perhaps."

"In the middle of the night."

Her lips parted with amusement. "A tourist with insomnia."

"That's a pretty big coincidence."

"Life, Jack, is full of coincidences."

I thought about that. And I thought about this woman who made art out of Dr. Watson's diaries and out of the deerstalker cap and out of Sherlock Holmes's cocaine bottle. Who made art out of honey and ash. I saw her moving the pieces around the way she had laid out the glass on the living room floor. She was, after all, Holmes's mother.

"Did Blackfriar know about the video?"

"He knew. He believed he had the only copy." She seemed to weigh her next words, and then she said, "He enjoyed watching it."

It took me a moment to get my voice under control before I asked, "What's going to happen to him?"

"We shall see. I imagine he will go to prison; even my husband is not untouchable. After that…" She gave a one-shouldered shrug. "A great many things could happen."

"What about Tom?"

"I understand he's arranging some kind of deal with the prosecutor. Regardless, he is no longer welcome at the Grange." Cecilia's smile was white, a bright sickle. "This family already has a Watson."

"And H?"

"My son is not well, Jack. I understand that you are attached to him, but he needs time to come to terms with what he has learned."

"He should stay at Walker."

"I don't think that would be good for anyone."

"You have to let him stay. If you don't, I'll—I'll tell everybody what I know. About this family. About you. About what you did, all of this, how you made it happen."

"Jack," she said, and she leaned forward slightly. In spite of my best efforts, I moved backward in the chair. She didn't raise her voice. It remained cool and untouched and clear, like winter sunlight. "You're forgetting: I'm the victim."

From what seemed like a long way off, I thought I could hear honking. Or maybe it was all in my head, that noise, the distant blaring sound.

"Come," Cecilia said. "I'll walk you out."

At the door, I looked her in the face and said, "Was it Fairfax?" I could see him in my mind's eye, the way he'd been in the photograph in Blackfriar's study: the silver eyes, the exact same hair. "Is he H's real father?"

Cecilia smiled. "Be safe, Jack."

And then another thought came to me, and it was so impossible, so ridiculous, that I wanted to laugh. But it ran through me like ice water in my veins. "It wasn't—was it Leopold? Was it Leopold Moriarty?"

"What an interesting question," she said as she shut the door. "You'll have to tell me, one day, what you did with Maggie's body."

Chapter 36

Elementary

The days dragged by with no sign of Holmes. Walker's campus emptied as students left, all but the few who stayed for the summer program. Rowe and Emma and Glo insisted that I come visit them over the summer, which was nice of them to say. But it turned out they weren't just saying it; the day after they left, plane tickets popped up in my inbox. *A gift from the three of us*, the note said. *See you in July*.

Dad and I were busier than ever, which was partly because we finally had free run of the campus, and there were always a million things to fix, and partly because I thought Dad was trying to work me into the ground again, the way he had in December. I thought maybe I should tell him that this time was different. It hurt, having Holmes disappear again. Hurt didn't begin to describe it. But it was easier, in some ways, knowing it was my fault. And easier, too, knowing that Holmes was safe now, that he was free of Blackfriar. If the cost was that I had to lose him, well, that was ok. I could live with that. Some days, I could even tell myself it was better this way.

And then, on a hot day at the end of May, I walked into the maintenance garage, and he was standing there. He looked like he always did: the oxford, the chinos, the immaculate chukkas. His only concessions to the heat were that he had cuffed his sleeves and undone the top button of his oxford. In his good hand, he carried the black doctor's bag that Tom had been toting around. I, on the other hand, was a red-faced, sweaty, filthy mess, who had spent the last four hours moving mulch by hand. And Jesus Christ, I thought with a high-pitched note I recognized as panic, my hair.

Dad was there too, a shop rag in one hand, head bent as he listened to Holmes. He'd been working on the bike, I figured—he'd pulled it out from where we kept it stored, and he'd taken off the chain. For a moment, neither Dad nor Holmes seemed to have noticed me.

Holmes was saying, "—cannot ask him to forgive me. You will understand, though. You will explain it to him and give him Dr. Watson's bag." He seemed to struggle for a moment before saying, "Please, tell him—"

Then he stopped, and he turned his head and looked at me.

I wanted to run to him. I wanted to touch his face, make sure it was really him. I wanted to hear his breathing, for Christ's sake. But my legs stayed locked, and I realized I had my hand in my hair, still trying to fix it. I pulled my hand free, and some mulch came with it, and somebody in charge of my voice said, "Um, hi."

So, that was it. That was officially how I died.

Amusement and compassion flickered across Dad's face—definitely more of one than the other—and he said, "Finish up here, buddy. I'm going to talk to Holloway for a minute."

Holmes threw him a questioning look, but Dad only nodded and tossed me the rag.

"But I—" I said. My legs still weren't working. "Shouldn't I—"

"Get the chain back on," Dad said as he herded Holmes toward the side door—a move, part of me noted in the background, designed to keep Holmes and me from crossing paths. "We'll be back in a few."

The door clicked shut behind them.

I did not get the chain back on. I went to the door, shouldered it open, and watched them walk up the canyon. The blue grama was getting tall, the seed heads bobbing in their wake. The air was hot and dry, and the pine trees seemed to shimmer with it.

"I said get that chain back on, son," Dad said. He didn't even have the courtesy to look back.

I let the door close. Then I opened it again, more quietly this time. They were still walking up the canyon, the blue grama brushing their calves. I could see the decision being made in Dad's body, and then his hand came up to rest on Holmes's nape, and after a moment, he slid his arm around Holmes's shoulders. Holmes, of course, immediately lost every shred of grace, and he walked like someone had replaced his joints with machine bolts. They stopped where a line of aspens grew, and the shade was plentiful, and the air was sweet. Dad kept his arm around Holmes, and he was talking in a low voice, and Holmes was perfectly still and listening. Dad glanced up, and I flinched and let the door fall shut.

The bike.

I had a hell of a time getting the chain back on. And then I realized that's because I was doing it backwards. So, I had to take it off again, and by the time I got it on—the right way, this time—my hands were a mess. I checked the tire pressure, which was stupid, because my eyes weren't working right and I couldn't read the gauge. I made sure the wheel was true and not pulling to either side. The panic hit me like a wave, coming out of nowhere. My face was hot, and I was sweating all over again, and I dropped the bike so hard that it bounced once. I ran to the door and threw it open. Because what if he was gone?

But he wasn't. He was standing there, and Dad was hugging him, and I knew what I was seeing because I'd gotten a few hundred of them, give or take, in my lifetime: Holmes was getting a dad hug. I figured he'd never had one before. Holmes didn't look stiff anymore; he was falling apart against Dad, crying into his chest, loud enough that I could hear the worst of the sobs that wracked him, even at that distance.

I tried to wipe down the bike. I couldn't even do that. I stood there with a bucket and a clean rag, and I stared at the water dripping from my hand. And finally, when I'd decided I didn't care what Dad did, didn't care if he told me to work on the bike, didn't care if he grounded me, didn't care if he decided I'd totally lost my shit and locked me up in a home, didn't care about any of it, the door opened, and Holmes and Dad stepped back into the garage.

Holmes was red eyed, but his face was soft and strangely clear, and he moved with that familiar, liquid smoothness. I knew the look on Dad's face because he wore it the last time he beat me at arm wrestling, after I'd done way too much buildup with the trash talk. That was how Dad looked when he was unbearably pleased with himself and making only a minimum of effort not to show it.

"Are you—" I started to ask. I took a step. I stopped. My legs were trembling, and I thought of a video I'd seen on TikTok, of a colt that had just been born. "How—"

Dad gave me another of those amused looks, but all he said was, "We're going to help Holloway move back into his dorm."

"But—" This time, I summoned up all my internal fortitude and managed a complete sentence. "It's summer."

Dad raised an eyebrow.

"Not that it's a problem—I mean, I want H to—I mean, that's great—"

"Son," Dad said.

I stopped and tried to remember how to swallow.

"Holloway is going to do Walker's summer program," Dad said.

And I, Boy Genius, said, "Oh."

Dad sighed. "Shake a leg. Go find him a spare toothbrush and some clothes he can borrow until his stuff arrives."

I looked at Holmes. My brain remembered how to swallow, and I did that a few times.

"Now, Jack," Dad said more loudly.

I sprinted to the house. I grabbed an unopened toothbrush from the hall. Then, triumphantly, my brain said, Toothpaste too! So, I grabbed toothpaste. I grabbed shirts and shorts and joggers and tried to carry all of it in my arms, and then I tripped on my backpack, and it all flew out of my arms.

A bag, that super-smart voice in my brain said. Maybe put it in a bag.

So, I did that.

When I got to Baker and shouldered open the door to 221, they were making the bed together, Dad helping Holmes with the sheets. Holmes looked at me, and his red eyes got a little wider. Dad made a disgusted noise.

"I put it in a bag," I said.

"For the love of God," Dad muttered. "You know, my son, we have all sorts of options. You could have used your backpack."

"I tripped over my backpack," I said. I was talking too fast, but I didn't know how to slow down.

Holmes looked at Dad, and Dad rolled his eyes, and Holmes gave that soft huff of a laugh.

"You could have used a suitcase," Dad said.

I blinked. I hadn't thought of a suitcase.

"Anything, in other words," Dad said, "except a grocery bag."

"I dropped them," I said.

"My only child is apparently having a stroke, Holloway," Dad said as he took the paper bag. "Please excuse us."

Holmes's grin was unsteady, gone almost as soon as it appeared. Then he looked like he was about to cry again.

"Do you want some time to yourself?" Dad asked Holmes.

I said, "No," a moment after Holmes did, and Dad gave me a dirty look.

To Holmes, he said, "Then I'll see you tomorrow."

Holmes nodded.

"Eight o'clock sharp."

"Yes, Mr. Moreno."

"Good man," Dad said. He gave Holmes another dad hug before he left, and Holmes's eyes were silver as he blinked away tears.

The genius in me chose that moment to say, "If Holmes is going to stay, and if I'm going to be a student at Walker, maybe we could get a room together. I mean, a double."

"Mother of God," Dad said under his breath. "Maybe you'd like a five o'clock curfew. How about that?"

That woke me up a little. "Five o'clock!"

"Think about it."

"Dad!"

He laughed. As he passed me, headed toward the door, he squeezed my shoulder and said, "My son, whom I love dearly, and who is the most important person in the universe to me."

I was staring at Holmes again, but I managed to say, "Uh?"

"Do not make me castrate you."

That definitely woke me up. Dad chuckled, but there was something serious in his eyes, and he held my gaze until I nodded.

"Door open, boys," Dad said. "I'm going to bang on the radiator and pretend I'm working while I spy on you."

"Oh my God," I said.

And then his steps were moving down the hall.

"Normal parents do not behave this way!" I shouted after him.

When I looked back, Holmes was smiling—that real smile, the true one, with all its wobbliness. He whispered, "Hello, Jack."

It took me a couple of tries before I got out, "Hi."

For some reason, that made his smile flare up again. He sat on the bed, and after a moment, he said, "Would you like to sit down?"

"I'm all dirty, and the sheets—"

"Jack," he said and made a desperate noise that might have been a laugh. "Please?"

So, I sat next to him. His arm was warm where it touched my arm. His leg was warm against mine. He smelled like that woodsy heat I dreamed about sometimes. His breathing accelerated, and then he was crying again, wiping at his face with one hand.

"Is it ok if I—" I started to put an arm around him, stopped. "Do you mind—"

Holmes turned into me, burying his face in my shoulder, and I looped an arm around him. He cried harder for a while, and I stroked his hair and tickled his neck. After a while, I realized we were lying on the bed, and his crying had slowed. And then it stopped. And then we had a situation. And down the hall, Dad was banging on the radiator, and I wondered if he'd been serious about that threat.

For a while, we lay like that, both of us pretending it wasn't happening. Holmes's breathing was slow and deep.

"We never went to prom," I said.

He sounded like he was about to start crying again.

"It's ok," I said. "It's ok. I'm just saying, you know. We didn't get to go. And I wanted to go with you. So, um, maybe next year, it'll be like a raincheck."

Holmes nodded against me. Then he got up onto one elbow. His eyes were redder than ever, and that wasn't supposed to be cute, but apparently Holmes could make anything look good.

"Jack, I know you can never forgive me, not for what I did when I betrayed your trust and took the safe, and certainly not for what my—for what Blackfriar did to your mother. All I can do is apologize—"

When I shushed him, he stopped.

"I'm sorry," I whispered. What I meant was, I'm sorry it was true, and I'm sorry I was the one who told you, and I'm sorry for what I took from you, because I can't give anything back.

He shook his head as tears came again. Somehow, he managed a choked, "You should not apologize. I should apologize—"

"I'm sorry, H. I'm sorry too."

With a wet laugh, he shook his head again. "That's what you say at the end of a fight."

I brushed some of his hair back into its part and nodded.

"I don't know how to undo what I did, Jack. I'm afraid I've lost you. I'm afraid if I've lost you again, it will kill me, and no matter how hard I try, I cannot—I cannot stop it from hurting."

"You didn't lose me. I'm right here." I carded his hair again and smiled up at him. "We're both right here."

He shook his head again.

"You didn't lose me," I said. "Did I lose you?"

Another shake of the head.

"Then we're ok," I said. "We can figure out the rest of it together."

I drew him back down, and although he resisted, it wasn't much. He lay in the crook of my arm, and we stared up at the ceiling, and after a while his body softened by degrees. I listened to his breathing. I hadn't known until today how much I missed it. He started to pick mulch out of my hair, not seeming to realize he was doing it, and I grinned in spite of myself.

Down the hall, Dad was still banging on the radiator, which maybe they should consider teaching in sex ed, because it was painfully effective.

"Do you know how Watson described himself?" Holmes asked. "John Watson, I mean. In his original accounts."

I shook my head. A little more mulch fell out, which made Holmes quirk a smile.

"He said, 'I was a whetstone to his mind.'" Holmes fell silent again. He cupped the side of my face and looked at me, and I didn't know what to call his expression. "But he was so much more. Sherlock Holmes was a brilliant detective, Jack. He would have been that regardless of other circumstances. But he was a good man—he was a happy man—because of John Watson."

He bent, and his lips hovered over mine, and I knew, once more, Holmes was giving me what he had never given to anyone else. I crossed that tiny, infinite gap and kissed him. His lips were dry. He tasted like Holmes. He was trembling, and I tried to tell him, each time our mouths moved against each other, that he was all right, that this was all right, that I would take care of him.

Holmes broke the kiss. He blinked slowly, and his voice was gravelly in a flattering way as he smoothed down my hair and said, "You are my soul, Jack Moreno. I do not know why John Watson wrote his stories that way, why he wrote himself so small, when he was so much more. I do not think I will ever understand. But I do not want to know what I would be without you."

I didn't know what to say to that, but I didn't think I needed to say anything. I lay there, arm around Holmes, and kissed him again. A few more times, in fact, until Dad started singing, "I've Been Working on the Railroad," in time with all that banging on the radiator.

When Holmes slid off me, he huffed another of those laughs.

"It's not funny," I said, tugging at my jeans. "See how you like it when you die of blue balls."

Holmes did laugh then, a real one this time, turning into the pillow to smother the sound.

When he'd recovered, I said, "I think I know."

The question formed itself in his face.

"About Watson, I mean. Why he wrote the stories that way." Holmes stayed silent, so I gave a lying-down shrug. "Because he loved him." I waited again. "Like I love you."

Holmes's breathing changed. He ran his knuckles across his eyes, and he said, "Do you? How can you, Jack? How, after everything?"

I gave another of those lying-down shrugs. His hair was the color of aspen leaves in autumn. His eyes were the color of the sky before dawn. He was mine for as long as I could hold on to him, and I planned on holding on for a long time. I cupped his cheek. My thumb found his cheekbone, and I wiped away another tear. It was a surprise and not a surprise at the same time. The way things feel when they're finally right. When everything comes together. When the end and the beginning meet. I grinned. "Elementary, my dear Holmes."

THE FACE IN THE WATER

Keep reading for a sneak preview of *The Face in the Water*, the first book of Iron on Iron.

1

"I'm not catastrophizing," Teancum Leon said as he wheeled his luggage into the Santaland Resort and Convention Center lobby. "I'm simply stating a fact: by coming to the middle of Missouri, we're statistically more likely to be murdered by hillbillies."

His husband, Jeremiah Berger, who went by Jem, smiled at an elderly couple passing them. But he said, "And."

"And if that murder were to be preceded by events like those in Deliverance, which, by the way, I still don't know why you made me watch—"

"Because it's amazing."

"—then we shouldn't be surprised."

When Tean paused to orient himself in the hotel lobby, Jem reached over to smooth down his collar. "And."

"And we would likely end up being made into masks of human skin."

"You didn't even watch Texas Chainsaw Massacre. You said it was too scary."

"So, you can see my point: this is objective reality. That's all."

Jem considered him. He seemed to be speaking to himself when he said, "We should have gotten you more tweed."

Tean blinked. "What?"

"More tweed. You're this bigwig—"

"I'm not and have never been a bigwig."

"—specially invited to attend a prestigious conference—"

"Missy invited me to be on her panel, Jem, at the annual conference for a third-tier association. Most of these people are hucksters. And I'm not even the keynote speaker."

"—and we should have gotten you those pants the horse guys have to wear, the really baggy ones. Only out of tweed."

"Jockeys?"

Jem smirked. "Boxers, but I wanted to surprise you." Before Tean could formulate a reply to that, Jem caught the eye of an older woman passing them. "This is my husband," Jem said. "Teancum Leon. He's a bigwig speaker who got invited to be on a panel."

The woman smiled at them and gave Tean a second look.

"I'm not—" Tean began.

"You can have his autograph for five dollars," Jem said over him.

And because he was Jem, the woman laughed. She even touched Jem's arm as she passed.

When Jem looked back at Tean, he said, "What?"

Tean refused to answer, but judging by the grin playing behind Jem's beard, Tean thought he already knew anyway. "And I don't know why I have to wear tweed—"

"You're not wearing tweed," Jem murmured. "A problem I intend to solve."

"When you get to wear—well, that."

That was a neon pink and green Beverly Hills 90210 t-shirt that fit Jem like a dream and vintage Adidas shorts (gray and purple because, well, Jem) and flip-flops.

"I seem to recall the last time I bought you a pair of shorts being told, 'I have chicken legs,' which, for the record, I disagree with, and I like how you look in shorts."

"That's not the point," Tean said. Although he felt like he might have lost track of what the point actually was.

Because the whole Deliverance-squeal-like-a-pig thing wasn't getting any traction, and the clothes thing had been a flop, Tean gestured at the lobby of the resort. True to its name, Santaland had gone all out with the Christmas decorations. Plastic Christmas trees, of course, filled every corner, shedding multicolored light from big, old-fashioned bulbs. Plastic reindeer perched in ornamental spaces overhead, looking down at conference-goers from where they bounded and leaped and frolicked in plastic snow. Plastic garlands draped the mantel of an enormous fieldstone fireplace, where orange plastic streamers shimmered. No actual fire in August, thank God— Tean was still soaked with sweat after the short walk from the car. Plastic elves wore jaunty plastic hats. And, of course, no fewer than eight plastic Santas were staged in various positions: in a sleigh, of course, and with a sack of toys over his shoulder. One appeared to be bending over and pulling down his red velour trousers. Background music played softly, and at least one of the hidden speakers had blown. It sounded like Irving Berlin had suffered a stroke. The only concession to the conference were signs and banners for the International Habitat Conservation and Protection Association.

"Do you know—" Tean began.

"You get one, so make it good."

For a moment, Tean floundered. He went with "They have too many bucks. If these were real deer, when they went into rut, they'd trash this place."

Jem made a face. "Really? That's the one you picked?"

"No, hold on—"

Laughing, Jem put a hand on his nape and steered him toward the registration desk. "You're going to have fun. You're going to cut open snails and ride walruses and throw fish back into ponds, and one of you is going to have to wear the shame antlers, and there will be so much animal urine, you'll be like a kid in a candy store."

"One time," Tean said, "I had coyote urine in my pocket one time, and it should be a lesson to you not to snoop, much less open things that don't belong to you."

Jem smiled at an older man passing them, and because he was Jem, the older man smiled back.

"If I'd smiled at him," Tean said, "he would have burned me at the stake."

"Get it all out of your system, or your friends are going to make you wear the shame antlers when you do the annual penguin dive."

"What are the shame antlers? What is a penguin dive?"

"Like you don't know."

"It's going to be three unbearably boring days, Jem. In fact, it's going to be so boring that we should turn around right now, and we can fly back tonight, and—"

"This lady is coming to talk to you."

"—and I'm going to tell her I've got giardia, and don't you dare contradict me."

"Never," Jem said through a smile as the woman reached them.

It had been years since Jem had seen Missy Bennett—since grad school, actually—and she'd changed. They both had, of course. She'd gotten rid of most of her dark hair (thanks to Jem, Tean knew it was called a bald fade), and she'd opted for a baggy t-shirt and jeans that accentuated the androgynous look. The heart-shaped gauges were new, but the earbuds worn around her neck weren't—and neither were the dark, friendly eyes.

"Missy—" Tean began, lurching into a hug when Jem propelled him from behind.

At the same time, Missy said, "Teancum—"

She laughed. Tean tried to extricate himself. Jem, when Tean glimpsed him out of the corner of his eye, was beaming.

When they separated, Missy turned toward Jem, holding out a hand. They shook, and Missy said, "You must be—"

But Jem said over her, "He doesn't have giardia."

It was an interesting experience, Tean thought through the distant ringing in his ears. He'd never been swallowed by a black hole in slow motion before.

Then Jem grinned and said, "I'm Jem."

And somehow, because he was Jem—again, over and over again—Missy only laughed and said, "Missy. I've wanted so badly to meet you. Ever since you made Tean get Instagram."

"He didn't make me get it," Tean said. "He stole my identity and created the account himself."

Missy's smile got bigger. "I see rings."

"Yes," Tean said, touching his gold band absently, "and it's always getting caught on something. With my luck, I'll probably get my hand ripped off during the walrus ride."

Missy turned a look on Jem.

"He's been under a lot of pressure," Jem said, slinging an arm around Tean. "Walrus fever."

Missy laughed again, as though that made sense—as though any of it made sense—and Tean decided he was going to become a hermit. Nobody ever came and bothered hermits, and if they did, hermits were legally allowed to shoot at them with .22s until they left.

"Did you register already?" Missy asked. "The desk is over here."

"Nope," Jem said as he urged Tean forward. Then, in a whisper, he added, "I know that look, Teancum Leon. You are not allowed to become a hermit."

"I can do whatever I want."

Jem actually snorted at that.

"Heather," Missy said as they approached the registration desk at the far end of the lobby, "this is Dr. Teancum Leon, with the Utah Department of Wildlife Resources. And this is his…" She let the sentence trail.

"Troublemaker," Jem said. "Jem Berger."

Heather was an older woman, white, with a wattle of crepey skin. Her color was bad, and although it was hard to tell because she was sitting behind the table, she looked too thin, with only a hint of residual weight around her middle. She searched through the badges until she found Tean's, and then she started putting together a welcome kit—a tote bag with a conference program, flyers from industry and academic journals, some sort of little spongy thing that was probably meant to be for stress.

"Do you know the environmental toll of printing waste—" Tean began.

Jem cleared his throat. When Tean shot him a look, he was innocently studying one of the plastic reindeer overhead, whistling "White Christmas."

"I can connect you with your dog," Heather said as she passed the bag over. She had a gravelly voice, and she coughed before continuing. "If that would help."

Missy made no effort to hide rolling her eyes.

"Like, long distance?" Jem asked.

"No, thank you," Tean said.

"How did you know we had a dog?" Jem asked.

"We're fine, thanks."

Heather smiled at them: yellow, crooked teeth. "I can sense him with you. A black dog. I get the feeling of bigness. Is he big? Does he have a big personality? His aura has melded with yours." She frowned. "Did you lose him recently?"

Jem's mouth opened in shock. "I did. How did you know that?"

"We didn't lose him," Tean said, taking Jem's elbow and trying to pull him away. "You took him for a walk without a harness, and he got stuck in the McCoys' fence."

"He's speaking to me right now," Heather said, closing her eyes and touching her temples. "He misses you a great deal."

Jem nodded at him with a grin, and Tean spotted the dog hair on his sleeve that had, against all odds, survived a full day of travel.

Brushing away the fur, Tean said, "If anything, he's getting so many treats that he's going to have diarrhea or bloat or pancreatic failure or diabetes by the time we get home. Maybe all of them."

"Yes, well, if you're worried about him—" Heather opened her eyes and fumbled for a card. "—I also perform remote healings."

"No," Tean said.

"I'm interested." Jem snagged the card. "Very interested. Thank you so much."

"Heather," a woman snapped. "I told you: this is a professional organization, and there's no place for that kind of nonsense here. If you're going to bother the speakers, I'll have someone else staff the registration table."

The speaker was a broad-shouldered, big-chested woman, her skin dark and lined from the sun, and she looked militant in a khaki shirt with epaulettes. The only thing missing, Tean decided, was a riding crop.

As she approached the table, Tean tugged Jem backward until they'd joined Missy. The woman planted herself in front of Heather. "What's the status of my room?"

Heather's shoulders curved in, and she sank down in the seat, not meeting the other woman's eyes. "The resort staff say it's all cleaned up, but they don't know how the cats got in—"

"Cats," the woman said and gave an unpleasant laugh.

"That's Yesenia," Missy whispered. "She's the president of the association."

It looked like Yesenia might have said more to Heather, but at that moment, screams erupted from the front of the lobby. They all turned to watch as two Santaland security guards—whose street cred, Tean considered, was probably undermined by the red jacket with white piping—dragged a struggling young woman toward the doors.

"No!" she was screaming as she kicked the air and writhed in their grip. "No! Let me go! It's not real!" Her labored breathing had the quality of real panic. "It's all a lie! I have to tell them!"

The automatic doors slid shut behind her, and the muffled screams slowly faded into the distance.

"Jesus," Jem said under his breath.

"I have to see to that," Yesenia said, striding toward the doors. "Don't let me catch you again, Heather."

Heather, still shrunken in her seat, sent a gray-faced scowl after the other woman.

"Uh." Missy gave an unsteady laugh. "Sorry about that, Jem. There are always people who show up at these kinds of events. The ones who think we're not doing enough. And the other side, who think we're doing too much already."

When Jem looked a question at Tean, he gave a tiny shake of his head: a silent answer of Yes, but not like that.

"I think we'll get our room," Tean said. "Grab our luggage, get unpacked."

"I'm so happy you're here," Missy said, wrapping him in another hug that, once again, Jem propelled Tean into. "Thank you for coming."

"It's really—"

"No, seriously, thank you."

Tean wondered if wriggling was ineffective; maybe he should duck and try to slip under her arms.

"It means so much to me," Missy said, and she sounded, all of a sudden, on the brink of tears. She released him then, stepping back, blinking rapidly. "Go on, get your room. But please, we have to grab dinner one of these nights. We have so much catching up to do. And I want to get to know Jem—I mean, I don't even know what you do."

"Real estate," Jem said. "I'm literally the most boring person you'll ever meet. Ask me about escrow accounts."

Tean couldn't help the laugh that erupted, and he changed it into a fit a coughing when Jem whapped him on the back.

They got the card keys to their hotel room, and they retrieved their luggage from the rental car. Even though it was evening, the air was so hot and humid that it felt like they were swimming in a broth of skin cells and off-gassing decomposition and redneck conservatism. Tean was explaining this to Jem in the elevator, at length, until he saw the smile on Jem's face and made himself stop.

Their room was clean, small, and cool, with the mini-split AC churring happily. It had a connecting door that, Jem checked, was securely bolted from their side. More importantly, they had a big bed, and even though they'd been together years, Tean blushed when Jem bounced on the bed, reclined on an elbow, and waggled his eyebrows.

"Come on," Jem laughed and flopped onto his stomach. "I want to call the girls."

Tean joined him on the bed as Jem placed the call. A moment later, the video started, and a giant, wet, black nose snuffled across the screen. Squeals of laughter filled the background.

"They thought that would be hilarious," Hannah said. Tean's friend—and co-worker at the DWR—appeared a moment later as Scipio, their black Lab, moved away from the camera. "Here they are. Scipio says hi, by the way."

"No, he doesn't," Tean said. "We could die in a fiery plane crash—"

He grunted when Jem elbowed him, and then the girls were there.

Sofia was ten, her hair still in the braids that Jem had done, and she was filled with a ten-year-old's outrage. "It's my turn on the Switch but Anahí won't let me have a turn even though she died and Hannah said when she died it was my turn!"

"Hi, sweetheart," Jem said and laughed.

The patter of feet announced Anahí, and Sofia sprinted away—doubtless, Tean decided, to reclaim the Switch. Anahí was only six, her dark hair short, a bow in it already falling halfway out. She was holding a slice of pizza—well, a fraction of a slice of pizza, since Hannah had clearly cut it in half for her.

"We're having pizza!" Anahí screamed and then ran away again.

"Are you being good?" Jem called after her, but excited screams were the only answer.

Hannah appeared a moment later, tucking chestnut-colored hair behind her ear. "They're being wonderful. Although nobody mentioned the exploding toy boxes."

"Just leave it," Jem said. "We'll pick up when we get home."

"They're not supposed to be having pizza," Tean said.

Until then, Tean hadn't known people could share an eye roll over FaceTime.

"Vegetables—" he tried again.

"We did pizza salad," Hannah said. "And yes, they both ate their salads. And they've both been wonderful. And in case you're wondering—"

"I'm not," Tean said.

"—they're much, much easier, and more pleasant, to be around than their foster dads."

"Thank you for taking care of them," Jem said. "I'll Venmo you some money for the pizza."

"Oh my gosh," Hannah said. "Do you want to talk to Scipio again?"

They disconnected. Jem kicked off his flip-flops and went down a rabbit hole on TikTok. Tean had trained himself to tune it out, but he was fairly sure, from the bits and pieces that filtered through, it was about animal psychics. Tean checked his email, did a quick scan of his paper, and then, when he realized it was total crap, decided to rip it down to the studs and start from scratch. It would be considerate, he decided, if hotels provided metal trash cans so you could burn things more easily.

"Nope," Jem said, kissing him on the side of the head as he took the laptop away. "Either we're going to do something incredibly wicked in this giant bed, without children or dogs or neighbors to distract us—"

"If you'd closed the blinds last time like I asked—"

Laughing, Jem kissed him again, on the mouth this time, a little slower. He leaned back, smiled, and said, "Take a shower, and we'll go to sleep. I'll ravish you in the morning."

So, they got ready for bed, and in the dark, smelling like Santaland soap (peppermint and rosemary, which was weirdly wonderful), with Jem warm around him, Tean should have fallen asleep immediately—they'd had an early flight, a layover, a long drive. But he twisted and squirmed and pushed the blankets down and pulled them back up again.

Finally, with a growl, Jem pulled Tean against him. He nuzzled into Tean's shoulder, and when he spoke, his voice was muzzy with sleep. "One."

Tean let out a tiny laugh in spite of himself.

"It'd better be a really good one," Jem mumbled.

"Do you know if people reused just two feet of holiday ribbon every year, we'd save 38,000 miles of ribbon? That's enough to tie a bow around the planet."

Jem's mouth was rough as he kissed Tean's shoulder and settled them together a little more comfortably. Tean was at the edge of sleep when, from a great distance, he heard Jem murmur, "With that much ribbon, imagine how many geese you could strangle."

Acknowledgments

My deepest thanks go out to the following people (in reverse alphabetical order):

Jo Wegstein, for helping with so many continuity errors and points of accuracy, for making me laugh about those wedge-shaped nipples, and for lending her expertise about so many things (like Zodiac's emergency lights!).

Mark Wallace, for catching my missing quotation marks, for helping me with the overall readability of the story (especially those long sentences), and for sharing his honest experience of the beginning chapters and of the ending.

Tray Stephenson, for asking about Blackfriar's tin eyes, for suggesting word order changes for clarity and emphasis, and for lending his editorial eye to my many errors.

Nichole Reeder, for helping me with staging (Jack with his back to the wall), continuity (Jack's age – and more), and for noting my new favorite word :-).

Pepe, for asking (as usual) such wonderful questions about—some of which I've tried to answer—and for giving me the great idea to bring back Ms. Prinze.

Cheryl Oakley, for asking tough questions about Cecilia and Noneley, for pressing me about the portable safe, and for catching so many of my typos – Paxton's raspier voice!

Raj Mangat, for helping me make Maggie's disappearance work so much better, for her feedback about Jack and H's first time, for making me laugh about Scipio/Scorpio, and for always being so kind and encouraging as I tried to tell the story I wanted to tell.

Steve Leonard, for meticulously inspecting (among other things) the timeline of events, for his kind words about Jack and Holloway, and for making me laugh about the new Ward and June Cleaver.

Fritz, for (among other things) suggesting I explain the solution to the combination, guessing at the meaning of my mixed-up sentences, and worrying about Ms. Albrecht's poor Elantra!

Austin Gwin, for (as always) being my go-to guy for help with cars, for gently correcting Jack's conversation with Ariana, and for help with my typos (who's for whose!).

Savannah Cordle, who—as usual—asked so many good questions (most of which I hope I answered), for her feedback about clarity in several key points, and for sharing my love of these guys right up to the end!

About the Author

For advanced access, exclusive content, limited-time promotions, and insider information, please sign up for my mailing list at **www.gregoryashe.com**.